"Dust of Death"
and
"The Stone Man"

TWO CLASSIC ADVENTURES OF

DOC SAVAGE

by Harold A. Davis and
Lester Dent writing as Kenneth Robeson

with a new historical essay
by Will Murray

D1605295

Published by Sanctum Productions for
NOSTALGIA VENTURES, INC.
P.O. Box 231183; Encinitas, CA 92023-1183

ISBN: 1-932806-77-6   13 Digit: 978-1-932806-77-9

Series editor: Anthony Tollin
P.O. Box 761474
San Antonio, TX 78245-1474
sanctumotr@earthlink.net

Consulting editor: Will Murray

Copy editor: Joseph Wrzos

Proofreaders: Carl Gafford and Matthew L. Schoonover

Cover restoration: Michael Piper

The editors gratefully acknowledge the contributions of Tom Stephens, Jack
Juka and the Lester Dent Estate in the preparation of this volume, and William
T. Stolz of the Western Historical Manuscript Collection of the University of
Missouri at Columbia for research assistance with the Lester Dent Collection.
Dust of Death restorations by Will Murray and Scott Cranford. *The Stone Man*
restorations by Will Murray.

Nostalgia Ventures, Inc.
P.O. Box 231183; Encinitas, CA 92023-1183

Visit Doc Savage at www.nostalgiatown.com and www.shadowsanctum.com

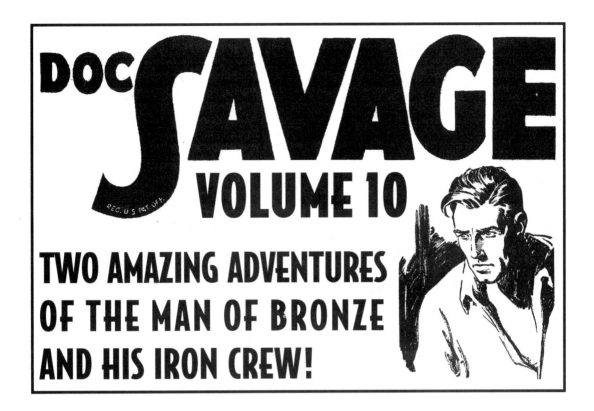

DOC SAVAGE
VOLUME 10

TWO AMAZING ADVENTURES OF THE MAN OF BRONZE AND HIS IRON CREW!

REG. U S PAT OFF.

Thrilling Tales and Features

DUST OF DEATH (writers' original manuscript text)
by Harold A. Davis and Lester Dent
(writing as "Kenneth Robeson") 4

RESTORATIONS IN BRONZE 74

INTERMISSION by Will Murray 75

THE STONE MAN by Lester Dent
(writing as "Kenneth Robeson") 77

Cover art by Walter M. Baumhofer and Emery Clarke
Interior illustrations by Paul Orban

*Two embattled nations find a new and deadly
foe in the queer, gray,*

DUST OF DEATH

A Book-length Novel Complete in This Issue

By KENNETH ROBESON

Chapter I
THE COMING OF TROUBLE

THE plane slammed down for a landing in a
way that stood the hair on end, and conveyed the
thought that the pilot did not care much for his life.
The ship sank out of the South American sky in a
power dive that made a moan which could be heard
for miles. It hauled out, went into a side-slip that
seemed more than a ship could stand. Then it landed.

The landing told things. The pilot was neither
reckless nor a fool. He was a wizard.

The man who got out of the plane stepped into
trouble, but that was not apparent for the moment.

The man who got out of the plane looked as if he
were about ready to die. Not that he was wounded,

not that he had any affliction. He was just a pale
bag of bones, and not a very large bag. His complexion was about as inviting as green bananas.

The man peered about. Then, quite suddenly, he
shoved a hand inside his greasy flying suit.

The flying field was jittery with heat waves. The
fighting planes—very modern military planes they
were—over by the army hangars were like baked
insects that had just crawled out of hangars that
were ovens.

Trouble was coming from the hangars in the
shape of a squad of uniformed brown soldiers.
There was trained precision in their advance, even
if they were in a hurry. Their faces were grim and
their rifles clean—cocked.

The officer in charge of the squad was dapper,

efficient, and, coming up to the flyer who had the look of an invalid, he presented a blue automatic, muzzle first. He spoke brisk and grim Spanish.

"This is a military airport, señor," he said. "No landings are permitted here. You are under arrest."

"Si, si, amigo," said the puny-looking flyer.

He took his hand out of his flying suit and it held papers, official looking. He passed them over.

The officer took them and read them, and his eyebrows went up, then down, and his shoulders did the same. He spoke English this time and it was not especially good.

"Our consul, he ees not have right for you thees military field to use," he said. "Eet ees not what you call—call—"

DOC

"Not regular, I know," said the flyer. "But suppose you call your chief, contact someone high up in the war department. I did a little telephoning before I started."

The officer did tricks with his eyebrows while he thought that over.

"I will see," he said. "You wait."

He took the papers, which the flyer had given him, and walked away briskly, going past the hangars and along the walk which led to the operations office. Before the war, the field had been a civil one and someone attempted to landscape the grounds. But, during the last year or two, the shrubbery had not been cared for and was growing wild and rank along the walk.

THE officer took quick strides, eyeing from time to time the documents which obviously held great interest for him. He shook his head, sucked his tongue, and spoke to himself.

"If this flyer's identity is as these papers say," he murmured, "it means great and amazing things are to come."

He turned a corner briskly. The path, virtually an alley, ran between thick walls of shrubbery on either side.

"If this man is who these say he is," the officer waved papers at himself, "the mystery of the Inca in Gray may be solved after all."

A man came out of the bushes into the path behind the officer. He came swiftly without much noise.

The man was bent over and his hands were across his middle as if he had a permanent pain there. A beggar, to judge by his looks. His hair was long. His *poncho* ragged, his fiber sandals frayed.

Unless the matter was given thought, it might not occur that the fellow was excellently disguised.

"Señor *soldado,*" the ragamuffin hissed, "I have something to tell, important."

The officer stopped, turned and, surprised, let the tall, stooped bundle of rags come up to him. He was unsuspicious. In the South American republic of Santa Amoza civilians treated army officers with respect. Not being suspicious was the officer's mistake.

The ragamuffin had a knife concealed in his hand. But the officer did not see that until he looked down at his chest and saw the hilt sticking out over his heart. Queerly, the army man kept his mouth closed tightly. But, after a moment, strings of crimson leaked from the corners of his mouth, a string from each corner at almost the same time. Then the army officer, in a slow, horrible way, got down on his hands and knees and lay on the knife hilt so that the point was shoved on through, and the point came out of the back of his neat khaki uniform.

He kicked as he died.

THE killer was a thrifty soul. He got his knife. Then he got the papers. After which he scampered away through the brush, making as little noise as he could.

Beyond the flying field was jungle, where there was rainfall down here on the coast where sat Alcala, capital city of Santa Amoza. Once in the jungle, the slayer ran as if his shadow were a devil. After a time, he came to a house, a very miserable looking hovel and apparently untenanted, but which held a modern telephone.

The telephone set-up was remarkable. Not the instrument itself, which was ordinary, but the box of apparatus through which its circuit ran. The device was what is known as a "scrambler" and it was ordinarily employed by telephone companies on government lines where eavesdroppers were not wanted. Only the proper unscrambler at the other end would make intelligible what went over the wire.

"Word must be got to the Inca in Gray," said the killer. "The thing we feared has happened."

"What do you mean?" demanded a coarse voice. They were speaking Spanish.

"Major Thomas J. Roberts just arrived at military field," snapped the slayer. "I thought I recognized him. I used my knife on a fool officer, and got diplomatic passes which prove the man is indeed Major Thomas J. Roberts."

"And who might Major Thomas J. Roberts be?" the voice over the wire demanded.

"Who was your father, my friend?" asked the killer.

"He was a man of Inca blood, of which I am proud," rapped the other. "And what has that to do—"

"I thought he must have been an ox," sneered the slayer, "for naught but an ox could sire a son so dumb. This man Roberts is more commonly known as Long Tom."

"And so what, insulting dog?" demanded the other. "Is this Long Tom *Señor Diablo* himself?"

"He is worse," declared the ragamuffin. "He is the assistant, one of the five assistants rather, of the one man our master, the Inca in Gray, fears."

"Continue, man of many words and little information," directed the voice on the wire.

"Doc Savage!" said the killer. "Long Tom is the assistant of Doc Savage."

There was silence. It was a long silence, as if the man on the other end of the wire had been hit a hard blow and was recovering. Then he began to swear, and his profanity was like the explosions of bundles of firecrackers. He started in a loud scared voice and swore until he ran out of breath.

"Wait," he said.

The killer waited. It was all of five minutes. Then the other was back on the line.

"The Inca in Gray will direct this personally," he said. "This Long Tom will be disposed of."

"Goodbye, son of an ox," the killer chuckled and hung up.

BACK at the military flying field there was excitement. For the body of the knifed officer had been found. It was orderly excitement, grim. For these soldiers of Santa Amoza were well trained— and long trained, for the war had been going on for four years already.

"Long Tom" Roberts was in the office of the field commander, standing stark naked, for he had been stripped as they searched him. He looked more than ever like a man who was waiting for a coffin. But there was nothing moribund about the Spanish he spoke. It was good Spanish. He used plenty of it, pointedly, loudly.

"Call Señor Junio Serrato, war minister of Santa Amoza," Long Tom bellowed. "He'll okay me. He knows I'm coming."

They finally did call Señor Junio Serrato, war minister, and what he said must have been emphatic and plenty. For the flying field officials turned suddenly apologetic.

"My treatment of you is to be regretted greatly. But you must understand our country is at war," the field commander himself said. "And the mysterious murder of the officer—"

There was much shrugging, in the middle of which Long Tom Roberts left. He took a horse-drawn hack driven by an old woman who looked like the Yankee conception of a witch. All gasoline was commandeered for military use in Santa Amoza and all ablebodied men were in the army. Long Tom eventually got into town.

Alcala, after the fashion of South American cities, was a bright-colored town, made brighter by the flags which hung in profusion. Bright sunshine made the white houses whiter and filled the streets with heat waves. Tourists would have ecstasized over the place.

But there were no tourists. There was war!

It showed in something besides the numbers of uniformed men. There was a grimness, chill in the faces, a thing as distinct as the snow-capped Andes, which could be distinctly seen inland.

Long Tom surrendered his conveyance, because marching squads of soldiers frequently held him up and he could make better time walking.

The walking, Long Tom concluded in short order, was a mistake. There were beggars; war makes beggars. Tattered and filthy and pleading, they tagged at his heels. He tossed them coins, knowing that was a mistake, for it drew more of them like sugar in the midst of flies. He tossed more coins, but they grew bolder, more insistent. They scuttled alongside him, tugged his clothing.

The presence of the beggars was not strange, for tropical cities are commonly infested with mendicants.

But suddenly it was strange. It was sinister. It had a purpose.

One whining rogue, ragged and dirty as the rest, shuffled up, arms held loosely at his sides, bare feet scuffing the dust of the unpaved street. Then, unexpectedly, his long arms were wrapped around Long Tom's slight figure.

"Spy!" screamed the beggar. "He is a spy!"

The mob burst out in a roar. The suddenness with which it happened showed this all had been arranged. Unclean hands closed upon Long Tom. There seemed to be dozens of them.

"Spy!" they shrieked. "Kill him!"

"Kill him!" a score echoed.

Then Long Tom—he who resembled an invalid—picked up the first beggar who had seized him. Using the victim as a club, Long Tom bowled over fully half a dozen others. It was a feat the burliest wrestler would not have blushed to recount.

In the next few seconds, Long Tom demonstrated some of the qualities which qualified him as an assistant to that man whose name was legend to the far corners of the earth—Doc Savage. Long Tom used his fists at first, and they landed with noises only slightly less than pistol shots.

A ring opened around Long Tom, in it the bodies of those who had become senseless. The mob roared, circled the man whose mild appearance was so deceptive.

"Kill him!" it bawled. "A spy!"

Then they closed in, and many knives appeared. They tore a stoop from in front of a house, and hurled these sizable rock fragments. Long Tom got one in the chest and it put him down.

Lying there, gasping, he drove hands into his pockets. They came out with small glass bulbs. He broke these in the street, and they made wet splashes which vaporized away almost instantly. It was gas, odorless, producing quick unconsciousness if breathed—a product of Doc Savage's inventive genius. Long Tom held his breath so as not to get any of it. He got up and ran.

Into a door, Long Tom dived, not knowing where it led. He was lucky. It admitted into a patio, and he climbed a palm tree to a roof, crossed that, got into another street, after which it was doubtful if a man in the mob could have kept up with him. He could hear them yelling.

"Spy!" they screamed. "Kill him!"

They shouted that as if it were something they had been told to shout. War-ridden cities are hysterical places, and mobs have executed spies in a patriotic frenzy and it has been passed off as something to be regretted, but not entirely unreasonable under the circumstances.

"Whoever hatched that murder scheme," Long Tom grumbled as he ran, "was clever."

Chapter II
THE GRAY DEAD

ALCALA, Capital of Santa Amoza, had the outward aspects of a backward city and a poor one. It was neither. Santa Amoza was a country rich in natural resources—nitrates and oil among others—and before the war a flood of exports had poured out of Alcala, the seaport, and a flood of gold had poured in. Alcala had been a rich field for American salesmen.

The government hospital was a typical example of just how modern Alcala was. The building was huge, white and of fine stone. The interior was also white and sanitary, modern to the extreme.

Long Tom Roberts was following a stern-faced male nurse down a hall and into a big room, where a man lay on a white cot.

The man on the cot was a mummy in bandages, except for his hands and his face. He had an interesting face. At some time or other his nose had made forcible contact with an object harder than its tissue and bone. The nose gave the man a face remindful of the countenance of an English bulldog. Inside the bandages the man's frame was probably angular and capable.

The bandaged man did not see Long Tom at first.

Long Tom grinned and said: "All wrapped up for shipping."

The bandaged man turned over. His blue eyes all but came out of his head. He tried to bound out of the cot and fell on the floor.

"Long Tom!" he howled. "You old corpse, you old rascal, you sonuvagun!"

"Ace Jackson," Long Tom chuckled.

Long Tom helped him back on the cot, and they grinned and mauled each other a little, shouting things which did not make much sense.

"Ace Jackson," Long Tom chuckled. "Same old Kiwi. Haven't seen you since you were flying a Spad, back in the Great War."

"Same here," chortled "Ace" Jackson. "Swell of you to drop in to see me, you pint of dynamite."

"I was down in Argentina on a hydro-electric project," Long Tom explained. "Buzzed up here as soon I heard that you had tried to do a bit of flying without wings. What's the idea? Been flying so long you thought you had sprouted wings?"

Ace Jackson looked suddenly grim and did not answer.

Long Tom stepped back and eyed the bandaged aviator seriously.

"It must have taken *some* sky battler to bring you down," he said dryly. "Did they gang you? I'll swear no one man could outfly you."

"The Inca in Gray may not be a man—I think sometimes," Ace Jackson said slowly and distinctly.

FOR the first time, Long Tom became aware there was a girl in the room. She was tall, dark haired. And her complexion had the utter fairness of the pure Castilian. She came forward when she saw that Long Tom had perceived her.

Long Tom had the sudden feeling that he was looking upon the most beautiful girl he had ever seen in his life.

Ace Jackson made introductions.

"This is Señorita Anita Carcetas, daughter of the president of this republic," he said.

"Holy smoke," Long Tom gasped elaborately. "The president's daughter!"

"Anita, I want you to meet Major Thomas J. Roberts, better known as Long Tom, electrical wizard extraordinary. And a lug who would rather fight than eat. And he loves his food. Where there's trouble you'll find Long Tom, and he's a pal of mine."

"I have not been so dazzled since I saw my first sunrise," Long Tom said gallantly.

His eyes told him things. These two were violently in love.

The girl was patting pillows, adjusting coverlets and bandages and otherwise making Ace Jackson comfortable. She was getting such a big kick out of it that Long Tom let her continue for a while. Then he spoke.

"You said something a moment ago," he reminded Ace Jackson.

The wounded flyer looked around the girl at him. "Eh?" he queried.

"The Inca in Gray," Long Tom explained.

Over Ace Jackson's face came an expression as if he had just met, face to face, a bitter and detested enemy.

"I guess it's a man," he muttered. "Sometimes, though, that don't seem so sure."

"Riddle me again," Long Tom suggested. "I like guessing games."

A thought struck Ace Jackson with all the visible effect of a physical blow. He reared up on the hospital cot, heedless of the girl's admonishing gasp.

"Gimme straight dope on something," he requested.

"Sure," Long Tom said.

"Did Doc Savage send you to Santa Amoza?" Ace Jackson asked pointedly.

Long Tom's answer was prompt.

"I came here solely to see an old pal, who had cracked up. And for no other reason," he said. "Now what is this ranting about an Inca in Gray? Is it a secret?"

Ace Jackson sat up rigidly on the cot.

"You won't believe this," he clipped. "But I'll give it to you, anyway."

"Go ahead," Long Tom invited. "I'm rather gullible."

"The Inca in Gray is responsible for this war!" Ace Jackson leaned back as if he had gotten something heavy off his chest.

Long Tom squinted at the bandaged aviator.

"I suppose this Inca in Gray is the nickname of some general of Delezon, the country Santa Amoza is fighting," the puny looking electrical wizard suggested.

"You don't get me right," Ace Jackson corrected. "The Inca in Gray is something—something horrible. No one knows whether he is from Delezon, or what."

Ace Jackson sat up on the cot again. He leveled a gauze-wrapped arm at Long Tom.

"I'll give you one example," he said. "At one time the Santa Amoza army apparently had Delezon licked. We had broken through their lines in a big drive, and were marching across the desert toward their capital. Then, one night, every officer of consequence in the expeditionary force died, mysteriously. It was the work of the Inca in Gray."

"Sounds to me like the work of an espionage agent," Long Tom corrected.

Ace Jackson shook his head. "This Inca in Gray has done horrible things; murder, butcherings, things deliberately calculated to stir our nation into a frenzy. Our enemy, Delezon, would hardly do that. General Fernanez Vigo, commanding the enemy force, is a straight shooter, even if he is hell on wheels in a fight."

Long Tom grunted. "I still say espionage."

"I'll give you another example," Ace Jackson said. "There was—"

Entrancing Señorita Anita Carcetas interrupted.

"Let me give you the example of Señor Ace Jackson," she said.

Ace Jackson scowled at his bandages. "I look like a swell example."

THE girl went on as if she had not been interrupted.

"Ace Jackson is commander of our Santa Amoza air force," she explained. "It was his idea that we take the war into the air. He organized our air force. Another man could not have done what he did. We were winning over Delezon, and it was due solely to Ace Jackson's genius."

"Am I blushing," Ace Jackson muttered.

"The Inca in Gray tried to kill Ace Jackson," the girl finished. "Tried to kill him because in another few weeks he would have won the war for Santa Amoza."

Long Tom shook his head. "This doesn't sound reasonable."

"I know it," Ace Jackson growled.

"Just who is this Inca in Gray?" Long Tom demanded.

"Mystery," Ace Jackson retorted. "Nobody knows. He is just a name that you hear whispered."

Señorita Anita Carcetas looked at Long Tom, but spoke to Ace Jackson, saying, "Ace, you might tell Long Tom what we were talking about this morning."

Long Tom interposed: "How did this Inca in Gray get you, Ace?"

"You know I never go up without going over my plane," Ace Jackson said. "I did this time not ten minutes before taking off. But a wing came off just the same. My parachute had been tampered with. It split, but evidently not as much as they had hoped. I got broke up some."

Long Tom nodded. "Now, what is this thing you were talking about?"

Ace Jackson opened his mouth to speak, then closed it. A door of the room had opened. A male nurse, the same one who had guided Long Tom, entered, carrying a glass of milk and some food on a tray. The nurse seemed very weary, as if he had worked long and hard hours. Perhaps that explained the small accident which now befell him. An accident innocent of itself, but one which was to have grisly consequences.

He stumbled. Milk and viands landed on Long Tom's coat.

"Thousand pardons, señor," the nurse gasped contritely, seizing a towel and mopping at the mess he had made. The towel did not help much.

"Forget it," Long Tom said.

"No, no, señor, I will clean it," the male nurse gasped. "Only a few moments will be required."

Long Tom grinned and removed his coat.

"Sure, sure," he smiled, "if it'll make you happy."

The nurse took the coat, still bubbling over with apologies—possibly the presence of the president's daughter had helped unnerve him—and, backing to the door, used one hand behind him to open it. He stood there bowing again and again, half in the room and half out.

No one noticed that the arm over which he had draped Long Tom's coat was extended into the corridor while the rest of his person was in the hospital room.

"I am so sorry, señor," he told Long Tom again.

"Forget it," Long Tom repeated. "Accidents happen."

The nurse backed into the corridor and shut the door.

Señorita Anita Carcetas said: "Poor fellow, he is doubtless overworked."

Long Tom asked Ace Jackson: "Now, what were you about to tell—"

A sound came from the corridor outside the door, an unpleasant sound, obviously a body falling. And there was one shriek, brief but hideous, in a man's voice.

Long Tom swung to the door and wrenched it open. Señorita Anita Carcetas made a shrill sound, expressive of utter horror. Ace Jackson got out of his cot, could not stand, and slumped to the floor.

Long Tom looked up and down the corridor. No one was in sight. Then the electrical wizard bent over the body of the man on the hallway floor.

The man on the floor was on his back, dead, with his eyes open and a terrible agony reflected in their still depths. It was the nurse. Long Tom's soiled coat was still draped over his arm.

But it was the dead man's face that held Long Tom's gaze. The face was gray, almost white. Long Tom looked more closely to ascertain what made the dead man's face gray.

What looked like gray dust coated the fellow's features.

Long Tom fanned with his hand close to the visage of the corpse and the gray stuff was stirred like dust in a little cloud.

"Get away from it!" Ace Jackson screamed.

Chapter III
SUBSTITUTED MESSAGE

WITHOUT turning, Long Tom rapped: "Why not touch it?"

"That man was killed by the Inca in Gray!" Ace Jackson shouted.

Long Tom spun around. "What?"

"The gray dust," Ace Jackson snapped, "is always on his victims."

Señorita Anita Carcetas said: "The death was meant for you, Señor Long Tom."

"I know it," Long Tom growled. "Only the coat on his arm was visible when he stood in the door. The killer thought it was me with my coat over my arm."

The word exchange had taken but a moment. Long Tom whipped glances up and down the corridor. He decided the fleeing killer would have gone to the right toward the exit. Long Tom ran in that direction.

He reached the entrance and saw a uniformed military guard there, rifle alert. The fellow must have heard the death sound.

"Did anyone pass?" Long Tom demanded in Spanish. The sentry said no one had passed and Long Tom turned back, trying doors to the right and to the left. There were cries, running footsteps from other parts of the hospital, these no doubt made by persons coming to see what the excitement was about.

It was in a big white operating room, banked with instruments, that Long Tom came upon an object of interest.

The object was a man; a rather small man who was attired in immaculate blue serge. He had Latin handsomeness and a mustache that was a dark neat line on his upper lip.

There was a distinct smear of gray dust on the right sleeve of his blue serge suit.

Long Tom rushed to the small man's side. The fellow was struggling to get up, his writhing lips bending and unbending his black line of a mustache.

"A fiend—cloaked, masked," he gulped. "He struck me down and fled."

He pointed to an open window.

Long Tom whipped to the window. There was no one in sight. The ground below was sun baked enough not to hold footprints, and there was shrubbery enough about to have concealed a small army.

Long Tom shouted an alarm and a soldier appeared, began searching the grounds.

Going back to the neat little man with the mustache, Long Tom studied the fellow narrowly. Abruptly, Long Tom seized the man's arm.

"Free me!" the other sputtered. "What is the meaning?"

"You were attacked," Long Tom told him dryly. "But that's your story. You haven't got a mark on you."

The man tried to speak. But Long Tom shook him, then marched him, angrily incoherent, back to the room where Ace Jackson had gotten back on his cot.

Ace Jackson's eyes flew wide and he said: "Don't mind who you manhandle, do you?"

"What do you mean?" Long Tom growled.

Ace Jackson pointed at the mustached prisoner. "No idea who this is?"

"I don't get you," Long Tom said.

"He is Señor Junio Serrato," Ace Jackson advised.

"For the love of mud," said Long Tom.

"Exactly," Ace Jackson agreed. "Señor Serrato is war minister of this nation!"

LONG TOM hurriedly released his captive. One did not drag war ministers around as if they were common culprits. For, in these South American countries, war ministers usually had more actual power than the president.

"I deeply regret my tremendous error, Señor Serrato," Long Tom murmured.

That was diplomacy. Regardless of what one thought, one did not accuse war ministers of crimes which there might be difficulty in proving they had committed.

Long Tom was somewhat surprised when Señor Junio Serrato took it graciously.

"It is no indignity to be handled roughly by a man who belongs to one of the most famous little groups in the world," he murmured. "I have heard much of Doc Savage and his five aides."

Long Tom was trying to think of something equally polite when there was an uproar out on the hospital grounds. They hurried to the windows and saw the squad of soldiers who had been searching the ground had made two seizures. They were bringing the prisoners in.

The captives were a Jeff and Mutt pair in stature. Both were well dressed.

"The *soldados* have made a mistake," war minister Serrato murmured at Long Tom's elbow.

"You know the prisoners?" Long Tom queried.

"Oh, yes," minister Serrato nodded. "Count Hoffe is the tall one. He is the representative of the European munitions concern which supplies our needs in arms and ammunitions."

"A salesman of death," Long Tom said grimly.

Minister Serrato smiled. "War must have its servants."

"The short one?" Long Tom suggested.

"Don Kurrell is his name," advised Minister Serrato.

"Another munitions salesman?"

"Oh, no." The war minister smiled again. "Don Kurrell represents the company which holds the Santa Amoza oil concessions. He is interested in seeing the war ended. His oil wells, I regret to say, are in the battle zone. Unless our nation wins, his concern stands to lose its investment."

The prisoners were ushered in shortly. The soldiers explained they had been acting suspiciously when caught.

Tall Count Hoffe removed his hat, displaying a close-cropped bullet head, and explained: "We were seeking shelter. We heard the excitement and feared there might be shooting."

"Just why were you here?" Long Tom asked them.

The two looked at each other, then eyed minister Serrato, and they all glanced at Ace Jackson.

Ace Jackson said: "I think everybody has the same idea."

"What is it?" Long Tom demanded.

"The thing I started to tell you," Ace Jackson grunted.

"Shoot," Long Tom invited.

"We want Doc Savage down here," Ace Jackson said. "We want him to smash this devil, the Inca in Gray."

THERE was talk after that, explanations of what was known of the Inca in Gray. But all of it added up to little more than Long Tom had already heard. The Inca in Gray was some mysterious power who was managing to keep the slaughter going for some unknown reason of his own.

"I'll see about it," Long Tom told them finally. "I'll cable Doc."

"Do you think he will come down?" Ace Jackson asked eagerly.

"You can't tell about Doc," Long Tom told him. "But this sounds like the sort of thing that would interest him."

Don Kurrel, the oil representative, had a mannerism peculiar to small men. He was continually drawing himself up, even rising on tiptoe as if to look taller. He did this now.

"I hope Doc Savage will come," he said. "All the world has heard of him."

Long Tom said: "I will cable," and left.

Hardly more than one minute after Long Tom had taken his departure, Count Hoffe clicked his heels, doubled his long body in a smart bow and said: "Believe me, I am truly glad that Doc may come to Santa Amoza. This unending slaughter is a terrible thing."

Then he took his departure.

Ace Jackson stared at the door after Count Hoffe had gone, and closed it. He muttered, "Sometimes I wonder about that guy. He's the only one I can think of who stands to profit by having this war go on and on."

"You mean that he might be the Inca in Gray?" murmured war minister Serrato. "That thought has occurred to me."

"And to me, too," broke in Don Kurrell. "That is why I have been palling up with the blighter. I am checking up on him."

"Learn anything?" asked Ace Jackson.

"No," said Don Kurrell.

Everyone left.

Those in the room would have been greatly interested in the actions of a strange figure in a nearby park some moments later. Even a close inspection would not show whether this form was that of man or woman.

An all-enveloping cloak of gray material, with a hood which completely concealed the features, furnished an excellent disguise. This form glided through the shrubbery, keeping out of sight, and stopped under a tree which grew out of the shrubbery. This tree was very large and ancient.

The actions of the mysterious skulker became rather unusual. The figure sank beside the tree, took out a notebook from beneath the cloak, and wrote something in it. The notebook had pages of thin, onionskin paper.

The note was rolled, and one hand, gloved, carried it into a hollow in the bottom of the tree. If the strange individual had made any sound thus far, it was lost in the cooing of pigeons, numbers of which swarmed the ancient park at all hours of the day, picking up scraps, perching in the branches of the trees.

The individual in gray removed his hand from the tree, and slunk away, vanishing from view.

Only a few moments later, a pigeon arose from the top of the tree. It was only one pigeon among many, and there was nothing to indicate to any onlooker that it was a carrier pigeon, which had come up from the hollow trunk of the old tree from a cote concealed in the base. Nor was there anything to show an observer on the ground that the bird carried a note sealed in a quill.

LONG TOM ROBERTS was also encountering pigeons, but they were only of the ordinary mongrel variety which hopped about in the streets and he paid no attention to them. Long Tom was thinking, mulling over in his mind what he was convinced was a fact, two facts rather.

The two facts were the two attempts on his life—the attempt of the beggar horde, and the strange incident at the hospital. Presumably, both attempts had been made by the Inca in Gray; and the motive was not hard to guess. Doc Savage was not wanted on the Santa Amoza scene.

This talk of the Inca in Gray was entirely new to Long Tom. But that was not strange. This war between Santa Amoza and Delezon had been going its bloody way for almost four years, yet it was quite possible that any number of people in New York had never heard of it. The newspapers, of course, had carried stories of the bigger battles, but almost nothing of the day-by-day fight. American editorials usually dismissed the affairs as sporadic squabbles over the jungle and desert tract that separated the two republics. Washington had, however, placed an embargo on the export of arms to the belligerents, hoping to stop the conflict.

"I'll bet Count Hoffe liked that," Long Tom muttered.

The electrical wizard turned into a cable office. He took a blank and wrote:

DOC SAVAGE
NEW YORK
EVENT VERY MYSTERIOUS STOP LEARN WAR BEING KEPT GOING BY MYSTERY INDIVIDUAL KNOWN AS INCA IN GRAY STOP MIGHT BE GOOD IDEA IF YOU CAME DOWN AND CLEANED UP
LONG TOM

Long Tom left the cable office and blissfully went his way, searching for a suitable hotel.

Some moments after Long Tom had left, when there had been approximately time for him to get out of earshot, a strange thing happened. A man came running wildly down the street with several others pursuing him. He turned into the cable office as if he thought it offered escape. There he picked up a chair and turned, at bay. The pursuers charged in. Promptly there was a mêlée. Furniture flew about. Desks were upset. The cable office attendants screamed for the police.

The police arrived eventually. But, by that time, the mysterious fighters had taken their departure. They had, in fact, joined the sinister figure which had dispatched the pigeon from the park tree.

"How did it come out?" the cloaked individual asked.

"Perfectly, master," came the answer.

One of the gang who had staged the fight turned over a telegraph blank. It was the one which bore the message Long Tom had written.

The hooded one chuckled when he saw this.

"You left in its place the one I gave you?" he asked.

"We did," said the other.

"It is well," the cloaked one said. "Had we merely stolen the message the cable attendants might have missed it."

"We did excellent work," bragged one of the fighters.

"True," said the cloaked one. "Your work is not done."

The other seemed surprised, and made a question with his eyebrows.

"Long Tom Roberts is now to be gotten out of the way," the cloaked one clipped shortly.

LONG TOM had finally found himself a hotel, but had discovered it necessary to go to the airport in order to get his baggage sent in. He had dispatched a single suitcase, which comprised his luggage, by a burro man whom the military had recommended as honest. Long Tom was now back at the hotel.

"My luggage get here, señor?" he demanded of the clerk.

The clerk smiled, all but bumped his forehead on the desk in a bow, and passed over Long Tom's room key.

Long Tom located the stairway and climbed to a hall which was dark after the brilliance of the sunlight outside. It took him a moment or two to locate the room that his key called for. He unlocked it and, his eyes still somewhat blinded, he swung the door open, then took a step inside.

Two men had been busy over Long Tom's open suitcase. They leaped to their feet. Knives came into their hands with grim suddenness.

Long Tom was afraid of no man with a knife. Anyway, there was a chair between himself and the pair. He could grab it, use it for a weapon.

But he did not reach the chair. The two over the suitcase had been there as bait to hold his attention. There was another man standing just inside the door. That fellow went forward, swinging an arm club fashion. His hand held a gun, held it by the butt. For nobody but a fool clubs with the butt of a gun. The weapon made unpleasant noise against Long Tom's head.

The two, who had been over the suitcase, caught the electrical wizard's unconscious form so that it would not make noise in falling.

A strange figure in a cloak now appeared, coming from somewhere outside. This individual examined Long Tom closely, making sure that he was senseless.

"Bring a trunk," the cloaked one ordered. "We are going to take him away."

"Is it safe, O Inca in Gray?" one asked.

"Keep your suggestions to yourselves," uttered their fantastic looking chief. "Get this Long Tom Roberts to the place at the edge of the city where I shall meet you."

Leaving his more than a little frightened assistants to handle the matter of removing unconscious Long Tom from the hotel via the trunk route, the Inca in Gray left the hostelry. He went to a cable office, the same one incidentally from which Long Tom's message to Doc Savage had been so cleverly filched. It was the siesta hour, so naturally the place was empty.

The Inca in Gray wrote out a cablegram to an individual in New York. Outwardly it looked like a very innocent cablegram concerning the possibility of getting the American government to make an exception in the embargo against the exportation of war materials in the case of fighting planes. Actually, the message was in a clever code and its true contents were concerned not at all with fighting planes or embargos.

The Inca in Gray met his uneasy assistants at an unfrequented spot near the outskirts of Alcala. They had Long Tom, who was bound and gagged, blindfolded and quite limp.

"Is he dead?" he demanded anxiously.

"Sleeping," sneered one of the men. "Twice I have used my gun on his head."

"He will sleep for a long time in the place where we are sending him," the Inca in Gray said grimly. "And Doc Savage in New York will never hear of him again."

<h2>Chapter IV
THE PERIL IN NEW YORK</h2>

NEW YORK was quiet under a blanket of fog, slightly wetted down by an occasional drizzle of cool rain. It was near six in the afternoon. The populace had gone home from work, and had not yet started for the theatres. It was as quiet as any daylight hour ever became.

But at one spot, rather peculiar sounds could be heard. They were on the eighty-sixth floor of a building which was probably the most pretentious skyscraper in the city.

"Oink!" The sound came with distinct regularity. "Oink! Oink!"

Two men sat in the eighty-sixth floor office from which the sounds came. One of them looked angry. He was a rather slender man, especially thin at the waist. But the thing about him that stood out was his garments. They were sartorial perfection. A typical sample of what was gaining for the wearer a reputation as perhaps the nation's best dresser.

"Oink!" came the sound. "Oink!"

The second man in the room kept his face straight with some difficulty. This man looked rather pleasantly like an ape in unkempt civilized clothing. He would undoubtedly weigh in excess of two hundred and fifty pounds.

The apish man was making the sound, doing it systematically and with painstaking care.

"Oink!" he tried again. *"Oink! Oink!"*

The dapper man blew up. He gesticulated with a slender black cane which he had been holding across his knee.

"Monk," he gritted, "just one more of those noises and I'm going to trim your toenails off right next to your ears."

"Now, Ham," the apish Monk murmured, "you should control that temper."

Ham got up and did something with his cane so that it became evident that harbored therein was a blade of fine steel which looked razor sharp.

"You've been making those hog noises to devil me," he said grimly. "You are hunting trouble and you are certainly going to get accommodated."

Neither of these men looked quite what he was. The man with sartorially perfect rainment, "Ham," was Brigadier General Theodore Marley Brooks, pride of the Harvard Law School alumni. The simian one, "Monk," was Lieutenant Colonel Andrew Blodgett Mayfair, admittedly one of the greatest industrial chemists.

These two—like Long Tom of the South American happenings—were members of Doc Savage's group of five aides. The spot where they conducted their quarrel was the anteroom of Doc Savage's headquarters. The present quarrel was no new one. It had been going on for years, dating back to the World War to a charge of pig stealing which the homely Monk had once framed against the dapper Ham by way of retaliation for a practical joke which Ham had pulled on him.

Monk squared off belligerently and picked up a chair as a defense against the sword cane. The quarrel sometimes reached the point where they struck blows, which was somewhat strange since Monk and Ham had each on occasion risked his life to save the other.

There was no violence this time. A voice spoke from the doorway.

"Something seems to have happened to Long Tom in South America," the voice said.

THAT voice was remarkable, not that it was loud or that it seemed to strive to be particularly emphatic. But it had a suppressed quality that induced thoughts of a mighty machine, murmuring under low throttle.

Monk and Ham both whirled to stare at Doc Savage as he came into the room.

Doc Savage held a cablegram in one hand. The hand was distinctive for two things. The tendons on the back were amazing. The hand had an unusual bronze color. The size of the hand was mentionable also, but was not especially striking because the rest of the man's size was in proportion.

An individual whose appearance was in keeping with his fabulous reputation was this man, Doc Savage. He would stand out in a multitude. There was more to it than his appearance. His eyes for instance—they were like pools of flake gold, stirred always by tiny winds. And there was also his hair, the hue a slightly darker bronze than his skin and straight, rather remarkably like a metallic skullcap.

Doc Savage offered the cablegram. Monk and Ham read it.

DOC SAVAGE
NEW YORK
      IN ALCALA SANTA AMOZA VISITING FRIEND ACE JACKSON STOP MAY SPEND SOME TIME HERE STOP EVERYTHING QUIET

LONG TOM

The cablegram had come from Alcala, Santa Amoza.

Monk, the homely chemist, squinted and scratched his bullet head.

"I don't see anything in that to make anybody think Long Tom is in trouble," he said.

"For once I agree with the ape here," Ham murmured. "I don't either."

Doc Savage's metallic features did not change expression. This was one of his characteristics. He rarely showed emotion.

"Have you overlooked the five-letter code?" he asked.

Monk started, and a ludicrous expression crossed his homely face.

"Sure," he grunted, "every sentence should start with a five-letter word. That's the touch to make sure members of our gang really send the messages."

Dapper Ham seized the cablegram which Doc had brought and examined it again.

"Every sentence doesn't start with a five-letter word in this," he snapped. "That means Long Tom did not send it."

Monk scratched in the bristles along his nape. "What do you reckon's behind this?"

"We will see what we can learn by cabling," Doc told him.

ON the street there was not much traffic and not many parked cars. Hence, there was plenty of room along the curbing. A small sedan wheeled into one of these open spaces.

Four men alighted. The fifth, who was behind the wheel, drove the car away. Those who had gotten out strolled over and ostensibly looked into a show-window. Above them towered the stone and steel monolith that housed Doc Savage's eighty-sixth floor aërie.

"Your instructions are clearly understood?" asked one of the men.

The others nodded. The leader paced the way into the skyscraper. He was a rather striking fellow, principally because of his size and shape. His lines were somewhat remindful of a box on stiff legs. He looked as hard as railroad ties.

Under one arm this man carried a bulky object, carefully wrapped in thick brown paper.

Once in the building lobby, the men separated. Two turned toward the elevator that would lead them to an observation tower above Doc Savage's headquarters, almost a hundred stories above the street level.

The other two members of the group strolled carelessly down the spacious lobby, stopping close to the entrance that led to the express elevator which carried passengers to floors eighty to ninety. They lighted cigarettes and leaned idly against the wall, conversing softly as if awaiting the appearance of friends.

Over in the observation tower elevator, the box of a man—he had the unmistakable look of a professional wrestler—and his companion were silent. The operator glanced at them with only slight curiosity, for dwellers in Manhattan become accustomed to strange types of humanity.

When the elevator stopped at the observation floor, the two passengers acquired admission tickets, walked out on the railed platform and gawked about. A few other persons were there, these obviously being tourists. The burly wrestler still carried his package as he mingled with the crowd. There was system in the mingling, however, for the pair worked around the tower and soon stood before a small door. They tried this and found it locked.

They waited until they were alone on that side of the tower. Then the wrestler brought out a bunch of keys—an assortment of skeleton keys. There was a faint click and the door opened.

The pair slipped through and closed the door behind them. Without hesitation they raced down a small set of steps into a room where the whirr and the click of machinery sounded continuously.

It was the room which held the mechanism that operated the elevators.

A mechanic rose quickly from his chair just inside the room with the machinery. But he was too slow. He did not even see the newcomers. The wrestler swung a great block of a fist, and the mechanic was senseless.

"You know what we do next?" the big box of a man asked.

He was looking about, plainly more than a little bewildered by the maze of wheels and cables that confronted him.

His companion nodded, a confident grin on his wizened face.

"I can handle the rest of it," he said. "I used to install these things."

With sure steps he threaded his way through the cables, pointed to one drum which appeared full of slender steel thread.

"This is the cable that holds up Doc Savage's private elevator," he said. "Unlimber that thing you're carryin'."

The big man grunted and unwrapped the parcel which had been under his arm. The other took it, stripped off the wrapping and revealed a compact metal-cutting torch of a type popular with safe robbers.

Eye-hurting flame from the torch began to play against the cable drum.

DOWN in the street level lobby, the two men who were leaning against the wall near the express elevator were beginning to consult their watches nervously.

"We got another minute," one said.

They were silent throughout the minute.

"Now," the first said. And the other nodded.

They walked to the endmost of the bank of express elevators and entered the cage.

The operator spoke to them quietly, saying, "This elevator goes only to Doc Savage's floor."

"That's where we're headed," one of the passengers responded.

Then the operator jumped suddenly and looked down. A gun had been jammed into his ribs.

"Get going," the hard-faced holder of the gun ordered.

The operator closed the door and started up. For an instant, the two passengers were speechless, their eyes intent on the operator. The latter moved his lever to the stop position. The button of the apparatus that would automatically level the cage at the eighty-sixth floor door was already pushed in.

A fist struck the elevator man callously under the jaw. He sagged, and one of the two passengers caught him under the arms. Holding him helpless, they hit him again and again, until his senses were thoroughly beaten out.

They lowered him to the floor as the cage stopped on the eighty-sixth floor.

The two passengers opened the door, made sure the corridor was empty, then propped the elevator door open with the use of small wooden wedges, which they had previously prepared. They moved silently down the corridor to the stairway. One of them turned and cupped his hands to his mouth.

"Help!" he screamed. "Help!"

Then the pair scuttled silently down the stairway.

The door of Doc Savage's quarters burst open. The giant bronze man was first through, Monk and Ham close on his heels.

"Somebody yelled!" Monk exploded. "Where was it?"

The open elevator door caught their attention. They ripped toward it, glanced inside.

Unexpectedly a small weird sound filled the corridor and the elevator cage wherein the beaten unconscious operator lay. The sound was tiny, exotic, a thing difficult of description. It was a trilling, in a sense, a minute, fantastic note that might have been the product of the wind through the spires of an Arctic ice field.

Monk and Ham looked at Doc Savage, knowing the bronze man was making the sound. They had heard it often. It was a small thing which the bronze man did unconsciously in moments of stress.

Doc Savage stepped into the elevator. Monk and Ham followed.

HIGH above, in the room which housed the lifting machinery, the two sinister men had been staring downward. The elevator cage had a grilled top and the interior was brightly lighted so that they saw Doc Savage and his two aides enter.

"Quick!" gulped the wrestler.

The other manipulated the cutting torch. He already used it sufficiently to nearly sever the cables. The finish of the job required only a moment. With the sound of a snapping fiddle string, the cable parted.

The cage fell away from the open door before Doc Savage and his aides could possibly get out. It gathered momentum. Doc worked the elevator control lever rapidly. It had no effect. Their speed increased.

Homely Monk jammed a thumb violently against the button which was labeled emergency stop. Nothing happened. His apish visage began to look as if whitewash were being pumped under the skin.

Floors went past in a grisly blur.

"Cable cut," Doc Savage said briefly. "Automatic stopping device jammed."

Ham, the dapper lawyer, said nothing, but brushed an imaginary speck of dust from his immaculate clothing as if he wanted to look his best when his crushed body was found after the elevator crashed to the bottom of the shaft, eighty-six floors below.

The human mind has an amazing faculty of working at lightning speed in moments of stress. Monk, his bowed legs outspread, his apish body braced in what he probably knew was a futile effort to absorb the shock, fully expected to die. It showed on his face. But there was something he wanted to say and his big mouth and his throat struggled over the words. To him, what he said seemed to come with infinite slowness. Actually, his words were rapid.

"Sorry I kidded you about that hog, Ham," he said.

"I know," Ham said with equal difficulty. "Forget it."

"You been—great pal, Monk mumbled.

Doc Savage's bronze features had not lightened. The paleness of fear, which might have been expected, was entirely absent. His features were almost weirdly composed. Nor did he speak.

Air was roaring about the cage as they plummeted. The senseless operator stirred a little on the floor, but he would never revive in time to realize what was happening.

The wild cage flashed past the ground floor. And a startled yell came from the starter outside as he realized what was occurring.

Things happened. A giant hand seemed to reach out and grab the elevator, gently at first, then with more violence. Air, passing the sides of the cage, made an ear-splitting scream. The occupants of the elevator went down as if mashed by a giant invisible hand.

And the cage was unexpectedly still, although it seemed, due to the freakishness of the human organism, that it was now flying upward.

Monk lay very still. Ham had fallen half across him.

It dawned on Monk that they were, miraculously, to go on living.

Monk gave Ham a shove that was not gentle.

"Get up and off me, shyster," he snarled.

Ham said, "You awful accident of nature," and got up.

They both eyed Doc Savage. Their expressions showed what they wanted—explanations.

"The bottoms of these shafts are of special construction," Doc Savage said. "They are completely enclosed and fit tightly to the sides of the cage. The compression of the air formed a natural shock absorber."

Monk started to say something, then looked down at his clothing, surprised. He had become soaking wet with nervous perspiration.

ESCAPE from the cage did not prove to be a simple matter. First, the top grille was bolted in place solidly and, being stout, it yielded but slowly. Springing upward, Doc Savage managed to seize an ornamental projection in the cage top. An observer would have sworn it offered no hand grip whatever. Yet, the bronze giant clung there and struck and wrenched repeatedly at the grating until it came loose. The metal was a stout alloy. He bent it back amid a squeaking and rending.

By this time, they had the shaft door open and faces were shoved through, shouting excitedly that an emergency truck had been summoned.

The sides of the shaft were of brick, and rough. Doc Savage mounted, the strength in his amazing hands making ample security out of microscopic handholds.

Even with his efforts, however, several minutes had elapsed before he reached the lobby. A crowd milled. More persons came in from the street, excitement drawn.

Doc Savage lost no time in getting the doors closed so that no one might enter or leave. There was a bare chance the culprits might be inside.

They were not. They had lost no time in leaving the skyscraper, had entered their little sedan and were driving fast when they got a glimpse of the bronze man.

The big wrestler and his consorts were not bad actors. They managed not to show enough excitement to attract attention.

"We've laid an egg," one muttered.

The wrestler began to curse, calling his own father and mother and immediate ancestors numerous unpleasant names.

"Count Hoffe in South America ain't gonna like this," another of them groaned.

The wrestler stopped abusing his ancestors.

"We sure gave the job a botching," he agreed. "Now Doc Savage will steam straight for South America."

"And the Inca in Gray will begin to lay eggs of his own," another man agreed.

"Don't worry," snorted the wrestler. "Any eggs the Inca in Gray lays will hatch out plenty of hell."

The little sedan took them out of sight.

AN hour later, Doc Savage knew that those who attempted to murder them had escaped. The bronze man went to his laboratory. He began assembling mechanical devices—the gadgets which he employed and which, on more than one occasion, had saved his life.

Monk, the homely chemist, stopped in the reception room to read a newspaper. It was a late edition. Filled with the vague heat of the presses, the dampness of fresh ink upon it. The attempt on their lives was headlined.

There was more in the newspaper, also—a paragraph which endeavored to convey to the reader just who and what Doc Savage was.

Doc Savage, the man whose life was attempted, is an individual of mystery. Little is known of him, because he goes to great lengths to keep out of the public eye. It is, however, well known that he is almost a physical marvel and a mental genius.

Doc Savage's profession is undoubtedly the strangest thing about him. Trouble is his specialty—other people's trouble. He is something of a knight in armor, who travels to the far corners of the earth to aid the oppressed, to right wrongs and to war upon those who seem outside the law.

Doc Savage, it is understood, does not work for pay. Yet, he always has fabulous sums at his command. The source of his wealth is a mystery.

Doc Savage interrupted Monk's perusal of the newspaper.

"You might get your portable laboratory together, Monk," he suggested.

The homely chemist squinted at the bronze giant. "Then we're going places?"

"We are," Doc agreed.

Monk frowned. "Do you think that fake cable with Long Tom's name signed to it, and that attempt to kill us had a connection?"

Whatever reply Doc Savage intended to make was interrupted by the appearance of a messenger, wearing the uniform of a cable company. He presented a blue envelope, which Doc opened, read, then passed to Monk and Ham. The missive was cryptic, expressive.

DOC SAVAGE
NEW YORK
    LONG TOM ROBERTS HAS DISAPPEARED
                        ACE JACKSON

The message was from Alcala, Santa Amoza.

Monk looked up from the missive and demanded: "This means we charge right down there, don't it?"

"It does," Doc agreed.

Ham asked, "Do we go by plane?"

"We will try the new stratosphere dirigible," Doc told him. "On a flight as long as this, it will probably be faster than our big plane."

Chapter V
FIRING SQUAD

AT about that moment, Long Tom Roberts, some thousands of miles south of New York, lay on his back and wished that Doc Savage were not quite so far distant. He also wondered where he was, what had been done to him.

A thundering roar was rattling in his eardrums. For some moments he had been wondering about that roar, being unable to tell whether it came from inside his head or outside. Splitting pains chased each other around inside his skull, and at times his eyeballs seemed full of sparks.

He got around to trying to move and found his arms and legs tied. A bit later, it dawned on him that he was jammed in a cramped compartment, small for his slender frame. He tried to shift his position a little.

Instantly, ripping swear words in *Español* crackled above him. He was kicked twice, very hard, in the side. Then a pair of heavy, booted feet pressed down on his middle and remained there, effectually discouraging further movement on his part.

Long Tom ... was ... plunging like a rock toward a mass of very green jungle some thousands of feet below.

Long Tom lay still and organized his thoughts. He was in a plane, an open cockpit type ship. That awful roaring which had tortured him so was the motor.

A riveting machine seemed to open up, almost over his head. The terrific din of it made such a pain in Long Tom's head that he gasped and shut his eyes tightly. The plane in which he was riding must be engaged in a fight.

There was a sound not unlike two cats having a violent fight in the rear of the fuselage somewhere. The plane's framework trembled perceptibly. Long Tom had been through enough aërial fighting to know what the sound meant. Machine gun bullets hitting their ship.

Long Tom's ears began to distinguish other sounds, which resembled firecrackers letting go in a well. That would be artillery. There was an occasional much closer *woof!* some of which cause the plane to sway, pitch. Archies.

Long Tom lay back and shut his eyes. He was not scared, not by the war anyway. He had been through too many of those. He did some reflecting.

Let's see. He had been knocked out in the Alcala hotel. Now he had awakened over the front lines of a war which, judging from the sounds, was no opera.

Long Tom, who frequently went out of his way to hunt trouble, seemed to have done very well in the present case.

The war front sounds were dropping behind. There was no more machine gunning, no more anti-aircraft. The plane flew quietly for some time.

Then arms caught Long Tom under the shoulder, yanked him up. Sunlight hit him in the eyes so blindingly that he was hardly able to see. He felt the ropes being ripped from his feet. A knife slashed the cords that bound his arms.

Instantly, Long Tom turned, tried to get a grip on his captor; but the confinement had made the pallid electrical expert very clumsy. He fared very badly in the fight which he started.

Powerful arms caught him about the middle, lifted him up. He was held over the side of the cockpit, the whole thing happening so quickly that he was distinctly astonished to find himself plunging like a rock toward a mass of very green jungle some thousands of feet below!

LONG TOM'S next actions were pure instinct. He reached for a parachute rip cord ring. When he did that, truth was, he did not even know whether he wore a chute. The head blows had left him very hazy. But the chute rip cord ring was there. He yanked it.

With a suddenness that wrenched his aching muscles, his downward plunge was halted by a billowing spread of silk that snapped out over his head. The parachute had opened, checking his fall.

Long Tom, however, failed to experience the feeling of relief which this happening should have induced. The shock of parachute opening had been too much for his shaky condition. It had knocked him out. He hung, quite senseless, in the parachute harness.

Long Tom, being unconscious, missed the excitement which his descent caused. The jungle land below was not far behind the front lines, and it was infested correspondingly by soldiers.

Naturally, no one shot at the figure in the parachute; but there was a wild rush for the spot where the silk lobe was going to drop.

Long Tom hit hard, but did not know it. He was also dragged a few yards until the silken bulb of the parachute caught itself on a small tree and spilled its air.

When Long Tom revived a few seconds later, he was out of the parachute harness and being held erect by several men. There were other men standing about, holding rifles. All of the men wore uniforms.

Long Tom was too dazed to be greatly concerned about anything. The uniforms did not impress him at first. Alcala had been full of uniformed men.

Those uniforms. Suddenly, he peered at them more closely. They were not like the uniforms he had seen in Alcala. They were entirely different, in fact. He realized what the difference meant.

"Blazes!" Long Tom gulped feebly.

He must be across the line in Santa Amoza's enemy country, Delezon.

The soldiers who had seized him were looking him over. The officer in charge wore a design on his sleeve which meant, if Long Tom guessed correctly, that he was a corporal.

"*Norte Americano*," said the corporal.

"*Si, si,*" Long Tom said in Spanish. "I'm an American. Where am I?"

The corporal laughed; it was not a nice laugh.

"Search him," directed the corporal.

Long Tom might have submitted to the search meekly, except that one of the soldiers, whether by accident or not, jabbed him slightly with the point of a bayonet. Long Tom's reaction was to take a swing at the handiest face. There was quite a tussle for a moment. Then they wrestled Long Tom down and held him.

The soldiers plunged hands into his pockets, turning them inside out, bringing to light everything in his possession. The possessions were a distinct surprise to Long Tom. He was, he discovered, carrying things he had never seen before.

There was, for instance, a small bottle with a poison label. There was a tiny camera with a very

LONG TOM

fast lens. There was a fountain pen which held, as the corporal in charge of the soldiers demonstrated, invisible ink.

"Boy, oh boy," Long Tom mumbled thickly. "Somebody has sure done carpenter work on me."

"What you ees mean, señor?" asked the corporal, who seemed to understand a little English.

"I've been framed," Long Tom said.

The corporal emitted another loud laugh even more ugly, if that were possible, than the first one.

"Eet ees plain you are spy, señor," he said.

"I've been framed," Long Tom repeated.

"You need more better story than that," said the corporal. "Mebbe yo ees t'ink of better one as we take yo to thees Señor General Fernanez Vigo."

"General Vigo, dictator-general of Delezon?" Long Tom grunted.

"Si, si, señor," agreed the corporal. "General Vigo, he ees like talk to spy."

GENERAL FERNANEZ VIGO proved to be in a dugout rather close to the thundery, crashing front line trenches than a general might be expected to keep himself.

General Vigo was the biggest and ugliest man Long Tom could recall having seen in a long time. General Vigo's inconspicuous khaki garb only accentuated his gargantuan aspect. No chevrons or insignia showed on his uniform. As a matter of fact, Long Tom reflected, such marks of rank would not be needed. For anyone who had ever heard of General Vigo would recognize him on sight.

General Vigo's laugh was also interesting. It sounded as if a turkey gobbler were gobbling.

The gobble was very loud and very amused as General Vigo listened to Long Tom's attempt to explain that the spy paraphernalia found in his pockets had been planted there without his knowledge, and that he had not jumped from the plane but had been thrown.

Long Tom gave it up, not having expected the story to be believed anyway, and fell to eyeing General Vigo. He had heard of dictators, political iron men, and had seen some. This was the first one who had looked the part. General Vigo, Long Tom recalled from newspaper stories, had started life as a bullfighter. And that could be believed.

General Vigo stopped his gobble and rumbled in surprisingly good English, "You are a spy. You are wasting your time to deny it."

Long Tom frowned at the world's ugliest man. "What happens to spies over here?"

"They are shot," General Vigo boomed promptly.

"Do they get a chance to defend themselves?" the electrical wizard countered.

"That depends on me," General Vigo laughed. "Sometimes, yes, if I get up on what you call the right side of the bed. Otherwise, no. We just go ahead and shoot them."

"How soon do you shoot them?" Long Tom asked.

General Vigo shrugged. "In your case, ten minutes."

Long Tom batted both eyes rapidly. He was quite positive General Vigo was not kidding him. The General looked very serious at the moment. Long Tom moistened his lips.

"Can you get a cablegram to New York?" he asked.

"Si si," said General Vigo in answer, and added, "Sure."

"Take a tip," Long Tom suggested. "Cable Doc Savage before you cut loose on me."

General Vigo looked like a man who has just discovered himself standing over a quicksand bed.

"Doc Savage?" he growled. "What do you mean, señor?"

"Ask Doc Savage to describe his aide Long Tom Roberts to you," Long Tom suggested. "Take a good look at me when you get the description."

General Vigo thought that over. That he had heard of Doc Savage, it was plain.

"You are one of Doc Savage's men?" General Vigo demanded.

"Right," Long Tom told him.

"What do you do down here, señor?"

Long Tom told him, making the recital as complete as he possibly could. He began with the moment when news of Ace Jackson's being in an Alcala hospital had come to him on the hydroelectric project far to the south.

General Fernanez Vigo was a man who seemed to enjoy his own ugliness. There was a large mirror on the dugout wall in front of his desk, and he amused himself as he listened to Long Tom's recital by making fierce faces at himself in the mirror.

Long Tom finished his recital, "And I have a hunch this mysterious power they call the Inca in Gray is behind my troubles."

General Vigo's face froze. For perhaps a score of seconds, he gave an excellent imitation of a man who had turned suddenly to stone. Then he turned slowly to Long Tom.

"Inca in Gray?" he said slowly and distinctly.

"Yes," said Long Tom. "Inca in Gray—"

"What do you know of the Inca in Gray?" General Vigo roared unexpectedly.

"Nothing," gulped Long Tom, startled. "You see I—"

General Vigo leaped to the mouth of the dugout, shouted, waved his arms. Soldiers came running. He bellowed orders at them in Spanish.

"This man has been found to be a spy!" he roared, "Take him to headquarters! He will be shot at once!"

LONG TOM had often boasted that he had a poker face, but it did not function very well now. He was already very low physically. His feelings showed on his face. The result was rather hideous.

The soldiers grasped Long Tom, hustled him out of the dugout, rushed down a long trench. Rifle bullets squeaked overhead. Exploding big-gun shells made the ground quake. Once, a considerable quantity of dirt was thrown over them by a hit nearby. They had to run to get clear, as the shell caved in the trench.

General Vigo, Long Tom reflected, was at least not afraid of showing himself where the action was hot.

Long Tom was taken well behind the lines, and was loaded into a motor van. This bumped and jarred and rumbled over a bad road, and probably no road at all, for a long time.

Because bouncing about on the van bottom was extremely uncomfortable, Long Tom managed to get to his feet, and this gave him a vantage point from which he could look out of the rear of the van. His impression that the truck was traversing what amounted to no road at all was correct. Scrawny jungle was reeling past. The van stirred up a great deal of evil looking gray dust. Long Tom almost shivered. The dust looked exactly like the dust of death which had been on the murdered man in the Alcala hospital.

Thatched huts began to appear on either side of the van. They were entering a village. The only residents seemed to be soldiers, weary looking fellows, probably back from a rest from the front. The thatched huts gave way to mud or adobe structures. Then there was a scattering of stone buildings. This must be the better part of town, although it was still not an impressive village.

The van stopped. Long Tom was booted out. The soldiers were not handling him any too gently.

A figure appeared before them—the ugliest man in the world, again. To arrive so soon, General Vigo must have come ahead of them in a fast car.

Rage stiffened Long Tom's frail-looking frame. He made a jaw at General Vigo.

"You're putting your neck out, you old bull-head," Long Tom advised him.

"What does that mean—putting my neck out?" General Vigo demanded.

"It means likely a head chopping," Long Tom assured him. "In other words you're asking for it."

"Hah!" General Vigo struck an attitude, his idea of the one which Napoleon is generally supposed to have originated. He gobbled a laugh.

"Me, you would threaten?" he rumbled. "Me, General Vigo, you would scare? Hah! I am not afraid. Me, I can whip the world!"

"You've been trying to whip Santa Amoza for four years," Long Tom said dryly.

Long Tom fully expected that to throw General Vigo into a rage. It did nothing of the sort, made General Vigo grin from ear to ear.

"A wise señor, eh," chuckled the dictator of Delezon. "I could like you. It is too bad I must shoot you."

Long Tom growled, "If you will get in touch with Doc Savage—"

General Vigo roared at his soldiers and waved an arm. The uniformed men picked Long Tom up, stalked with him toward a high adobe wall.

THE prospective shooting of a spy is a spectacle calculated to grip the attention of everyone in the vicinity. This probably accounted for the fact of no one noticing the peculiar actions of one man observing the tableau.

This observer was not much to look at. He had a pocked face, was undersized, but, somehow, there was an air of evil about him. He was careful to get in no one's way and attract no attention, but this man kept a very close watch on what was happening to Long Tom.

General Vigo led the execution squad with the victim directly to the adobe stockade. This was very high and the walls seemed to be thick. There were embrasures to permit the mounting of machine guns along the top. It was obviously a fort.

The entrance through the wall was narrow, to make defense easier, and the aperture was closed by a door of heavy timbers. This opened. Long Tom was shoved through.

The stockade interior was occupied by numerous large buildings, most of them with barred windows. Long Tom was not given much time to look around. They hauled him across the court and he found himself standing before a wall.

The electrical wizard twisted his head to get a look at the wall. What he saw caused him to swallow. The wall was full of pits which had been made, no doubt, by rifle bullets. So here was where they shot their spies.

"A blindfold?" General Vigo inquired, much too politely.

"Yes," Long Tom said promptly.

General Vigo seemed surprised, but before he could speak, Long Tom explained.

"I don't want to be looking at the fellow who kills me," he said. "He might have bad dreams."

Contrarily enough, that struck General Vigo as extremely funny. His roar of laughter echoed off the walls, and sounded exactly like the noise of a farmyard turkey.

"Ready!" he bawled at the execution squad.

That shouted word was very loud. It carried beyond the compound wall and reached the ears of the crowd which had gathered outside. These curious

HABEAS CORPUS

Habeas Corpus is an Arabian hog who is not very big, but makes up for his size in other ways.

Habeas' master, Monk, got him in Arabia. Monk's story is that Habeas Corpus' former owner, an Arab, had sold the pig because Habeas had been making a nuisance of himself by catching hyenas and dragging their carcasses up to the house. It was possible that either Monk or the Arab exaggerated, of course.

But Habeas Corpus is unique among shoats, although it seems he was permanently stunted in youth. Monk has spent many long hours training Habeas, and the result is that the pig possesses a brain which is remarkable. Habeas also knows certain signals, conveyed by movements of the hands, or even a winking of the eye, and will do all of the things which he has been taught the signals mean he is to do. These secret signals of Monk's account for some of Habeas seemingly human intelligence.

When not otherwise engaged, Habeas Corpus can usually be found annoying Ham in some manner.

---

persons had not been admitted to the stockade. Apparently no spectators were allowed. A tense silence settled over this small throng.

"Aim!" They all heard General Vigo shout the word.

If anything, the tension, the silence, increased.

On the outskirts of the listening crowd stood the insignificant man with the pocked face, the fellow who had been observing the proceedings with such interest. He strained his ears.

"Fire!" came General Vigo's command.

It was almost drowned by a volley of rifle shots. In the midst of the ragged fusillade, everyone in the listening throng distinctly heard a cry of agony, exactly such a scream as a man would utter when he feels death lead in his vitals.

Silence followed that.

STRANGELY enough, only one man in the throng outside the stockade smiled. Everyone else was sober. Death was not a pleasant thing.

But one man smiled, and that man was the pock-faced, curious spectator. After permitting himself the smile, he turned and scuttled back among the huts. He lost himself in the shabbier part of the village.

In one respect this village resembled the capital city of Santa Amoza, Alcala. It had stray pigeons. There was not a great number of them, but, nevertheless, there were pigeons.

So no one noted one particular pigeon which arose shortly from the village and winged in the direction of Santa Amoza. Certainly, no one caught the significance of the bird, because carrier pigeons look very much like ordinary pigeons.

Long Tom Roberts was dead. The bird carried word of the end of Doc Savage's aide.

Chapter VI
ATTACK IN THE AIR

THE air speed indicator needle stood near three-hundred-miles-an-hour; but the instrument was not entirely reliable. Not that it was defective—up here in the stratosphere there were wind currents, terrific in velocity, which carried an aircraft hither and yon so that only by celestial observation could speed be reliably calculated.

Doc Savage, a giant of bronze, leaned over a lighted map board, marking their position.

"At this speed, we should be in Alcala, capital of Santa Amoza, in another three hours," he said quietly.

Monk, a grotesque, baboon figure in the vague light of the stratosphere airship control cabin, lifted a furry hand to stifle a yawn.

"This chariot sure can travel," he muttered sleepily.

No clouds were about them, for they were too high. A cotton mass of vapor was some thousands of feet below. It was night. The clouds underneath had the aspect of silver which needed polishing in spots. Overhead, the sky looked remarkably black, the stars unnaturally bright.

Ham, dapperly clad as usual, was in the rear of the control room, applying a bilious looking substance to the tip of his sword cane. The bilious concoction was a drugged mixture which would produce abrupt unconsciousness should a victim be pricked. Ham finished his task and came forward.

He said, "Doc, if you wish to get some sleep, Monk and myself can handle the craft."

Doc Savage shook his head. "Not tired. You and Monk turn in."

Ham nodded agreement, turned, and immediately stumbled over something that emitted a startled grunt.

Monk's bulky form straightened, his homely face contorted with what, if it was not rage, was an excellent imitation.

"Be careful, you fashion plate!" Monk howled. "You kicked that hog on purpose."

Ham sniffed and managed to do it with great dignity.

"Get your insect out of the way," he requested.

The homely Monk, registering great indignation, began to examine the object over which Ham had stumbled. This was a pig. The shoat was one of striking appearance, having a scrawny body, the legs of a dog, an inquiring snout, and ears which induced thoughts of a young elephant.

The pig was Habeas Corpus, Monk's pet.

Monk picked Habeas up by one over-sized ear, looked him over, and sat him down again, then glared at Ham. The dapper lawyer glared back. They did this as a matter of habit. Not only did they never speak civilly to each other, but they invariably looked as if they were on the point of indulging in mutual murder.

Doc Savage had resumed his position calculations. The speed of the dirigible and more especially the velocity and vagary of the air currents made frequent checks necessary. The lighter-than-air craft was much more subject to being swept off its course than would have been a heavier plane.

OUTWARDLY, this stratosphere dirigible gave little indication of its true nature. It was more perfectly streamlined, of course, and there were no projections on the hull, no motor gondolas or control cabins. Everything was inside. Internally, however, the ship was vastly different from the ordinary type.

Skin and framework were of extraordinarily light, strong metal. High-speed Diesel motors, driving propellers, furnished propulsion in the ordinary manner. However, installed in the stern were experimental rocket tubes with which Doc Savage had been experimenting. The rocket method of propulsion was not as yet feasible, being too violent for take-offs and landings. But it could be used in the stratosphere to attain terrific speed. The gas which gave the dirigible buoyancy was, of course, non-inflammable, and had other qualities.

In the control cabin, airtight, special oxygen and heating apparatus took care of air pressure and warmth.

All seemed peaceful, safe, aboard the unusual aircraft. But appearances are deceptive.

Dirigibles are, of necessity, complicated craft, with many structural intricacies. In this one, for instance, there was a little tunnel of a catwalk running underneath from bow to stern, and another on top. There were various chimneylike tunnels with ladders. It was possible to reach almost any part of the gas bag by this system of passages. They were there so that repairs might be made easily while in the air.

They furnished an excellent hiding place; and, as such, they had been taken advantage of.

Two men crouched in one of the tunnels. Both of them had been with the gang which attempted to murder Doc Savage with the elevator trap in New York City. One was the burly fellow whose physical build somewhat resembled that of a box with short legs.

It was very cold up here in the stratosphere. The two skulkers, stowaways in fact, were blue, and almost too stiff to shiver. They had to hold hands over their mouths so that breath could warm their blue lips, in fact, before they could whisper to each other. They had been doing this for the last few moments, preparatory to a conversation.

"We can't hold out much longer," whispered the box-of-a-man's companion.

The burly fellow tried to agree with a nod, but was so cold he could hardly manage even that slight motion. "We're gonna freeze stiff," he said.

"This is a helluva hiding place," the other complained.

"We was damn lucky to get away with even this," the burly fellow told his companion earnestly.

"This Doc Savage ain't such hot stuff," said the first. "He didn't find out we were aboard."

The other man now managed a pronounced shiver which was not due entirely to the cold.

"Don't fool yourself," he mumbled. "The bronze guy took off in a heck of a hurry for South America."

They were silent for a time, suffering from the chills. Moving their arms and legs did them little good. They had not stowed away entirely unprepared, it might have been noted. Each had a small rubber bag, which was one of the chemical heating pads frequently sold by drugstores. That these were losing their potency was evident.

"We gotta do somethin'," said the small man.

The box of a fellow nodded. He crawled to one side, taking great care to avoid noise, and peered down through a tiny opening which he had made in the dirigible's skin. He joined his companion hurriedly.

"Looks like Santa Amoza below," he grunted. "It's time we opened our keg of nails."

The small man got up hurriedly. His expression was vicious, bloodthirsty, and just a bit uneasy.

"You think this is gonna work?" he grunted.

"Sure," said the other. "It can't fail."

They crept downward.

DOC SAVAGE, plotting a Sumner line in the course of his navigation calculations, abruptly heard a slight sound. He heard it twice before giving it much attention. The noise was metallic, not a clanking, but a grinding and gritting, such as might have been made by pliers working upon metal.

Doc Savage swung a glance at the instrument panel. The dirigible was being guided by a robot pilot, a gyroscopic affair, not greatly different from those employed in big planes. The dirigible was exactly on its course.

Doc Savage abruptly decided Monk and Ham were not making the noise. Monk and Ham, in fact, were probably asleep.

The bronze man left the control room, went down a passage which was narrow, barely wide enough to permit him to pass, in fact. On either side were compartments, some of which were used for sleeping quarters. The majority of the compartments, however, had been converted into storerooms or equipped as laboratories for work with electricity or chemistry. Nowhere was there wasted space.

Doc Savage's progress was slow. He was tracking down the source of the grating sound. This was not easy. The motors which drove the airship were, by no means, absolutely silent.

Doc Savage reached the compartment which Monk and Ham used for sleeping. There were two of these, one on either side of the central passage.

The bronze man at once noted a strange fact. There were fastenings on the outside of the compartment doors. These were now secured. Monk and Ham, it appeared, were each locked in. Whether they were asleep could not be told. It was by no means silent enough for snores to be heard.

Doc Savage was looking at the barred doors when another door directly ahead of him opened. This door led into the after catwalk which ran up to the tail where the rudders and elevators were affixed.

A small man with a pinched face that would have been an excellent visage for a movie villain, stepped out. He held his hands up, empty. He looked scared, in fear of receiving immediate bodily damage.

"Wait," he shrieked. "Lemme explain."

He jerked both hands back of him and upward as if trying to indicate something above.

That was a trick. It was a bit too obvious. Doc Savage spun.

Another door down the corridor behind Doc Savage had opened. A huge man, with the body of a box and a face of no intelligence, had stepped out. This one had a revolver.

Doc Savage found himself looking into the muzzle of the gun. There had been no time to do anything.

"Just hold it," said the little man who had first appeared. He now took a gun from his clothing.

Doc held it. He stood very stiffly. However, a close observer might have noted certain large arm muscles swelling in the bronze man's coat sleeve. The sinews coiled, bundled, swelled up, strained against the coat fabric.

But the two captors were too canny. They wrenched small oxygen respirators—gas mask affairs—from inside their shirts and clamped them to nostrils and lips. They must have used these previously on such occasions as the dirigible had gone so high into the stratosphere as to reach air that would not sustain human life.

Doc Savage relaxed. The big muscles in his arms subsided. These two men must know a few of his tricks. In a concealed pocket in his coat sleeve Doc Savage carried tiny glass balls of an anaesthetic which produced quick unconsciousness once it was breathed, but which lost its potency after being in the air a few moments. He had been on the point of breaking the balls with his arm muscles to release the gas.

"Just one more trick," said the box of a man, "and it'll be too bad for you."

The box of a man, it was clear, was not nearly as stupid as he looked.

The two came close, but did so very carefully. Their hands snaked into Doc's pockets, ran over his person. The hands brought nothing to light.

"Huh!" grunted the box of a man. "He don't even carry a gun."

"Don't let that fool you," muttered the other.

They made gestures with a plain meaning. Doc Savage turned, walked toward the control cabin. The guns made twin pressures against his back. He reached the control room, stepped inside.

A giant firecracker seemed to go off on top of his head.

IT was one of the few times when the bronze man came close to being taken completely by surprise. The fact that he was so nearly deceived was probably due to the noise of the dirigible's engines. This covered most of the sounds which the box of a man made as he clubbed with his gun. Not all of them, however.

Doc moved enough to evade much of the blow's force. He went down because that is what they would expect him to do, but he did not go entirely flat. While still slightly above the floor, he seemed to explode.

Spinning, Doc Savage got one of the box man's

legs. He jerked. The fellow went down; but the manner of his descent furnished a surprise.

The box man was a wizard with his strength. He was uncanny. Not only did he have terrible strength, but he knew how to do fantastic things with his hands; and he was only a little slower than chain lightning.

The box man landed full on top of Doc Savage, and his blunt, stubby fingers were instantly in the bronze man's neck, exerting horrible pressure on certain particular nerves and spinal segments. His legs went around Doc's middle in a peculiar scissors which completely stopped breathing.

Doc Savage's hand gripped the man's head, twisted it one way, then the other, so rapidly that the fellow could not get strain in it, then roared bull fashion; but the fellow's neck muscles had surprising strength.

The fellow hit Doc, a very scientific blow which brought pin points of light into the bronze man's gold-flaked eyes.

Doc got hit again.

The bronze man wilted. The tenseness went out of his body and arms, and his head sank until his arms touched the floor.

The box man looked very glad and his grip did not relax. He hit again and again. Then he got Doc's throat, and for long moments he kept his position, squeezing, legs crushing. Finally, he began to relax, sensing victory, and a slow grin slit his square dumb-looking countenance.

"I guess I ain't so bad," he gloated between labored breaths.

His legs loosened and he started to lift himself from Doc Savage's limp body.

Then the bronze volcano exploded. As if he had been a mere featherweight, the box man felt himself tossed into the air, slammed down with a headlock, lifted and whirled in what is commonly known as an airplane spin, a very dangerous predicament in which to be, crashed to the floor.

The box man looked very piqued indeed. He had fallen for an old trick, which had been rather well acted. His squarish body hit the floor with a shock that distinctly shook the dirigible from end to end. He emitted one great squawk, and he did not get up.

Doc Savage did not stand and watch. He flashed for the small man. The latter had been an observer, a gleeful one at first, a discomfited one now. He was trying to get his gun into action.

The little gunman was canny, much more canny than it appeared on the surface, as it later developed.

The fellow dropped his gun, spun and ran. He got out of the control room, banged the door behind him.

Doc did not pursue him. There was a very good reason for that. The box man had only been resting, recovering from his dazed condition. He was on his feet, roaring, berserk. The fellow charged, closed with Doc Savage and began to use more of his innumerable tricks.

The fellow did not get along so well now. Time after time he found himself thwarted. He could get his hands on Doc Savage, but trying to employ some of his deadly holds was about as easy as trying to thread a needle with an eel.

The man registered more and more uneasiness. He had snarled at first. Now he was silent, grim, fearful. The truth had dawned on him.

Doc Savage was merely playing with him.

It was not desire for amusement which motivated the bronze man's dallying. This fellow, Doc had discovered, was a master of physical combat tricks. He was the most dangerous thing in a hand-to-hand fight the bronze man could recall ever having encountered.

It was not often that the bronze man encountered a foe physically his match, and it was somewhat a pleasure, painful perhaps, to work out with the fellow, and it was also an education.

Doc Savage had been educating himself at strange things for a life time.

THERE had been method in the flight of the box man's small companion; but there were no observers to note that. The lean, evil-faced fellow had climbed upward to a spot immediately above the control cabin where there was a second cubicle which held the apparatus that conditioned the air in the control rooms.

The man produced a flashlight. He seemed not unfamiliar with machinery as he worked his way through the banks of mechanism, stopping beside the battery of tubes which carried the air into and out of the cabins below.

The small man began to work with valves. In a moment the man had shut off the oxygen supply.

He hurriedly retraced his way toward the control cabin.

In the cabin, Doc Savage and the box of a man were still at it. That the bronze man was up against a very accomplished opponent was evident in several bruises which he now carried. His skin was broken in a place or two.

But the box of a man was growing weak at the knees. Shoulders hunched to protect his jaws, he sidled back and forth, striving to escape the bronze man rather than approach him. His thick arms darted out repeatedly. There was still speed in them.

Unexpectedly, Doc caught the fellow's wrists, yanked, and the man came toward him helplessly. The blocky man grasped wildly at his opponent. The next instant he was giving an excellent imitation of an attempt to stand on his own face on the floor. He never did know by just what process he had been tripped, up-ended in that fashion.

The squarish fellow rolled over. He was whipped. He made no effort to get to his feet.

Doc Savage watched warily, as if suspecting a trick. He was breathing more rapidly than usual, which was another thing that showed how strenuous the scrap had been. His physical condition was excellent.

So slowly that it was almost imperceptible, the bronze man's face began to change expression. His lips seemed to set more firmly together. For a moment, a small weird sound was audible over the moan of the engines in their special enclosed compartments. It was very vague this sound, a trilling, an uncanny note, one which defied description, except that perhaps it might be likened to the exotic noise of a wind filtering through a tropical forest.

The bronze man took two rapid strides toward the controls. Then his knees collapsed slowly. He went to the floor.

He fell almost directly before the instrument panel, one dial on which registered the air condition. The needle on the oxygen portion of this dial was over on the red section, which meant dangerously low.

Back in the cabin there was a great clamor, a beating of fists on metal, howling and shouting. Monk and Ham had been aroused; but they had found themselves locked in their compartments and the doors were solid.

The blocky man's small, wizened companion appeared, gliding toward Doc Savage's prone form. The fellow now wore his small oxygen supplying device. The man made sure Doc Savage was unconscious. Then he listened to the uproar Monk and Ham were making. That seemed to cause him to become uneasy.

The box man, the terrific fighter, was lying motionless, gasping a little. The small fellow walked over, drew a revolver, and quite casually knocked his associate senseless.

THE small man got binoculars, peered downward through the survey port in the bottom of the control cabin. There were lights below, slightly ahead. The fellow seemed to recognize them. He grinned thinly, and immediately went to the radio apparatus.

The man was no stranger to radio, his movements proved. He studied the outfit briefly. Then, without hesitation, he turned the proper knobs, got the transmitter and receiver in operation. He took his mouth from his oxygen apparatus to speak into a small microphone.

"Reporting," he said calmly.

He turned to a certain wavelength on which there must have been a listener. For there was no wait, no preamble whatever.

"Report," said a voice over the receiver.

"Message to the Inca in Gray," said the small man over the radio. "White Legionnaire number two reporting capture of Doc Savage's dirigible."

That was all. He waited. Several moments passed. Monk and Ham still made a great deal of noise trying to get out of their cabins, but failing. As a matter of fact, those cabins had been constructed with the idea that they possibly might serve as prison cells on occasion. Escape from them was almost impossible.

A message came over the radio. It was not in English, that message, but in a code which would have been absolutely unintelligible to a listener. The small man in the dirigible, however, seemed to understand perfectly.

"Message to Inca in Gray," he said finally. "Instructions understood."

He shut off the radio apparatus, arose from the desk, and again examined Doc Savage. The bronze giant's chest was not moving. He seemed to be lifeless. Showing a callous indifference, the small man paid no attention to his late companion, the burly fellow whom he had cracked over the head.

Running now, the small man made for the portion of the dirigible where they had hidden themselves since the craft had left New York. From a spot where it had been concealed among the girders, the fellow hauled out a bundle, and this, it developed, held two articles.

One of the articles was a bomb.

The other was a parachute.

The man carried the bomb, scrambled downward, sought out the most vital part of the ship, exactly amidships. He placed his bomb, showing some knowledge of explosives in the act. A clockwork detonator was attached to the infernal machine. The man set this. Then he fled.

His hands trembled with haste as he fastened the parachute harness. Then he all but fell down into the control cabin. Light, non-shatterable glass extended all around the control cabin floor. Most of it was immovable; but there were sections on either side which could be raised, hatch fashion. The man worked at one of these, got it open.

Cold air, air many degrees below zero, rushed into the ship. The man shivered. The man thought of something, leered and hurriedly opened the other hatches. He had made it three to one that Doc Savage and the others would die. There was a lack of oxygen, the bomb, and this cold, which would soon freeze them.

The man hesitated and then calmly stepped through one of the open hatches, counted the usual ten seconds very carefully, then pulled the ring of the rip cord. The chute sprouted whitely above him.

He fell very rapidly, and the clouds which had at first seemed nearly carpet smooth became rugose, nodular, a forest of bulbs and clefts of vapor.

Off ahead a short distance the clouds ended. Beyond these, so small as to be barely distinguishable, more of a blur than a definite array of dots, were the lights of Alcala, capital of Santa Amoza.

The clouds followed the man descending by parachute. The fellow was cold, stiff, in fact.

The man had been trying to glance upward, but he had long ago lost sight of the airship. Minutes passed. Again and again he stared upward. He seemed to be waiting for something.

The something, judging from his intense attitude, was slow in coming. The fellow looked worried. A frown of concern grooved his forehead.

Suddenly it came. There was a flash, distinctly lighting the clouds about him. Following that, some moments later, there was a sound remindful of a great crack and whoop and gobble of thunder. Echoes of that tremendous report romped through the cloud bank.

The man in the parachute seemed satisfied. He sighed.

He made an expert landing in a patch of tall brush which scratched him somewhat. He disengaged himself from the parachute in a great hurry. Then he scuttled away.

Chapter VII
AN OFFER TO SURRENDER

SOUNDS of that titanic explosion in the sky were heard over the entire city of Alcala. It caused some thousands of people to promptly rush to their bomb-proof cellars. For aërial bombing raids were not unknown in Alcala. Others of the populace swarmed into the streets, these being sold to curiosity exceeding the demands of safety and good sense. They stared at the sky, hoping to see the spectacle of an air raid.

The observers saw what seemed to be great streamers of flame dropping through the sky, flaming fragments falling toward the earth from a tremendous height perhaps. These burned themselves out long before they reached the ground. Searchlights around Alcala pointed lean white fingers into the sky, and waved about hungrily, trying to locate possible raiding planes from Delezon. Anti-aircraft guns barked a few times. Quiet finally returned.

Under cover of the excitement, however, certain sinister movements had been going on. Various men who always kept to the darkness and took great pains that their faces should not be seen had been moving toward a certain common spot. It was not difficult for them to move about undiscovered for Alcala, after that first explosion, had been promptly darkened in anticipation of an air raid.

Almost in the shadow of the rather impressive presidential palace of President Carcetas the meeting occurred. The spot was the deserted home of a certain wealthy man who had been in sympathy with the enemy country of Delezon and had found it wise to flee some two years previously. Except for a muttering of passwords there was no other sound as the men met.

Eventually, however, there was a stir of activity, a muttering.

"The master comes," someone whispered.

"The Inca in Gray," another breathed.

A moment later, their sinister master stood among them. No *fosforos*, the little paraffin matches popular in Santa Amoza, were struck. Nor did anyone thumb on a flashlight. To have done so would probably have meant prompt shooting or a knife, and it would have disclosed nothing anyway.

The Inca in Gray was disguised simply and effectively. A long shroud of gray cloth, so dark a gray that it was almost black, encased the figure from head to foot. There were no eyeholes, but the cloth of the hood was thinner so that the eyes inside could peer out through the fabric.

The Inca in Gray spoke in a voice that was painstakingly altered so as to be unrecognizable.

"Has White Legionnaire number two arrived?" was the question.

The small man who had left the bomb in Doc Savage's dirigible now stepped forward and identified himself. He launched immediately into a description of his feat.

"There was T.N.T. in that bomb," he finished, speaking Spanish with the difficulty of a man who has just learned it. "You can take all of that airship that they'll find and put it in your eye."

The Inca in Gray was ominously silent.

"A little more respect in your manner, please," said the voice back of the hood.

Although the voice of the disguised mastermind was excellently disguised, a close listener might have detected one possibility. The English which the being spoke was better than the Spanish. The English words came more freely.

The assembled followers of the Inca in Gray seemed to know what they were there for. No orders were given.

The Inca in Gray simply said, "We will act now, señors."

The meeting dispersed.

THE sinister cloaked figure of the Inca in Gray appeared alongside the presidential palace shortly afterward. There were no lights, but sentries could be heard shifting back and forth in the darkness.

The Inca in Gray listened to the sounds the sentries made. Some moments of this was sufficient to furnish an excellent idea of the beats the fellows patrolled. The vague form that was the Inca in Gray scuttled forward.

Then came a bit of bad luck. One particular sentry had been pacing a regular course. Now, desire for a smoke suddenly seized him and he stopped, popped a cigarette between his lips, struck a *fosforo*. The glow of the match showed the Inca in Gray, a rather hideous apparition in the darkness.

The sentry tried to shout. He leaped backward. He was too slow. With a frenzied speed the Inca in Gray was upon him. One furious blow was struck, a heavy military pistol being the implement.

The sentry went down and made no sound thereafter.

Sudden, violent as it had been, the conquering of the sentry had been executed with comparative stealth. There was no alarm. The Inca in Gray eased away, a ghostly apparition in the warm night.

Santa Amoza had been at war a long time; and war means that political leaders must take more than the average precautions against an assassination. President Carcetas had, as a move to protect the life of his daughter, caused a tall, thick screen of shrubbery to be thrown up around the palace verandas.

Pretty Señorita Anita Carcetas was at this moment resting herself on a veranda, where she not only was hidden from the street, but from anyone in the palace grounds as well. The young woman was reading the local newspapers which were filled with the usual claims that Santa Amoza had the enemy, Delezon, practically whipped.

The young woman actually considered herself perfectly safe. If she heard a faint sound behind her, she dismissed it as being made by a servant. A large pad of cloth was over her mouth before she was aware of danger. The cloth was saturated and reeking with a well known hospital anaesthetic. The young woman struggled furiously. She could not see her captor. She kicked backward, contacted shins.

For a moment she got her face free of the wet cloth. She emitted piercing screams, and, because she had gotten a glimpse at the grim covering of her assailant, she jumped at a correct conclusion.

"The Inca in Gray!" she screamed. "Help!"

Then her attacker got the soaked cloth back over her nostrils, lifted her and carried her way. The anaesthetic had her senseless before she had been taken far.

EXCITEMENT ran like fire through the presidential palace. Sentries dashed about. An attempt was made to turn the lights on, but it was discovered the power lines had been cut. The enforced darkness only increased the confusion.

President Carcetas of Santa Amoza dashed out of his private office. He asked questions of an excited sentry.

"Señorita Anita—"

"Carried away," the soldier blurted.

President Carcetas became very pale at that.

"Stop this wild dashing about," he roared in Spanish. "Order all streets in the vicinity of the presidential palace blocked. Have squads of soldiers search the houses. Notify the police. Quickly!"

The soldiers scurried away.

President Carcetas had one thing that political leaders frequently do not have. He looked the part. When his picture appeared in the rotogravure sections of New York newspapers, as it occasionally did, it was not necessary to read the cut lines below the photograph to know that here was a president of a South American republic. President Carcetas could also have been taken for an elderly Irishman, although he was pure Castillian. His skin was fair, but a bit sun browned. He had a great shock of white hair, somewhat remindful of a basket of cotton on his head. His eyes were piercing, but overshadowed by eyebrows that somehow made one think of miniature black foxes. President Carcetas' eyebrows were very expressive. The rest of his face seemed to be grim and, at the same time, kindly.

President Carcetas moved to the left wing of the presidential palace and soon stopped in front of a closed door. He lifted his hand and knocked, got no answer, knocked again. His black eyebrows ran up on his forehead. He hesitated, then turned the knob and entered.

At first glance, it appeared the room was vacant. Sheets and blankets had been thrown back from the bed, as if had been slept in. A taboret near the head of the bed was upset. A glass of water that had been on it had wetted the carpet.

A groan sounded. It was muffled.

President Carcetas' eyebrows ran down, then up, and he sprang forward, hot lights in his piercing eyes. He sank beside the bed, looked under it, and a moment later pulled a bound figure into view. The fellow was gagged, but removal of this speech impediment took only a moment.

The bound man who had been under the bed was long and lean. The hair on his bullet-shaped head was close cropped.

The man was Count Hoffe, munitions salesman. His presence at the presidential palace was no mystery. President Carcetas of Santa Amoza had been placing a new order for munitions, and terms had needed discussing. Hence, Count Hoffe had remained at the palace for the night.

"What happened?" President Carcetas demanded.

Count Hoffe groaned. An ugly bump showed on the side of his head. One of his eyes was all but closed, and a small stream of scarlet crawled from one nostril.

"A sinister figure in a gray cloak was creeping through my room," Count Hoffe explained. "When I awakened, he struck me down."

"Did you see the face of this assailant?" Carcetas asked.

Count Hoffe hesitated, moistened his lips.

"I did."

"Who was it?" President Carcetas barked.

"The information will not be pleasant," Count Hoffe mumbled. "It will be a shock."

"Who was your attacker?" the chief executive of Santa Amoza requested grimly.

"Ace Jackson," said Count Hoffe.

PRESIDENT CARCETAS was genuinely shocked, it was plain. His jaw dropped and his eyes widened.

"Ace Jackson," he said grimly. "Are you sure?"

Count Hoffe nodded painfully. "I am sure."

"But Ace Jackson is lying in the hospital badly burned," reminded President Carcetas. "He could walk only a few paces."

Count Hoffe was free of the fastening rope now. He sat on the edge of the bed and held his head in his hands.

"You might have the hospital called to see if Ace Jackson is still there," he suggested.

President Carcetas barked an order. One of his many secretaries immediately got in touch with the hospital where Ace Jackson had been confined. The secretary came scampering back with a surprised look on his face.

"Ace Jackson is gone," he said.

"Now we know the identity of the Inca in Gray," Count Hoffe growled.

President Carcetas said nothing in reply. He seemed to be too deeply stricken for words.

The section of the city in which the presidential palace stood was now in an uproar. Machine guns had been erected in the streets. Lines of soldiers blocked the thoroughfares. No one was allowed to enter or leave.

Squads of soldiers were searching houses regardless of whether the occupants wanted it or not. President Carcetas dashed here and there. He waved his arms; he shrieked. His demeanor was altogether that of a man on the verge of going to pieces.

This was surprising. President Carcetas was ordinarily a taciturn man who kept his temper. Ordinarily, he never flew into rages, and because he kept his head level his decisions were usually just. This was what made him probably the most genuinely respected president Santa Amoza had ever had.

Now, however, President Carcetas was a different man. The seizing of his daughter had done that. If he remained in his present condition, he would be unfit to guide the destinies of the republic. He was, in fact, liable to commit all kinds of blunders.

"Why should the Inca in Gray seize my daughter?" he screamed repeatedly.

Count Hoffe took pains to shake his own head sorrowfully. If he had any ideas on the subject, he did not voice them.

President Carcetas, snapping frightfully at those who tried to comfort him, made his way to the room where the sentry knocked unconscious by the Inca in Gray was being revived. The soldier had received a terrific blow. Restoratives were only now affecting him. He stirred feebly, moaned.

President Carcetas sat over him and shouted. "Who struck you, fool?"

This was the first time anyone could recall having heard President Carcetas address one of his soldiers abusively.

The recovering sentry noticed the rage of the chief executive and shivered.

"It was a figure, a beast in gray, señor *Presidente*," he gulped. "I had no chance."

"Did you see the individual's face?" roared President Carcetas.

"I am not sure," spoke the sentry. "But I think—"

"You think what?" Carcetas was frankly frantic.

"I think it was Señor Don Kurrell, the oil man," said the sentry.

THE effect of the soldier's words was that of a minor explosion. Ominous mutters went up.

Count Hoffe, disbelief on his militaristic features, shouted, "That must be a mistake! It must have been Ace Jackson!"

"It resembled—Don Kurrell," insisted the sentry.

If President Carcetas had been imitating a madman before, he put much more zest in the performance now. He all but bowled his chief of staff over, shouting, "Get Don Kurrell! Have him brought here at once!"

Soldiers scampered out, entered fast official cars, and these roared away. It was well known that Don Kurrel maintained a suite in Alcala's finest hotel.

Within twenty minutes, the officer in charge of the soldiers sent to get Don Kurrell telephoned. He was speaking from Kurrell's hotel.

"Don Kurrell has not been seen all evening," he reported.

President Carcetas went into a fresh spasm at this. He ordered guards all over the city quadrupled. He directed that the airport be watched, the trains be searched, that all automobiles be stopped and thoroughly examined.

It was plain that President Carcetas was becoming no calmer as time passed. Indeed, his past years of self-control seemed to be reacting unfavorably. He was growing more jittery, more violent.

Official cars had been making a great deal of noise in their going and coming, but this was nothing to the uproar of sirens which now accompanied the arrival of an expensive foreign limousine, trailed by four military automobiles bearing a personal bodyguard of soldiers. There was a coat of arms on the foreign limousine for everyone to see and thereby know who rode within.

Señor Junio Serrato, minister of war, commander in chief of the armies of Santa Amoza, was the man who was second in power to President Carcetas. War minister Serrato's face wore a worried look as he alighted and dashed into the presidential palace.

He got a jarring greeting from President Carcetas.

"Where have you been?" howled the chief executive of Santa Amoza. "When I need you, you are not around!"

"Shut up!" said war minister Serrato, with equal brusqueness. "Read this. It was shoved under the door of my home."

Serrato presented a folded paper for the other's inspection.

> To be delivered to President Carcetas:
> Your daughter is by now in my hands. In the room next to her a firing squad will be oiling rifles. Whether or not the girl stands before this firing squad depends on President Carcetas. If Santa Amoza surrenders to Delezon, the girl will be released unharmed. If there is no surrender, she will, I can assure you, be shot.
> General Fernanez Vigo,
> Dictator-General of Delezon

President Carcetas' hands seemed to die in a limp way. The paper dropped from his hands to the floor.

"Vigo—has—Anita!" he gasped.

War minister Serrato, his Latin handsomeness somewhat stark, made a grim mouth. He rubbed a fingernail over the thin line of his black mustache.

"What moves shall we make?" he asked.

President Carcetas drew himself up. He was very pale as if about to faint.

"Order an unconditional surrender immediately!" he snapped.

War minister Serrato's mustache jerked a little. Determination came over his face, settled there so heavily that it made his features almost ugly.

"No!" he snarled. "Santa Amoza will never surrender!"

TENSION CAME into the room, a tension which was as real and which affected everyone as if it had been a cold wind. There were present a number of old generals who had been through revolutions before the day of President Carcetas. These canny old fellows drew to one side and dropped hands to the guns which they wore at their belts. They became expectant, tense.

President Carcetas was glaring at war minister Serrato. The chief executive of Santa Amoza looked somewhat stunned, and, for a moment, his calmness was almost deadly.

"You heard my orders," he said grimly. "We surrender."

"I heard your orders," minister Serrato told him. "We do not surrender!"

President Carcetas blew up.

"You are no longer a war minister!" He turned to the soldiers and screamed, "Arrest this man!"

The officers present had obeyed President Carcetas for a long time. Habit got the best of them. They moved forward.

War minister Junio Serrato drew himself up. His little mustache was a straight line, and he now made a speech that went down in Santa Amoza history.

"Wait!" he said. "The future of Santa Amoza depends on what we do within the next few moments. The situation which confronts you has behind it, I believe, more than meets the eye. I refer, of course, to the sinister depredations of this mysterious fiend known as the Inca in Gray."

War minister Serrato paused to look over the assemblage. They had stopped, were listening to him.

"The Inca in Gray has seized Señorita Anita Carcetas," Serrato continued quietly. "There was a purpose behind that seizure, a purpose that is plain. The purpose is about to be accomplished. President Carcetas is a man whom we all love and revere and respect, but he is not himself now. He is a man driven insane by danger threatening the one he loves. I do not censure him for that. No one can. But I do not think you, the generals who have fought with me, or I, should permit the surrender of Santa Amoza. For that is obviously the thing the Inca in Gray intended to happen."

That was all he said, but it was enough to make the others think. It was a crucial moment. President Carcetas did the thing which really swayed the course of action.

Waving his arms, screaming shrilly, President Carcetas shouted, "Santa Amoza must surrender! The life of my daughter depends upon it!"

That decided the assembled generals. Thousands of men had already died in the war. It was a terrible decision which confronted them, but they, as soldiers, saw their way clear. The life of one person, even of attractive Señorita Anita Carcetas, must not lose everything for Santa Amoza.

President Carcetas was seized. They carried him, screaming, gibbering to a secluded portion of the presidential palace.

Señor Junio Serrato looked on quietly. If there was elation in his heart, he hid it. He did not look like a man who had just become actual ruler of Santa Amoza.

Count Hoffe, munitions salesman, had been an obscure onlooker. Count Hoffe had taken pains to stand well in the rear, but it was purely by chance he positioned himself near a tapestry. He had paid no attention to that tapestry. When a voice now reached his ears, he did not, at first, realize it was coming from behind the hanging.

"You have just witnessed a rather unusual revolution," said the voice, which was low and cultured. "Should war minister Junio Serrato himself be the Inca in Gray, he could not have planned more skillfully. By this one stroke, he has made himself all powerful in Santa Amoza."

Now this speech was one which might well prove not to be the healthiest of utterances. Men have been shot for less.

Count Hoffe turned to see who had spoken. His eyes flew wide. He actually jumped some inches off the floor.

"Doc Savage!" he squawked.

Chapter VIII
SABOTAGE

COUNT HOFFE'S shout was very loud and very surprised. It promptly drew all eyes to the giant bronze man who had just stepped from behind the tapestry, which, incidentally, covered a window that admitted to the palace grounds.

No one said anything for several moments. Perhaps the silence was due in part to the impressive presence of the bronze man. For, as he stood there, his giant size, the strange power in his flake-gold eyes, his combination of bronze skin and slightly darker bronze hair, were very impressive.

War minister Junio Serrato stepped forward. His thin mustache warped a smile. He executed a brisk bow.

"Santa Amoza is honored," he said. "May we hope that you had an interesting trip down?"

"It proved to be interesting enough," Doc Savage said dryly.

War minister Serrato caught the double meaning, promptly demanded, "What do you mean?"

Doc Savage was a student of human nature, and knew a great deal about the most effective methods of going about obtaining his ends. A frank statement of his position frequently avoided misunderstanding and difficulties. So he told exactly what had happened including the attempt on his life in New

York and ending with the dirigible flight southward after he had learned Long Tom was missing. He described the fight in the dirigible. That part was interesting.

The airship control cabin, it seemed, was equipped with emergency oxygen apparatus, which went into operation automatically when the main source of supply failed. The emergency equipment had saved Doc Savage's life. In fact, he had only been unconscious for a brief period, reviving in time to observe the small man leaping with the parachute.

A hasty search had located the bomb, and it had required no great skill to disconnect the clockwork mechanism so that the infernal machine would not explode.

"We carried the thing to a hatch, reset the clock mechanism and tossed it overboard," Doc explained. "It went off in the air, far below us. That was to lead the would-be killer to think his plot had succeeded."

"Where is your dirigible?" war minister Serrato asked.

"In the stratosphere above Alcala." Doc explained. "It seemed advisable to let our mysterious enemies think we were dead. An auxiliary plane brought me down to earth. Monk and Ham are with the dirigible."

"You say you employed—an auxiliary plane?" War minister Serrato seemed puzzled.

"A very small craft carried inside the dirigible," Doc told him. "Not a new procedure, as you may know."

"Where did you leave the plane?" the other queried.

"At a small airport west of the city," Doc replied.

War minister Serrato smiled slightly, but without humor. "You got past the presidential palace guards quite easily."

"They nearly caught me several times," Doc corrected.

Serrato seemed to be considering that. When it became apparent that he was to have nothing more to say on the subject, Doc Savage spoke.

"Long Tom—Major Thomas J. Roberts," the bronze man reminded. "His whereabouts is the most important thing to me at present."

War minister Serrato looked grim at that, his mustache an upside down arc. "We have, as you might expect, an espionage system in the enemy country of Delezon."

Doc Savage's flake-gold eyes were steady. "And your spies have reported what?"

"That Señor Long Tom Roberts was yesterday shot as a spy," Serrato said.

DOC SAVAGE'S expression, strangely enough, did not alter in the slightest at that; but a moment after he had heard the news concerning Long Tom, there was a sound in the room, a small eerie mysterious sound, a trilling. It might have been the note of some fantastic tropical songster, so vague that it all but defied recognition, and possessed of a ventriloquial quality which made it seem to come from everywhere. It trailed up and down some vagrant scale of its own and died away.

"This report was reliable?" he asked.

"Quite," war minister Serrato nodded. "There's not the slightest doubt."

"Tell me what you know of this Inca in Gray," the bronze man suggested abruptly.

War minister Serrato blinked, then replied. The bronze man listened silently to the review of the sometimes rather horrible activities which were delineated. The tale told a very definite story of its own. Time after time the Inca in Gray had smashed offensives which had seemed certain to give victory to Santa Amoza.

"That makes it seem as if the Inca in Gray were a representative of your enemy, Delezon," Doc suggested.

War minister Serrato nodded his head. "We have thought so, but there has never been proof."

Doc Savage said nothing more, but turned toward the door.

"What do you plan?" Serrato demanded.

"A visit to General Fernanez Vigo, general dictator of Delezon," Doc Savage said.

The other's thin mustache was a rapidly bending line. "But—"

"General Vigo executed Long Tom," Doc said quietly. There was no rage in the bronze man's voice, no crashing wrath; but the controlled tones held something else, held a quality so chilling, so determined that war minister Serrato took a step backward. He bowed.

"The facilities of Santa Amoza are at your disposal," he said.

"Thank you." The bronze man hesitated. "My preference is to work alone."

HAM

He stepped through the same window by which he had arrived, and, although there were guards in the grounds, and in the surrounding streets, his departure was undiscovered. The bronze man was a master of stealth, a wizard at going places without being seen.

There were a few lights along the streets of Alcala now. The night was hot, and even a military edict could not keep doors shut and windows shuttered. Even an excellent system of street-lighting, however, would not have made the avenues of Alcala, especially in the poorer section, easily traversed after nightfall. Over in the old town, on the west side, streets were all narrow, and, more often than not, rough, some lined with debris.

Could an observer have noted the progress of the bronze man, that person would perhaps have sworn that Doc had the eyes of a cat. As a matter of fact, the bronze man possessed something better than that.

He wore goggles of peculiar construction—they had lenses fully as large as condensed-milk cans. In one hand he carried a box of a device which resembled an oversized magic lantern. The lens of this was very large and almost intensely black. It seemed to give off no light—which was deceptive. The box was a lantern for the projection of light rays outside the visible spectrum, and the goggles, amazingly complex, made it possible for the bronze man to see with this unusual light.

Hence, although he traveled through what was apparently intense darkness, he could actually see with fair distinctness what went on about him.

Running easily, he sped through the streets, dodging obstructions, making fast time toward the small airport on the outskirts of the city. He was careful to keep clear of pedestrians, and when he saw cars coming he ducked into darkened doorways.

He reached the airport. He came on the scene silently, using the "black light" lantern. That

Doc Savage picked up the fallen fellow as though he were weightless and whirled him, club fashion.

accounted for the fact that he took a number of men by surprise.

THERE were seven of them. They wore civilian garments, and it was necessary to no more than look at them to understand why they wore such clothing. A recruiting officer, even in war time, would hesitate to pass such ugly looking specimens as these.

They drew near the plane. Without seeming to change his stride, Doc Savage's speed increased. He made no noise. Although he could see clearly, there was intense darkness around the little airport, and the eyes of the men, of course, failed to register the presence of the black light.

Doc Savage closed in on the rearmost. He could hear them talking.

"Hurry, *amigos*," the one who seemed to be in charge was saying. "There is little time."

"Why does the Inca in Gray wish the plane destroyed?" one muttered.

"That is the question of a child," sniffed the other. "Have you not heard of the aërial push against Delezon, which Ace Jackson this afternoon ordered from his hospital bed?"

"I heard many planes in the air," one grunted.

"There are no other aircraft in Alcala for Doc Savage to use," said the first speaker. "Hence, if we destroy this ship, he will have to remain in Alcala."

That was not all Doc Savage would have preferred to hear, but they were starting to wreck the ship. That would have to be stopped. The bronze man drove out a beam of an arm. A man moaned, dropped under the blow.

Doc Savage picked up the fallen fellow as though he were weightless, and whirled him, club fashion. When he released him, two more men were bowled over.

Doc Savage whipped backward, making no noise, circling. He still held the black light lantern, but now he placed this on the ground, its rays playing on the group about the plane. Then he charged.

A man tried to drag out a flashlight. Doc went to him, clipped him alongside the temple. The fellow fell.

The survivors were shouting, charging about madly, falling over the fallen forms of their companions.

One, by the rankest of good luck, got a grip around Doc's neck. The bronze man reached back, grasped his assailant, whipped him swiftly. The man screamed in the air. The shriek was ended with a hollow, unpleasant sound as his body hit the ground.

There were two survivors now, and they got frightened. They put their heads back, their chests out, and ran. Nature probably invented fear as a stimulant to make her children move swiftly when there is need to do so. These men were frightened, and thought death was at their heels, and they probably ran faster than they ever had before.

Doc Savage was delayed a moment when one of the men who had already gone down in the fight strove to get to his feet. He sank when Doc Savage clipped his jaw, and remained down, only breathing showing that he was alive.

Doc Savage pursued the two who had fled. Fast as these two traveled, Doc Savage was swifter. He did not, however, catch them until they had covered all of two hundred yards. The breath was coming out of their lungs with whistles like the barking of small dogs.

He felled them as they ran by pulling up alongside them and using his fists. The first sank easily. The second made a ball out of himself and went head over heels with a loud slapping noise.

Doc Savage was examining them when he heard a plane motor roar into life.

DOC SAVAGE straightened, listened. It was a plane, certainly. Its roar was coming from back at the field. There was a bass crash of power about the motor that enabled Doc to recognize it instantly— his own plane!

The bronze man ran toward the field. What had happened was unexpected. The men he had left there, his assailants—six out of the eight—would certainly still be senseless. He knew how hard he had struck them.

Doc was heading for the unusual lantern which projected the black light, and which he had left on the ground at the scene of the fight. He found it, picked it up, and twisted a rheostat on it making the beam stronger. Ordinarily, he did not use it full strength, because the small, powerful batteries would be quickly exhausted. He doubled around shrubbery, raced through a clump of palm trees, and the invisible rays from his lantern picked up the plane.

The ship was in motion, traveling rather fast, wavering a little uncertainly. The wavering was due to the fact that the tail was carried a little too high; the stick must be lashed forward. That, of course, had been done to keep the ship from leaving the ground.

With speed increased, the ship headed for the opposite side of the field. The tarmac was rather large, somewhat rough. The ship bounced. It must be doing close to a hundred miles an hour now on the ground.

Palm trees lined the opposite side of the field. Straight for these the little all-metal craft scudded.

With devastating force the ship hit the palms. Wings snapped off. The motor left the craft and went on ahead like a bullet. There was a spectacular crash, a *whoosh!* as the gasoline caught. The flames spread, not only enwrapping what was left of the plane, but climbing the palm trees and turning them into pillars of fire.

Doc Savage did not go toward the ship; it was ruined, of course.

The bronze man had kept on running throughout the whole thing. He merely changed his course now, veering toward the spot where he had left the six unconscious men. His strange light device picked them up an instant later. He counted, all six of them. They were exactly as he had left them.

But no! Not as he had left them. They had been alive.

Now they were dead.

Doc Savage was still using the black light. The aspect of things, as viewed with this light was somewhat unnatural, high-lights and shadows being more starkly emphasized; but it was certain that the six were dead.

There was something else also, a weird appearance of the skin, a vague glow somewhat like phosphorescence. Doc Savage switched off the light, removed the goggles, and extracted a small flashlight from his clothing. He thumbed it on.

The instant he looked at the six dead men his strange trilling came into existence. The sound seemed smaller, more eerie than ever, and it persisted only a moment.

A grayish powder covered the hands, the faces of the dead men. The stuff might have been an unclean dust.

The mark of death by the hand of the Inca in Gray!

Doc Savage went swiftly to a knee. Reaching into a pocket, he extracted an envelope, not an ordinary paper envelope, but one of a varnished silk, both water and air proof.

He did not touch the powder, but with blades of grass brushed some of it into the envelope. He rolled the top of the envelope tightly and fitted over it a metal clamp, which rendered it air-tight. He pocketed this.

He had been listening; and now he heard the sound he had expected to hear. A man moving.

DOC SAVAGE advanced toward the sound. He made no effort to move noiselessly, but his progress was almost silent. His keen ears caught the sound of more motion ahead of him. Someone was creeping away.

Doc donned the goggles, turned the infra-light projector on again. The invisible rays—invisible to the unaided eye—disclosed no one. The skulker was inside the undergrowth which surrounded the field.

Doc Savage decreased his speed slightly as he entered the growth. That was necessary to maintain silence. He heard his quarry more often. The fellow seemed to be moving faster, attempting to get away from the vicinity.

With a burst of speed that was a bit dazzling, had there been light to observe it, Doc Savage shot forward. He discerned a crouching, running figure. The marauder was quickly overhauled.

The bronze man struck no blow. He merely grasped the fugitive's arms just above the wrists, lifted the fellow and slammed him to the hard ground.

They remained thus an instant. Neither spoke. Neither moved. Then Doc Savage transferred both the fellow's wrists to the vise grip of one bronze hand, and with the other hand extracted his electric flashlight and brushed off the goggles. He switched the flash on.

The captive was a tall angular mummy of bandages. He had a face that looked as if it had gone through many a fight. His nose was particularly flat, giving his countenance the aspect of an English bulldog.

The captive grinned widely.

"I've heard a lot about you," he said. "An' I'll tell the wide-eyed world that you live up to advance notices."

"Who," Doc Savage asked, "are you?"

"Ace Jackson," the prisoner said.

Chapter IX
CRACK-UP

DOC SAVAGE'S fingers, clamping the man's wrists, did not loosen. The grip was tight and painful. The grin disappeared from Ace Jackson's face and he writhed a little.

"Take it easy," he requested. "After all, I'm supposed to be an invalid."

"Why did you wreck my plane?" the bronze man asked, and there was something terrible in the contours of his voice.

"You got me wrong," Ace Jackson grunted. "I didn't."

Doc Savage pulled the flyer toward him, powerful fingers holding the other easily. He searched the man. Two big military automatics came to light. Nothing else.

"You fled," Doc Savage reminded his captive.

Ace Jackson blinked. "I was hunting my pal."

"Talk sense," the bronze man requested.

Ace Jackson scowled, "Say, ain't you bein' kinda rough on a friend of Long Tom's?"

Doc Savage told him, "It would be much more convenient if you stick to answering questions."

"I seem to be in bad," the flyer blurted.

"You are," the bronze man agreed. "Count Hoffe seems to be quite sure that you knocked him out in his room and tied him up."

Ace Jackson's grin was boyish. "Seeing you're such a pal, I won't deny that."

The bronze man said nothing, did nothing, but small strange lights were in his flake-gold eyes as he asked, "Do you mind explaining?"

"Something happened to Long Tom Roberts, and when something happens to my pals, I generally try to do things," Ace Jackson said grimly. "I think the Inca in Gray got Long Tom. I ain't got no proof. I just think it. So I been looking around. I was frisking brother Hoffe's room when he woke up, so I chilled him."

"Any reason to suspect Hoffe?" Doc asked.

"Nope," said Ace Jackson. "I just wasn't overlooking any bets."

Doc Savage suddenly slapped Ace Jackson's arm and chest lightly. He slapped numerous spots. Only twice did the flyer wince.

"You are supposed to be very badly burned," Doc Savage told him. "Actually, you seem to be in fair condition."

Ace Jackson flushed, quite distinctly. He moistened his lips; he wrinkled the flat nose that gave his face the bulldog aspect.

"Lookit," he muttered. "If you had a pretty girl who came to see you every day and held your hand and stuff like that, wouldn't a hospital look pretty good to you? Fact is I coulda been out two weeks ago, but I been doing a little faking."

Doc Savage said nothing, looked at the man. Ace Jackson grinned wisely, plainly hoping his story would be believed.

"That's straight," insisted the flyer. "But, for gosh sake don't tell Anita."

"What were you doing here?" Doc Savage asked abruptly.

"I was following a guy," said Ace Jackson.

"Who?"

"Don Kurrell," Ace Jackson grunted.

"You suspect him, too?" Doc queried.

"I'm a very suspicious guy," said Ace Jackson. "And I suspect everybody. The plain nasty truth is I haven't got ideas enough to suspect anybody in particular."

"Granted that Don Kurrell is the Inca in Gray," Doc Savage said, "what would be his motive?"

"Plenty," said Ace Jackson. "He's an oil man. These oil guys pull all kinds of stunts. He may have a deal with old General Vigo of Delezon whereby, if Vigo whips Santa Amoza, Don Kurrell's company gets oil concessions in the combined republics."

"Any proof of that?" Doc asked.

"Nope," Ace Jackson admitted. "But you never can tell."

A hoarse scream sounded suddenly, startlingly. It was wordless, but it did not need words. It was a plea for help. Ace Jackson leaped erect, although his wrists were still in Doc Savage's grip. They moved toward the source of the scream, and Doc Savage still held the flyer.

They could hear a body plunging through the undergrowth, undoubtedly the one who had screamed. The fellow was coming toward them. He came into view an instant later.

He was a short plump man, and, when he saw them and stopped, he did a small peculiar thing, evidently a habitual mannerism. He drew himself up on tiptoes, as if to look taller.

"Don Kurrell!" Ace Jackson barked.

DOC SAVAGE'S flake-gold eyes appraised Don Kurrell. There was nothing particularly distinguishing about the small man who represented a European oil concern, except his diminutive size and his small efforts to make himself appear as large as other men.

"What is wrong?" Doc Savage asked.

Don Kurrell took hold of the bronze man's arm as if to draw strength and encouragement from the contact.

"You are Doc Savage?" he gasped. "I've heard much of you, have seen your pictures."

"What is wrong?" the bronze man repeated.

"The Inca in Gray is trying to kill me," Kurrell gulped.

"Just now?" Doc queried.

"Twice," Don Kurrell said rapidly. "Once at my hotel, when I escaped. I started to go to the presidential palace, but on the way I heard soldiers talking. I learned that I was suspected—the Señorita Anita Carcetas had been kidnaped, and I was accused."

When he heard the words stating that Señorita Anita Carcetas had been kidnaped, Ace Jackson looked as if he had been struck with a whip. He seemed too stunned to speak. If it was acting, it was good.

Don Kurrell continued rapidly, "I also overheard the soldiers say that your plane was here. So I came to head you off to talk with you. I need your help. I want you to clear me. I'm in deadly danger."

"Why should the Inca in Gray try to kill you?" Doc Savage queried.

"I do not know," Don Kurrell said. "That is absolutely true. I do not know. And this other thing, this charge of making away with the girl. Why, they may shoot me on the mere circumstantial evidence of that soldier's word that the man looked like myself."

Ace Jackson screamed suddenly, "Anita gone! You did it!"

The flyer wrenched free of Doc Savage and pitched himself headlong at Don Kurrell. He was so much larger than the oil representative, so much more of a fighter that he would have made short shrift of his victim; but Doc Savage got between them, did things with his arms and one leg, and Ace Jackson was suddenly flat on his back, gasping for breath.

"Easy does it," Doc Savage said.

Ace Jackson screamed, "Damn him! He's the Inca in Gray!"

SILENCE followed that, an interval during which Ace Jackson's hysterical shout seemed to echo through the night.

Don Kurrell retreated a step as if the very force of the accusation had knocked him back. Next he did a quite senseless thing. He began to brush his bedraggled clothes. He was not trying to make himself look tall now. He seemed very small, almost pitiful.

"You—why I—" Suddenly he straightened. Up on his tiptoes he went. He drove an arm out rigidly at Ace Jackson.

"You!" he barked. "Why haven't I really thought of you before?" Excitement made him almost inarticulate.

"Meaning what?" Doc Savage asked abruptly.

"Meaning that I should have thought of Ace Jackson before," Don Kurrell snapped. "He is a paid war pilot, a mercenary, and he always seems to be on or near the scene when the Inca in Gray is active. He is the man who kills with the strange gray dust. He is the man who had Señorita Anita Carcetas kidnaped. Ace Jackson is the Inca in Gray!"

Ace Jackson stood and took the accusation, but his bulldog face was purpled and his mouth worked strangely.

Doc Savage's flake-gold eyes missed no move of the little tableau. If he believed one or the other of these two, his expression betrayed no evidence of the fact.

"Can either of you men prove your opinions?" Doc asked.

They only glared. It was plain they could not.

Doc Savage grasped each by the arm and hurried them through the undergrowth. They struggled a little, not against the bronze man, but trying to get at each other to land blows. Doc managed to keep them apart, without seeming to put forth much effort.

They reached the spot where the other two members of the party of eight, which Doc had overpowered, had been left.

The two forms were still on the ground. Ace

Jackson looked at the pair and emitted a sharp gasp. Don Kurrell, looking also, seemed to lose some inches of his hard-fought-for stature.

The two were dead, horribly so. On all parts of their exposed skin the grisly gray dust, which was the special mark of the death of the Inca in Gray, lay filmed.

Doc Savage separated Don Kurrell and Ace Jackson, released them, then bent over the two bodies. There had been no time to search the others, but there was opportunity to examine these. The bronze man went over them carefully, wearing rubber gloves, which he drew from a pocket, and which he carried for numerous purposes—handling electric wires, leaving no fingerprints, working with chemicals. Removal of the victims' clothing uncovered no marks that might have brought death. Yet, their features were contorted, their eyes staring and hideous. Death, when it had come upon them even while they were unconscious, had been no pleasant thing.

The examination took some time, and when it was over, Doc Savage guided Don Kurrell and Ace Jackson back to the tarmac of the flying field. There they all got a surprise.

A flashlight blazed unexpectedly.

"What seems to be happening here, Señor Savage?" said a smooth voice.

War minister Junio Serrato stepped from the shadows. When Doc had last seen him, the war minister of Santa Amoza had been neat and immaculate; but now he was somewhat disheveled. He had perspired. He wore no coat. There was dirt on his shoes, and his hair, and one trouser leg.

The man evidently seemed to think some accounting for his appearance was due.

"I came to the airport to see that you got away safely," he said. "I saw the burning plane. I tried to extinguish the flames, but unsuccessfully."

Doc Savage did not nod. Nor yet did he show in any way that he might disbelieve the story.

"Your guards came with you?" the bronze man asked.

"I came alone," said war minister Serrato. "It was quicker."

The manner in which he snapped out the words gave a hint that the questioning was not exactly welcome.

Doc Savage's metallic eyes sought the sky, which seemed perceptibly lighter. Dawn was coming.

"There are no planes at all available in Alcala?" he murmured questioningly.

"Correct." War minister Serrato scowled at Ace Jackson. "This man ordered all planes to the front. He did so without consulting me."

Ace Jackson put out his jaw and said, "The air force of Santa Amoza is a separate unit. That was my understanding when I took it over. What I say goes, and I don't have to ask anybody."

War minister Serrato smiled much too grimly and said, "It is possible that arrangement will be changed."

Ace Jackson snorted. He turned to Doc Savage.

"There's one plane here," he said. "It ain't such a hot bus. It's my old barnstorming Jenny that I flew up here in. But it's here and you're welcome to it."

Don Kurrell made himself tall and yelled, "It is probably a death trap!"

"Little man, I'm gonna reach down your throat and get your liver, if you keep that up," Ace Jackson threatened.

Doc Savage interposed, "The plane will fly?"

"It will fly," Ace Jackson admitted. "It's an old puddle jumper and it looks like it came over with Columbus. It's got about enough ceiling to clear a barbwire fence. But there ain't no barbwire fences where you're goin'. An' it's got a machine gun that'll really shoot."

"Take me to it," Doc Savage requested.

The bronze man walked away from the others, went to a clump of brush at the edge of the field. He took from the brush a small bag which he had concealed there when he first arrived in his own plane. Carrying the bag, Doc walked back to the others.

War minister Serrato, it developed, had a car waiting some distance away. They went to the machine and Serrato drove. His driving was hard on the nerves.

Doc Savage rode in front, and shortly war minister Serrato found occasion to lean over and whisper in his ear, "Don Kurrell and Ace Jackson—each accused the other of being the Inca in Gray. What do you wish done about that?"

"Nothing," Doc Savage said.

War minister Serrato swore expressively under his breath and said, "If it is vaguely possible that either of those señores is the Inca in Gray, I will have them both shot."

"No," Doc Savage said.

War minister Serrato thought that over, meantime driving so recklessly that twice Don Kurrell in the rear seat cried out in mortal terror, incidents that made Ace Jackson laugh callously. Finally Serrato ridded himself of a typical American expression, but one which had spread over most of South America.

"O.K." he said.

DOC SAVAGE said nothing when he saw Ace Jackson's old Jenny. Probably that indicated as much as anything that had gone before just how great was the bronze man's self-control. The Jenny was an airplane, although there might have been some who would have looked at it and promptly made denial. In contrast to the sleek streamlining of Doc's little ship that had been destroyed, this one gave the impression of a slow moving and clumsy snail.

In comparison with a modern fighting ship, this crate looked as antique as the glorified kite with which the Wrights had startled the world at Kittyhawk.

Doc Savage checked the engine. It was old, but had recently been overhauled. It might hold together. He put the small bag behind the stick.

There was nothing decrepit about the machine gun, however. This was nearly new, and modern as they came, and the ammo belts were fully charged. Doc removed the canvas cover and checked this also. It was on a Scarf ring. No Bowden control wires to rust out in the tropical dampness. You simply pulled the trigger. It was not synchronized to shoot through the prop.

"With cowl guns sunk through the prop, you gotta aim at your ship," Ace Jackson explained. "You're damn lucky to keep this old hen in the air, much less aim her at anything."

Ace Jackson whirled the prop. Doc shouted, "Contact." The motor gave one loud bark and stopped. They tried again. It caught, banged and whanged and shook the whole ship. Dust and leaves fell off the wings.

Doc Savage looked at the instrument panel. Bullets had done for the altimeter some time in the past. The tachometer read thirty-three hundred, which was obviously a lie. The oil gauge was knocked out entirely.

"You just smell of her," Ace Jackson explained. "When she begins to stink, she's too hot. An' you look around for a place to squat."

"Pull the chocks," Doc Savage requested.

Ace Jackson got the blocks from under the wheels. He had to squall to make his voice heard over the motor racket.

"Good luck!" he said.

The ramshackle motor barked harder. The ship seemed to try to shake itself to pieces, after which it moved forward, gathered speed. Doc went forward with the stick, and began to think the tail would never come up. Then the bus was off. Doc banked. The plane went back over the little field, sounding like a boiler factory.

Of those looking on, Ace Jackson alone knew that they had just seen something of a miracle.

"For the love of little billygoats!" Ace Jackson gulped. "That guy's a wizard. He got her off with a fourth of the run I usually have to take."

That, coming from Ace Jackson, was a compliment indeed.

Doc Savage gave the throttle more notches, which, if it did nothing else, made the motor more noisy. He held the stick back in a steady climb. When Ace Jackson had said the old ship's ceiling was enough to clear barbwire fences, he had exaggerated a little, but not much.

Doc Savage glanced upward. But the light of dawn is tricky. There were a few clouds. He failed to see his stratosphere dirigible, which was not unexpected. The airship was probably up there higher than any modern commercial plane could rise.

Doc Savage experimented with the throttle. He lashed the stick, climbed up and did things with the carburetor so that the motor lost some of its racket and settled down to something vaguely resembling a hum. Its performance now would have astounded the already surprised Ace Jackson. The old ship had found its master.

The craft also gathered more altitude. The sun came up, and the height of the plane saved Doc from feeling the sudden terrific heat that daylight brought; but he knew the tropics, and the green jungle below was deceptive in its appearance of coolness.

But the jungle did not extend far. Ahead there was desert, spotted with scrawny bushes and out in that was a line of haze, a vague transparent rope. Doc Savage had seen battle lines before. This was the front. The haze was dust stirred up by big shells. Some of it was the smoke of battle of which poets write. Before long he could discern tiny lines dug into the blistering soil. The trenches.

Unexpectedly, a rattling, snarling and jarring sounded from the left wing bank of the ship. Doc looked. Splinters were falling off the wing. Fabric was peeling back.

He had seen that phenomena before, too. Machine-gun bullets.

THE BRONZE MAN was no stranger to bird battling tactics. He acted before he looked, booting the rudder, slanting the stick. His ancient chariot seemed to grunt and slide sideways. It got out of the lead storm.

Doc glanced upward then. Three planes were attacking him. They had come out of the sun, and it was no reflection on his ability that they had taken him unawares. The human eye is not made that can look into the sun and pick up a plane.

They were modern, foreign built, these attacking ships. They came down like buzzing meteors. One held its course. The other two angled out.

If Ace Jackson's old Jenny had behaved surprisingly well before, it began to perform miracles now. It rolled, went into a slip, then a dive, and suddenly a perfect Immelmann turn. The three attacking ships popped past while their pilots stared in surprise.

Doc Savage looked closely at them. He saw enough to tell him what he wanted to know. War planes of Delezon and Santa Amoza would be marked. These carried no identification whatever.

Doc took the right-hand ship. Out of its Immelmann the old Jenny curled half over and seemed to wiggle itself into a groove. Bronze fingers wrenched the machine gun around on its Scarf ring. A little redbird seemed to perch on its muzzle and sing with a voice of thunder. Every fifth bullet was a tracer. That helped; but it did not account for the wizardry of the shooting. Only iron nerve, alloyed muscles and much practice could account for that.

Motor cowling fell off the enemy ship. The propeller lost a blade, only one blade, which was more unfortunate for a ship with a racing motor. It tore itself from its mount, or almost so, before the pilot could shut it off. It hung like a thick scab on the snout of the plane as the craft gyrated downward. The pilot lost control, then regained it. He should be able to manage a landing he could walk away from.

The outcome of the scrap surprised the other two planes. Doc Savage was close to them before they could get their wits together. They banked furiously, evaded him. Their ships had cowl guns. That was a handicap, perhaps not in ordinary bird battling, but certainly against a marksman of the bronze man's ability.

The two ships flew side by side while the pilots thought of ways and means. Then Doc Savage did something that looked foolish. He executed a maneuver that put him directly ahead of the two planes, below them. All they had to do was dive, riddle him.

They sloped down to get their meat. The pilots were excited, eager. There was a moment when they could not see the Jenny, the old ship being below the noses of their war craft. During that moment when he was out of sight, Doc Savage doubled over, got something from a small bag which he had placed beside the control stick. The objects resembled grenades. And after he threw them over they did explode, but softly. They threw off not chilling fragments of steel, but a bluish vapor.

Doc Savage threw the old plane into the beginning of what an expert might well have sworn would be suicide maneuver—an outside loop; but he rolled as he went into it, down and under.

The two attacking ships followed him. Both were confident. Probably they never saw the small clouds of blue vapor. These had widened, spreading rapidly. The planes flew into them.

Both motors stopped, not together, yet not more than thirty seconds apart.

Doc Savage looked back and saw the propellers come to a standstill. His metallic face held no expression. The grenades he had thrown had contained a highly expanding gas. This stuff had been drawn into the motors of the two attackers. It had simply caused a chemical reaction which had rendered the gasoline mixtures non-explosive. Both engines would have to be thoroughly cleaned before they would run again, since the vapor would congeal on carburetor intakes and cylinder walls.

The pilots of the two planes promptly nosed down. They were in no danger, provided they could find a spot for a dead-stick landing.

Luck was with them. There was a spot where they could land, a clearing, the only one for miles. The first plane to be disabled was already dropping into it. The pilot of that ship did not do so bad, considering the circumstances. He did not quite kill himself, but he thoroughly wrecked his ship.

The other two ships came down fast, fishtailed away speed, and dead-sticked passably.

Doc followed them down. His assailants, there was more than slight reason to believe, might be killers dispatched by the Inca in Gray. What else could account for the planes bearing no markings? Doc Savage intended to land to question the fellows.

But the occupants of the three planes had other ideas. They worked furiously at their cowl machine guns. These, it developed, were of a type which could be dismounted quickly. They rested them over the fuselage and began firing. They were not bad gunners. Their lead scabbed fabric off the Jenny.

Doc Savage banked away like a hawk grown suddenly wary. Then he made a most unwelcome discovery.

His gasoline tank had been punctured.

HE got the Jenny clear of the open space where the three planes had landed. Then he stood up in the cockpit and looked about for a suitable spot to set his own ship down. There was none nearer than several miles. The brush below was a scrawny thick mat patch on the edge of the desert.

The planes had moved a good bit during the sky fight. They had crossed the lines. This spot was well in Delezon territory.

Doc Savage reached his decision in short order. Trying to make a landing back in the clearing in the face of those machine guns would be suicide. He straightened the ship out, pointed it for the nearest patch of desert, and lashed the stick.

Scrambling forward, he hung in what for anything less than muscles of trained metal would have been an extremely dangerous position. He tore away fabric, got at the gas tank. The hole was large and it was too late to do much about it. Most of the gasoline was gone. Doc stuffed a handkerchief in the aperture the bullets had made.

The engine began to cough, sputter. The Jenny grew logy. Then its nose went down. It was like a stricken bird.

There were moments when it seemed the bronze man would not make it; but he was successful. Onto the desert at the edge of the growth he settled. There was soft sand, no helping that. The old tires rolled on top for awhile; then they went in.

The ancient Jenny grunted, did a stand on her nose. There was a loud crash as she broke her back and the wings went off. Fine sand in a cloud enveloped everything.

Chapter X
THE KILLER LAUGHS

THERE was an upheaval in the wreckage while it was still settling, and Doc Savage's head protruded from the cockpit of the broken and torn Jenny. The non-shatter glass of his goggles was crashed in, but, when he removed them, his eyes were unharmed. He stripped off his flying helmet, exposing his straight bronze hair which was like a metal skullcap. He listened.

There was shouting, but it was distant; soldiers undoubtedly. Having seen the planes come down, they would arrive before long. Doc Savage got out of the wreckage hastily. His clothing had suffered. He was cut in a place or two. He secured the bag which had been behind the control stick.

The brush had looked thick from the air, but it looked even more dense from the ground. Doc Savage did not dash directly into it, but walked in backwards, and he carefully erased each footprint which he left in the sand. This required some moments, for he did a thorough job.

The voices were coming closer. Their barkings were in Spanish. Doc grasped the boughs of a small tree, swung up, whipped to another with the accomplished ease of a circus aërialist, and vanished from view.

A squad of Delezon soldiers trotted up. Dust clung to their uniforms and made mud on their sweating faces. They gathered, cackling in Spanish, about the wrecked Jenny.

The sergeant in command of the squad looked puzzled after he had made an examination. There should have been a body in that wreckage, but there manifestly was none. Scratching his head, the sergeant inspected the sand. He failed to detect a sign of footprints.

"*Diablo!*" he gulped. "This is strange."

"A plane without a pilot!" Another soldier crossed himself. "It is, indeed, impossible."

"Impossible is correct," snapped the sergeant. "Scatter. Search the brush."

The soldiers tramped into the brush—that is, they all tramped but one. This fellow was tall, heavily built, and he had avarice in his eyes. The purpose of his lagging behind soon became evident. He was after loot. He dug into the plane wreckage, striving to reach the instruments. Had he known just how worthless those instruments were, he might have been a little less ambitious.

His whole attention was concentrated on his thievery. He did not see a giant bronze figure ease out of the underbrush, tread silently through the sand toward him. He realized nothing was wrong, until he was seized from behind. Then the knowledge was a bit tardy.

The husky Delezonian soldier struggled briefly, terrifically, only to go limp, and that without as much as seeing his attacker.

Doc Savage shouldered the fellow and carried him from view. It would not do to have the marks of a dragging body found.

Minutes passed, hot, blistering minutes. Soldiers began to come from the underbrush. More than one of them was drenched with perspiration. That jungle was terrible in heat such as this.

The sergeant appeared and demanded, "Find anything?"

He was assured they had not.

Then some one had a stroke of brilliance and volunteered, "*Bueno!* I have it. The pilot of this plane leaped with a parachute. Probably he leaped miles from here and the ship came on to crash."

"*Si, si,*" agreed the sergeant. "I believe you are right. Fall in. We will continue our march."

The rest of the soldiers now came out of the jungle. Among them was the tall, heavy-set individual whose shoulders drooped slightly. This man drew only one or two glances, those casual.

He looked exactly like the soldier who had lagged behind to loot the fallen ship.

The squad of soldiers seemed to be bound back from the lines for a period of rest. They looked as if they badly needed it.

IT was a long march, marked by nothing noteworthy, except its monotony, the heat, and the tongue-lashings of the sergeant whose disposition seemed to have been curdled by the terrifically hot sun. As they neared the village which General Vigo of Delezon was using as general headquarters, they were enveloped almost continuously in dust stirred up by marching soldiers, rumbling motor trucks and galloping cavalry horses. There was hardly any wind and, hence, it was impossible to escape the dust by walking on the windward side of the trail.

The trails were exactly that. Small trees had been chopped down, boulders and dirt rolled in the gullies, and a few crude, heavy bridges had been constructed. It seemed to be necessary to keep squads of men working on the road continually to keep it passable.

As they entered the general headquarters village, the tall, heavy-set, stooped soldier with the squad began to loiter behind. Discipline was lax so he got away with this. It would have taken a close observer to have detected the slightest difference between this man and the one whom he resembled so closely.

They entered the squalid outer fringe of the village. The usual swarm of dogs and camp hangers-on greeted them, and discipline became even more lax. The burly soldier with the stoop fell even farther behind. His fellows drew ahead. He made no effort to overhaul them, instead he turned off abruptly into a side street.

Now his pace changed. He moved slowly, warily.

It was, however, certain that he would be challenged by the Delezon equivalent of military police. Numbers of these gentlemen, wearing their distinguishing arm bands, were on the streets. Two of them, looking neat and cool despite the heat, confronted the burly soldier unexpectedly with a challenge.

The heavy, stooped soldier glared at the two M.P.s. The soldier was caked from head to foot with dust, and his visage was muddy; his eyes, habitually thin slits as if from exposure to the tropical sun. He put out a jaw at the two military policemen and sneered his contempt.

"You are looking at a man," he said belligerently. "I have fought the heat, the fever, the insects, and the enemy. I would enjoy fighting two fat old women such as yourselves. One side! Let a man pass!"

Had it been anywhere but South America, these words would have precipitated a prompt fight. As it was, the M.P.s scowled and drew aside. Not only were these soldiers returning from the front accorded extra privileges on order of General Vigo, but the hardships of the front sometimes rendered the soldiers a little mad. It was not healthy to fool with them.

The tall, heavy-set soldier went on, still with his stoop. He used somewhat more care and was not again challenged.

It was not difficult for him to locate the building used by General Vigo for headquarters. This was a large structure, evidently a private residence prior to the war. Strangely enough, it was of modernistic construction, boxlike, with very large windows.

The burly soldier loitered past the front of the headquarters. Numerous soldiers were about. He mingled with them. There seemed to be no reason why he should not do this.

But there was, it developed, a reason.

So unexpectedly that it was like lightning out of a clear sky, he was covered by rifles. Three Delezonian officers had suddenly presented the weapons, muzzles first. The pieces were cocked.

The burly soldier lost a little of his stoop, blinked foolishly at the guns and the men who held them.

"Would you please try to escape, señor?" invited one of the officers.

The burly soldier ignored the invitation. He merely continued his dumb blinking.

"Take him to General Vigo," directed one of the officers.

GENERAL FERNANEZ VIGO, general dictator of Delezon, had appropriated for his office what had once been the sunroom of the modernistic house which was so out of place in this humble village.

General Vigo was walking angry circles around a shiny glass and chromium table, putting each foot down with a violence that shook the floor. General Vigo wore two pistols and a bayonet. His uniform, which bore no insignia, was torn and ripped in several places. There was a bandage around his head, and another around one arm. That very afternoon General Vigo had personally led a charge into the Santa Amoza trenches.

General Vigo managed to do a spectacular thing such as this occasionally. It inspired his soldiers, probably accounted for the good showing which Delezon, a potentially weaker country than Santa Amoza, had made in the war thus far.

General Vigo stopped his pacing when the prisoner was brought into his presence.

"Bueno!" he howled. "One of you we have finally captured!"

The prisoner executed several snappy salutes and gulped, "I do not understand."

"Oh, yes, you do!" roared General Vigo. "I ordered your detachment of soldiers back from the front especially so that you could be arrested. You slipped away from the squad, and we thought you had become suspicious. But no, you were merely out prowling."

The bulky soldier looked utterly astounded. He swallowed several times.

"I do not understand," he mumbled again.

General Vigo made a fierce face at him.

"You are a spy, an employee of the Inca in Gray!" roared the general dictator of Delezon.

Soldiers gripped the prisoner. Sharp points of bayonets pressed against his back. Any attempt at escape would have been suicidal.

"No, no, mi amigo," the prisoner stuttered. "This is not true."

"What!" Fabulously ugly General Vigo waved an arm, shrilled, "Search him!"

They began to strip the prisoner. The coat came off first, then the shirt. A hissing of surprised gasps went up.

"Caramba!" General Vigo exploded, eyes bulging. "Such muscles on a man I have never seen before."

They finished stripping the prisoner, and, when they stood back, more than one man was pop-eyed with amazement. They had uncovered a physical giant, a man of incredible muscles. The officers who had brought the prisoner in shivered a little, and wondered if they had not just had one of the narrow escapes of their lives.

Most striking of all, perhaps, was the remarkable fineness of the prisoner's skin texture and its striking bronze color.

General Vigo stared. He worked his thick shoulders inside his coat as if trying to get rid of an invisible weight which had just settled upon them.

"Who," he demanded, "are you, señor?"

"Doc Savage," the prisoner said quietly.

General Vigo had a fit. He jumped up and down. He screamed and beat his own chest with his fists.

"Doc Savage!" he shrieked. "So you are working for the Inca in Gray!"

General Vigo jumped up and down some more, mauled himself, and slavered a little in his rage.

"No!" he howled. "You, Doc Savage, are probably yourself the Inca in Gray!"

DOC SAVAGE had schooled himself to show no emotion unless he so willed. So the fact that his countenance now remained inscrutable did not mean he was unsurprised. He was learning things.

According to previous information, the Inca in Gray had been an affliction peculiar to the republic of Santa Amoza; but here was General Vigo of Delezon flying into a rage over the name of the Inca in Gray. That angle would bear investigation.

"What is the Inca in Gray?" Doc Savage asked.

General Vigo went through the motion of a grotesque jumping jack.

"He is a devil!" he screamed. "He is a fiend, this Inca in Gray! He is a tool of Santa Amoza!"

"Will you be more specific?" Doc requested.

"Some of my leading generals have been murdered, murdered strangely with a weird gray dust on their faces and hands," General Vigo snarled. "There has been other sabotage. And, worst of all, there is the uprising."

"What do you mean?" Doc Savage queried.

"The natives, the uncivilized Indians of the jungle," General Vigo growled. "For generations they have been peaceful and have given no trouble. But lately they have gone on the warpath. They are raiding our villages."

He paused, scowled darkly at Doc Savage.

"It is the work of the Inca in Gray," he continued. "The Inca in Gray is a devil. He has convinced the natives that he is the leader destined to bring back their ancient power and glory."

Doc Savage persisted, "What ancient power and glory?"

"The natives are descendants of the Incas," General Vigo advised. "They have a natural hate of all white men. The Inca in Gray has capitalized on that."

Doc Savage was silent a moment.

"Would it be any use," he queried, "to assure you that my presence here is for the purpose of ferreting out the Inca in Gray—and ascertaining what happened to my aide, Long Tom?"

General Vigo's expression changed slightly. He looked as if he half believed the bronze man.

"Turn on the machine," General Vigo told one of the orderlies. "We will examine this man's clothing."

The orderly went into the next room. In a moment, a weird hum sounded from the chamber.

Doc Savage stood calmly as the clothing he had worn was picked up and carried into the next room. Doc Savage was marched after the clothing. His guards kept their guns ready.

A queer machine stood in the adjacent room, a large box of an affair from which wires ran to a generator on the floor. Both the box and the generator were making the humming noise.

"Guard the door," directed General Vigo. Then the general dictator of Delezon frowned at Doc Savage. "You know what this device is?"

Doc nodded. "Certainly. An ultraviolet ray machine."

"Then you probably guess why I have it?" suggested General Vigo.

Again the bronze man nodded. "The device will bring out hidden messages on cloth, paper and—"

"Enough," grunted Vigo. Then to his orderlies, "Examine the clothing."

They seized the uniform which they had removed from Doc Savage and held it under the black lens of the ultraviolet lantern, a piece at a time. The shirt, the trousers, the blouse, revealed nothing.

Far from looking disappointed, General Vigo seemed a bit relieved.

Under the ultraviolet lens they shoved the undershirt which Doc Savage had taken from the burly soldier he had overpowered back by the wrecked plane.

And on the undershirt appeared a crude map, and row after row of figures.

AN enraged roar came from General Vigo. He was plainly surprised; and even Doc Savage, with his great composure, was momentarily moved into a flicker of annoyed astonishment.

Doc Savage knew instantly what had happened. There had been no chance to tamper with his clothing after he had taken it from the burly soldier. Therefore, that soldier had been a spy. Probably there were many of these in Delezon. It had been the bronze man's misfortune to impersonate one of them.

The writing on the undershirt had been done with invisible ink; but few invisible inks are impervious to detection with ultraviolet light. This one certainly was not. When the room was darkened, the writing glowed out distinctly.

General Vigo examined the map. He seemed to swell with rage.

"Our front line!" he snarled. "It shows our gun emplacements, our supply roads, our airports—everything!"

Doc Savage began, "The clothing came from a man whom—"

"Silence!" roared General Vigo.

Doc Savage did not grow silent. He raised his voice, and its thunder beat down the objections of the general dictator of Delezon. The bronze man talked, spoke rapidly, heedless of the bayonets which menaced him at first. And General Vigo, because there was nothing else to do, listened, heard him through.

Doc Savage told the whole story, omitting nothing, beginning with the attempt on his own life in New York, telling the adventure on the dirigible, and ending with an account of exactly what had happened in Santa Amoza. He got several surprising reactions from General Vigo.

"I did not seize Señorita Anita Carcetas!" howled General Vigo. "I do not have to kidnap women to win my wars!"

"But there was a message to minister Serrato, saying that you had the young woman and that she would be executed unless Santa Amoza surrendered," Doc told him.

"It was no message from me, señor!" General Vigo shouted. "Someone else must have sent it. Either that or war minister Serrato lied."

"There are certain indications pointing to minister Serrato as the Inca in Gray," Doc Savage said.

General Vigo was obviously engaged in deep thought. He turned off the ultraviolet lantern, then took several slow turns about the room, hands locked together behind his back. The jumping about he had done in his rage had opened his head wound, and a string of crimson was crawling out from under the bandage, drops staining the front of his uniform and the floor, unnoticed.

Suddenly he stopped, cracked an order at his officers.

"Assemble a firing squad," he directed.

Small lights came into the bronze man's flake-gold eyes.

"You do not believe me?" he queried.

"I believe you are Doc Savage," said General Vigo.

Doc began, "Then why—"

"I also believe you have turned fiend," snapped General Vigo. "I am convinced you yourself are the Inca in Gray. You have been plotting, carrying on a devilish campaign here in Delezon. What your motive is, I do not know. You might tell me that before you are executed."

Doc Savage was silent through a long moment.

"There are some men with whom it is senseless to argue," he said.

That was about as near Doc Savage ever came to insulting anyone. He made it a policy not to engage in personalities.

"Don those clothes," General Vigo snapped.

Because there was nothing else to do, Doc Savage obeyed.

He was hemmed in by bayonets and rifles and escorted from the headquarters building.

Their appearance outdoors caused a wave of excitement. Word spread hurriedly. Another spy was to be executed. It was the Inca in Gray himself. A roar went up at that information. The Inca in Gray, it seemed, was a name synonymous with terror in Delezon. The crowd, not all of it soldiers, surged closer.

DOC SAVAGE, closely guarded, was marched toward a high stockade, the adobe walls of which were perforated along the top for machine gun emplacements. The only door in the wall of this fort was narrow. They headed for it.

Mingling with the crowd of onlookers, making himself inconspicuous, was the small man with the pocked face and the evil grin. Without being too forward about it, he was gathering all the information he could. The pock-faced fellow craned his neck time and again and managed to get several good looks at Doc Savage. Once he was close enough to hear General Vigo speaking.

"This is taking a weight from my mind," General Vigo was rumbling to Doc Savage. "Only yesterday I executed your aide, Long Tom. For a time that preyed on my conscience. But now I know I did right. You are the Inca in Gray, and he was your assistant."

Doc Savage walked with a steady tread, his bronze features showing no slightest sign of fear. He did not argue.

The bronze man was led through the narrow door into the enclosure, the same enclosure into which Long Tom had been escorted some hours previously. Doc was marched to the same bullet-pocked wall against which Long Tom had stood. He was backed against it. The soldiers withdrew.

"A bandage for your eyes?" General Vigo asked bluntly.

"No," Doc Savage said distinctly.

The door through the stockade was closed. The firing squad lined up before their victim.

Outside the stockade, the pock-faced little man

with the evil face mingled with the throng. He kept a hand tucked behind an ear, listening intently. He managed to pick up the ominous commands from within. General Vigo was giving the execution orders himself.

"Ready!" roared the general dictator of Delezon.

"Aim—"

"Fire—"

A volley of shot blazed out, frightening pigeons off the roofs of nearby buildings.

In the comparative silence that followed, a strange sound was heard. It was a trilling, small, eerie, fantastic, carrying from within the stockade in amazing fashion. It might have been the song of some exotic feathered thing of the jungle. The trilling was quite distinct at first, but it faded slowly, seeming to go away into nothingness until only the memory of its weird tremolo remained.

THE small, pock-faced spectator crept away as soon as he could do so without attracting attention. He went directly to a squalid house in the poorer section and entered. The house, after the South American fashion, had a patio, a tiny court in the center. The dwellings of Delezon had these patios, regardless of how poor they might be.

Shortly, a pigeon arose from the patio. The bird attracted no attention, for there were other pigeons in the village, and their resemblance to the carrier breed of bird was close enough to cause confusion.

No one paid much attention to pigeons anyway.

Chapter XI
DISASTER

DOC SAVAGE'S stratosphere dirigible hung motionless considerably more than a score of thousands of feet over Alcala, capital city of Santa Amoza.

Monk, the homely chemist, was using the device, which, for lack of a better name, was called the "infra eye." This was simply an elaboration of the portable apparatus which Doc Savage had used in the darkness. It consisted of a projector which sent out light waves of a wavelength invisible to the human eye downward. There was a scanning panel for observation purposes.

Monk had been observing for some time. His small eyes were acquiring a strained squint.

"Wonder what's happened to Doc?" he grumbled. "That fire we saw a few hours ago on the edge of a flying field, I wonder if that could have been something happening to his plane?"

"Our orders were to stick up here until we got some word from Doc," Ham said shortly. "Doc wanted this Inca in Gray, whoever he is, to think the dirigible had been destroyed."

Monk went on with his muttering. "No planes have left Alcala except that crate that looked like an old Jenny. Blazes, I expected some word from Doc before now!"

Monk reached suddenly for a powerful telescope, one of Doc's own design. Then he seized the controls of the airship, manipulated them, and the craft began to descend.

There was a bank of fleecy clouds below. This hid the earth completely as far as inspection with the naked eye was concerned. The infra rays however penetrated the dense cloud bank, which was the reason they had been using the rays.

"What is the idea, you missing link?" Ham demanded.

"I see something," Monk told him. "Shut up."

The ship sank, altimeter needles marching slowly backward. There was almost no sound since the motors were turning over very slowly. They entered the clouds.

"Someone will see us from below," Ham snapped.

"Use your head," Monk retorted. "This bus is camouflaged so you can't hardly see it from below. An' that infra eye ain't so hot when you want to make a detailed inspection. I saw somethin' I'm gonna use this telescope on."

The clouds began to thin out. The ship had penetrated to the under side.

"Hold 'er," grunted Monk.

Ham took the controls and leveled the dirigible out.

Monk opened a floor hatch, lay down beside it, and focused the powerful telescope carefully. He seemed very interested in what he was studying. It was noticeable that the telescope was not pointed directly at Alcala which was almost below, but was slanted off to one side—toward the battlefront, in fact.

"Well," Ham snapped, "do I get a look?"

Monk surrendered the telescope reluctantly.

Ham focused the lenses to his own vision.

"Just a plane," he said.

"Yeah, but watch how it's actin'," Monk grunted. "An' notice them little patches of white vapor behind it."

Ham inspected the patches of vapor which had been mentioned. These were very vague, and were some distance behind the plane.

"Smoke from anti-aircraft shells," said the dapper lawyer. "What is queer about that?"

"Just keep watching," Monk advised.

Ham watched. He had not been doing that long when he stiffened.

THE plane they were observing was behaving somewhat uncertainly. It did not stay level. Numerous times it slipped. Once it fell off in a short spin before it was hauled out.

"Something wrong with the plane," Ham said.

Monk nodded. "Practically unmanageable. Probably some of its control wires have been shot away."

They continued to watch. It was doubtful if the dirigible could be distinguished with the naked eye from the earth below. Powerful glasses might have revealed it, but even that was a bit doubtful, due to its camouflaging.

Monk leaped to the controls, adjusted them, sent the airship toward the front lines. This enabled Ham to observe the strangely acting plane more distinctly.

Unexpectedly a puff of white smoke came from the tail of the ship. The craft veered, straightened. Another puff of smoke appeared. Then a third.

The plane flew some distance. Then smoke appeared again. This time it came for a longer interval. It stopped. A moment later it resumed.

"Catch on?" Monk grunted.

"Dry up," Ham said. "Watch this."

A few moments later the plane had deposited three balls of smoke in the air, three rather long wads of smoke, then three more balls.

"Continental code," Monk barked. "I can read it with the naked eye now."

"S. O. S." Ham agreed. "It means whoever is down there wants help."

"Think it's Doc?" Monk demanded.

The two men exchanged glances. The usual animosity with which they inspected each other was missing. They seemed to reach a common conclusion without the use of words.

"Down we go," Monk grunted.

The homely chemist lunged to the controls. He wrenched the throttle levers open. The motors blurted out a great howl. He stroked another lever. A scream came from the tail portion of the dirigible. The rocket tubes had been put into operation. The airship began to give an excellent imitation of a bullet as far as speed was concerned.

Details of the scene below took on distinctness. The earth seemed to swell. The frontline trenches became discernible.

The plane, it developed, was farther away than had first appeared. It was, in fact, well within Delezon territory, and would be deeper in Delezon before they overhauled it, for it was flying at a good speed, although its behavior was as erratic as before.

Monk seized the telescope, focused it, stared.

"It's Doc!" he barked.

"How can you tell?" Ham demanded.

"He isn't wearing gloves," Monk explained. "His hands look like bronze."

They began to manipulate the dirigible's con-

trols, shutting off the rocket tubes first. This was necessary in order to decrease the speed of the craft so that it would not overshoot the plane below. They managed this very efficiently. The airship drew alongside the plane, slightly above it, perhaps a hundred yards separating the two aircraft.

Monk used the telescope again, readjusting the lenses for the short distance. What he saw caused him to emit a bark of surprise. He lunged to the rudder wheel of the dirigible, turned it and whipped the airship almost alongside the plane. He stared again.

"That guy ain't Doc!" Monk yelled. "He's got make-up on so he'll look like Doc."

The plane suddenly shed its erratic manner of flight. The pilot delved into his cockpit and came up with a hand machine gun.

"A trap!" Ham shouted. "Take 'er up!"

MONK hit the altitude controls of the airship. The big, reinforced alloy metal bag jumped.

Simultaneously, a shattering roar came from the side of the control cabin, a sound as of many drumsticks beating very hard. They looked at the windows. These were becoming cobwebbed with cracks. The glass was bullet-proof, and obviously machine-gun lead was crashing into it.

Shadows of an attacking air squadron swept over them like a dark cloud. The ships zoomed, circled and came back again. Their machine guns were winking red eyes on the cowl. There were half a dozen of these ships, and not one of them bore a marking to designate it as belonging to the military force of either Delezon or Santa Amoza.

Their lead made a great drumming and roaring on the dirigible. It was not, however, doing a great deal of damage. The control cabin was proof against anything less than a field gun shell. The gas bags, the dirigible's skin, of course, could not be made bullet-proof, due to the necessity for lightness. But puncturing the bags would do no great damage. For the gas cells were coated inside with a spongy substance which expanded and closed all but the largest of apertures.

Monk had the altitude control lever far back. The ship was all but standing on its tail. He jerked other levers. The rocket tubes began to make moaning sounds.

"They ain't gonna faze us," Monk grunted.

Ham nodded and snapped, "Notice the lack of markings on the ships. They must be followers of this mysterious Inca in Gray."

"Whoever he is, that Inca in Gray ain't no piker," Monk mumbled. "He does things on a big scale."

The dirigible was beginning to leap upward in the sky.

There was a moan off to one side as an attacking plane came down, then hauled up swiftly. A small bomb detached from its under side, and came boring for the dirigible.

"Watch it," Ham yelled.

Monk wrenched the controls. The big dirigible, for all of its terrific speed, veered abruptly. The bomb—it must have weighed in excess of a hundred pounds—missed them, and hurtled down to dig a great pit in the jungle below, well behind the war front of Delezon.

Monk peered downward at the pit the explosive had made, mentally visualizing what would have happened if it had struck them. It was not a pleasant mind picture.

Suddenly Ham was screaming again. "Drop 'er! Drop 'er!"

Monk looked up, too late. One of the planes was rushing toward them. It was almost upon them. The pilot was out of the cockpit, hanging on with one hand, using the other hand to handle the stick and guide his ship.

He was going to crash them, ram them deliberately with his own plane. It was a desperate expedient, and probably the only one which would insure success under the circumstances.

At the last possible moment, the enemy pilot pitched clear of his plane. He was a cunning fellow. He held his body so that the very force of the air and his momentum caused him to hurtle downward under the dirigible.

The plane hit the gas bag squarely. It buried itself almost completely in the cellular structure of gas compartments and girders. The concussion was terrific. Flame burst from the plane, which had been turned into a missile. This fire, however, was almost instantly snuffed out, for the gas which furnished buoyancy to the airship was not only non-inflammable itself, but was effective as fire extinguishing vapor in smothering flames.

Both Monk and Ham were stunned by the impact.

SHOCKS have rather a strange effect upon the human system. A shock will produce unconsciousness, while another and similar shock, perhaps of lesser violence, will, under the proper combination of circumstances, have the effect of returning that consciousness. It was thus with the crash as the dirigible struck.

Not all of the ship's buoyancy had been lost. So that it did not fall very hard. The jungle cushioned its landing also, and the stout metal framework of the control room preserved Monk and Ham. A loud hissing came from the ruptured pipes of the mechanism which conditioned air.

Monk's sturdier constitution caused him to come to his feet first. He listened. The planes were moaning about overhead.

Came a jarring explosion. Fifty yards distant, earth and tree fragments spouted upward. The earth gave a distinct jerk. It was a bomb dropped by one of the planes above.

Ham was sitting up. There was in his eyes that unclearness which indicated he still did not fully comprehend what was occurring.

"Ham!" Monk shouted, then slapped the dapper lawyer's face.

Ham growled, "I'll skin you alive for that," and came to his feet.

"Run for it!" Monk barked. "They're laying eggs on us!"

The homely chemist opened the hatchway and stumbled out into the thick jungle growth, closely followed by his more slender companion. Staccato rattle of machine guns sounded overhead, and bullets pattered in the brush about them. They ran.

A squealing grunt from behind brought Monk up short.

"Habeas!" he cried, and turned.

"Forget the hog!" Ham barked.

That suggestion was proof that Ham had almost completely recovered himself.

Monk shoved out a foot, upset Ham ignominiously in the brush, and yelled, "That hog is worth six lawyers!"

The homely chemist plunged back through the undergrowth toward the stricken ship, heedless of danger from bombs and machine-gun bullets. His long, apelike arms stretched ahead of him to part the dense jungle creepers.

Ham got up from where he had fallen when Monk tripped him, scowled darkly, then followed the homely chemist. He drew near the dirigible wreck in time to see Monk disappear into the hatchway.

Almost simultaneously, a squad of men in clothing almost unbelievably dirty and bedraggled burst into view and ran for the fallen dirigible.

"Monk!" Ham shrieked. "Watch out!"

The men, it appeared, were armed. They lifted rifles. These whacked. A storm of bullets drove Ham into cover.

Inside the dirigible, Monk was bawling angrily. He burst out of the wreckage, carrying the pig, Habeas Corpus, by one saillike ear. It could not be said that Monk gave Habeas the gentlest of treatment. The instant the homely chemist saw the armed men, he hurled the pig through the air into the nearest clump of brush.

Then Monk doubled around the dirigible wreckage in a frantic effort to escape.

"Run!" Ham bawled encouragement.

Then Ham suddenly discovered that he had

more to do than vocally encourage Monk. There were more of the strangely shabby men in the jungle. They were creeping up on him. They were, in fact, only a few yards distant. Now they rushed.

Ham was no unskilled fighter. Particularly was he adept at use of his sword cane, but that had been left behind in the excitement. It was somewhere in the ruined airship. Ham struck out furiously with his fists.

But he was fighting men who were not afraid, and who had some ability. They swarmed over him. He was hopelessly outnumbered and beaten down, tripped, held.

"Monk!" Ham shrieked again. "Run for it! I'm all right!"

There was a crashing and thumping and struggling in the brush nearby, and after that had continued a while it approached. A swarm of men were bringing a captive.

The prisoner was Monk.

He looked at Ham and growled, "So you're all right. What a liar!"

In the brush, Habeas Corpus grunted anxiously.

"Ah, a peeg," one of the dirty, disheveled men murmured in bad English. "We shall have fresh meat."

Two or three of the men were deployed. There was brief, tumultuous struggle, followed by several startled squeals.

"Got heem," said a voice.

"Caramba!" grunted another, "Eating heem will be like eating leather and string."

"Put heem in thees pen," someone suggested. "We well feed heem well—"

"Blast them guys!" Monk struggled violently.

"Take it easy," Ham suggested.

THE man who seemed to be in charge of the party approached them, looked them over. The fellow's face was not a nice thing to examine. He smirked evilly at them.

Then the fellow walked a few yards away into an opening in the jungle, and, with his arms, made signals to the planes which still buzzed about overhead. The pilots of the ships observed, waved back. After that the aircraft moaned away over the jungle and their sound was soon lost to hearing.

The leader of the jungle party came and stared down at Monk and Ham. He jerked his head in the direction taken by the departing planes.

"They will bear good news to our master, The Inca in Gray," he said.

Somebody in the back of the group laughed, spoke in Spanish.

"And they will return bearing even better news, let us hope," this man said.

"Si, si," the first man agreed. "The Inca in Gray

is striking fast now. It will not be long until his plans are completed and his ends are gained."

Monk, who could speak Spanish, put in, "And what end is this Inca in Gray after?"

The homely chemist received a resounding kick for his temerity in putting the question. Eyes pain blurred, Monk looked at Ham. The glance the dapper lawyer returned did not hold much sympathy.

The captors now began to hold a consultation. They spoke loudly, frankly, and as they did so, they watched their prisoners as if enjoying the reaction which the words produced.

"Would it be better to kill them now?" one ruminated. "Or should we receive orders from the master, the Inca in Gray?"

"Now," a man voted.

"No, no," said another.

"Why not?" demanded the first. "They are our enemies. Death to such."

"I know," said the first, "but the Inca in Gray prefers to know all and to direct all moves. It is to our advantage to receive instructions. The prisoners will be killed anyway, of course."

"That is as it should be," said another. "They are followers of that bronze man, Doc Savage."

The man who said this spoke the words somewhat nervously, much as one might mention a very real personal devil. This caused some of the others to chuckle mirthfully.

"Our brother has the heart of a flower," they laughed. "He fears a dead man."

"I do not," insisted the other.

"Doc Savage is dead," he was reminded. "And you fear him."

Chapter XII
THE HUMORIST

DOC SAVAGE'S death, to paraphrase the statement attributed to a famous man of letters, was somewhat exaggerated.

Doc Savage was in a room which was not merely dark. It was black—black with an intensity that seemed to deny the possibility of any light existing anywhere. This darkness was the more noteworthy, because somewhere outside there should be brilliant tropical sunlight.

The bronze man was in a dungeon somewhere under the compound's walls. He had been there some time. Long Tom Roberts was in the dungeon with him.

Long Tom was talking, had been talking in exactly the same tone and repeating many of the same words for some time. Long Tom was not a man who indulged in profanity. He was using no swear words, but he managed to put into his monotonous voice a good deal of gripping vituperation.

Long Tom had ridded himself of opinions concerning the hot weather, Santa Amoza, Delezon, General Vigo, the Inca in Gray, South America in general, and had now gotten around to those gentlemen who are frequently blamed for wars.

"Munitions makers," Long Tom intoned, "they suck the blood from nations . . . . murderers of the masses . . . . they've got me here . . . . fiends . . . ."

It was strange talk for Long Tom. It was exactly such conversation, in fact, as might be attributed to an insane man. There was a madness in the tone, too. The guards outside, hearing the interminable condemnation exchanged knowing glances. They had heard men go mad before in these dungeons. It did not, however, usually happen so soon.

However, a close listener might have detected another sound which was almost drowned by Long Tom's interminable talking. This was a series of low whizzings. These tiny noises kept up steadily. The guards outside were not close enough to hear them.

Long Tom finished with munitions makers and went back to the Inca in Gray for conversational matter.

"Infernal devil," the pallid electrical wizard mumbled, "killing people . . . . no visible reason . . . . something big must be behind him . . . ."

A guard pacing outside shivered. The air down here was stifling for want of ventilation. The guard tried to smoke a cigarette, but it stuck to his lips. He felt thirsty.

The dull monotone of Long Tom's incantation went on and on, sentences disjointed, thoughts half phrased. Under it, the small mysterious scraping and buzzing continued.

The buzzing was inside the dungeon. Suddenly a tiny pin point of light appeared. This grew to an irregular slit, but very slowly. Minutes were required for the phenomena. The slit lengthened, changed direction. It assumed the shape of a "U" lying on its side.

The lock was being cut out of the heavy door.

Doc Savage spoke in a low voice.

"It is ready," he said simply.

Long Tom ceased his mumbling.

"Whe-ew," he said in a perfectly normal voice. "It's about time. I was running out of things to talk about."

LONG training had put an incredible power in Doc Savage's fingers. The cracks in the door which afforded his only grip were not large, but, employing them, he managed to swing the heavy portal inward.

Dim light from outside filtered into the room. Falling across the floor, this luminance disclosed the ingenious drill which the bronze man had fashioned from two belt buckles—his own and Long Tom's. A piece of wood, ripped from a bench, provided a handle. Long Tom's interminable conversation had been to cover the sound the drill was making as it cut around the lock.

"Come," said Doc Savage. "But be careful about the noise."

"I know," Long Tom breathed. "The guard."

With a stealth and lack of noise that a tomcat would have envied, the bronze man stalked along the dim passages. He could see the sentry shortly. The fellow had gone to a water bucket, which stood on the passage floor, and was drinking. He was taking the water noisily as some diners take their soup.

There was no noise, no struggle of consequence, after Doc Savage seized the man. Bronze fingers simply found nerve centers on the back of the fellow's neck, squeezed, and the man became unconscious. Doc laid him gently on the ground.

Closely trailed by Long Tom, the bronze man worked upward. The inside of the stockade wall, which looked so thick, was hollow, in part, being honeycombed by stairways, passages, and small rooms. These afforded them a method of reaching the top.

They came out through a small door upon the runway which ran around the inside of the stockade. A single good leap would put them atop the stockade. Doc Savage made it. He extended a helping hand to Long Tom, for it was quite a jump.

They did not kill time. The drop below them was not a thing to be taken casually. One thing was in their favor, however. The stockade wall was not vertical by any manner of means. It sloped outward, and, although it could hardly be climbed from below, one might slide down it and friction would somewhat delay the descent.

"Let me tackle it first," Doc Savage said. "And be careful."

Without perceptible hesitation, the bronze man stepped over the edge of the wall. There was a loud whizzing sound as he went down. This attracted the attention of a soldier across the street. The fellow stopped and stared, mouth open. Apparently, it did not occur to him to shout, or to unsling the rifle which he carried across his back.

The shock absorbing qualities of tremendous leg muscles came into valuable play as the bronze man hit the packed ground at the foot of the stockade wall. He did not try to remain upright, for that would have been impossible. He let himself go down, almost flat, but he was up again instantly.

"Now," he called to Long Tom.

Long Tom patently did not like what was ahead of him. He made a fierce face, sucked in a full breath, and stepped off the edge. He had used the best judgment. Friction burned him through his clothing. His skin was blistered in several places.

The next instant he was on the ground. Doc Savage had caught him, cushioned in part the shock of his landing.

They ran.

Across the street, the soldier came to life; he emitted a howl that would have done credit to an Andes jaguar. He fought to get the gun off his back.

Doc and Long Tom leaped toward him. They reached the fellow before his rifle came into use. They fell upon him. Doc used his fists and the man was abruptly silent.

There was a doorway nearby, open. They dived into this, carrying the soldier. The room was empty. They left the soldier.

A door took them into a patio from which they climbed onto a roof, and eventually reached the next street. It was the hot part of the day, the siesta hour. Even the war could not break the habits of the Delezonians. Most of the soldiers were having their hour or two of slumber.

"Where now?" Long Tom demanded.

"This way," Doc Savage said. "We have a job to do."

AROUND the headquarters of General Vigo there was quiet. A single sentry paced patrol, and his manner was drowsy. He stopped frequently to perch on the veranda rail and smoke.

There were bushes immediately below the veranda rail. The sentry sighed and drew deeply on his cigarette.

The next instant he was off the rail. He made almost no sound. The bushes fluttered only slightly as he disappeared into them, drawn by a pair of corded bronze arms.

For some moments Doc Savage worked on the nerve centers at the back of the fellow's neck. The sentry became limp, and seemingly slept. Smoke, which he had drawn out of a cigarette, curled slowly from his lips and nostrils.

Long Tom whispered, "That was nice."

"Wait here," Doc Savage breathed back.

The bronze man made a cautious survey. No one was in sight. The shouting of the soldier who had observed their escape from the compound had failed to attract attention. Two things could explain this. The Delezonians were a people who naturally did a great deal of shouting over trivial things. There was also some drinking among soldiers back from the front on leave.

Doc Savage eased over the veranda rail.

The windows of General Vigo's quarters were open. Gliding to them, Doc noted the layout of the room. The door to the corridor was next to, and at right angles to one of the windows. The bronze man went to this window. He eased through, crossed the room, and caught sight of his quarry.

General Vigo was alone, leaning over a map into which he was sticking colored pins. He chanced to be standing so that he was almost certain to observe Doc Savage as the bronze man entered, and he gave no sign of intending to move.

Doc Savage had no intention of waiting until General Vigo decided to shift his position. The unconscious sentry might be discovered at any moment, or they might find that he and Long Tom had escaped from the stockade dungeon. The bronze man flexed the muscles of his throat in peculiar fashion.

"General Vigo," he called in Spanish. His voice was different, meek and mild as if it were a common soldier speaking. "Come quickly, I wish to show you something."

Now, remarkably enough, these words did not seem to come from Doc Savage, but from the other side of the room in which General Vigo stood. Doc was using ventriloquism. General Vigo faced the spot from which the words had appeared to emanate. A door was there.

Seeing no one, General Vigo snapped, "What is it? Who wants—"

His voice was abruptly choked off by corded bronze fingers which had clamped upon his throat. General Vigo was no weakling. He struggled violently, kicking backward, driving his fists. Doc Savage received two terrific blows. He kept his throat grip.

The bronze man hit General Vigo, not as heavily as he intended, on the jaw. Vigo only struggled more violently. Doc tried again with his fist. Fist and jaw, meeting, made a sound as of two hardwood blocks colliding violently.

WHEN General Vigo awakened to sit up and rub his jaw and make numerous ugly grimaces, there was scrawny brush about him. He listened. He could hear plane motors and, straining his neck, could see indistinctly a number of his own military airplane hangars. He was, he decided, near the airport on the outskirts of his headquarters village.

General Vigo looked at Doc Savage. The bronze man stood nearby. His metallic features were expressionless. Long Tom was on the opposite side.

General Vigo looked as if he wanted to swear. Instead, he grinned.

"It is not healthy to kidnap the general dictator of a country the size of Delezon," he said.

Doc Savage began speaking.

"Why did you fake those executions?" the bronze man asked.

"What executions?" General Vigo demanded.

"Those of Long Tom and myself," the bronze man elaborated. "You stood me against that wall, and, in a very loud voice, gave the order for the firing squad to shoot. They fired into the wall, but far to one side of where I stood. Long Tom says you did exactly the same thing in his case."

"For which you owe me thanks," General Vigo grunted.

"And for which you owe us an explanation," Doc Savage told him.

General Vigo shrugged. "The reason is simple."

"Suppose you explain it," Doc told him.

"I desire the end of the Inca in Gray," General Vigo snapped. "I would not hesitate to shoot the devil. But I did not want to execute innocent men. I do not believe in executions. Therefore, I arranged the fake shooting. The men in the firing squad can be trusted. Word would be spread that you were dead. To all intents and purposes, you *would* be dead."

"Which would get you what?" Doc queried.

"If the Inca in Gray suddenly dropped out of sight, after, for instance, I had pulled my little execution trick on you, that would be suspicious, eh?" General Vigo demanded.

"So that was the reason," Doc said.

"It was," the general dictator of Delezon growled. "And now, suppose you let me go, señor."

Doc Savage shook a slow negative. Then he stared steadily at General Vigo.

The bronze man's eyes were capable of doing strange things. Nature had given them an unusual appearance; but long practice had given them a good deal more power, had enabled them to express things. The flake-gold eyes had almost as much ability to express emotion as had the face of an experienced actor. The bronze man's eyes were grim now, and utterly threatening.

General Vigo squirmed uneasily.

"*Dios mio,*" he mumbled hoarsely. "I believe you intend to kill me."

That was exactly the impression Doc Savage had been trying to create.

"You have," the bronze man said, "one chance to live."

"What is it?" growled General Vigo, somewhat weakly.

"Do as you are told," he was advised.

General Vigo swallowed several times. He said nothing.

Then Doc Savage did a totally unexpected thing. He drew from his clothing a heavy automatic military pistol and extended it to General Vigo. The latter took it, and looked stunned.

General Vigo would not have admitted it himself, but he was scared. Just how frightened he was, how thoroughly cowed, was evident from his action now. He held the gun in his hand, but made no attempt to use it.

"The weapon is not loaded," Doc Savage said.

"You will walk behind us, pointing the gun at us as if we were your prisoners. We will walk on to the airport. You will ask for your special plane; presumably, you have one, have you not?"

General Vigo nodded. He was watching the bronze man's eyes. That was a mistake, but the general dictator of Delezon had no way of knowing that he was subjecting himself to what was literally a hypnotic spell.

"I have a private plane," he admitted.

"Walk," Doc Savage directed.

General Vigo got up. Doc Savage and Long Tom strode a little ahead of him, one to the right and one to the left, maintaining such a position that they could watch the man behind them.

They marched out on the tarmac of the Delezon military airport.

SENTRIES challenged the moment they were in view. General Vigo gave what was evidently the password for the day, and he added for good measure, "These men are my prisoners."

The sentries passed them.

They approached the hangars. Their presence was observed, and officers came out, lined up, saluted. The commandant of the field advanced.

"My private plane," General Vigo told him. "Get it ready for the air at once. I will fly it myself"

The officer looked dumbfounded, saluted, said, "But you cannot fly, general *mio*."

General Vigo got himself out of that very nicely. He put his ugly face out and growled, "Do not question my orders. I will show you whether or not I can fly."

General Vigo's plane was a five-place cabin ship, an American job, modern, fast, new. A single twist of the propeller started the motor roaring. Long Tom and Doc Savage climbed into the cabin.

There were two bucket seats for pilots forward. Doc Savage took one of these. Controls were before both. General Vigo got into the other bucket.

"Good work," Doc Savage told him.

General Vigo scowled, looking very much as if he had just eaten a full meal of green apples. He stuck his unlovely visage out of the plane window and bawled an order. The chocks were pulled.

General Vigo grasped the control wheel; but Doc Savage did the flying. The motor bawled. The plane ran across the field, picked up its tail, and jumped.

Doc Savage headed the ship for Alcala, capital city of Santa Amoza. The motor droned steadily. It was a good motor with plenty of power to spare. Long Tom, back in the cabin, kept silent, but watched the jungle and desert below. They crossed the ropy haze of death that was the frontline trenches, and there was no incident to mar the smoothness of their flight.

"See if you can find binoculars," Doc Savage called from the controls.

Long Tom searched, probing through door pockets, and in little compartments above the seats.

"You will find them toward the rear," General Vigo shouted gruffly.

Long Tom looked, located the binoculars, and passed them to Doc Savage. There was a glass hatch immediately above the control cockpit. This was grease-smeared from the motor. Doc Savage opened it for clearer vision and focused the binoculars at the sky. There had been clouds earlier in the day, but these had dispersed. The heavens were an inverted bowl of white and heat.

The bronze man evidently did not find what he was looking for. He passed the binoculars back to Long Tom.

"Keep an eye open for the stratosphere dirigible," he suggested.

Long Tom nodded and worked with the fastening which secured the cabin windows. He did not have his window open when Doc Savage's voice came again, a grim crash.

"Never mind," the bronze man said.

Something about the words, or perhaps it was the sudden grimness in the bronze man's voice, caused Long Tom to spin and stare. Doc Savage was looking at something ahead, to one side, on the earth. Long Tom followed the bronze man's glance.

It was the dirigible—the wreckage of it, rather. Doc Savage banked the plane sharply, sent it toward the crash scene.

The dirigible now looked like nothing so much as a silver egg which dropped urgently in the jungle. The egg aspect, however, did not persist for long. The true size of the stratosphere craft became apparent as they drew closer. Then, too, they could see that the aërial vessel had hit with a great deal of force.

Doc Savage put the plane very low. Wind from the propeller stirred the jungle leaves as they hurtled along. It was obviously his intention to examine the dirigible as closely as possible.

They flew past the airship.

Long Tom spoke in a voice that might have come from Death himself.

"No sign of them," he said. "They must have been crushed in the cabin."

DOC SAVAGE banked the plane, went past again. Their second scrutiny was no more availing than the first. Nor did a third show them a sign of life. Doc Savage backed on the stick and the ship took a little altitude. They looked for a spot that would do for a landing.

The jungle ran for miles. Clearings were scarce, small; but there were a few. The nearest was at least two miles distant.

The clearing, when they reached it, caused Long Tom to shake his head. It was smooth enough, but it was terribly small. Doc Savage sent the plane for it. Long Tom shuddered. They would not make it, even with the bronze man's magnificent flying skill.

But they did make it. The craft jerked into what seemed a certain stall just at the edge of the clearing, coasted out of that, went into a slip, straightened, then, miraculously, seemed to have almost no momentum when it landed.

Long Tom got out and looked around and his neck got red. They had something near two hundred feet to spare.

"Long Tom," Doc Savage said, "want to watch the plane?"

Long Tom knew the answer that was expected to that one.

"Sure," he said.

"Take it into the air at the first sign of an attack," Doc Savage directed.

"Sure," said Long Tom. The heartiness in his own voice surprised him. He did not feel it. In fact, he was quite sure that he could never fly a plane out of that small clearing.

Doc Savage seated General Vigo in the plane in one of the wicker seats, and lashed him there. He made the tying a secure job.

"Merely to avoid any complications," the bronze man said.

General Vigo replied with some words from the vocabulary of a Delezonian mule driver. General Vigo had been describing himself profanely under his breath for some little time now. He was trying to figure out what had made him act so meekly before, back at the flying field, when he had so readily complied with the bronze man's demands. The general-dictator of Delezon could not understand it.

The effect of hypnotic influence was just a little beyond the conception of General Vigo's blunt nature.

Doc Savage moved to the jungle, disappeared. The growth was very dense, hot, full of insects. The bronze man took to the trees, the upper boughs of which interlaced to a large extent. He traveled now in a fashion somewhat amazing.

His agile climbing, his breath-taking swings from one bough to another, the long drop through space from one bough to another, were hardly exceeded by a swarm of jungle monkeys which he passed within a few minutes. The monkeys, chattering excitedly, followed him for some little distance, made great uproar.

An individual with less knowledge of animal nature would have thrown sticks at the little beasts, with the result that they would have been excited even more. Doc Savage simply put on speed, hurtling from one tree to another, running along swaying boughs with the ease of a tightrope walker. He had removed his shoes. His feet, his toes, it might have been noticed, were possessed of a remarkable prehensility which adapted them somewhat to the unusual mode of travel. He left the monkeys behind.

He reached the dirigible.

Some twenty minutes he searched the wreck and its vicinity. He found footprints, plenty of them. Scores of men, most of the m barefooted, had swarmed around the ship. The bronze man found empty machine gun shells, but, since these frequently lay where there were no human tracks, he knew that they must have been dumped from grabsacks attached to airplane machine guns.

Monk and Ham's trail he finally found. He traced it out. He came to the spot where they had been captured; and there he found ominous signs.

There were scarlet stains on the trampled leaves, leakage from human bodies obviously. There were two indentations where forms had fallen. Doc studied these. They about fitted the statures of Monk and Ham.

BEFORE continuing his hunt, the bronze man removed from the dirigible lockers a small metal case equipped with carrying straps. He carried this and continued his search. Tracks lead away from the spot, footprints in profusion. He studied these closely. Nowhere did he find a print which could be identified as belonging to Monk or Ham. He would have recognized these had they been there. For the bronze man retained in his remarkable memory accurate knowledge of the sizes of footprints made by all of his men.

He lost the trail. The fact that he did was no reflection on his ability at following spoor. The footprints joined unexpectedly a jungle trail which seemed to be a route much in use by soldiers and light artillery in going to and from the frontlines.

A good deal of traffic had used the trail recently. A squad of cavalry came up while Doc Savage searched and the bronze man withdrew to cover to let the Delezonians pass. When they had gone, he continued his hunt.

It was hopeless. The party which had captured Monk and Ham and might be carrying their bodies must have gone in one direction or the other, but it was impossible to tell which. Their footprints had been blotted out completely.

Doc Savage returned to the spot where he had left Long Tom, General Vigo and the plane. Nothing had happened there. Doc took the controls while Long Tom untied General Vigo. The ship taxied to the edge of the clearing, came about with one wheel braked, and stood there with both wheels braked while the motor revved up. With the wheelbrakes released, the craft was off like a shot. It took only a few leaves off the trees as it got out of the clearing.

Doc Savage flew directly to the trail, followed it toward the rear for several miles. He saw marching soldiers, artillery, more cavalry. He flew low and inspected them. No sign of Monk or Ham.

The bronze man flew back toward the front, still hunting, but with equal futility. He flew very low, but the plane was not shot at.

"Was the capture of Monk and Ham reported to you?" Doc asked General Vigo.

"No!" snapped General Vigo. He sounded too angry to be lying.

Doc Savage lifted the plane, headed it toward the front and the republic of Santa Amoza, which lay beyond.

Ugly General Vigo looked curious and uneasy.

"What crazy things are you going to do now?" he demanded.

"We are going to try to promote a merger," Doc Savage told him.

"Merger?" The general dictator of Delezon scowled. "Talk sense, señor."

"Santa Amoza and Delezon have a common enemy," Doc Savage told him.

"I still do not understand, *amigo*," Vigo growled.

"The Inca in Gray," Doc Savage said.

General Vigo blinked, wet his lips. He understood.

"Si, si," he said slowly. "But I do not understand this merger talk."

"Think," Doc Savage directed him. "Take everything into consideration. The Inca in Gray has been harassing you. If you will analyze the crimes of this mysterious mastermind, you will find that they have come at such times as it seemed you were on the point of whipping Santa Amoza. Is that true?"

General Vigo thought briefly. "It is. *Caramba!* It is."

"Exactly the same thing has happened in Santa Amoza," Doc continued. "The Inca in Gray has been keeping this war going."

General Vigo performed a typical American gesture. He scratched his head.

"This thing, señor, she is just a bit too incredible to believe," he mumbled.

"The Inca in Gray has a tremendous organization," Doc Savage said. "This is no small thing. Whatever the Inca in Gray is after, it is big and undoubtedly will affect the lives of many people."

Vigo nodded, then barked, "What about the merger?"

Doc Savage did not answer. He sent the plane toward Santa Amoza.

Chapter XIII
CHEMISTRY

A SMALL but rather important thing happened in the jungle some miles from the wrecked dirigible after Doc Savage had taken his plane out of sight. A pigeon arose. It did not behave as an ordinary wild pigeon would have. It flew in circles until it had attained a considerable height. Then it lined out—flew straight for Santa Amoza and its capital city, Alcala.

One who knew carrier pigeons would have recognized this bird, from its actions, as belonging to that type.

Monk and Ham had watched the bird released. Both Monk and Ham were very much alive, although somewhat battered. They had been beaten, but they had not been entirely on the receiving end of the punishment, it was evident from the battered countenances of several of their captors. Some of these had noses which had been recently bloodied. It was, as a matter of fact, the drippings from these proboscises which Doc Savage had found.

"They tied a note to that pigeon," Monk growled. "Wonder what it was?"

"How would I know?" Ham demanded sourly. "Did you notice them showing it to me?"

The two prisoners fell silent, listening. Four guards were with them. All the rest of the party had departed, the departure being coincident with the appearance of a plane which had cruised back and forth a few minutes ago.

Monk and Ham, having been under the mat of the jungle, had not seen the plane, hence had no way of knowing Doc Savage had been in the craft. Nor did they have the slightest inkling that the decreased number of their captors meant that some of them had dashed off madly in an attempt to apprehend the bronze man as he examined the dirigible. Thickness of the jungle had thwarted this attempt, the expeditionary force not even getting close enough for Doc Savage to become aware of their presence.

Monk listened to the grunting of his pig, Habeas Corpus. The shoat was tied to a tree in the nearby jungle.

His tether was a wire. It was rather long, and Habeas, by moving to the end of it, could stand a few feet within the tiny clearing where Monk and Ham were being held.

The shoat appeared now, stood looking at his master, Monk, big ears distended.

Probably that was what gave Monk his big idea. The homely chemist rolled over on his side, spoke in a low voice to Ham. He used Mayan, a language which very few people outside Doc Savage and his five aides understood.

MONK

"Get ready for some fireworks," was the gist of what Monk said in Mayan.

Ham glared as if Monk had just told him they were going to poison somebody, but that was only Ham's manner. He made it a point never to be polite to Monk.

Monk faced Habeas Corpus.

"Señores," said the pig in Spanish. "I object to this treatment."

Nature has neglected to give pigs human voices, so it was manifestly impossible that Habeas did the speaking; but it certainly sounded as if the speech was coming from the porker.

The guards were dumbfounded. One even dropped his rifle. Two of the officers crossed themselves superstitiously.

"Si, si, amigos," Habeas continued. "For an ordinary hog this sort of treatment might be in order; but for one of my undeniable abilities—"

It was Monk, of course, throwing his voice. The homely chemist had long ago learned ventriloquism from Doc Savage.

The byplay might have been ridiculous, comical under other circumstances, but here in the jungle, coming in the surprising manner which it did, falling upon the ears of men who were probably superstitious to start with, it had its effect.

It gave Monk and Ham a chance to heave unnoticed to their feet.

MONK and Ham were both bound, ankle and wrist; that, by no means, meant they were incapable of movement. They could manage quite respectable leaps, and they did so.

Monk howled as he jumped. His war whoop was one that might have been made by a dozen men. Monk always liked his fights noisy. He crashed his bound hands down on the neck of a guard. The fellow collapsed.

Ham took a second guard in the same fashion, striking the fellow near the base of the skull. Two of the captors were left. Monk took one, his tremendous strength working to great advantage. Ham got the last man down. The fellow was no easy victim. He knew something of wrestling. He closed with Ham and began to do painful things to the dapper lawyer's slender frame. Ham twisted frantically, doubled, and suddenly managed to get the man's head between his knees. That was perfect. Ham's bound ankles made it unnecessary to hook his toes for leverage. He squeezed. The victim's tongue began to come out.

Monk and Ham got to their feet almost together and Monk grinned from ear to ear.

"You gotta admit that hog has his uses," he said.

Ham sniffed. Rather than give praise to Habeas, he kept silent. Monk went over and untied the wire from around the neck of Habeas Corpus.

"Let's see how you can run, hog," the homely chemist grunted.

They started to run through the jungle. They ran without the slightest attention to direction, giving all of their attention to keeping the noise down, making speed. After perhaps a mile of that, they devoted another half hour to wiping out their trail. They did this by crawling through the matted tree tops, by wading in a small stream which they found, and by stepping where footprints would not remain. They did this very assiduously, having had their fill of being prisoners. They did not want their late captors to overhaul them.

Came the inevitable time, however, when they had to decide where they were to go.

"Santa Amoza," Ham said.

They agreed on that. At least, Monk did not object.

They looked at the sun. The solar orb was just enough off center to cause some doubt as what might be south, the direction in which Santa Amoza lay.

Monk leveled an arm, said, "That way."

"Wrong," Ham objected. "It's this way."

Ham pointed in a direction almost opposite from that indicated by Monk.

"You're crazy, you shyster," Monk accused. "Weren't you ever a Boy Scout? Can'tcha tell directions?"

They proceeded to express audibly and quite vehemently various unflattering opinions of each other's abilities as jungle guides. Neither was willing to admit the slightest chance that the other might be right, which would not have surprised anyone who knew them.

"A weak mind goes with a strong back," Ham told the huge, apish Monk finally. "I am going my own way."

The sun was pouring down relentlessly from the heavens, and while it did not quite penetrate the thick jungle growth, it made a great deal of heat. Monk flailed his arms at a swarm of tiny flies that stung like hornets.

"Go your own way, you animated law book," Monk muttered. "I'm goin' where I know Santa Amoza is."

Without a backward glance, Monk plunged ahead in the direction he had chosen. Habeas Corpus, the pig, grunted unhappily, eyed Ham with what seemed to be an air of expectance, then arose and trotted after Monk, waving his oversize ears at the pestering flies.

Ham, although he would never have admitted it, was nonplused.

"Go ahead, you hairy idiot," he shouted. "I hope the flies eat you."

An insulting grunt from Monk, and an equally insulting echo from Habeas was the only reply.

HAM promptly sat down to rest from the strain of the argument. It was very hot. He had merely to shake his head, and drops of perspiration fell off. He sat there, firmly resolved he would go the way his own judgment told him that Santa Amoza lay.

Sounds of Monk's progress ceased. The jungle became silent, and its silence was not pleasant. Ham, in the course of a few minutes, fell to glancing about nervously, experiencing that not uncommon feeling that he was being watched by unseen eyes. His lips tightened. This was no country for one man to tackle alone. Neither himself or Monk.

Ham reached a decision. It hurt him, but he arose and grudgingly turned his steps in the direction taken by Monk. There was a faint trail left by the chemist and his redoubtable pig.

Ham was very alert. There was no sound about him; but the impression he was being followed grew. Great jungle trees overhead created an artificial twilight, and in the dimness objects were difficult to discern with clarity. Ham stopped repeatedly to listen.

He heard a crashing ahead.

"Monk," Ham opened his mouth to call, but closed it grimly. Jungle terror or no jungle terror, he intended to have some fun with Monk. He would devil the apish fellow, make him think he was being attacked.

Ham crowded on as noiselessly and as rapidly as possible. He peered ahead intently, and soon he was rewarded.

Through the trees he could see stooped massive figures moving along the ground, pushing creepers and jungle vegetation aside with long, hairy arms. The light was very indistinct; but that stooped, apelike stride was unmistakable.

Ham's smile spread. He picked up a rock, scuttled

forward into a thicket in which the apish form had vanished, drew back his arm and hurled the rock. It smashed into the brush.

The rock smacked through the leaves. It hit something—undoubtedly flesh—with a thump that to Ham was a wholly satisfying sound.

Ham expected to hear a prompt howl from Monk. He was disappointed. There came a high shriek, a great crashing of brush. The noise came in Ham's direction, and Ham's eyes all but fell out. He looked at what came out of growth.

It was a monkey. But such a monkey.

It was larger than a chimpanzee, but smaller than a gorilla. It had no tail and its hair was rust colored.

Strangest of all was the astounding resemblance which the newcomer bore to Monk.

The strange anthropoid advanced toward Ham, making small mumbling sounds which were very like those Monk made on the occasions when he talked to himself.

"Scat!" Ham gasped, and retreated. He promptly had a bit of bad luck. His heel caught in a root and he fell.

The simian marvel bounded toward Ham.

"Scat, drat you!" Ham exploded.

Ham was frankly scared as the creature sprang upon him, but his fright evaporated suddenly as the big simian flung its arms around him and clung there, whimpering, scared.

Ham looked intently into the visage of his new friend. He could not help laughing.

"Monk's twin brother or I hope to kiss that pig Habeas," he gulped.

The simian chattered amiably and Ham got to his feet. The chattering made considerable noise.

"Go away," Ham directed. "One creature looking like you around me is enough. Monk will not want any competition."

The tailless anthropoid bounded up and down—a thing Monk did when he was mad—and gave no indication of holding any thoughts of departure.

Ham scratched his head and ruminated aloud, "I wonder how you tell one of these things to beat it."

The simian made amiable chattering noises.

"Scat," Ham directed. "Shoo. Sooey. Beat it. Vamoose. Go along chop chop."

None of this had any effect. Ham tried clucking as he were driving a horse. That did not work either.

Ham gave it up and fell to studying the creature. He was struck once more by the uncanny resemblance which this jungle dweller bore to the homely chemist, Monk.

At that point came an interruption. Accompanied by a faint noise of shuffling leaves and shifting weeds, the pig Habeas Corpus appeared. The shoat caught sight of the anthropoid. Habeas promptly stopped. His big ears went up like sails. He grunted rapidly. Plainly, Habeas did not think a great deal of Ham's new companion.

The feeling seemed to be mutual. The tailless simian seized a stick, rushed at Habeas, and gave the porker a resounding whack. Habeas fled, emitting a series of wild grunts.

That decided Ham. He sat down and laughed, laughed until tears came into his eyes. His predicament was completely forgotten in the glowing light of a great decision.

"I am going to keep that funny looking baboon as a pet," he declared. "Boy, will that burn Monk up. And will it give that pig, Habeas Corpus, something to do besides chew holes in my clothes whenever he can find them."

The tailless simian, having chased Habeas from the vicinity, came ambling back, carrying a stick over one shoulder, gun fashion. Ham struck an attitude, relaxed, scratched his head, then straightened.

"I christen thee Chemistry," he told the simian.

The remarkable looking anthropoid clucked happily as if the new name were perfectly agreeable.

Laughing to himself, Ham struck out again on Monk's trail.

CHEMISTRY followed Ham closely. When the jungle floor became tough going, Chemistry took to the trees, but still kept close, swinging along easily.

"Come down here," Ham directed.

Chemistry only sat on a limb and looked stubborn. Ham gave it up and listened. There was no sound. Strangely enough, the feeling that unseen eyes were watching him still persisted. Despite the heat, he shivered slightly. Afraid of nothing he could see, the dapper lawyer was nevertheless experiencing vague misgivings, feelings which he knew, having studied psychology, must be a result of the instinctive fear of the unknown, handed down from ancestors who had lived in such jungles perhaps millions of years ago.

Ham shook himself violently as if to rid himself of the fear, then called loudly to the ape, Chemistry. The homely simian was a companion at least.

Instead of coming out of his tree, Chemistry abruptly began to chatter amiably, then swung forward at a rapid pace. Ham, for no good reason that he could explain, took out in pursuit. Swinging overhead, unhampered by clinging vines and brush, Chemistry made the better time. Occasionally he disappeared almost entirely. Ham expressed unkind opinions of Chemistry under his breath. He picked up a short stick. It would be just as well if Chemistry, at this point, learned some discipline.

Something appeared ahead. In the vague light, it looked like Chemistry. Ham let fly with his small club.

"O-o-ow," howled a familiar voice. "Who done that?"

"Monk," Ham called, "it's me!"

"It would be," Monk said disgustedly. "Fine business, throwin' clubs at me. It's a wonder I didn't shoot you."

"Didn't know it was you," Ham snapped, and added so as not to be misunderstood, "If I had, I'd have thrown a bigger club."

"Who'd you think it was?" Monk growled.

"Chemistry," Ham said and burst into laughter.

"Chemistry?" Monk exploded. Then he eyed Ham intensely. "You gone crazy?"

A frightened squealing from Habeas Corpus interrupted them. Both men wheeled, ran a few paces through the jungle, and came upon a strange sight. Chemistry had captured Habeas Corpus. He was holding the pig, and diligently searching his hide for sign of interesting vermin.

Monk emitted a roar, picked up the most convenient stick. Ham grasped his hairy arm, restraining him.

"Wait, Monk!" he barked.

"Wait nothing," Monk gritted. "I'll teach that funny lookin' baboon to pick on Habeas!"

"That baboon," Ham snapped, "is Chemistry."

"What?" Monk squawked.

"Chemistry is my new pet," Ham declared. "And striking him is the same as striking me."

Just what action Monk would have taken never did develop, for at that moment Habeas managed to bite Chemistry, an expedient which resulted in his escape.

"Chemistry," Ham said, "is some animal, don't you think?"

Monk exhibited symptoms of a spasm.

"Don't tell me you're gonna keep that—that—thing. Why, he looks like nothing else on this green earth."

"I mistook him for you at first," Ham said pointedly.

Monk squawled, "I won't stand for it."

"You'll not only stand for it," Ham retorted. "You'll like it."

Habeas shoved his nose out of the jungle. Chemistry jumped at the pig. Habeas hastily took flight.

Monk began rolling up his sleeves.

"That blasted thing don't go with us," he said. "If I gotta, I'll take both you and your baboon apart—"

Chemistry emitted a sudden weird squeaking sound and leaped toward Ham. He crouched beside the dapper lawyer, knuckles resting on the ground, little eyes roving nervously over the surrounding jungle. He was scared. An instant later, Habeas Corpus scuttled out of the undergrowth and stopped near Monk's feet.

"Blazes!" Monk breathed. "Somethin's around here."

They both carried rifles which they had taken from their late guards. They lifted these weapons, waited, listened.

"Whatcha reckon it is?" whispered Monk.

Ham shook his head, and, in a whisper equally as thin, said, "Don't know. But maybe—" He broke off suddenly.

There came a dull noise, a whistle and a *plop*.

HAM had been standing beside a tree. He ducked wildly, slamming flat upon the ground. An inch from where his neck had been, in the bole of the tree, there quivered a tiny, feathered dart.

"Poisoned arrow!" Monk bellowed angrily. He started to leap forward.

"Don't," Ham yelled. "They may be all around us."

Monk halted, stood perfectly still, rifle ready. There was intense silence. Chemistry broke it with a shrill, almost human cry. The unusual simian leaped, wrapped small, hairy arms around Ham's head.

Ham later decided that Chemistry had made a gesture at protecting him—at least so he took occasion to assure Monk; but at the moment, all that Ham could make out was that Chemistry's embrace was keeping him from seeing.

"Blazes!" Monk barked suddenly, somewhat horribly.

Ham freed himself from Chemistry's embrace. He had been blinded for only a moment; but unpleasant things had happened in that interval.

Completely surrounding them, having materialized like ghosts, stood a ring of natives. These were small men, somewhat wizened in their faces. In their hands was the deadly blowgun used by the uncivilized dwellers in these jungles.

"Don't start shooting," Ham gasped.

"Think I'm a sucker?" Monk growled. "We ain't got enough shells to take even a fourth of these little guys."

Chapter XIV
MORE TO DIE

A NATIVE, somewhat taller and a bit more intelligent looking than the rest, stepped forward. He wore a fierce scowl, and he jabbed his arms several times at Chemistry. Then he spoke suddenly, rapidly.

The native's rattling jargon left Monk's face blank.

"He says to drop our weapons," Ham told the homely chemist, and let his own rifle slip from his hand.

"Good night," Monk grunted. "What language is he talkin'?"

"Listen closely," Ham retorted. "If you can't pick out enough words to give you the meaning, you're as dumb as you look."

The native leader was cackling again. Monk listened intently. From an expression of deepest gloom his features changed to radiance, almost joyful.

"Mayan!" he exploded. "It's not the same Mayan language we know, but it's Mayan."

"Right," Ham agreed.

"Then we're among friends," Monk chortled.

The statement was somewhat strange, but had a foundation in an adventure they had gone through early in their association with Doc Savage. It was this episode which had resulted in the bronze man's acquisition of his almost limitless source of wealth.

In a remote valley in the Central American mountains dwelled a lost people—the pure descendants of ancient Maya. In the valley was a gigantic treasure of gold, the major wealth of ancient Maya, probably the richest empire known to history. Doc Savage and his aides had penetrated this strange lost valley, had done a great service for the Mayans there. Out of gratitude many honors had been heaped upon the bronze man, most concrete of which perhaps was the agreement to supply him such gold as he needed. Doc Savage had but to go to a powerful radio transmitter, broadcast a few words in Mayan at the noon hour on certain seventh days, and, a few days later, a pack train laden with gold would come out of the Central American mountains. These treasure loads, frequently amounting to millions, were deposited to the bronze man's credit; and no white man but Doc Savage and his aides knew the source.

"If they're Mayans, they're buddies of ours," Monk insisted.

The leader of the natives was barking again. His syllables were rapid, explosive. He lunged suddenly, and captured Chemistry. The homely simian chattered and squeaked but did not struggle violently. In fact, Chemistry seemed familiar with their captors.

Men stepped forward, surrounded Monk and Ham and seized them firmly.

"Friends, did you say?" Ham asked Monk sardonically. "Oh, yes, you can notice it very plainly."

Monk scowled first at Ham, then at Chemistry.

"It was that blasted thing you picked as a pet," he declared. "It squawked and hollered and these guys heard it. That's how they found us."

The natives were chattering volubly now.

"Listen," Ham told Monk.

Monk strained his ears, an intense pucker on his brow. He could pick up quite a few words.

"Chemistry seems to be their sacred ape or somethin', as near as I can make out," Monk grunted.

"Exactly," Ham said. "And that is why our lives have been spared. The sacred ape was friendly with us. That's why they spared us."

"You made that last up," Monk accused. "They didn't say nothin' of the kind."

The argument was broken up by their captors. Ropes made of twisted vines were wrapped around their chests, imprisoning their arms. Neither Monk nor Ham attempted to escape. Not only would it have been useless but probably fatal. Those blowguns and poisoned darts were not things to be trifled with.

Ham now spoke, attempting to use the guttural jargon of the natives. They seemed to understand him, but they did not give him the courtesy of an answer. The leader of the little men only shrugged his shoulders.

"If Doc were only with us," Monk grumbled, "I'll bet he could get some action."

The natives now grouped about them, waved arms indicating that they were to move through the jungle. Before long, paths became discernible. They were narrow paths, evidently used by these small men. The march pushed forward at more speed.

The chemist and the dapper lawyer were silent. Neither would admit that he was worried, but they were far from cheerful. Not only was there the matter of their own predicament. There was their lack of knowledge of what might have happened to Doc Savage, to say nothing of Long Tom.

Habeas Corpus brought up the rear of the cavalcade. The homely shoat was not interfered with. Chemistry had been released by now and swung along, sometimes on the ground, sometimes in the trees. From time to time Chemistry plucked hard tropical fruits and pegged them at Habeas, making the pig's life miserable.

The small natives had fallen silent. As a matter of fact, the intense heat was not encouraging to conversation.

"I wonder what happened to Doc Savage?" Monk groaned finally.

The words had a startling effect on the leader of their captors. He halted and looked at them, small eyes wide, wizened face curious.

"Doc Savage?" he asked.

The men obviously could not speak English, yet the distinctness with which he managed to speak Doc's name was startling. He got every syllable correct.

Monk nodded, a broad grin overspreading his face. "Yeah, buddy, Doc Savage. Have you heard of him? He's our chief."

Monk had spoken English, deceived by the clarity with which Doc Savage's name had been spoken. He had gotten the mistaken impression that the native leader could also speak English.

Then, realizing his words had not been under-

Monk began rolling up his sleeves. "That blasted thing don't go with us," he said …

stood, Monk launched into Mayan, speaking slowly so that these people could understand his version of the tongue.

"We are followers of Doc Savage, the man of bronze," he told them. "He is our leader, our chief. Do you understand?"

A fierce expression crossed the native chieftain's face; but there also was awe and fear mingled with the ferocity. The wizened fellow jabbered excitedly, waving his arms at his fellows so that they all drew

around. They all jabbered, some of them jumping up and down. The proceedings became a bedlam.

The rapidity of the talk got beyond Monk's ability. He turned to Ham, who possessed a better knowledge of Mayan.

"What are they sayin', Ham?" he demanded.

The lawyer's face had hardened, acquired a grim set.

"We seem to have run into bad trouble, Monk," he said grimly. "In fact, when you opened your mouth, you put your foot right into it. I cannot catch all they are saying, but they are afraid of Doc Savage and they have orders to kill any of his men. Wait, listen."

There was an interim when Ham strained intently to catch rapid words.

"These natives are followers of the Inca in Gray," Ham exploded finally.

FOUR hours later, Monk and Ham were in no better position. They were very near the exhaustion point. Their little captors had kept traveling at full speed, and had seemed not greatly affected by the terrific heat, whereas Monk and Ham had all but melted down.

Chemistry and Habeas Corpus were still having their difficulties. Chemistry, long arms trailing, stalked along keeping close to Ham, only separating himself from the dapper lawyer to set off in pursuit of Habeas at intervals.

A subtle change began coming over the small natives and it was not induced by their frequent glances at the sun which was flirting with the horizon and giving promise of the coolness of night.

The reason for their excitement became evident a moment later. They were nearing a village. It was obviously a temporary settlement. Bamboo was the principal structural material of the huts. The roofs were thatched, and the floors consisted of platforms a few feet off the ground, this latter structural detail no doubt an expedient to discourage snakes and small animals. None of the huts had walls.

The leader of the natives jabbered. Small but strong hands seized Monk and Ham, propelled them toward a hut which was in the approximate mathematical center of the village.

"Notice anything strange?" Monk whispered.

"Yes." Ham nodded. "There isn't a woman about the place. This is purely a war party."

"A war party of the Inca in Gray, señor," interrupted a new voice in Spanish. It was not a strange voice. They had heard it before. Both Monk and Ham started, spun.

Standing beside one of the jungle huts was a man—one of the gang which had captured them when they got out of the crashed dirigible. This fellow made a small gesture. Several other men appeared. These, too, had been members of the party from which Monk and Ham had escaped.

"You are surprised, señores?" a man queried.

"Bugs on you," Monk growled.

The man showed them his teeth.

"You will wait here for a time," he said. "Shortly you will be joined by Doc Savage."

Monk started. "What's that?"

"The great Doc Savage will be with you before long," said the other. "The Inca in Gray has planned it thus, and the plans of the Inca in Gray have a way of working."

"What do you mean?" Monk growled.

"Shut up, Monk," said Ham. "Don't give him the satisfaction of being able to stand there and brag."

Habeas Corpus, who had ventured near, suddenly squealed and fled with Chemistry in close pursuit.

"Ah, the peeg," murmured the man who spoke in Spanish and a little bad English. "He shall yet roast in my pot."

Monk bellowed angrily, tried to throw himself at the speaker despite the fact that he was a prisoner. The little natives held him back. The white man— he was undoubtedly white, as were his companions, although some of the latter might not be of pure blood—laughed and strode away. The natives forced Monk and Ham along. Mongrel dogs ran forward, nipping at their heels. They chased Chemistry into the trees, ran Habeas through the brush; but Habeas was a match for dogs. Bristles erect, tusks bared, the pig charged, emitting a series of locomotive grunts. The dogs fled. That seemed to encourage Habeas. He trotted over belligerently and sat under Chemistry's tree, as if inviting the latter to come down. The tailless monkey threw overripe fruit at him.

Monk and Ham were conducted to a hut, one side of which was shaded by a curtain formed by stacking large palm fronds. This curtain prevented their seeing inside the hut. Their wrists and ankles were bound. They were lifted, tossed onto the upraised floor.

"Good evening, señores," said a weary feminine voice.

Monk turned his head, found himself looking at one of the most beautiful young women he had ever seen. She was tied as securely as were Ham and himself.

"Who are you?" the homely chemist exploded.

"Señorita Anita Carcetas," said the young woman, who was obviously a prisoner.

MONK gave every inclination of a man temporarily stunned.

"The daughter of the president of Santa Amoza," the homely chemist blurted.

"Yes," said the young woman. "And you?"

Monk took another look at the young woman and this had the effect of getting his voice. Monk was very susceptible to feminine beauty; and it was Ham, a little less vulnerable, who spoke.

"The missing link here is Colonel Andrew Blodgett Mayfair, better known as Monk," he said. "I am Brigadier General Theodore Marley Brooks, although I am usually called Ham, a nickname I do not like. We are associated with Doc Savage."

The girl was seized with sudden excitement.

"Then Doc Savage is in Santa Amoza?" she gasped.

"Or Delezon," Ham admitted. "We do not know for sure where he is."

The young woman strove to sit erect, but failed.

"You think he will be able to aid us in our present predicament?" she asked.

"Of course he will," declared Ham, knowing that was the proper thing to say.

Monk had discovered that, if he took his eyes from the girl's attractive features, his voice would return. He did so and asked a question.

"Will you tell us," he requested, "what this is all about?"

The girl nodded and spoke swiftly. Words fairly poured from her lips. She told them about the depredations of the Inca in Gray, dwelt upon the mystery behind the sinister master mind's manipulations. She sketched briefly some of the rather hideous crimes committed by the Inca in Gray.

In particular did she describe the fantastic death of the gray dust.

Monk took this all in with great interest. It was their first opportunity, incidentally, to receive a general story of what was behind the affair. Both Monk and Ham nodded comprehension.

"The Inca in Gray has been trying to get us out of the way," Monk said.

"And doing fairly well at it," Ham added.

A faint noise came from outside the hut, from the jungle nearby, in fact, a small scurrying sound. Monk's head came up but he could not see what made the noise.

"Have you anything else to tell us?" Ham asked the girl.

She shook her head. "Only that the Inca in Gray is deadly, and is really responsible for this long war. He has kept the war going for some awful purpose of his own. That makes him responsible for thousands and thousands of lives."

Again came the sound of a scurry, a rustle, and a sharp grunt as though of pain. Monk began to look uneasy. He struggled against his bonds but it was useless.

"What about this death of the gray dust?" Ham asked the girl.

The young woman shuddered. "It's—it's horrible. I saw one victim of it. There was nothing to show where the dust came from, how it got there. It was simply there. The expression on the dead man's face—he must have perished horribly." She shuddered several times.

The scurrying and fluttering in the brush broke out again. There was a shrill squeal. Monk lunged against his bonds, fighting to free himself, but getting nowhere.

"They're tryin' to catch Habeas," he groaned.

The squealing and grunting became louder as did the smashing about in the brush.

"Get heem!" yelled a voice in bad English.

Habeas Corpus dived into the hut, took shelter behind Monk. An instant later Chemistry lumbered in, grabbed Habeas and he held the shoat in close embrace.

The pig hunters now appeared. They were the white men. A few of the natives were with them. They approached Habeas purposefully.

But the natives got between the white men and Chemistry and Habeas. They jabbered excitedly.

Ham listened to the cackling conversation, then glanced at Monk, panted, "Get that?"

"Yeah," Monk growled. "They say your dang baboon obviously don't want Habeas hurt. So therefore these other guys have got to leave Habeas alone."

"Chemistry," Ham said, "has probably saved Habeas' life."

"I hate to admit it," Monk mumbled. "But I believe you're right."

There was tension for a few moments, the white men plainly angered at the objections of the natives. The fact that they were greatly outnumbered was something they evidently kept in mind. They backed down, shrugging, showing forced grins.

Habeas showed his gratitude for being saved by biting Chemistry's rather humanlike big toe, which made it necessary for the pig to flee wildly into the jungle.

"Habeas," Ham said, "has about the same disposition as the guy that owns him."

IT must have been half an hour later, and the sun was nearly down, when the arrival of a messenger was observed. This fellow spoke rapidly. There was a hum of grim excitement. Natives and white men approached the hut where the prisoners lay.

The fellow who could speak bad English came forward and addressed the captives.

"Word has come from our master, the Inca in Gray," the man said. "You are to be consigned to pits."

Monk looked puzzled, eyed Ham, demanded, "What does he mean—pits?"

The girl, Señorita Anita Carcetas, emitted a short strangled cry. "The ant pit."

"Huh?" Monk eyed her.

"You—you have heard of it," she choked. "A pit—ants—honey—"

Hardened though he was, Monk felt himself grow chilly. He had heard of that method of torture, one used by only the most ferocious of barbarians. It was a slow horrible thing, incredibly cruel. It kept a man alive hour after hour, while he was being literally eaten alive.

Ham had evidently heard about the ant pits, too. Pallor was on his not unhandsome features. But he said nothing.

Rough hands seized the prisoners, yanked them to their feet, pulled them into the red light of the dusk. Monk saw that the girl was being brought along also.

"Hey!" he bellowed. "You gonna do that to a woman?"

"It is the word of the Inca in Gray," said the white man.

But, at this time, the messenger thrust himself forward. He spoke volubly and vehemently.

As a result of the messenger's exhortations, the girl was separated from the other two prisoners, and placed back on the raised hut floor.

The Inca in Gray, it seemed, had not only not ordered her death, but had given specific instructions that she be kept alive. Monk and Ham were marched away.

"*Adios,*" the girl called after them in a voice that she tried to keep firm. "You are as I imagined Doc Savage's men would be—very brave."

"This is gonna come out all right," Monk managed to shout back at her.

A moment later the village was left behind. There was a swarm of natives around the two captives. The fellows were excited; but, strangely enough, theirs was not a bloodthirsty excitement. In fact, there was some surly talk on the part of the small brown men.

"That surprises me," Ham murmured to Monk, "these natives are not so anxious for the torture."

Monk frowned. "You mean they're doin' it just because the Inca in Gray ordered it?"

"That's the idea," Ham agreed. "They do not like it. It seems that these natives are really hillmen, men out of the mountains. Some of them are saying that torture is below their tribal honor. They claim it is resorted to only by the low and hated jungle Indians who eat locust and other insects."

They came to a clearing. This was not large, but was absolutely bare, and it was hot, insufferably hot, although the sun had all but disappeared.

The torture pit was in the center of this clearing. Men who had gone ahead were scooping it out. There was nothing particularly terrible or ominous about its appearance, it being merely a shallow hole dug in the baked ground.

Stout pegs were driven into the bottom of the pit when it was completed.

Rough hands seized Monk and Ham, shoved them down into the depression. They were shoved flat. Their ankles and wrists were untied, then tied again, this time to the stakes. They now lay on their backs, spread-eagled, helpless.

The leader of the white men stood at the pit edge. He seized a short spear from one of the natives. This did not have a poisoned tip. He flicked it down. It came so close to Monk that it nicked the flesh of one arm. The homely chemist gave no sign.

"*Diablo,*" howled the white man. "Thees ees no essport. Bring on thees honey."

Small natives appeared carrying jars. These held the honey. Streams of the stuff were poured back and forth across Monk and Ham, and up and down the sides of the pit.

"You understand what thees ees for?" asked the white man who spoke bad English. The fellow's face was a grinning, hideous mask. It contrasted starkly with the visage of the little natives.

The white man was enjoying this. The natives were not.

The men carrying the honey jars now walked away through the jungle, streaming the sweetish substance after them, leaving a trail.

HAM looked at the homely Monk and demanded, "Know anything about ants?"

"No," said Monk. "And I don't care about starting my education now."

The white man with the sadistic complex laughed at them.

"You will learn much about ants," he said. "They like honey. They will follow this trail. They will come upon something they also like—live meat."

The little men came back with the honey jars empty and grunted that they distributed the stuff in long lines through the jungle, where it was almost certain to be encountered by ants.

The white man growled an order, and they all marched away.

Monk ruminated aloud, "Wonder what kind of ants they got down here?"

"Army ants," Ham told him. "I've read about them. They eat everything. They march over you. They cover your whole body. You know how one ant stings when it bites you. Well, thousands of them—"

"You can save the rest of that," Monk told him. "I got an imagination of my own."

There was silence. It was broken once by the rumble of a jungle drum, close at hand. Evidently, the small natives were signaling in this fashion. A few minutes later, from the infinite distance, another drum rumbled. The sounds were throbbing and seemed to adhere to no particular pattern, but both Monk and Ham knew that the sounds conveyed a message. It was always mysterious, these drum languages of the jungle people. White men seldom fathomed them.

"Look," Ham barked suddenly.

It seemed they had been there for hours, yet it was not yet intensely dark, which meant that not a great deal of time had passed, since twilight did not last long in the tropics.

A single ant was crawling around the edge of the pit, following the honey. It worked downward slowly, seeming to have no particular idea. It came close to the two bound captives.

Monk, with his hairy fingers, managed to pick up a small quantity of dirt. He flung it at the ant. The insect scurried away. It seemed to have a purpose now. It went directly over the edge of the pit and disappeared.

"You made a wrong move then," Ham told Monk.

"Why?" the homely chemist demanded.

"Did you ever read anything about these army ants?" Ham demanded.

"No," Monk said.

"They have ant scouts," Ham told him. "You should have let that insect come close, then made sure that it didn't leave to get its fellows."

Monk wet his lips. He felt suddenly cold. This was strange. For the heat in the little clearing must be terrific. Only a few times in his eventful career had Monk felt as he did now, and always that had been when death was close.

"The Inca in Gray!" Monk mumbled. "Damn him, whoever he is!"

Chapter XV
POLITICS

THE Inca In Gray was a cloud that had covered Delezon and Santa Amoza. Invisible this cloud, true, but so real that it had touched every citizen of the two republics. The Inca in Gray had become a symbol of terror, just as the bat is the symbol of the night. The Inca in Gray was as symbolic of death as the skull and crossbones. Yet none knew what he— if the Inca in Gray was a man—thought. Never was motive or goal cloaked in more diabolic mystery.

General Fernanez Vigo was expressing his personal opinion of the Inca in Gray.

"A clever fiend," he said.

Doc Savage, Long Tom said nothing. The bronze man was flying the plane. It was General Vigo's private ship, and it had just taken off in the dusk from an outlying spot in the jungle. The ship, the three men had waited there all afternoon, waiting for darkness.

The waiting had puzzled General Vigo. He had asked questions about it.

"Our purpose demands that we reach Alcala, capital of Santa Amoza, unobserved," Doc Savage told him.

So they were in the air now in the gathering darkness, with the plane motor encouragingly a-thrum. The jungle turned black below. Red light, like diluted lighter fluid, enveloped the plane itself for a time. Then that darkened also. The moon, which had been overhead all the time, brightened as if it were a silver porthole behind which an electric light had been turned on. Doc flew steadily. He kept the stick back until the ship had gained every inch of altitude of which it was capable.

Long Tom, with the binoculars which had been in the plane, kept a close watch on the earth below, searching for lights. He found them eventually.

"Ahead," he said. "I think it is Alcala."

Doc Savage took the binoculars, made a scrutiny of his own.

"Right," he agreed.

"What do you men plan to do?" General Vigo demanded impatiently.

Doc Savage said nothing.

"Quit asking questions," Long Tom suggested.

General Fernanez Vigo had been absolute ruler of Delezon just long enough to lose his liking for men who talked back to him. He put his ugly visage close to Long Tom's pale countenance, and seemed inclined to use his fists. He had, however, the good judgment to change his mind.

Doc Savage flew the ship for a time in silence. Then he reached over unexpectedly and cut the switch. The motor stopped. The silence which followed was almost startling. Then air moaned past the flying wires as the ship slipped into a long glide.

General Vigo knew something of flying. He looked uneasy and mopped his forehead.

"Me, señors, I do not like these night landings," he said.

"Quit grouching," advised Long Tom with scant respect for the dignity of a general-dictator.

ALCALA was a vaguely phosphorescent haze on the earth below. The haze brightened. Separate lights became discernible although there were not many of these, and, no doubt, they would be extinguished before long, due to fear of air raids.

Doc Savage selected a spot well beyond the outskirts of the city. He evidently remembered it from his previous flight over the metropolis. It was a vegetable field, smooth enough for a landing.

The plane swooped down, three-pointed perfectly. There was only a slight drumming as the wheels bounced over ruts made by vegetable rows. The ship stopped, so perfect was the judgment with which it had been landed, directly in the shadow of a cluster of large trees. It was not likely to be seen there.

"Any houses close?" Long Tom demanded.

"None," Doc Savage replied.

General Vigo growled, "You must know the country around Alcala pretty well."

"Picking up secluded spots such as this," Doc Savage told him, "becomes a habit when you have been in trouble as much as myself."

PRESIDENT CARCETAS, elected chief executive of Santa Amoza, was an old man. He was also a broken man. His spirit was shattered. His morale was at the lowest of ebbs.

This was somewhat surprising, because President Carcetas' past life had been a hectic one, a violent one. He had fought in revolutions, always on the side which he believed to be right. Twice he had been exiled, only to return in triumph, finally to reach this highest position, that of president of his beloved Santa Amoza. He had always been a fair man; but no one had ever accused him of softness or lack of courage. There had been those who claimed he had no soft spot, that he was an iron man.

They had been wrong, and the evidence was before them, if they cared to look. The loss of his daughter had wrecked President Carcetas. It had pulled the plug of the cask of his courage.

President Carcetas sat alone now in his study in the presidential palace. There was a knock at the door and, without looking up, he said, "Come in."

War minister Junio Serrato entered. Serrato's shoulders were back and he walked sprucely. He looked confident, sure of himself. He looked a bit proud also, and there was reason for that. For he was now the Iron Man of Santa Amoza. He was the power behind the throne. If he played his cards right, he was a power greater than the throne.

"The executive committee is holding a special night meeting," he said. "They await your presence."

President Carcetas turned slowly in his chair and looked at the war minister. President Carcetas' eyes were those of an old and beaten man, either that or he was an excellent actor.

"What is the executive committee discussing?" he asked.

"You have forgotten?" war minister Serrato exclaimed, and looked surprised. "It is a matter of financing further purchases of war material. Count Hoffe's company, as you know, has demanded that we strengthen our credit."

President Carcetas seemed to think that over in a semi-detached way. He nodded slowly.

"I will be there shortly," he said.

War minister Serrato hesitated, then shrugged elaborately. "Very well," he said and went out.

President Carcetas took his head in his hands and sat there. He might have been engaged in deep thought. Once he got up and went to a small mirror, examined himself.

The lights went out.

It was intensely black in the room, no ray of light penetrating. Somewhere a clock was striking. It was a musical clock and it struck rapidly, the chimes playing a tune. This sound persisted for several minutes, and it was almost exclusively musical. For the clock was a museum piece, almost priceless, which had been the property of the rulers of Santa Amoza for generations.

The lights were out all over the presidential palace, in fact. There was not much confusion at first. Then guards began to scamper around, searching for the source of the trouble. Flunkies ran here and there.

Finally the light came on.

An orderly ran to the door of President Carcetas' office, knocked, was bidden to enter, and did so.

"I wished to make sure that your excellency was safe," he said.

"Thank you," said President Carcetas.

President Carcetas now sat before the desk. About his shoulders was a long cape which he wore on state occasions, and which had been hanging on an ornamental tree near the door. This cape was very long; it was crimson lined; and bore only a single decoration, a design which indicated the wearer was supreme commander of the armies of Santa Amoza. That ornament was a lie as far as present conditions went, for war minister Serrato was really the one who led the armies.

The orderly departed.

President Carcetas now did a strange thing. He went to the mirror again, began to examine his own features, exactly as he had been doing when the lights went off. He did not seem to be satisfied. He drew from his clothing a pencil of the type used by actors. With this he carefully added a line to his countenance.

President Carcetas was deliberately making himself look older.

Satisfied, he turned out the lights and left the presidential mansion.

THE extraordinary meeting of the executive committee of Santa Amoza was in full progress. This actually meant that the full government was functioning. Santa Amoza had a parliament, with the conventional upper and lower houses, but this was not in session now; and, when it was not in session, governmental functions, even those of extraordinary nature, were handled by the executive committee. There was an air of grimness over the place.

On a rostrum sat the individuals who were serving as chairmen. Members of the executive committee occupied comfortable seats in the middle of the room. Arrayed around the room were military guards—and three spectators. The spectators were Ace Jackson, Count Hoffe, and the oil man, Don Kurrell.

War minister Serrato had the speaking platform. He had a harsh, rasping voice such as a fighting man might be expected to have.

"I have just come from President Carcetas," the war minister was saying. "He will join us shortly, but, before he comes, I wish to make a request of you gentlemen. President Carcetas has just suffered a great shock. The misfortune to his daughter has been almost more than he could bear. He is, I deeply regret to say, not himself. His condition is something that you men can understand. I know you gentlemen, understanding this, will make the proper allowances."

A clever man was war minister Serrato. He knew that President Carcetas was dearly beloved. He had many friends. These friends would be quick to spring upon anyone whom they suspected of opposing the president, or conspiring to take away his authority. War minister Serrato was by far too clever a man to antagonize those friends, especially if he could gain his ends by exercising the proper amount of guile.

There was a stir at the entrance. All eyes went in that direction. Many kindly smiles came on weary faces.

"President Carcetas," someone breathed.

President Carcetas came forward, still encased in the long gray robe. He walked slowly as if he bore an infinite burden, and he did not remove the cloak.

He walked straight to the speakers' platform, mounted it, faced the audience and lifted his arms, commanding attention. He began to speak in excellent, distinct Spanish. He was noted as an orator. Never had he spoken in a manner that carried more weight.

"I have something to say," he said. "Please listen carefully, for it is very important."

One of those proverbial pin-drop silences followed his words.

"We have been fighting our neighbor republic of Delezon for almost four years," he continued. "Many brave men have died on both sides. The murder of one of our border patrol, presumably by Delezon soldiers, was the cause. It was a case of our honor demanding satisfaction. If there was honor to be avenged, gentlemen, it has been avenged. If there was pride to be assuaged, it has been assuaged. And yet the fighting has gone on and on."

He paused. It was so quiet that no one seemed to be breathing.

"Gentlemen," said President Carcetas, "we have been fools. We have been pawns. We have been like chessmen, played by a sinister master."

War minister Serrato broke the silence.

"What do you mean?"

"That first border killing that started the war was not committed by soldiers of Delezon, there is every reason to believe," said President Carcetas. "It was committed by another, a sinister mastermind, who was deliberately scheming to start the war. And he succeeded. That was the first touch of a sinister hand. But it was not the last. Time and again things have happened which have kept the war in progress. This master chess player, this dread monster of greed, who for some unknown purpose of his own has done his best to keep the conflict in progress, is a name well known to most of you."

He paused for the proper dramatic effect.

"I mean the Inca in Gray," he said bluntly.

There was a pronounced murmur from his audience. Men looked at their neighbors. Quite a few lips were moistened.

"The Inca in Gray has been working in Delezon, exactly as he has here in Santa Amoza," continued President Carcetas.

"How do you know that?" demanded war minister Serrato.

Instead of answering, the president of Santa Amoza held up his arms so as to command greater silence.

"I will ask a man to speak to you now who knows conditions in Delezon, as no one else does," he said.

He paused again.

"I present," he said, "General Fernanez Vigo, dictator-general of Delezon."

General Vigo walked from the door to the speakers' platform.

THE shock of the words and the unexpected appearance of General Vigo created much the same effect as would have been secured by a mass electrocution. Eyes and mouths flew open to their widest. A few persons half arose in their chairs. Yet, so general was the shock, that not a move was made to intercept General Vigo.

General Vigo began to speak the instant he was upon the platform.

"We have a common enemy—the Inca in Gray," he said bluntly.

The words were so unexpected, the mere presence of the commander of the enemy forces so astounding, that no one said a word or made a move.

"I am here to demand something, gentlemen," said General Vigo. "I demand a truce. I demand more than that. I demand peace. And I demand your cooperation. We must join hands, and together stamp out the organization of this mysterious monster who calls himself the Inca in Gray."

General Vigo's words carried great weight. Squat, heavy-set, his ugly face set in firm lines, he was a figure to command respect. The very unthinking courage in his manner was also something that impressed.

General Vigo continued speaking.

"This war has been a hideous mistake," he said. "Peaceful neighbors have been turned into bloodthirsty enemies through no fault of their own. I ask you, gentlemen, to cooperate in stamping out this Inca in Gray."

He surveyed them. The startling effrontery of his presence was still holding them spellbound.

"There will be no difficulty over peace terms," he said. "Delezon demands nothing. Further than that, we will do our bit toward making restitution toward those who have lost most in this ill-famed struggle."

It was a very nice speech. It was having its effect. Should General Vigo say a few more words along this line, and he had them all ready to speak, a mass vote might well end the war.

But General Vigo's speech was never finished. Came a scuffle from the door, shrill cries. A man was trying to get in, a wizened, pock-faced fellow who wore civilian clothing. The guards had grabbed him, were holding him.

It was Don Kurrell, the oil man, who acted first. He sprang toward the struggling group. The man who had tried to get in was gasping out something. He had difficulty ejecting the words, for one of the guards had a hand over his mouth.

But Don Kurrell understood what the fellow was trying to say.

Kurrell spun, lifted his voice to a piercing scream that carried to every portion of the committee room.

"You are being tricked," he screamed. "The man who spoke to you first is not President Carcetas."

Everyone heard those words. The import of them silenced the uproar which had started.

Don Kurrell bellowed. "Examine the man who looks like President Carcetas. You will find that his hair is not white. It is powdered."

It was war minister Serrato who acted now. He chanced to be standing very close to the man whom they all had taken for President Carcetas. Serrato sprang forward. He was very quick.

Serrato grabbed at the white hair with one hand, snatched at the cloak with the other. The results were illuminating. The hair was indeed made white by powder. And the cloak, coming away from the figure, revealed not the wasted, gaunt form of President Carcetas, but the figure of a bronze giant who obviously had tremendous physical strength.

The bronze man was recognized instantly.

"Doc Savage!" the shout went up.

Chapter XVI
FLIGHT AND PURSUIT

TUMULT seized the committee room. Those present were already emotionally tense. They blew up. They went to pieces.

Doc Savage, abandoning any pretense of further impersonation of President Carcetas, spun to General Vigo.

"Look sharp!" rapped the bronze man. "We are in real trouble!"

General Vigo used an expression which he must have gotten from American movies. "You're telling me?"

The mob surged toward them. General Vigo found himself grasped by the arms, but struck about furiously, freed himself and retreated. Doc Savage was beside him. They managed to reach a window which was shuttered. They broke the glass and tore the shutter loose. Guns crashed behind them as they dived through.

"Kill Vigo!" voices screamed behind them. "Kill Doc Savage! They tried to trick us!"

"Find President Carcetas!" other men screamed.

Doc Savage and General Vigo ran. A slight figure joined them almost immediately. It was Long Tom.

"What went wrong?" Long Tom demanded.

"That is somewhat of a mystery," Doc Savage said. "Someone appeared who knew that I was masquerading as President Carcetas. The fellow had the look of one of the Inca in Gray's men. He has been about before."

Long Tom grunted, "But how'd they know about President Carcetas? Nobody saw us grab him in his study. And we left him bound and gagged."

"Someone must have happened upon him," Doc Savage said.

The three dashed down narrow streets, doubling to the right, then to the left. Abruptly, Doc Savage stopped.

"Long Tom, General Vigo," he suggested, "go get President Carcetas. At least see if he has freed himself. Meet me at the plane."

"Right," Long Tom agreed. "But what do you plan?"

It was not often that Doc Savage explained moves which he contemplated; but he did so now.

"Don Kurrell," he said, "the fellow acted strangely. In fact, he gave himself away."

"You mean that Don Kurrell is the Inca in Gray?" Long Tom demanded.

Doc Savage did not answer. He was gone into the night. The bronze man moved swiftly, furtively, he took the housetops and traveled there whenever he could, because it was safest.

He was retracing his steps to the meeting place of the general executive committee.

The bronze man reached the building. There was great excitement in the vicinity. Angry, shouting groups paced about. Doc watched.

He saw no sign of war minister Serrato, Ace Jackson, Don Kurrell, or Count Hoffe.

Then, some five minutes later, he discovered Don Kurrell.

The short oil man was standing on the outskirts of the crowd, unconsciously indulging in his small habit of drawing himself up on tiptoes to seem taller. His eyes were very busy. He was plainly watching proceedings.

Don Kurrell, after a time, wheeled, looked about as if to make sure no one was watching him, then sidled away. He turned into a darkened side street. He walked very rapidly, looking back often.

Don Kurrell, if he were actually trying to ascertain if anyone was following him, was a novice at the game. Not once did he observe the shadowy figure that was Doc Savage keeping close tabs on his progress.

DON KURRELL, it was evident, had some very definite destination, and was in a hurry to get there. He confined his pace to a walk only so long as he was in the excitement zone where there was likelihood that soldiers, seeing a running figure, might shoot and ask questions afterward. Once he was clear, Don Kurrell ran. For a small fat man, he had very good wind. He reached the edge of the city without being challenged.

He still ran, down a rutted lane at first, but soon he left the lane to cut across truck farm land which had been cleared from the jungle surrounding Alcala. He covered some three miles.

His final destination proved to be an enormous barn, exactly such a building as might have been found on a prosperous Missouri farm. The barn looked innocent enough, but appearances are deceiving.

Planes were being wheeled out of the barn. There were three of these ships, cabin jobs. They were of the type which had wings that could be folded back against the fuselage. This explained how three of them could be stored in a barn.

Don Kurrell ran directly to the group about the planes.

Doc Savage, of necessity, used caution in approaching the spot. Before he was close, the wings of the planes had been hinged out in position, and most of the passengers were aboard. Two of the motors had started. A third motor now started.

Doc Savage tensed. For an instant, he seemed on the point of rushing forward.

Then a man threw a lighted flare from one of the planes. This was evidently to furnish a degree of illumination for the take-off. The flare lay on the ground and burned brightly.

It would disclose Doc Savage before he could come near the plane. The bronze man remained where he was. It was the only wise course.

The light also illuminated with remarkable distinctness the features of those seated in the planes' cabins.

Some of the occupants of the three craft were swarthy, evil-faced fellows, plainly satellites of the Inca in Gray.

Some faces in the planes, however, belonged to the last persons who might reasonably have been expected to be seen there.

President Carcetas, Ace Jackson, Count Hoffe, Don Kurrell, all were seated in the planes.

The ships were in motion. The pilots were not unskilled. They took just the proper run, then lifted the ships off, climbed in conservative fashion, and were lost in the night.

The three ships roared away in the direction of Delezon.

LONG TOM and General Vigo were beside General Vigo's private plane where it had been left outside Alcala when Doc Savage joined them.

"We did not find President Carcetas," said Long Tom.

"Someone must have found him and freed him," General Vigo added.

That was no surprise to Doc Savage. With a few crisp sentences he conveyed to General Vigo and Long Tom what he had seen—the three planes, their occupants.

"Ace Jackson was aboard?" Long Tom gulped. "I can't believe it."

General Vigo swore in Spanish.

"I know Count Hoffe personally," he growled. "The man sold munitions to both Delezon and Santa Amoza. But it is hard for me to believe that he was working with the Inca in Gray."

"And President Carcetas," Long Tom muttered. "I can't understand this."

"The whole affair is coming to a head," Doc Savage told them. "Come. We have very little time to spare."

They got into the plane, and Doc Savage lifted it into the air. He did not turn on the lights at wing tips and tail, but flew in darkness and flew high. From time to time he used the binoculars, attempting to pick up the planes ahead.

General Vigo's ship was faster than any of the three cabin craft. Its motor was larger, its streamlining better.

"Think we'll catch 'em?" Long Tom mumbled.

The bronze man did not reply. The question did not seem to be one that required an answer.

After they had been in the air some time, Doc Savage leveled a bronze arm. "There."

Long Tom used the binoculars. He employed them for some moments, shaking his head at first; but finally he nodded.

"I see them," he said. "They're heading for the jungle."

Doc Savage got out of the control bucket, motioned Long Tom to take the stick.

"Follow them," the bronze man directed.

Long Tom nodded, and took over the handling of the plane.

Doc Savage went back into the rear. The bronze man opened the metal case which he had gotten from the wrecked dirigible. This held Monk's portable laboratory.

Doc Savage took from a pocket a small object which, unrolled, proved to be the envelope—the waterproof, airproof envelope of rubberized fabric—into which he had, many hours previously, scraped some of the weird gray dust, which always was to be found on the faces of the victims of the Inca in Gray.

The bronze man began to work over the chemical laboratory. His manipulations were complex. General Vigo came back and stared, but could make nothing out of the proceedings, shook his head and returned to help Long Tom watch the planes ahead.

Hours later, it seemed—although the interval could not have been that long—Doc Savage came forward.

"What have you been doing?" Long Tom asked.

The bronze man seemed not to hear. Long Tom did not repeat his question. Doc Savage had a small habit of seeming to go suddenly deaf upon occasions when he was asked questions, which, for reasons of his own, he did not desire to answer.

They flew on.

"Look!" Long Tom pointed. "The three planes are landing."

It was true. The ships, barely distinguishable in the bright moonlight, were coming down.

Doc Savage took over the controls of their own ship. He promptly cut the motor, and began a long, silent glide to the jungle beneath.

Doc Savage selected a clearing almost three miles from where the other three ships had landed, and he came toward it from a direction opposite the spot where the other three ships had descended. It was not likely that they would see him. He was careful in putting the ship down, not making much noise.

The three of them alighted.

"Now what?" asked Long Tom.

General Vigo spoke up before Doc Savage could make an answer. Until this point, General Vigo had played the part of a brave man, but he had had a hectic night, possibly the most eventful one in his existence.

"I balk, señores," he said.

DOC SAVAGE'S flake-gold eyes became intent upon General Vigo. "What do you mean?"

"Let me go back to my camp." General Vigo suggested. "We will need help in fighting this Inca in Gray, and I will bring it. I assure you this war will stop. You've shown me things tonight."

"No," the bronze man said.

General Vigo bristled. His face, in the moonlight, became even more ugly.

"Why do you want me with you?" he demanded.

"We may need your assistance," Doc Savage said.

Long Tom, hearing that, suppressed a desire to snort. If any individual on earth was less in need of assistance than Doc Savage, that person would be hard to locate.

Abruptly, Long Tom frowned. Doc Savage wanted General Vigo with them. Could it be the bronze man had learned General Vigo was the Inca in Gray? The bronze man might have proof that fell a little short of absolute certainty. In that case, if Doc's actions in the past were any indication, the bronze man would not reveal his suspicions until they were shown as irrefutable facts.

General Vigo mumbled and muttered to himself.

"I do not like it, señores," he said at last. "But I will go."

They marched; crawled, described it better. They had lights, but it was not wise to show them.

It was not long before Long Tom started thinking of Monk and Ham.

"They're in a jam," he muttered, "even if they're only lost."

Chapter XVII
THE GRAY DUST

MONK and Ham, at that exact moment, were in a predicament, which they would have exchanged gladly for the mere difficulties of being lost in the jungle. The two men lay in the bottom of the torture pit, and the ants were just beginning to arrive. The insects had been a long time coming. That was not strange, and evidently not entirely unexpected to their captors. The wait for the arrival of the ants seemed to be a part of the torture, the mental portion of it. The physical torture was beginning now.

Monk squirmed furiously, gnashed his teeth, as he felt the first terrible bite. He was not gagged, and he could guess the reason why. Their captors—the white men, for the natives seemed none too enthusiastic about the grisly affair—would want to hear his screams of agony.

There was strange excitement back in the native camp. Men shouted. Orders were cried out. Shadowy figures moved through the night, but it was very dark under the jungle foliage where the moonlight did not penetrate.

Monk heard the sounds, and, more to take his mind off his present predicament than anything else, he spoke of them.

"Somethin's happenin'," he said.

Ham was also in agony. Not many of the ants had arrived as yet, but they were coming in a slender stream that was like a living rope crawling down the pit side.

"They probably have scouting parties out in the surrounding brush," Ham said. "They may be changing shifts."

He was wrong. That was apparent a moment later, when men shuffled up to the pit. Among them was the leader of the white men. He scowled down at them.

"Word has come that the Inca in Gray wishes to be present at your deaths," he said.

"Kind of the guy," Monk growled.

The white man laughed. Brittle and harsh, the sound was like glass breaking. "I think I shall stand here and watch you suffer for a while, señores. The runner who brought word of the Inca in Gray's coming said nothing about treating you gently."

And the man did exactly what he threatened. He crouched on the pit edge, from time to time using a flashlight to watch the work of the ants.

The electric flashlight had a queer effect upon the small natives. Each time the brilliant white beam lashed out, they started back, as if they considered it magic. This amused the white man, and he entertained himself by throwing the glaring rays over the natives themselves, sending them scampering into the brush. However, when he suddenly discovered a tiny poison dart clinging in the leaves beside him, he gave up his fun.

The jungle drums began to thump in the distance, the sound going on and on in monotonous syncopation. The natives listened to it. Then they gathered about the white man, and they chattered, making fierce little faces. Monk and Ham could understand what they said for their speech was an offshoot of ancient Mayan.

"The Inca in Gray is drawing close," was the gist of what the drums were saying.

Monk and Ham were untied, taken out of the pit, the ants carefully brushed off them with leafy twigs. Then they were escorted back toward the little village with its ramshackle, unwalled huts. Bound hand and foot, they were flung upon the floor of the hut in which lay Señorita Anita Carcetas.

The young woman greeted them as if she had never expected to see them alive again.

"The Inca in Gray himself is coming," Monk told her. "Listen."

They could hear sounds, crashing of the brush for the most part, then tramping of feet, and a file of figures came into the clearing. A small fire, perhaps with ceremonial significance, had been lighted in front of the hut. The newcomers filed toward this.

In their lead walked a sinister figure encased in a gray cloak. The Inca in Gray himself!

The night was hot, travel through the jungle rigorous. The Inca in Gray had thrown back the hood of the strange cloak, so that his features were recognizable.

Monk, Ham, Señorita Anita Carcetas, stared. Their eyes came wide, disbelieving.

"The Inca in Gray is—the last person on earth I would have suspected," gasped Señorita Anita Carcetas.

Chapter XVIII
JUNGLE

DOC SAVAGE was making slow progress through the jungle on the trail of the Inca in Gray. This was not his fault. Alone he would have had no difficulty in traveling at a good speed and eluding any possible natives. Even with Long Tom alone as a companion, their pace would have been much swifter.

General Vigo was the stumbling block. It had been many years since the dictator-general had taken such strenuous exercise as this. Travel through the jungle called for tremendous endurance. Time after time, Doc and Long Tom were forced to halt, to wait until Vigo regained breath enough to move on. A worried frown was on Long Tom's unhealthy looking face.

"I'll stay with Vigo, Doc," he suggested. "You go ahead."

Doc Savage shook a negative. "We will stay together."

He did not explain why. There were several reasons, not the smallest of which was that General Vigo and Long Tom, if left alone, probably could not follow the trail made by those who had come from the three airplanes.

Doc was following that trail now, and it was vague, difficult to trace in the darkness. Had there been daylight, the task would have been simplified greatly.

General Vigo complained loudly, "*Amigos*, I am thinking seriously of telling you both to go where they burn brimstone. *I* have enough of this."

"Not so loud," Long Tom hissed angrily.

But the loud voice which General Vigo had used had already done its damage. Long Tom heard no sound from the jungle about them, but he suddenly found the metallic grip of Doc Savage's bronze fingers upon his arm, and was bundled hurriedly and silently to one side. General Vigo, surprised at the rough treatment, tried to object, but found a hand clamped over his mouth and received a thorough shaking, which impressed upon him the necessity for silence.

The three men came to a stop, concealed quite a number of yards from their previous position. They waited, listening.

A faint rustling of underbrush sounded shortly. A few yards ahead was an open space where moonlight filtered through the jungle foliage. Two natives appeared, slipping along silently through this moonlight patch. Each little aboriginal held a short blowpipe in his hand. Darts, poison-tipped, they carried in bamboo sections which had plugs, bottle fashion.

Doc Savage's metallic hand found Long Tom's shoulder in the darkness. The hand squeezed, long and short squeezes which transmitted a message in the Continental Code. The sallow-faced electrical wizard made no response, but the touch of his hand upon Doc Savage's person telegraphed a reply. "O. K."

The little natives stood in the clearing as if they liked the moonlight better than the jungle. They moved about; obviously they had heard General Vigo's voice, knew that quarry was near. One little fellow stopped close to a tree only a few paces from where Doc Savage and his two companions were concealed. The other native moved ahead.

Long Tom grimaced disgustedly in the darkness. By separating, the two little jungle men had complicated things. For, when one was seized, the other might be able to give an alarm. Doc Savage touched Long Tom, telegraphing with his fingers.

Obeying that silently transmitted command, Long Tom leaped, caught the closest native from behind, and snapping his fingers down on the fellow's windpipe, cut off an outcry.

Long Tom had moved swiftly, but his speed was slow motion compared with the bronze man's action. Doc Savage whipped around the edge of the clearing, keeping in shadow, and was suddenly upon the second native. The little brown fellow did not even succeed in turning, nor could he yell. Doc Savage's fingers did something very briefly to the back of the fellow's neck, and he dropped, asleep for the time being.

When Doc Savage returned to Long Tom, the electrical wizard had succeeded in making his own victim senseless.

General Vigo muttered, "*Bueno*. Now they cannot give an alarm—"

Long Tom took hold of General Vigo's throat with both hands.

"You open that trap again, and I'm gonna wring your neck," the electrical wizard said.

General Vigo still had some fight in him. He bristled indignantly, and combat seemed imminent; but a breathed warning from Doc Savage brought them up sharply.

"Listen," said the bronze man.

They listened. Other groups of natives could be heard approaching.

ALL noise of the approaching natives suddenly ceased. Long Tom's anxiety increased. General Vigo's bluster was completely broken, and he was remarkably silent, face down. The three men wriggled through the underbrush seeking to escape.

Birds were fluttering about in the jungle, and that itself told the story. The natives had spread, had encircled the spot. Doc, Long Tom and General Vigo were completely surrounded.

A strange, weird cry echoed through the night. It was picked up, repeated until it came from all directions. The little natives called out to each other. The reason for the noise, at first a mystery, became apparent.

A light sprang up in the jungle. It was a torch which had been lighted. Others blazed, dozens, scores of them.

Soon a ring of lighted brands completely surrounded the spot where Doc Savage and the other two lay.

"Thees ees bad," choked General Vigo, forgetting his English in his excitement.

In charge of the natives was the small chief who had headed the party which had captured Monk and Ham. He gave orders quietly, speaking the offshoot of the Mayan language which was the tongue of his people.

"We have them surrounded," he said. "There is no doubt of that."

Warriors, armed and ready, stood behind the men who held the torches. There were hundreds of the natives here, enough of them to annihilate a small army. Yet, they made no effort to advance. In fact, they did not seem at all bloodthirsty.

"They cannot escape," a tiny aborigine whispered.

The leader murmured agreement, "No. And a runner has been dispatched to the Inca in Gray and should return shortly, telling us what we shall do with these three men whom we have surrounded."

"Sending the runners was unnecessary," grunted the first. "The Inca in Gray will decree only one fate for these three. He will ask their death."

"It is true," agreed the first.

"Then why did you send the runner?" the second native queried curiously.

The first shrugged and did not make his reply immediately.

"These men are not our enemies," he said at last. "Death is all right for an enemy, but why should we kill men whom we do not hate?"

"These men are enemies of the Inca in Gray," the other reminded him. "And the Inca in Gray has promised us, if we help him, that our mountains, the homes of our ancestors, shall be returned to us, and the glory of our people shall once more be what it was in the ancient days."

"The Inca in Gray is a white man," said the first. "White men often speak with forked tongues."

"That is all too true," muttered the other.

There was the sound of a man approaching rapidly through the jungle. A native runner appeared. He was breathing heavily.

"The Inca in Gray is sending one of his men with the dust of death," he said.

None of the little brown men showed any enthusiasm at that. They waited. As their firebrands burned up, they replenished them, keeping a ring of brilliant illumination about the place.

A party arrived through the jungle. A man detached from this group of new arrivals and came forward. He was a white man. He could not speak the tongue of the natives, but the latter seemed to know a few words of Spanish, and with gestures supplementing these Spanish words, the white man managed to convey his wishes.

The white man's party had brought the dust of death. They desired to make use of it.

Some of the torches were now extinguished. The ring of natives began to move. Gently, ominously, their line crept forward. Shadows flitted from tree to tree, from bush to bush, small, innocent-appearing shadows, but each was a tiny man armed with as deadly a weapon as the jungle has ever produced—blowguns. Light from the torches made a red, hideous luminance.

It was General Vigo who first broke under the strain. "Get back, you devils," he growled at the natives.

There was action then. White men detached from the native ring. They charged forward. They held in their hands strange packages, and shortly their figures were lost in the darkness.

No one watching on that occasion could have told just how the death of the gray dust was inflicted. The devilish operation went forward in darkness, silence, except that there were grunts, cries.

After a bit, the white men retreated.

"Eet ees feeneesh," one mumbled in bad English.

THE little brown dwellers of the jungle seemed to have an unnatural fear of the gray dust, which was not hard to understand. They drew back, listened. But there was no sound, no stirring from the center of their ring. They lighted more of the torches, and, by exchanging shouts, fired their own courage. Then they advanced.

The light of their torches soon shone upon three prone forms. Guttural exclamations came from the little men. They were not pleasurable sounds, and they were certainly not triumphant, as they surveyed the three inert forms.

The leader signaled his little men, and called out, and they kept their distance from the three bodies. They looked upon the three forms with curiosity.

One was a giant, a herculean bronze figure. The second man was pallid, small, rather unimpressive. The third man was a burly and ugly fellow attired in the army uniform of Delezon, a uniform which bore no rank insignia.

But it was not the prone, motionless figures which held attention.

On the face of each was a fine, grayish powder that gave the motionless bodies a horrible aspect. It was plain that even the little aborigines felt an eerie, creeping sensation, for they drew back, exchanging uneasy glances.

"The death of the dust," one mumbled.

"The Inca in Gray," said another, "has taken more victims. In truth, this Inca in Gray has no respect for life."

With one accord the natives retreated. They kept their eyes downcast.

"The three white men are dead," they said. "We might as well return to the camp."

They moved off, accompanied by the white man who had brought the death by dust, and after a time the noises of their going were lost in the sounds which are always in a jungle at night.

Chapter XIX
THE INCA IN GRAY

THE small brown warriors had left no lookouts behind. Had they done so and had the watchers been alert, they might shortly have seen a happening which, no doubt, would have greatly surprised them.

Doc Savage lifted his head as if to listen more intently, then got to his feet.

"They have gone," he said softly.

General Vigo whipped erect. There was a madness in his manner as he wrenched out a handkerchief and brushed furiously at his face getting rid of the gray dust.

Long Tom also seemed uneasy.

"You sure the stuff won't get us after all, Doc?" he demanded.

"The chances are that it will not," the bronze man said. "It would have taken effect before now."

Long Tom began, "Just what is this gray stuff, and just what—"

"We should he moving," Doc Savage cut in.

The bronze man set out through the jungle, following the natives who were returning to their village.

The trail was a hard one, and it was hot, for the

night seemed to have brought little coolness to the jungle. Doc Savage and his companions, however, made good time. They were close behind the natives and the white men when they entered the village.

More fires had been lighted in the village. These furnished considerable illumination.

From the muck beside one of the thatched huts a man came toward the new arrivals. Clad in long flowing robes tightly girdled about the waist the figure was rather indistinct, shapeless. The robe was gray. It had a hood with a mask-like attachment that almost completely concealed the features.

The Inca in Gray!

"What have you to report?" asked the Inca in Gray in Spanish.

One of the white killers with the native party replied in the same language.

"There were three of them," he said. "We got them all."

"Who were they?" asked the Inca in Gray.

"Doc Savage," replied the other, "his aide called Long Tom, and the third man was General Vigo."

That the Inca in Gray was astounded was evident, even though none of his features were visible. The folds of the robe shook as if the wearer were trembling uncontrollably.

"Where are their bodies?" the Inca in Gray demanded.

"We let them lay," he was advised.

"Fools!" screamed the figure in the gray gown. "You should have brought them. I will not believe the bronze man is dead before I see his body dismembered before my eyes!"

The spokesman of the killers squirmed uneasily.

"The gray death," he mumbled, "was all over them. We were afraid to carry them."

The Inca in Gray was screaming now, "You could have made litters! You should have brought them! Go back and get them!"

Rage was pouring from the robed figure. Curses roared into the night, curses in the offshoot Mayan, in Spanish, in bad English, and in good English. The Inca in Gray was a master linguist.

The natives quailed fearfully as did the white followers of the Inca in Gray.

They retreated, anxious to return and get the bodies of their three victims.

"Wait!" shrilled the Inca in Gray.

The cloaked figure summoned the others close. Words were exchanged, low-voiced words that did not penetrate more than a few yards.

Doc Savage, Long Tom and General Vigo, concealed in the brush nearby, failed to catch what was being said. They strained their ears to the utmost, but it was to no avail.

The natives scurried off, accompanied by their white companions.

All seemed very anxious indeed to get the bodies of the three men who were supposed to be dead.

CAREFULLY concealed on the edge of the village, Doc Savage watched the natives as they departed. The voices of the little brown men came clearly in the night. They were frightened. The rage of the strange gray being, who was their master, seemed to appall them.

Doc Savage stirred, coming quietly to his feet. Long Tom and General Vigo also got erect.

"We will try to reach the huts," Doc Savage breathed.

They eased forward. The night was well along, and the moon was preparing to vanish. Its disappearance would be followed by a thick darkness, and would greatly complicate attempts to move without noise.

They reached the first of the huts. There had been no sound. Over by one of the fires was a small cluster of natives. These were seated or lying on the ground for the most part, evidently tired out by the night's exertions.

Doc Savage reached the largest of the huts. The shadows were almost incredibly dark. Almost nothing could be seen of the interior of the hut. Doc Savage straightened, intending to search the structure.

Came a sudden gasp from behind him. It was General Vigo. The burly, ugly-faced dictator-general of Delezon cried out in horror. His fists made sounds as they struck lusty blows. A shrill angry squeaking echoed the blow sounds.

Long Tom had matches in his pocket. He struck one. There was no longer need of furtiveness. The noise had aroused the little brown natives.

General Vigo was engaged in a furious struggle with a very homely tailless monkey. The thing must have come upon him silently in the night and given him a great start.

"Chemistry!" came a voice from inside the hut.

The speaker was Ham. Doc Savage plucked matches from Long Tom's hand, sprang into the hut. He struck one of the matches.

The elevated hut floor was littered with bound human forms. Monk and Ham were both there. There was attractive Señorita Anita Carcetas, and her father, President Carcetas of Santa Amoza. There was war minister Junio Serrato, and there was Count Hoffe, the munitions salesman. Ace Jackson was also a prisoner.

Only Don Kurrell, the oil man, was missing. Doc Savage began wrenching at the bonds which secured the prisoners. These were of stout fiber cord, woven by the natives. They were not weak, yet they snapped under the metallic fingers of the bronze giant as if they had become inexplicably rotten. Monk heaved to his feet, free.

"They got Habeas Corpus tied under the next hut," he howled and dived outside.

The little brown men had scattered from their fires. Grabbing up their blowguns and poisonous darts, they had disappeared from sight.

Monk came back from the adjacent hut, carrying Habeas Corpus by one oversized ear.

A remarkable unlovely tailless monkey was dancing around General Vigo, making squeaking sounds. Long Tom leveled an arm at the animal.

"What's that thing?" the electrical wizard demanded.

"Chemistry," Ham advised. "My new pet."

Long Tom snorted, "I thought Monk was your pet."

Ham windmilled his arms to restore circulation. "Chemistry will keep me company when Monk's not around. They look so much alike."

There came a small clicking sound. It was very much as if a match had been dropped on a hard concrete floor, but its cause was nothing so harmless as that.

"Poison darts," Doc Savage rapped. "Tear down the thatch roof of the hut. Use it as a shield while we work into the jungle."

The bronze man had freed all the prisoners now. They began tearing the thatch from the hut roof, intending to use it as the bronze man had suggested.

Long Tom voiced a conviction which he had reached.

"Don Kurrell is missing," he said. "That means he's the Inca in Gray."

"But his motives?" gasped Señorita Anita Carcetas.

"Undale!" shouted General Vigo feverishly. "Hurry, hurry, mi amigos. We must get away from here."

Then came disaster. It struck so suddenly that the shock of it paralyzed them. From all around the clearing rifles cracked; bullets storming through the thatched roof of the hut forced them flat on the ground. Poisoned darts began to arrive in a deadly rain. There seemed to be scores of enemies about the clearing.

"The Inca in Gray!" Long Tom exploded. "He did not go to find our bodies. He was too clever for that. He figured we might have faked our deaths and would come here, so he spread his men around the place, set a trap."

"Keep down," Doc Savage said. "Keep the thatching over you. The darts will not penetrate it."

Count Hoffe shrieked. "We are trapped! They will kill us!"

"We don't need anybody to tell us about it, brother," Monk growled at him.

"Quiet," Doc Savage said.

They all fell silent.

The bronze man now began to speak, smooth, guttural words that came swiftly from his lips. He was not speaking Spanish or English but the language of ancient Maya, the pure, untainted tongue of the race which is conceded to have once been the most powerful in the Western World.

He was reciting a chant, a chant that was in the nature of a benediction. Centuries ago these same words had been used by the rulers of ancient Maya to address their subjects. The words belonged to the Kulca, the forbidden language, the language which could only be spoken by rulers, by the high sorcerers.

The chant had a remarkable effect. The little brown natives around the clearing had been shouting out, yelling their war cries. Now they fell silent, ominously silent.

General Vigo rumbled, "Say, what is this—"

"Shut up!" Monk admonished him. "Maybe you didn't know it, but Doc was once made a big shot among the Mayans, and ordained a son of Kukulcan, the Feathered Serpent, or something like that. These little brown fellows are Mayans, even if they have slipped a lot from the old days. Listen."

Doc Savage ended his chant. He began to speak straight Mayan.

"You have been used as dupes, O men of Maya," the bronze man said loudly, his voice probably carrying to every one of the listeners. "You have been used by this one who calls himself the Inca in Gray, and who is no Inca at all, but a treacherous killer. He has doubtless promised you rewards for your assistance, but have the men of ancient Maya brought forth descendants so weak that they must help the like of this Inca in Gray? Are you dogs to fight in hopes of being thrown a bone?"

The bronze man fell silent, and it was the turn of the little brown men around the clearing to talk. They shouted at each other, excitedly at first, then angrily. The gist of what they were saying was plain from their voice tones alone. They had enough of the Inca in Gray. They had enough of him before this last incident, for that matter.

Came a strangled yell from the edge of the clearing. The hooded figure shot into view, running madly.

"The Inca in Gray!" Long Tom yelled.

"Blazes," Monk exploded. "He's coming to us!"

The cloaked, hooded figure arrived. He stripped the covering back from his head and it was Don Kurrell, the oil man, and he shrieked, "I am not the Inca in Gray! I was only fool enough to help him!"

Don Kurrell stopped. His face was horrible in the faint light that came from the fire on the other side of the clearing.

"I was promised concessions for my oil company, if I aided the Inca in Gray," he blurted. "I'm only small fry!"

General Vigo got up and roared, "Your lies will not save you! Here's where you get justice!"

General Vigo had plucked one of the poisoned darts from the thatch. He lunged, holding the dart point first. Its venomous tip was buried in Don Kurrell's neck.

Don Kurrell screamed and tried to run, but got only a few paces before he fell, in the throes of the sudden hideous death which the little darts brought.

The end of Don Kurrell did not get much attention. Other things were happening.

Doc Savage lunged at General Vigo. The latter retreated.

"It's Vigo!" rapped the bronze man. "He is the Inca in Gray!"

THERE was bedlam around the clearing edge, screaming, and shouting and shooting. The little brown descendants of ancient Maya had obviously turned on the white followers of the Inca in Gray. They were fighting to the death.

General Vigo fled madly. He had a start of a few yards. That accounted for Doc Savage not overhauling him immediately.

General Vigo demonstrated himself as being perfectly familiar with the huts. He plunged into one, vanishing from sight in the shadows. Doc Savage followed him.

There was silence for a moment after the two figures disappeared, silence that seemed to those in the clearing, despite the uproar of the fight going on all about them and in the jungle, to drag ominously.

A scream sounded then. It was long and penetrating and there was a shake in it, a ripple of utter horror. That scream must have all but taken the vocal cords out of the throat of the one who uttered it.

Monk emitted a howl and rushed for the hut. Ham ran over to the fire, picked up brands for light. He came with the illumination to the hut.

Inside the hut, Doc Savage stood on the raised floor.

General Vigo was slumped on the floor, dead obviously.

Gray dust—the gray dust that was the special death of the Inca in Gray—covered both the features of Doc Savage and General Vigo. Vigo was dead. Doc Savage was quite patently alive. The bronze man stepped out of the hut.

"Keep away," he said, and began brushing the dust off his features.

Monk swallowed several times and managed to gulp, "But why didn't the stuff kill you?"

"The gray dust," Doc Savage said, "is not dust at all. It is a tiny parasite, poisonous, a parasite peculiar to certain portions of this jungle. The little bugs are almost of microscopic size. Actually, they do not bite. They sting, and, strangely enough, after they sting, they die."

"But they didn't get you," Monk persisted.

"Merely because of an anaesthetic which I mixed in the plane, enroute here," Doc Savage explained. "A plentiful application of the stuff on my skin, just before we entered the clearing, was a precaution in the event someone should try to use the gray dust. We used it back in the jungle when we were trapped, but the effects of that application had worn off General Vigo. And actually, the gray dust there was only faked, so Vigo was not afraid, even if my mixture had not been effective."

Long Tom jabbed an arm at General Vigo. "But why was he playing the part of the Inca in Gray? He was committing depredations on his own side, the same as against Santa Amoza."

"No," Doc Savage said. "You will remember that we saw no proof of any plotting of the Inca in Gray against Delezon. We had merely General Vigo's word for it, and General Vigo, along with the rest, was a consummate liar."

President Carcetas of Santa Amoza put in explosively, "Then General Vigo's aim—"

"—was trying to smash Santa Amoza," Doc Savage said. "He wanted to control both countries. It was a case of greed, coupled with a mind of devilish ingenuity."

There was still noise of fighting around the clearing, but not as much of it as before. It diminished rapidly. Finally it seemed to be in only one spot, one man resisting. That fellow tried to flee through the jungle. Sounds told the story as plainly as if they had been watching. The natives pursued him. The man's one scream was a sound that would be remembered. After that, silence.

Ace Jackson and Señorita Anita Carcetas were a little to one side. They had their arms around each other.

The little brown men began coming out of the jungle, slowly, keeping their eyes downcast, as if they had done something which they regretted. Their attitude was unmistakably friendly.

President Carcetas of Santa Amoza looked at them, said, "The war will now come to an end, of course. General Vigo was the Iron Man of Delezon. No one can carry on in his place, and, in the peace terms, I shall see to it that these little men, these descendants of Maya, are well taken care of for the service they have done this night."

PRESIDENT CARCETAS of Santa Amoza proved to be as good as his word. Delezon, as he had predicted, did go to pieces following the end of General Vigo. Peace terms were easily reached and they provided an ample reservation of Delezon's richest territory for the native descendants of Maya. The little brown men were satisfied. That is what they had been after all the time.

Doc Savage and his aides did little but act in an

advisory capacity as peace was restored. Monk and Ham in particular came under the lazy spell of the tropics. This disgusted Ham. He cast about for some way to restore his usual vitality. He hit on an idea.

"A sea trip," he decided. "We will charter a yacht for a rest."

He sounded the others out on the yachting jaunt idea. Doc Savage had experimental work which he wished to take up in New York; Monk, contrarily enough, agreed to go with Ham so the yachting trip went into the planning stage.

Monk and Ham had no way of knowing it, but that yachting jaunt was to precipitate them into an adventure a good deal more strenuous than the matter of the Inca in Gray. They were, in fact, to become embroiled in one of the most incredible adventures of their eventful career. On an island in the Pacific they were to find mystery, terror, things they could not understand. They were to fall into what amounted to the jaws of death.

But the yachting trip looked peaceful to them here in Santa Amoza. They went forward with plans for it to the accompaniment of much loud quarreling.

The day before they were to leave Santa Amoza, something happened that moved Monk deeply—and painfully. The chief of the tribe of the little brown descendants of Maya appeared. He brought with him Chemistry, the most remarkable looking sacred monkey.

The little Mayan made a long speech, an involved oration, but the gist of it was that Chemistry was being presented to Ham as a gift, and would Ham accept?

"Will I?" Ham smiled widely. "Chemistry'll be worth his weight in gold, if he does nothing but keep that hog, Habeas, away from me."

Monk watched the gift giving with open mouth. Monk's groan probably disturbed the condors on the Andean mountains.

THE END

RESTORATIONS IN BRONZE

As previously revealed in these pages, more than two dozen of Lester Dent's novels suffered significant deletions, usually at the hands of Morris Ogden Jones, an assistant to *Doc Savage* editor John Nanovic. During the 1930s and 1940s, Doc Savage novels that ran long were routinely cut to make room for short stories and other backup features.

With the kind permission of the Norma Dent Estate and through the considerable efforts of Will Murray, Scott Cranford and William T. Stolz of the Western Historical Manuscript Collection of the University of Missouri at Columbia, we have restored more than 4,000 words of previously-unpublished material from Lester Dent and Harold A. Davis' original manuscript for *Dust of Death*.

I'd like to formally thank Will Murray and Scott Cranford for their Herculean efforts restoring *Dust of Death* to Lester Dent's original vision. Scott is an avid Doc Savage collector, and the proud owner of Walter Baumhofer's original 1933 cover painting for *The Man of Bronze,* as published on the first issue of *Doc Savage Magazine* (which will be reproduced early next year on the 75th anniversary reprint of Doc's premier adventure).

"I'm very happy that the excised text has finally been restored," Scott Cranford explains. "I think it makes the novel better by including small details that add much more flavor. It's been a dream come true for me, as a fan of Lester Dent and Doc Savage, to be able to assist with the re-publication of the Doc Savage novels." We're also grateful to super-collector Jack Juka who provided the scans for this volume's covers, and as always Tom Stephens for OCR work and scans of the interior illustrations.

While I'm on the subject of restorations, I'd like to once again thank graphics wizard Michael Piper for his continuing work restoring the cover art for our Doc Savage and The Shadow reprints.

We'll return next time with two more Doc Savage classics: *Cold Death* and *The South Pole Terror,* followed by *The Squeaking Goblin* and *The Evil Gnome,* and then a Pat Savage double-feature reprinting *Brand of the Werewolf* and *Fear Cay.*

Early next year, we'll be celebrating Doc Savage's 75th anniversary with two very special volumes. In February, we're reprinting *The Man of Bronze* and *The Land of Terror,* the first two Doc Savage novels. March will see the pairing of *Up from Earth's Center* (from the final issue of *Doc Savage Magazine)* and *In Hell, Madonna,* a 1948 Man of Bronze adventure that remained lost until it was unearthed by Norma Dent and Will Murray, and published by Bantam in 1979. As special bonuses, we'll be reprinting *In Hell, Madonna* with the never-before-published illustrations that Edd Cartier created for the story back in 1948, along with "Doc Savage, Supreme Adventurer," a novelette by John Nanovic that served as the template for Dent's first Doc novel.   —Anthony Tollin, series editor

INTERMISSION by Will Murray

Dust of Death is laid against the backdrop of a long-forgotten border dispute that was still raging when Lester Dent wrote this Doc Savage adventure in 1935.

The Chaco War was a four-year conflict between Bolivia and the Republic of Paraguay. An oil war, it was fought for control of petroleum deposits believed to be simmering under the Gran Chaco region.

After years of friction and border skirmishes dating back to the 1920s, the Chaco War broke out in 1932 when, on orders from President Daniel Salamanca, the Bolivian army attacked a Paraguayan garrison at Vanguardia. A grinding ordeal followed, in which the guerilla tactics of Paraguay enabled the tiny country to hold off powerful Bolivia.

For this story, Dent has given Bolivia the name Santa Amoza, while Delezon stands in for Paraguay. All other characters are fictitious as well.

Dent never mentions the Gran Chaco specifically, and of course the names of the two warring countries are fictionalized. But in a working draft of the previous novel, *The Majii,* Dent pulled no punches when he hinted at the upcoming story:

Small voiced Monk was not having a blind fling at prophecy when he said: "I'll bet before I quit having bad dreams about this Rama Tura, we'll be up to our necks again."

But, if he could have foreseen the grim battle that waited for Doc and his men in the war torn plains of the Gran Chaco in South America, Monk's tone might not have been so nonchalant.

To end the needlessly, long drawn out slaughter of a futile war, Doc Savage went to South America. But he found there another war, a fight waged in mystery and terror. Men died horribly, and not by guns. Gray dust was the pall of the victims. A dust that lay thick on silent bodies.

Doc Savage and his men were to wonder how long it would be before that grim gray mantle lay over their own lifeless bodies.

And in the Gran Chaco the bronze man and his aides were to meet the strangest of all the queer persons their quest of danger had led to knowledge of. A man who wasn't human—a descendent of the Incas. They were to learn strange things from this man.

Dent foreshadowed this story in *The Majii* when Long Tom, about to leave for South America, is persuaded by Doc to join in that adventure. Long Tom is said to be in South America in *Quest of Qui* and *Mystery Under the Sea,* but because the novels were written and published out of order, this tiny thread of continuity was lost on readers.

Complications forced Dent to delay *Dust of Death.* He jumped ahead to *Mystery Under the Sea,* and blurbed it at the story's conclusion:

Trouble—it would be in South Ameriica next, although [Doc] had no way of knowing that. There would be more than trouble on that venture. There would be mystery, weird, uncanny.

Two South American countries were at war, a war that had lasted the best part of four years, bloody, violent, that war had been. But above the war, overshadowing it, striking terror into the most hardened soldier was—*Devil in Dust!*

But more problems arose with the story, forcing another delay.

Dust of Death was one of the earliest Doc Savage novels Lester Dent subcontracted to his old Tulsa *World* crony, Harold A. Davis. After Dent made modest changes—such as changing the Blue Inca and his white dust to the Inca in Gray and his gray dust of death—the manuscript went off to Doc editor John L. Nanovic.

And just as quickly came flying back.

Nanovic felt the story was padded and full of indiosyncracies, which Dent derisively dubbed "godawfulisms." So Lester did something remarkable: he sat down with Davis' manuscript and redictated it via his Ediphone dictation machine, verbally changing and revising the text page by page as he went along.

As Dent explained to Davis, "It was necessary to get Doc Savage into this story more, so I changed the order of the chapters, threw out a good deal of action, substituting other action. This does not mean that your method of handling was off. It was merely simpler to handle it in this manner as I went through, redictating the story."

Dent's secretary, Martin Baker, then transcribed each wax cylinder Dent produced.

It was a drastic revision. Only shreds of Davis' prose survived the savage rewrite. Dent changed Davis' original title "Death by Dust" to "Death in the Dust." This is the story that introduced Chemistry, the unclassifiable ape Ham Brooks adopts as a counterweight against Monk Mayfair's pet pig, Habeas Corpus. In Davis' draft, Chemistry was called Test Tube. Dent also altered the identity of the story's master villain, apparently in mid-story, because some scenes implicating Count Hoffe late in Chapter IV were revised.

Under pressure to write as many Doc novels as fast as possible, Dent went overboard. *Dust of Death* became one of the longest Doc Savage novels ever written. When the editors went to work on it, *Dust of Death* was severely pruned, including but not limited to some of the Mayan elements which tie this tale to Doc's origins. For this Nostalgia

Ventures edition, we've painstakingly restored it to its full length, including the original teaser blurb forecasting *The Fantastic Island,* which John Nanovic replaced with one promising Laurence Donovan's *Murder Melody.*

This adventure is packed with pulpy air action. The image of Doc Savage flying a World War I-era Jenny after arriving in South America via his stratosphere dirigible seems incongruous today. But pulp magazines like *Sky Birds* and *Flying Aces* were still popular in 1935, and Dent had written for them earlier in his writing career. So Lester was digging into his bottomless bag of pulp tricks once again.

As for the stratosphere dirigible, it's the same airship first flown in *Land of Always-Night.* In an anticipation of the later Cold War Space Race, the U. S. and Russia in the 1930s were vying to establish a high-altitude stratospheric ascent record. At the time *Dust of Death* was written, the Russians had just set a record of 52,800 feet. In November, the U. S. broke it with *Explorer II,* which ascended to 72,395 feet and enabled the team inside its pressurized gondola to see the curvature of the earth. This record stood for 21 years.

Street & Smith records show that *Dust of Death* was paid for on June 14, 1935. Ironically that was only two days after a ceasefire went into effect in the Chaco War. The conflict was over. Paraguay was seen as the winner, eventually claiming most of the Chaco Boreal. But war casualties exceeded 100,000 dead, and the economies of both nations were ruined as a direct result.

In a final irony, no oil was ever discovered in the disputed territory. The Chaco War had been fought for nothing.

The Stone Man dates from 1939. A newspaper clipping revealing the chemical discovery Dent mentions in Chapter XVII was the seed from which this story grew.

During his busy writing career, Lester Dent travelled to virtually every state in the Union. His explorations took him all over the U. S. southwest, into Colorado, Arizona and environs. Although *The Stone Man* begins in the air over Arizona, and Dent is deliberately vague wherein the Grand Canyon badlands this tale climaxes, his outline points to southwestern Utah—which may explain the stray Mormon or two mentioned in passing.

To say any more would spoil the story. *The Stone Man* is one of those Docs which received some unnecessary editorial pruning, and we've restored a scene or two unseen for almost 70 years.

Will Murray is the literary agent for the Estate of Lester Dent, and collaborated posthumously with the Man of Bronze's principal writer on eight Doc Savage *novels, beginning with* Python Isle.

**Lester Dent dictates
a Doc Savage novel.**

THE STONE MAN

By KENNETH ROBESON

Young, white-haired supermen in a land beyond the mists!
A Complete book-length novel

Chapter I
BAD MAN FLEEING

SPAD AMES was a man who was an authority on certain subjects, and concerning the matters on which he was posted, he knew just about everything that was to be known, which was undoubtedly fortunate, because otherwise they would have hanged Mr. Spad Ames a long time ago.

His specialty was avoiding the law.

His specialty certainly was not stone men. Not only was he not posted on stone men; he would not have believed such stuff. Spad was a realist.

He would have looked at you with those cold lobster eyes of his and said, doubtless:

"Stone men—ah, get t'hell away from me! That's crazy talk."

The phenomena—the word phenomena was a

mild description of it too—came to Spad Ames' attention in a roundabout way, and when he was not expecting anything like men of stone. As for the additional developments, which were hair-raising enough to make the stone-man business seem believable by comparison, Spad wasn't expecting those, either.

In keeping with his habit of knowing much about certain subjects, Spad Ames had calculated that the United States Border Patrol plane for that part of the Arizona-Mexico border would be safely grounded in El Paso on Friday. This was not entirely guesswork on Spad Ames' part; he had taken a precaution of pouring acid into the gasoline tank of the Border Patrol plane, so that engine valves and pistons would be eaten into a useless state.

But the Border Patrol dealt unkindly with Spad Ames, and double-crossed him by transferring another plane, a new and fast craft equipped with two machine guns, to that portion of the Mexican Border Patrol.

It was two o'clock in the afternoon when this new type Patrol craft sighted Spad Ames' plane.

"The dirty blankety-blank sons of black-eyed toads," was the mildest thing that Spad Ames said during the next few minutes.

Waldo Berlitz was less voluble, not being a fellow who talked a great deal. Waldo was a thick man and a wide one, and extraordinarily handsome, except that one of his ears was missing. A Mexican gentleman had removed the ear with a sharp knife a year or two ago, during the natural trend of a discussion about the Mexican's missus. A man less of a gentleman than the Mexican would have inserted the blade between Waldo's third and fourth ribs.

Waldo Berlitz was the other half of the smuggling combination of Spad Ames and Waldo Berlitz.

"How fast will this thing fly?" was all Waldo had to say.

Not fast enough, it developed. The Border Patrol craft was a late job, and it began overhauling them.

"There is a cloud over west," Waldo said, pointing. "We better get in it and unload."

Spad Ames nodded grimly. He was scared.

PART of their cargo—two cases of narcotics—would not have been such a problem. The narcotics were in powder form, and they would have spilled the incriminating stuff overboard, thus ridding themselves of the evidence.

The refugee—the other part of their cargo—was a different proposition. They needed a cloud to get rid of him. The refugee was a poor fellow from Austria who hadn't been able to obtain a visa to enter the United States, so he had paid Spad Ames a thousand dollars to be smuggled in. The refugee crouched in the cabin, pale and somewhat airsick.

The cloud was not large. White and fleecy, it hung all alone in the hot vastness of the Arizona sky. It was somewhat like a lost sheep.

Spad Ames dived his ship into the cloud.

"Work fast," he yelled at Waldo.

Waldo said to the refugee: "Get down on the cabin floor." As the refugee obeyed, Waldo struck him with a monkey wrench, hitting several times so that some of the contents of the upper part of the refugee's head stuck to the wrench.

With great speed, Waldo then rolled the refugee's body through a trapdoor in the floor of the plane. The trapdoor had been put there for the specific purpose of jettisoning cargo according to the old Number One rule of smuggling—first get rid of the evidence. Waldo also hurled the wrench overboard.

There was good reason for Waldo's speed. They needed to get the job done while their plane and the pursuing ship were hidden in the cloud.

The cloud was even smaller than it had seemed, and with sickening unexpectedness, the two planes popped out of the other side.

The pursuing Border Patrol got an excellent view of the body falling from Spad Ames' craft.

An officer even leaned from a window of the Border Patrol ship and took pictures of the scene with a miniature camera. The photograph would show the falling body, and the identification numbers of Spad Ames' ship.

Spad Ames opened and shut his mouth. For suddenly he was sick with terror. Trapped, not for smuggling, but for murder!

Waldo came back and sat down and asked: "Do they use a gas chamber, the electric chair or the rope in Arizona? I've forgotten."

If Waldo was trying to be funny, it was a raw time for a gag, Spad thought.

Spad Ames was a long man who slouched when he walked and frequently glanced back. He had a weather-beaten red face, an unusually high forehead—sign of receding hair, not brains, although he had brains, too—and in addition to the cold lobster eyes, he had a mouth so lipless that, when seen from a distance of a few yards, he appeared to have no mouth. Spad was a bad actor himself, but sometimes he was afraid of Waldo Berlitz, who gave the impression of never seeming to think the way a normal man should. Nothing Waldo planned to do ever seemed to worry him, and he never appeared concerned after he did it.

Spad Ames banked around and sent their plane back into the clouds. The Border Patrol ship fired on them, its machine guns thrusting out long whiskerlike processions of tracer bullets which came disturbingly close.

A cloud game of hide-and-seek then lasted about half an hour.

Spad Ames would have liked to flee toward Mexico; he got no chance. And finally when a faint bank of clouds appeared, far to the north, he made for that refuge in desperation. Luck, which distributes favors evenly to saint and devil, gave them a long start on the Border Patrol plane; their pursuer wandered around in the cloud for some time after they left before sighting them and taking chase.

Spad Ames peered backward, then batted his throttle open to the last notch.

"How many horsepower is this motor?" Waldo asked.

"Six hundred and sixty horses," said Spad. His face was the color of a concrete road.

"Come on, horses!" said Waldo.

The clouds got closer, and so did the Patrol ship. The latter climbed slowly, then suddenly dived, and its machine guns shook their iron rumps and cackled.

The storm of lead caused some of the instrument panel to jump out in Spad's lap. But the plane kept flying. It got into the clouds.

These clouds were thin, and the Border Patrol ship managed to follow them for all of three hours, part of which time they flew back and forth and up and down, and the rest of the time flying straight ahead at full speed.

The refugee's body slipped through the trapdoor of the plane and hurtled down, down …

Finally, they lost the Border Patrol plane.

"Where are we now?" Waldo asked.

"How would I know?" Spad Ames snarled. "The compass was shot to pieces."

SPAD AMES was in a bad temper in spite of their escape from the Border Patrol officers who had photographed them committing a murder. For a few moments, he had been elated. Then he had noticed that the needle of the fuel gauge was knocking against the pin on the empty side.

Waldo tried placidly to light a cigarette, but the bullet holes in their ship let in such a draft that he could not make a match function.

"Oh, well," he said, and discarded the cigarette.

The engine faltered in its roaring. For a few seconds, it sounded like a motorcycle. Then it stopped.

"What goes on?" Waldo asked.

"Get the parachutes!" Spad Ames barked. "We're out of gas."

The plane went whistling down out of the clouds in a long glide while Waldo ambled back to get the parachutes. Waldo returned empty-handed.

"Full of holes," he reported.

"What?" screamed Spad.

"I said," explained Waldo, "that our parachutes were hit by a burst of machine-gun bullets from that Border Patrol plane, and they're full of holes. You can use one of them if you want to. I don't think I will."

Spad Ames' mouth worked, but he was too sick with terror to get out words. He could only level an arm, indicating the terrain below.

An aviator's nightmare. At first glance, there did not appear to be a spot where a hawk could have landed, much less a plane. Everything was straight up and down, and came to points. There did not, from this height—the height was rapidly growing less—appear to be a shred of vegetation anywhere.

"We're over the Grand Canyon badlands somewhere, it seems to me," Waldo said.

The colors of the earth were mostly yellow, pale orange and chocolate.

Spad Ames banked clear of the spiked tip of the first peak. He avoided other peaks. There seemed to be miles of canyon space below him, although undoubtedly it was no more than two or three thousand feet. There seemed to be fog down here, and compared to the fairly bright late afternoon sunlight on the peaks, the gloom was that of night, or of an infinite cavern. At least, it was an unpleasant place—and a strange place for fog.

It was horrible. The human body is so constituted that it does not actually sweat blood, which was probably a good thing for Spad Ames. He would have perspired himself dry of the vital fluid.

"Spad—" Waldo said.

Spad Ames was surging up in the bucket seat and straining against the safety belt like a man being electrocuted. He couldn't say anything.

"—pick a soft spot," Waldo requested.

Waldo scrambled back in the cabin and scooped up cushions and the ruined parachute packs and fashioned a crash pad in front of himself, a preparation which he had barely completed when the plane began knocking itself to pieces on the rocks.

SPAD AMES had been knocked senseless a number of times during his hell-colored past, and on each of these occasions his period of blankness had been made hideous by nightmares of being shoved into a gas chamber of the type used in some states to execute criminals. He had once witnessed such an execution, and apparently it had given him a permanent case of the subconscious creeps.

Now, when Spad Ames regained his senses and realized that his mind had been a blank, and not haunted by gas-chamber nightmares, his first frightened conclusion was that he had died. The fact that his eyes were seeing only complete darkness heightened the possibility that he was now a disembodied soul.

"Hell and damnation!" he snarled.

Sound of his own robust profanity made the situation more real. He reached out, and found twisted metal with his fingers. He seemed to be lying under a portion of the mangled plane.

There was sand underneath. He dug with his hands, made room to use his arms, then heaved. Metal grunted, whined and shifted a little. He kept trying. Some time later, he managed to crawl out.

There were matches in his pockets, so he struck them and searched, but did not find any trace of Waldo Berlitz. However, part of the plane was buried deep in the sand.

"Waldo must be mashed under there," Spad muttered. "Serves the dirty buzzard right."

Spad Ames had never liked Waldo Berlitz, and he'd held a suspicion that the feeling was mutual.

Spad wandered away for a few rods, trying to ascertain in exactly what surroundings the plane had crashed. He could see stars overhead, but apparently there were great sheer walls everywhere else. The air was dry, and rather hot. Nothing whatever seemed to grow in the vicinity; at least, Spad Ames did not stumble over anything in the darkness that resembled a growing plant.

When he came back to the plane, he saw Waldo Berlitz at once. Waldo was sitting on a rock, examining a black arrowhead by the light of a match.

There was something strange about Waldo's manner.

Chapter II
STONE MAN BURNING

THE sand was soft—the plane had fallen in the bed of a canyon—and Spad Ames managed to approach without making any particular sound until he could look at the arrowhead which Waldo was inspecting.

The arrowhead, about the length of Waldo's longest finger, was thin and streamlined. It had striking perfection of line. Its color was black, a peculiar polished kind of black.

Spad had intended to speak up and ask why the infernal blazes Waldo had gone off and left him, Spad, pinned under the wrecked plane. But he held his words. Waldo, unaware that Spad stood behind him, was showing a distinctly peculiar curiosity in the arrowhead.

The match went out, and Waldo struck another with almost frantic eagerness. Indian arrowheads were plentiful through the West, and Spad had seen Waldo kick a number of them contemptuously with a boot toe in the past. So Waldo's absorption in this particular arrowhead seemed strange.

"It stopped the river," he muttered.

This remark did nothing to enlighten Spad Ames. He stood there, puzzled, watching Waldo turn the arrowhead over and over in his hands and peer at it as if the thing were some kind of a puzzle.

"It stopped the river," Waldo repeated to himself.

Then he began to swear. Waldo was cursing his inability to understand why the arrowhead had stopped a river, Spad Ames realized, and this did not contribute much toward clarifying the growing mystery.

Spad Ames decided to ask questions; he stepped around boldly into the match light. Waldo yelped in astonishment and the nervous jerk of his fingers sent the match arching in the darkness.

"You're kind of jumpy, ain't you?" Spad suggested.

"I—uh—" Waldo said, swallowing.

It was the first time Spad had ever seen Waldo speechless.

"By the way," Spad continued, "what is that thing you were looking at? Arrowhead, isn't it?"

"Oh—just a piece of rock," Waldo said, far too quickly.

"You generally do a better job than that of lying, Waldo."

"It was only a rock."

"Let's see."

"I—dropped it somewhere."

Spad Ames was tempted to hand Waldo a couple of hard rights to the jaw, because the fellow was obviously lying.

"Incidentally," growled Spad, "what was the idea of going off and leaving me fast under the wrecked plane?"

"Did I do that?" Waldo asked queerly.

Strangeness in Waldo's voice caused Spad to strike a match for himself. Waldo's eyes were too wide and there was a foolish expression on his face.

Spad Ames thereupon made a slight error, and concluded that Waldo had suffered a bump on the head in the plane crash, and that this had addled his wits.

"Sit there and rest, Waldo," Spad advised. "I'll see if I can find the seat cushion and make a fire out of it. By that light, I'll examine your head."

While Spad Ames was feeling around for the seat cushions, Waldo silently removed one of his shoes and took off a sock. He filled the sock with sand. Then Waldo crept over and brought the sand-filled sock down on Spad Ames' head with a round-house swing.

THIS time, Spad Ames held no doubts about merely having been unconscious because he had his usual nightmare of being thrust into a lethal gas chamber. On this occasion, in the beast-dream, they got him as far as jamming his head in the chamber door, and he was fighting them wildly when he awakened with a splitting headache. He lay for a minute, getting it all clear in his mind.

Spad got to his feet, but his legs shook and bent and let him collapse on the sand again. He ground his teeth.

"I'll kill him for that!" he snarled, dragging a revolver out of his clothing. "I'll blow him apart!"

Once when the plane crashed he had been knocked out, and again by the sand-filled sock, and his head did not feel so good, nor did his gangling body seem to want to cooperate with his pain-seared brain. He struggled to get himself organized.

"I'll blow him to pieces," he said grindingly.

Rage jacked him onto his feet, and he staggered a few yards through the darkness, then came to a stop, snarling with futile wrath. He had no idea which way Waldo had gone, did not know where to search. He stood there, pointing his gun this way and that, so inflamed with rage that he wanted to hear a sound, and shoot at it.

When sound did come, he failed to shoot. Instead, he jumped a foot, and would have jumped higher, had his strength permitted. Weakened as he was, he fell to his knees, where he remained, wincing while the shrieking noise ripped again at his eardrums.

Spad Ames was experienced. Once he had held a man close to his chest with his left arm and with his right hand had thrust a knife again and again into the victim's back while the fellow screamed his life out in Spad's ear. These present sounds had somewhat the same rip to them.

Waldo's voice. No doubt of that, because Waldo had a whanging tone that was as distinctive as a police whistle.

Waldo screeched his lungs out for fully a minute, which was a long time to keep screaming steadily, then silence fell.

Spad Ames crept toward the source of the shriek to investigate; he took his time, because he had no desire to rescue Waldo, but rather wished to satisfy an intense curiosity as to what had led Waldo to emit such a banshee squall. Spad listened, but heard nothing. Finally, he lighted matches, and discovered that the sand was grooved and gouged as though a struggle had taken place. Spad, down on his knees, tried to ascertain what had made the tracks, and found the arrowhead.

It was the same arrowhead, black, polished, exquisitely made, which Waldo Berlitz had been examining with peculiar interest.

"I'll be darned," Spad grunted.

The unexpected weight of the arrowhead caused him to emit the exclamation.

"Gold!" he chortled excitedly, and scratched the arrowhead with the sharp metal sight of his gun.

But it was not gold, as its weight had led him to hope. He couldn't tell what it was. Heavy, though.

A few moments later, he found Waldo's body, although he did not immediately touch it and get burned.

AT first, Spad was almost relieved to find Waldo's body. Lurid explanations for the scream had been galloping through his mind—possibly a bear had grabbed Waldo; maybe the bear was still around—so it was a relief to find the body, apparently unmarked.

The smoke arising from the body was something that Spad Ames noticed at once, but he thought it was merely a small breeze blowing dust.

Spad Ames summarized the whole situation aloud, as he saw it.

"The guy got bopped on the head when the plane fell," Spad muttered, "and was knocked nuts. Then he had a screaming fit and fell over dead." He rubbed his jaw and grinned. He had an idea. "I'll put Waldo's body in the plane wreckage," he chuckled, "and make it look like there never was more than one man in the ship. I'll fix myself an alibi somewhere, and get out of that murder the Border Patrol saw us pull." While he was being happy over that, he got another good thought. Waldo usually carried a large roll of money on his person.

Spad Ames, getting down on his knees to search Waldo for money, touched the body. Instantly, he squawked and snatched his hands back. Then, because there was a terrible burning sensation in his hands, he jabbed them repeatedly into the sand.

His next thought: something had bitten him. He found his matches—his fingers stung so that he could hardly hold a match—and made light. There was no rattler or scorpion on or around the body. There was just the smoke.

Smoke! Not dust swirled by the night wind, as he had thought at first, but something else. It was like—well, smoke was the word that most closely described it.

Rage jumped through Spad Ames. He did not like things he could not understand. He held the burning match in his left hand, seized his gun in his right and struck the body of Waldo Berlitz. It was purely a gesture of rage. But the effects were horrifying.

Spad Ames shrieked, sprang up and ran wildly. He took no particular direction; he just wanted to get away from there. He crashed into the canyon wall, bruising his face. But even that agony could not wipe from his mind the impossible thing that had happened when he struck the body of Waldo Berlitz.

For the body—the clothing, too—had broken, as if turned to glass, or brittle stone.

SPAD AMES was a badly battered specimen. He found he could not readily rise. His fingers, where they had touched Waldo Berlitz's strange body, were still full of stinging sensation, and he kept wiping them on the sand.

After a while, he was aware of the sound of water running.

The running water was weird, too. He had noticed no sound of a stream earlier, but now there was no doubt about it. The flow of water seemed to start gradually, then increase, until there was a sizable stream gurgling and splashing.

"I must be going crazy," Spad mumbled, believing it.

But when he got the strength, and struck a match, he saw that the river was no phantasm. It poured out from the base of the cliff-steep canyon side into which Spad had dived in his flight.

Spad said: "Well, that ain't so damn mysterious. Just an underground river."

When his match burned out, he struck another to continue his examination. A few yards from the foot of the cliff, the stream was fully twenty feet wide and two or three feet deep, and had worn a considerable channel in the stone.

Out of a hole at the cliff base the water spouted with geyser force, boiling, throwing up foam. The escaping water filled every inch of the opening.

"At least," Spad mumbled, "I won't die of thirst."

Spad Ames touched the body, then squawked and snatched his hands back in a hurry!

He had been afraid of that.

Then he noticed the second arrowhead. This one was black, also, but much larger—more than a foot in length—and seemed to be inlaid in the cliff face. Or was it carved and painted on the cliff? Spad stepped closer to see. Inlaid, he decided.

The striking resemblance of this large arrowhead to the small black one intrigued him. Spad fished the smaller arrowhead from his pocket, held it close to the inlay on the cliff for comparison.

"What the devil!" Spad exploded.

The water had stopped running. The roaring, splashing flow had ceased with weird unexpectedness.

Swiftly, the water flowed away and the gaping hole out of which it had been coming was left exposed.

Spad stood there, too startled to swear, until curiosity got the best of him. He crouched with a match beside the hole, and leaned to peer into it.

He made a mewing sound, and in his first spasm of effort to get up and flee, he skidded on the water-slick rocks and went over and over. Spad Ames knew, now, what had made Waldo Berlitz scream in such a horrible way. He felt like screeching himself, and did try, but could only emit awful mewing noises.

What he had found in the hole came out and overpowered him.

"Oh, mother!" Spad Ames croaked, just before he became unconscious.

Which was as near as Spad Ames had come to a prayer in many years.

Chapter III
THE ADMIRABLE MR. LOCATELLA

WHEN the United States government assigned several billion dollars for the building of roads, one of the things it accomplished was to make the Navaho Indian trading post of Cameron, Arizona, more accessible. Hitherto there had only been a wagon track across the Painted Desert to Cameron; this was improved, and during the season, a stream of tourists began to flow. A sparse stream, it was true; three or four cars a day was a fair average.

The trading post, a picturesque structure, perched on the edge of a crack in the desert, a crack that seemed a couple of thousand feet deep and so narrow at the top that a man could throw a rock across, and in the bottom flowed the Little Colorado River. There was a suspension bridge, the crossing of which was nothing for nervous old ladies.

In all directions to the horizon was heat and the disappointing baldness of the Painted Desert. To make the speeding tourists say, "Oh!" and "Ah!" there was now and then a herd of grazing sheep,

tended by a Navaho squaw and one papoose or more, and sometimes the beehive-shaped hodags in which the Navahos wintered.

Seven weeks and three days after the United States Border Patrol plane chased Spad Ames and Waldo Berlitz northward, there was something else to interest one tourist, however. The unusual article was a man lying on the road. Apparently the man was unconscious or dead. His hair was slightly white.

The tourist stopped his car and alighted to examine the poor unfortunate.

The man lying on the road lunged up and smacked the tourist on the head with a rock. The tourist collapsed. The man with the rock then ran to the car, but the tourist's wife and daughter got out and fled. They were long, lean women and they were scared. The would-be assailant with the rock failed to catch them, although he swore terribly and hurled his stone after them.

The man then entered the car, turned it around and drove toward Flagstaff. He did a good deal of cursing because he had to leave the tourists behind where they would be picked up by the next passing car.

There was a lunch basket in the tourists' car, and the man wolfed the contents of this. After eating, he stared grimly ahead, looking a little sick. He was thinking of his diet for the past three weeks. It had consisted of pack rats, gophers, rattlesnakes, and once, a jackrabbit. Principal item had been the rattlesnakes, which were easy to catch.

At Flagstaff, the man got a break. An eastbound freight train was pulling out; he swung into a box car.

There were two hobos in the box car, and that night, he bludgeoned them in their sleep, and got a dollar and eighty-three cents and a better pair of shoes. In Marceline, Missouri, a division point on the railroad, he robbed a plumber, and to his astonishment, got over two hundred dollars in cash. When he got to Chicago, he took a plane on to Newark airport, and a taxicab from there into New York City, to the office of Herman Locatella.

"Hello, Herman, you slimy bat," he said, and sank into a comfortable chair.

Herman Locatella stared at the man and said, "I don't know you!" indignantly.

HERMAN LOCATELLA was a man who took pains not to know a great many people. Socially, in particular, there seemed to be very few persons whom he considered worth knowing. He was a prize snob, but there were plenty of snobs in New York who liked that sort of thing, so Locatella did a remunerative law business.

Herman Locatella dressed the part; his attire was

correct for every occasion. That morning, he had worn the correct striped trousers, morning coat, lap-over fawn vest and ascot tie. Just now, however, he was planning to attend the horse races with one of his snob clients, so he had changed to sports attire consisting of woolly brown trousers, checkered sports coat, and scarf knotted at the throat. He maintained a dressing room off his sumptuous office for making these changes.

On the desk rested a folded newspaper which contained an article on the society page, stating that Herman Locatella, society lawyer, was beginning to be mentioned as the best-dressed man in America.

"So you don't know me," growled the visitor disgustedly.

"I never saw you before." Herman Locatella fingered the telephone. "Will you get out of here, or shall I call the police?"

"Why not call the Kansas City police?" the visitor asked dryly.

Locatella jerked his hand away from the telephone; he also became noticeably pale.

"Sure, telephone the K.C. district attorney, too," continued the visitor. "And the F.B.I. in Washington would be another good one to call."

Herman Locatella licked his lips and did not find anything satisfactory to say.

The grim-faced invader continued: "All of them would like to hear from you, wouldn't they, Locatella? Of course, you might have to tell them you were known, until a few years ago, as Nate Spix, or Spix the Mouth. You are only charged with being the brains behind about three murders and half a dozen bank robberies."

Herman Locatella got up and opened the door to make sure no one in the outer office was listening. He locked the door and strode back to his desk.

"Damn you!" he snarled. "Somebody might have heard you!"

"So now you know me?"

"Spad Ames—of course I know you." Locatella clenched his fists. "And I'm not worried about you yelling copper. Two months ago there was a newspaper story about the Border Patrol looking for you. Murdered a refugee you were smuggling in, didn't you? You're crazy to come walking in here. You should be in South America, or some place that doesn't have extradition."

Spad Ames showed his teeth in what was not exactly a grin. "Do I look like I used to?" he asked.

"You've changed," Locatella admitted. "Your hair is white."

"What I've been through," Spad Ames said grimly, "would change anybody."

THE two men knew each other well, from dealings in the past. There was silence while Locatella,

looking almost comically suave in his fancy clothing, poured drinks.

"What changed you?" he asked. "You look as if you had been through something tough."

"I lived on rattlesnakes for almost a month," Spad Ames said sourly.

"That almost makes you a cannibal, doesn't it?"

"That's not funny to me." Spad Ames eyed his drink, then poured it in the metal wastebasket. "I don't trust you. We might as well understand each other about that. Whether you trust me or not, I don't give a damn. You're going to help me, anyway."

Locatella made a regretful clucking sound.

"That is too bad," he said, "but I have given up criminal practice. I would not touch—"

"I want about twenty men," Ames interrupted. "They have got to be strictly tough ones. They have got to know machine guns and bombs and gas."

Locatella still wore a pure-as-pure expression, but his interest sharpened.

"Where would I get twenty such men?" he asked.

"You could get them without trouble, I haven't the slightest doubt."

"Hm-m-m."

"I will want two large planes, and pilots. I want the planes equipped with bomb racks, and I'll have to have expert bombers. Preferably men who had experience in Spain or China."

"How much are you willing to pay for this?"

"That's also where you come in."

"I come in?"

"You pay for it. In return, you get cut in for twenty-five percent."

Herman Locatella leaned back and opened his mouth; it was obvious that he was going to rip out a derisive laugh. But he changed his mind. He leaned forward and stared at Spad Ames intently.

"You know, Spad, I never liked you, but I did have respect for your judgment. You always had a good sense of values. So I'm not going to laugh. Instead, I'm going to ask what in the hell you plan on doing?"

"You said you read about the Border Patrol plane chasing me a couple of months ago."

"Yes."

"Well, it chased me out over the Grand Canyon badlands before we got away, then we ran out of fuel and crashed. We cracked up in . . . What do you know about that Grand Canyon country?"

"It's pretty wild, I've heard," Locatella admitted. "Personally, I wouldn't know, because I don't go in for roughing it."

"Some of that country," Spad Ames said, "is practically unexplored. Oh, I know that a boat or two has floated through the Grand Canyon, and planes have flown over some of the country. But there is a hell of a lot of it that white man never set eyes on. We landed in some of that unexplored country and we found—well, it's what I'm going back after that we found."

"You found—"

"For two reasons, I wouldn't tell you."

"Why not?"

"Too fantastic," Spad Ames said levelly. "I'm not crazy, but you might think so if I told you what I located. I'm the only white man who ever got in there, and out again. And I'm going back—with planes, at least twenty men, and the most modern bombs and poison gas."

"Twenty men," Locatella muttered, "is practically an army."

"We'll need an army. That black arrowhead may help—" He stopped the sentence in the middle.

"Black arrowhead?" prompted Locatella curiously. "What black arrowhead?"

SPAD AMES made no answer, and the two men sat looking at each other. They understood each other. Spad was not going to reveal more information, and Locatella knew it. Locatella also knew that he was being offered something big here. Spad Ames had a bad record with the law, but he had never been one to go off half-cocked. If anything, his fault was underestimating and using too much caution.

"Fifty percent," Locatella said suddenly.

"Twenty-five."

"You're crazy. Since when did bankrolls start taking twenty-five percent cuts?"

Spad Ames stood up and pounded the desk with his fist and began yelling. "The hell with you, then!" he shouted. "I'll go out and knock off an armored truck or a bank messenger and get the dough myself."

Herman Locatella knew now that he was being offered a good thing. He was being presented with a pig in a poke, but he knew other men who had accepted blind propositions from Spad Ames, and they had found it profitable.

"Sit down," he said. "How soon do you have to have the men and planes and stuff?"

"Quicker the better."

"Tomorrow morning be soon enough?" Locatella asked, and grinned.

He was proud of his ability to get such things as this done; he was even more proud of having kept underworld connections while pretending to be a Park Avenue barrister whose main love was fancy clothes.

Spad Ames nodded, and they shook hands. "Could you get some of the men together tonight?" Spad asked.

"Tonight?"

"I've got to snatch two—well—students."

"Kidnap them, you mean?"

"You might call it that. But don't get excited. They're not ordinary students, exactly."

"You mean that they're Indians?" Locatella asked, guessing.

Spad Ames shook his head queerly.

"I'm not going to launch into a lot of explaining about two—ah—strange people." Spad growled. "The whole thing is fantastic. I told you that."

"Do these two have names?"

"Mark Colorado, and his sister, Ruth—that is what they call themselves."

"Are they Americans?"

Again, Spad shook his head queerly. "I don't think," he said thoughtfully, "that you could say they had any nationality. They're from—well, never mind."

Locatella chuckled. "You're not hinting around that they're from Mars, or the moon or somewhere?"

"You'd be damn surprised if you knew," Spad Ames advised grimly. "That's all I can say."

Locatella was consumed by curiosity, but he restrained himself.

"Let's go out and see people," Locatella suggested. "We'll collect some of the right people if we can, then come back here to talk over details. This room is soundproof."

Spad Ames looked around approvingly. "No chance of anybody hearing us in here, eh?"

"Not a chance," Locatella assured him.

Chapter IV
HANDS OUT OF DARKNESS

HERMAN LOCATELLA was in slight error concerning the privacy of conversations in his sanctum. It was true that the room was of soundproof construction, as well as being, with its wood-paneled walls, sufficiently expensive looking to impress the Park Avenue set.

However, a good electric drill, working from the adjoining suite, had chewed away the wall without penetrating the wood paneling. And to the paneling, a sensitive contact type of microphone had been attached, so as to pick up all the conversation in Locatella's office.

Wires from the mike led to an amplifier, the output of which fed into a phonographic recorder which was of unusually ingenious design, being equipped with a record changer. As soon as one record was full, it was automatically removed and another blank substituted. The records were of the large fifteen-minute type, hence four of them were used per hour.

The man who had installed this complicated eavesdropping device happened to be in the adjacent offices at the moment. He had plugged in a telephone headset, and had listened. He now removed the headset.

"By Jove!" he remarked. "The peacock did finally turn out to be a buzzard."

He seemed much pleased. He was a broad-shouldered man with a waspish waist and the wide, flexible mouth of an orator. Most striking thing about him was the impeccable correctness of his clothing; he was somewhat more perfectly garbed than Herman Locatella, which was saying a great deal. There was no other comparison between the two, however, except that they were both lawyers.

This man was Brigadier General Theodore Marley Brooks, eminent product of the Harvard Law School, and unquestioned leader of male fashions in America—leader, that is, until of late, when his position had been menaced by an upstart named Locatella. Brigadier General Theodore Marley Brooks was called Ham by those who were his very good friends, or who could outrun him.

Ham Brooks picked up an innocent-looking black cane.

"Come on, Chemistry," he called. "We have tidings to bear."

Chemistry was Ham's pet chimpanzee; or it was Ham's contention that Chemistry was a pure-blooded chimp, although anthropologists were inclined to call the animal a what-is-it.

Ham and Chemistry departed a back way; they simply stepped out of the window onto a roof which could not be seen from Herman Locatella's office suite, and descending through a roof hatch, finally came out on a side street where Ham had a car parked.

Ham rode to one of the impressive skyscrapers in the midtown business district, took an elevator to the eighty-sixth floor of this building, and passed through a door. Small letters on the door said:

Clark Savage, Jr.

Ham struck an attitude.

"Bark, gentlemen!" he ordered. "Bark!"

The two occupants of the reception room scowled at him.

One of them was remarkably wide, remarkably short, and even more remarkably homely. He had small eyes, a very wide mouth, features that had been mistreated by other men's fists, and a hide covered with bristles which resembled rusting shingle nails.

He was Lieutenant Colonel Andrew Blodgett "Monk" Mayfair. Without in any way looking the part, Monk was one of the greatest living industrial chemists.

The second man who scowled at Ham was a huge framework of bones and gristle who had two outstanding features, the first of which was a sad, funeral-going expression, and the second a pair of fists so large they could hardly be inserted in gallon pails.

He was Colonel John "Renny" Renwick, eminent engineer, and noted for his habit of knocking wooden panels out of doors when he felt playful.

Monk and Renny, along with Ham, belonged to a group of five who were assistants to Doc Savage.

"COME on and bark!" Ham ordered impatiently.

Monk and Renny glared at him, their necks getting red.

"Arf!" Monk said.

"Bowwow," said Renny unwillingly.

"You didn't get down on your hands and knees when you barked," Ham said. "Do it the way we agreed. When you lost the bet, the understanding was that you were to get down on your hands and knees and bark whenever you saw me for the next week."

Monk, losing his temper, shook a fist wildly. He had a small childlike voice ordinarily, but rage caused it to lift and take on the stridence of a steamboat siren.

"You been overdoin' it!" he squawled. "You been goin' out of your way to meet us on the street and places."

Renny, who had a voice like the roar of a pained bear in a deep cave, put in his bit. "You turn up in restaurants where we're eating, and expect us to bark."

Monk howled: "And last night, you turned up at that lecture I was giving before the Chemical Institute, and I had to get down and bark, with all them dignified big shots watching. A fine shyster trick!"

Renny roared: "Let's dress him down with a chair."

"Let's," Monk agreed.

Ham made a wild jump, got across the reception room and through a door, which he slammed and locked before the pair of irate wager losers could reach him.

"At least," he remarked cheerfully, "they're not welshers."

Ham had fled into the library, a great vaulted room filled with the bluish glow of light from fluorescent bulbs, and packed with bookcases containing, for the most part, scientific tomes.

"Doc," Ham called.

"In here," came a voice from the adjoining laboratory. The voice had a deep, controlled quality that made it striking.

Ham entered Doc Savage's laboratory, the lair of

scientific magic where Doc Savage concocted many inventions and devices, some of them bordering on the fantastic, which he used in his strange career. It was a vast room; the sunlight slanted in through the great windows—three walls were composed almost entirely of glass—and sprang in glittering reflections from the array of retorts, chemical glassware, microscopes, and electrical mechanisms. A great deal of the stuff was so complicated that Ham had no idea of its nature.

"What was all the noise?" Doc Savage asked.

Ham grinned. "Oh, Monk and Renny and the bet they lost. They bet me Harvard wouldn't win last Saturday. Now they're squawking."

DOC SAVAGE—Clark Savage, Jr., although he was rarely called that—was wearing a transparent plioflim garment which covered him from head to foot, so evidently he had been working in the test chamber which stood in the center of the great laboratory. He was, Ham happened to know, endeavoring to perfect a selective germicidal disinfecting agent which would be effective in epithelial tissue, where a certain type of cancer was its inception.

Ham, looking at Doc Savage, felt a little awe. He had never lost that feeling when he came into Doc's presence, although they had been associated for a number of years. The feeling possibly came in part from Doc's appearance. Doc Savage was a giant of a man, and possessed of even more physical strength than his size indicated: the great sinews which occasionally sprang out on the backs of his hands, or the cables that stirred in his neck, hinted slightly at his fabulous muscular ability. An ability, incidentally, that was carefully developed and maintained by a daily two-hour routine of exercises.

Doc Savage was unusual. His eyes, like pools of flake gold, seemed to have magnetic power. His skin had been burned by tropical suns until it had acquired a permanent bronzed hue that was striking. His features were regular, the cheek and jaw muscles having that lithe appearance which is noticeable about the faces of character actors. His hair, of a bronze slightly darker than his skin, lay as smoothly as a metal skull-cap.

A man of mystery, almost a legend as far as the world was concerned, this big bronze fellow.

He was most famous, probably, as the man who had given his life to the strange career of righting wrongs and punishing evildoers, frequently traveling to the far corners of the earth to do so. These feats, being spectacular, got public attention. Less well known, but more likely to go down in history, were the bronze man's unusual contributions to science and medicine, some of them possibly a century ahead of his time.

Ham Brooks, who was capable of making a young fortune each year practicing law, had become associated himself with Doc Savage for the same reason as had the other five aides. Ham liked excitement and adventure and his association with Doc Savage was abundantly productive to both.

"I've got something important, Doc," Ham said. "You remember a lawyer I once told you about—name of Herman Locatella."

"The one upon whom you have been eavesdropping?"

Ham nodded, then he shoved his jaw indignantly in the direction of the reception room. "Monk has been going around saying I got a mad up on this Locatella because he was mentioned in the newspapers as likely to—er—displace me as the best-dressed man. But that's a low-life lie! I'm not that vain."

Which was possibly a slight exaggeration on Ham's part; where clothes were concerned, if he was not vain, then the word had no meaning. Also, any libel on homely Monk's character which Ham spoke could be disregarded. No one had ever heard either of them give a courteous word to the other, except by accident. They squabbled perpetually, and spent their spare time thinking up gags to pull on each other. All of which meant they were actually the best of friends.

HAM stood looking self-righteous and hoping he was deceiving Doc Savage—but doubting it. This big bronze man, who rarely showed emotion, was exceptionally hard to deceive; misleading Doc Savage was so difficult that Ham at times suspected Doc might be able to read minds.

"This Herman Locatella," said Ham, "pulled a crooked deal on one of my legal clients. So I put a microphone in his private office and attached a recorder to it. That way, I began checking up on the rascal."

Ham now told what he had overheard as a result of his eavesdropping.

"Mysterious business, seems to me," Ham finished. "And this Herman Locatella, bird of fine feather, turned into a buzzard."

Doc Savage's metallic features had shown no particular emotion during the recital—which meant nothing, since he had a carefully developed ability to keep his feelings where they belonged, in his mind.

"Planes, bombs, gas," Doc Savage said quietly. "And a black arrowhead."

"The black arrowhead puzzles me particularly."

"Does it make sense to you?"

"No," Ham admitted. "But it interests me. It looks like the kind of a thing we usually investigate."

"What would you suggest?"

"If we get a move on," the dapper lawyer said,

"we may reach Locatella's office in time to over-hear the plans they make to seize these two—er—strange people, as Spad Ames called them. Mark and Ruth Colorado, he said their names were."

"We will take Monk and Renny along," Doc said quietly.

But Monk and Renny were missing from the reception room.

"I wonder where they went?" Ham grumbled. "They'll hate to miss this—and I'll hate not having them there. Monk knows I've been watching Herman Locatella's office, and he's made cracks about it. I'd like to see him eat the cracks. Boy, have I been getting revenge on Monk lately!"

Ham chuckled over his bet while a private elevator lowered them to the garage which Doc Savage maintained in the basement of the huge building. They selected a taxicab which seemed as ordinary as the thousands of other cabs on New York streets, the armor-plate body and the oversized engine being cleverly constructed to give an uninteresting effect.

It was getting dark.

THE night had become completely dark by the time they climbed through the hatch onto the roof which adjoined the building housing Locatella's office.

"Over this way," Ham breathed. "You cross the roof to the window of a room where I've got my recording apparatus."

The roof had a covering of thick asphalt compound in which gravel was embedded, and the gravel crunched slightly under their feet. Dark clouds rolling out of the west had packed overhead, and there was chill fog which absorbed the city lights.

Ham stopped suddenly. "What was that?"

It had been a small squashing sound.

"Probably a pigeon egg rolled out of a nest up in the eaves," Ham decided. "That's what it sounded like."

Then Ham grasped his throat and made a strangled noise.

"Gas!" he exploded.

He realized ponderous figures were suddenly rushing upon them.

"Locatella must have found out about me!" Ham barked, and tried to bring his sword—the innocent-looking dark cane which he carried was a sword cane—into action.

The assailants, instead of rushing directly upon them, raced around them. The circling maneuver puzzled Ham until he discovered the reason. The attackers had some kind of a net, probably an ordinary fishing seine of strong twine, and they enveloped Ham and Doc with this. They fought the

cords, broke a few, but were jerked from their feet.

They lay there and struggled with the net until they had to breathe and take the gas into their lungs and become unconscious. Ham, trying to yell for help, managed to emit a shrill and eerie wail, and always afterward it seemed to him that he passed out while still making the sound.

Chapter V
THE MYSTERIOUS COLORADOS

THE wail of a noise that Ham made carried to the ears of Spad Ames, and Spad looked puzzled.

"What was that?" he growled.

"A tomcat," Herman Locatella said. "Or maybe a drunk."

Herman Locatella was feeling proud of himself as he sat behind his desk, tipped back in a chair, cigar tilted up in an amber holder, and adjusted his bow tie. He had just changed to full evening garb in the little dressing room adjoining his office.

Spad Ames dismissed the wailing sound out of the night and went back to studying his new gang—or the seven members whom Locatella, to Spad's astonishment, had managed to assemble within two hours. Spad was a judge of certain types of character, and he approved of the seven. They did not look too obviously like thugs, not sufficiently so to alarm a policeman. Not that they resembled honest businessmen. They might have been a group of perfectly honest and dressed-up truck drivers or waterfront roustabouts.

They had arrived one at a time, and Spad had been listening to Locatella state their qualifications, which consisted mainly of a string of penitentiary records.

"You'll do," Spad said. "The pay is one hundred bucks a day, payable at six o'clock each day. Locatella, here, is the bankroll. He pays you. I give the orders."

They watched him. They were not afraid of him. He was glad of that; he could make them afraid later, if necessary. There was only one of them about whom he had doubts.

That one seemed a little young, and he was going out of his way to act tough. He had sneered at Spad when he came in.

"Any of you got a gun?" Spad asked.

"I have," said the young one insolently. "What about it?"

"Give me the gun," Spad Ames requested quietly.

The youngster drew the weapon with a flourish and tossed it over. It was a nickel-plated pistol of the $8.98 variety, with practically all the barrel sawed off.

Spad Ames hit the young man. He struck open-handed. The young fellow upset. He was quick,

The attackers had some kind of net—and they enveloped Ham and Doc with this!

seemed to land on his feet, instantly lashed back at Spad Ames. Spad dodged. He gave the youngster a knee in the midriff; when the fellow doubled and gasped in agony, Spad grabbed the front of the coat and slammed him into a chair.

"In New York, don't pack a rod except when you need it," Spad said grimly. "Once the cops find a heater on you, they can hold you in the can until you rot."

The young man cradled his middle, said nothing.

"Give him a hundred bucks, Locatella," Spad ordered.

Locatella removed five twenties from his billfold and passed them over, without objecting.

"Now," Spad told the youngster, "you can take that dough and do a scram. Or you can stay, take orders and stick that lip out at somebody besides me."

The young man folded the money, doing so slowly, and by the time he pocketed it, had thought over the matter.

"I'll stick," he said.

Spad handed back the nickeled gun, said: "Throw that thing in the first river you come to. It's only good for noise."

Now Spad strode back and forth a few times. He had put on a good show, and he knew it. He'd had experience at handling men like these. Because he was going to use them immediately, he had to impress them—convince them that he knew what he was doing, that he was tough, but also fair, according to their standard. He had done so, he believed.

He made a little speech.

"We're going up against something pretty fantastic," he said, "so if you see something you don't understand, keep your shirts on."

He pulled the strange black arrowhead out of his pocket and showed it to them.

"Whenever you see anybody with one of these"—he shook the black arrowhead—"grab them right away. If you can't take them alive, kill them. And be careful. Anybody who has one of these black arrowheads isn't—well—they're not what you think they are."

They looked at him blankly.

"There are two people attending Phenix Academy," Spad Ames said. "They are named Mark and Ruth Colorado. We are going to get them tonight, and hold them as prisoners."

He gestured, and they all filed out of the office.

"You know where the Phenix Academy is?" Spad asked Locatella.

"Sure," Locatella said. "Uptown."

PHENIX ACADEMY was not widely known, for the good reason that it did not need to advertise itself—it did not use such devices as, for instance, a high-powered football team to make headlines in order to get students. Athletics were not even included in the curriculum; there was no gymnasium. There were not even any classrooms of the conventional type. Instead, there were laboratories.

Phenix was a modern venture in specialized higher education. Diplomas were not necessarily tickets of admission. Instead, one examining board ascertained how much the applicant actually knew, and another board, composed of psychologists, weeded out those who only wanted to learn a lot, and use the knowledge to get rich. Phenix Academy was trying not to turn out fortune-makers. There were students in Phenix who had never been in a high school, much less a college. And Phenix had turned down stellar graduates of Yale, Harvard and Heidelberg. So the institution had a strange bunch in attendance.

Strangest of all Phenix students were Mark and Ruth Colorado. They had arrived quietly one day some months before, plainly dressed, and wearing something suspended on thin steel hairs around their necks.

"What previous education have you had?" they were asked.

"We understood one merely had to take an examination here," Mark Colorado said.

The examining officer had been a little irritated. These two were too confident.

"You'll get tested, all right," he snapped.

Results of the tests were peculiar.

"Amazing minds," reported the general science examining board. "Both brother and sister have an astounding fund of scientific knowledge which has come from books, apparently. And almost no workaday knowledge."

Reported the board of psychologists: "We are somewhat puzzled. Both applicants seem to know practically nothing about civilized customs. They might almost be persons not of this world at all. They refuse to tell anything of their past. In spite of strange circumstances, we suggest acceptance, because they unquestionably have the most brilliant minds of any Phenix applicants to date. We recommend observation, however."

Mark and Ruth Colorado puzzled the examining boards, and they became an enigma to professors and students.

Both Colorados were perfect physical specimens. Both had entirely white hair. They were also of extremely fair complexion. They were not, as some at first supposed, albinos; for the term albino is applied to individuals whose features lack coloring pigment, and usually includes colorless eyes. The Colorados had deep-blue eyes of striking alertness and—it was often remarked—of eaglelike ability.

Ruth Colorado was breathtakingly beautiful. As was expected, none of the male students learned anything whatever when she first appeared in classes. But the girl had nothing to do with men. None succeeded in dating her, although practically all tried.

Particularly noticeable was the way that both Mark and Ruth Colorado kept to themselves; and they rarely ventured off the campus.

Once a professor of languages heard them conversing in a strange tongue. The professor went home and got a headache trying to identify the lingo—he'd thought he had a smattering of every language being spoken, enough knowledge to identify the tongue, at least, but this one defeated him. When he asked the Colorados about it, all he received was a strange blank smile. And he got the idea they were worried because he had overheard them.

On another occasion, Mark Colorado went downtown for dinner with some of the men students. They discovered that Mark Colorado seemed a little shy on previous experience.

The dessert course came.

"What is this?" asked Mark Colorado.

"Ice cream," someone explained, staring at him curiously.

"Oh."

They took in a movie, and the strange white-haired fellow stared with rapt attention.

"Like the show?" one of the others asked.

"I never saw one before," said Mark Colorado.

They did some wondering about Mark and Ruth Colorado at Phenix Academy. "We recommend close observation," the board of psychologists had said. But the observers couldn't quite make up their minds.

Both Colorados still wore the thin steel chains around their necks, and one evening Mark and Ruth Colorado went swimming and onlookers got a chance to see what was suspended on the chains. Two black arrowheads.

It was noticed that both Colorados seemed to like to walk alone about the campus grounds at night.

Ruth Colorado was taking one of these nocturnal strolls, alone, when Spad Ames lunged out of the darkness and trapped her with his arms.

SPAD barked, "Help me, guys!" and the rest of his men rushed to his aid. If it struck any of them as foolish that a long wolf of a man like Spad Ames should need help to seize one girl, they were disillusioned, for Ruth Colorado got hold of one man's arm and twisted it out of joint, practically yanked an ear off another, and did a quantity of lesser damage before they threw her, gagged her, and hauled her into thick bushes.

A man folded a handkerchief over a flashlight lens and put a glow on the girl.

"I never saw white hair like that before," he muttered. "Except it's maybe a little like Spad's."

"Give me a hand!" croaked the man whose arm the girl had twisted. "She got my arm out of joint."

Spad Ames yanked strong cords out of his pockets and tied the girl, taking care with the knots, testing each binding carefully.

He seized the thin stainless steel chain around the girl's neck and dragged the black arrowhead into view. Snatching the arrowhead quickly, he pocketed it.

During the fight, Herman Locatella had remained in the background where he would not be seen and identified, but his curiosity had overcome prudent caution, and he had stepped close enough to glimpse the article on the steel chain.

"Hey," he said. "What was that you grabbed?"

Spad Ames scowled at him. "You afraid of getting that monkey suit mussed? Why didn't you help us?"

"I'm doing my helping with dollars. Remember?" Locatella tapped Spad Ames on the chest with a stiff forefinger when the latter stood up. "Don't try to shove me around, Spad. What'd you find? Another arrowhead, wasn't it?"

Spad Ames ignored the question. He leaned over the girl, produced his own arrowhead, and let her see it. Her eyes widened. She was impressed.

"Where is your brother?" Spad Ames asked.

"Why should I tell you?" The girl spoke slowly, as if English was not her natural language.

Spad shook the arrowhead to draw her attention to it.

"I carry this talisman," he said. "And I have come out of the mists, as did you and your brother. I am a messenger. Now talk. Where is your brother?"

Moved by these magic words, in a low voice the girl described the exact location of her brother's room.

Spad Ames selected three men. "You guys come with me. Locatella, you keep the girl. We'll come back to this spot."

He vanished in the darkness with his men.

Locatella, who was as intrigued as a Fiji Islander who had just been shown a firecracker, got down beside the girl. He gave her his biggest smile, the one he gave his client just before he charged an outrageous fee.

"I'm your friend," he whispered to the girl. "That fellow who just left is a liar and a crook."

"Yes," the girl whispered back, calmly enough. "He is very bad."

"I want to help you, but I'm puzzled," Locatella said. "You tell me the truth, and I'll see what I can do. What did the stuff about coming out of the mists mean? And what are the black arrowheads?"

"You are puzzled?"

"I'll tell the cross-eyed world. I can't make heads or tails out of this thing."

"Swell."

"Huh?"

"You are as big a crook as your friend," said the strange white-haired girl. "And when your friend reaches my brother, he will die, and the secret will die with him. We had suspected your friend would come, my brother and I, and we have prepared."

"Spad Ames will be killed?"

"He will become as a rock which gives off mists, and any who touch him will suffer great pain."

HERMAN LOCATELLA straightened and did some fast thinking which led him to a conclusion. He couldn't understand the mystery, but he was convinced there was a great deal of profit involved somewhere. Spad Ames seemed to be the man with all the information. It wouldn't do to have Spad killed at present, although ordinarily the demise of Spad Ames would not have been much mourned by Locatella.

As a matter of fact, Locatella had made up his mind to double-cross Spad Ames at the first opportunity. He suspected Spad had the same idea.

"Watch her!" Locatella snapped. "I'm going to warn Spad."

Locatella galloped away. He had heard Ruth Colorado direct Spad to Mark Colorado's room, so he knew where to find his compatriot. Spad and his three helpers were creeping down a hallway when Locatella overhauled them.

"What the hell!" Spad Ames said unpleasantly. "You trying to watch every move I make?"

Whispering, Locatella told Spad what he had learned from the girl. The whisper was to prevent the three hired strong-arm men from overhearing.

Locatella finished his low-voiced information by suggesting: "Why don't we send one of the dopes in first? If anything happens to him—well, it'll be him it happens to."

"Remind me to keep an eye on you," Spad Ames said dryly. "You are becoming very smart."

They selected the most burly of the strong-arm men for their goat. They stood close to him and both of them patted his back.

"This Mark Colorado knows me by sight," Spad Ames said. "You barge in there and grab him, on account of if I went in, I wouldn't get to first base because he'd know me." Spad passed the man a stout sock filled with sand. A stout sock full of sand was Spad's favorite blackjack; in an emergency, the sand could be emptied, and a policeman could

HERMAN LOCATELLA

hardly call a sock in a man's pocket a deadly weapon. "Bop him one with this," Spad advised. "Tell him you are the electrician inspecting the lights."

The man walked to Mark Colorado's door, knocked, and was admitted when he mumbled that he was the electrician.

He did not come back.

"That don't look so good," Spad muttered, after about five minutes.

"Does this Mark Colorado really know you by sight?" Locatella asked in a low voice.

"Not that I know of."

"Why don't we all barge in, then? One man can't lick all of us."

Waiting had made Spad Ames impatient. "Let's do that," he growled.

THEY walked to Mark Colorado's door and knocked. There was no response.

"It's the night watchman," Locatella called in a loud hearty voice intended to inspire confidence. "Have you seen anything of a man pretending to be an electrician?"

"That was a good lie," Spad whispered admiringly.

It got no answer from beyond the door, however. Spad then tried the door, which proved to be unlocked. It swung open easily.

It was quite dark within, so Spad and Locatella—they were taking no chances themselves—had one of their hired helpers reach in and turn on the lights. Nothing happened, so they entered.

They found themselves in a large, pleasant room with a carpet on the floor and comfortable furniture. There were books on the table, a radio near the window. The window, Locatella noted, was locked on the inside, and there was only the one.

"Where is everybody?" a man muttered.

"Try the bathroom," Spad suggested.

The bathroom was in darkness also, so a man reached inside and snapped on the lights, after which there was some hesitancy about entering. Finally, Spad Ames got a hand mirror off the table where the books lay, and held it inside the bathroom, periscope fashion.

"Empty!" he said.

They examined the bathroom thoroughly. They examined the room. The one closet was empty, too, and there were no more doors. Locatella raked startled fingers through his hair.

"Nobody in here, and no place they could have gone," he said, and stared at Spad Ames.

"Don't look at me," Spad muttered. "I can't explain—"

At this point, the corridor door slammed. All of them jumped wildly, then rushed for the door, the same one by which they had entered. They found it locked.

"We're fastened in here!" Spad barked.

Locatella whirled, ran to the window, flung it up, and put a leg through it, preparatory to jumping. He drew the leg back hastily.

"We're four floors up," he gasped. "I forgot that."

The lights went out suddenly, and he finished the statement in the dark. They stood there, surrounded by complete blackness, until one of the men, his lungs irritated by holding his breath too long, began coughing. Spad Ames swore at him.

"Kick the door down!" Locatella snarled. "Why did I ever get messed up in this thing in the first place?"

"We make a racket, and they'll call the cops," Spad warned. "We'll all wind up in the can."

In the blackness of the room, someone began shrieking as if trying to get his lungs out of his chest. It was a cry such as Spad Ames had heard before: on that night weeks ago, after the plane crash in the canyon, Waldo Berlitz had made such sounds as these.

Chapter VI
BLACKJACK FIGHT

LIEUTENANT COLONEL ANDREW BLODGETT "MONK" MAYFAIR, the chemist who was a member of Doc Savage's group, was thinking of a great many things to say, and saying them as fast as his tongue could manage.

"It was all a gag, I tell you," he repeated at five-second intervals.

Big-fisted Renny Renwick, the engineer, was looking speechless and sheepish.

"All a gag," Monk insisted.

Doc Savage and the dapper Ham Brooks had finally revived. The gas that had overcome them was a type producing no harmless effects, although their period of unconsciousness had extended more than an hour.

"You two hooligans," Ham told Monk and Renny scathingly, "could walk under a caterpillar and not touch fuzz."

Monk wailed: "How was we to know Doc would be with you? It was a gag, I tell you. Renny and me got tired of that hands-and-knees-and-bark business. We knew you had been eavesdropping on this Locatella, so we laid for you here on the roof. We didn't know Doc would be along."

"What were you clowns figuring on doing with me?"

Monk and Renny hesitated, then both suddenly burst into laughter.

"We were going to take your clothes and leave you to wake up on top of that statue of Columbus at the corner of Central Park," Monk chuckled.

"Take my clothes?" Ham yelled. "Leave me naked in that conspicuous spot!"

"Except for a fig leaf," Monk explained. "I had the fig leaf. Brother, if you think finding a fig leaf in this town is easy, you can guess again. Renny had the ladder—snagged it from a fire house."

Renny let out a pleased rumble. "Can you imagine what the newspapers would have said? America's best-dressed man introduces fig leaf as latest style! Or something like that."

"That was a low-down trick!" Ham snapped.

"It was no lower down than the way you crooked us on that Harvard bet," Renny rumbled.

Ham started. "You—er—found out about that?"

"Yes," Renny thumped, "we did. And I don't mind your roping Monk with your gags, but you don't need to include me."

Ham had been afraid they would find out the truth. Some days before, he had rigged a microphone onto a radio over which Monk and Ham had been listening to a broadcast of the Harvard game; cutting the mike into circuit, Ham had described a different and entirely imaginary game wherein

Harvard lost. Then he had walked in innocently, pretending not to know the game was over, and deliberately irritating Monk and Renny, had offered to bet Harvard would win. To his glee, they had taken him up—and had to pay off by kneeling and barking whenever they saw Ham.

"Well, it was good barking while it lasted," Ham said cheerfully.

They went on and climbed into the office in which Ham kept his eavesdropping apparatus. Ham put on the telephone headsets and listened.

"Locatella's office seems to be empty." Ham frowned accusingly at Monk and Renny. "You've ruined our plans. You delayed us, and the crooks got away."

Monk snorted. "Your recording device was working, wasn't it? All we've got to do is play it back."

THIRTY minutes or so later, as a result of listening to the conversation from Locatella's office which the recorder had repeated mechanically, Doc Savage brought his car to a halt at the edge of Phenix Academy campus. They had made very fast time, and the abruptness of their stop made the tires whistle. They listened.

"Sounds like a war," Renny rumbled.

From around the Phenix Academy buildings were coming loud voices, a few shouts, and a series of irregularly spaced shots. Two searchlights, so powerful that they threw beams which were like white rods, were fanning slowly over the buildings.

"Something goes on," Monk agreed.

Before they could get out of the machine, a man came dashing through the darkness to their car.

"Are you cops?" the man asked.

"No," Monk said. "We're just curious—"

"Not cops—that's nice." The man showed them a viciously waggling blackjack made of a sand-filled sock, and put the blinding beam of a flashlight in their eyes. "Unload, you yaps! Get out of there—quick!"

"Hey!" Monk exploded. "What's goin' on?"

"Out with you! We need this car."

Monk blurted: "He's only got a blackjack—"

"Easy does it," Doc Savage said quietly.

Doc opened the door and got out, and his three men followed him, Monk banging the car door angrily.

The bandit with the blackjack lifted his voice. "Come on, guys!" he barked. "Here's a heap we can use for a scram."

Spad Ames and Locatella scrambled out of the campus shrubbery. They were followed by one man carrying Ruth Colorado. Four more brought up the rear, holding the corners of a stout blanket in which lay the final member of the raiding party.

The man they carried was in a peculiar condition. He was doubled, as if in agony. His body—it was obvious no life remained in him—was as rigid as stone. Also, it seemed to be steaming from head to foot.

The taxi headlights, helping out the fog-discouraged glow of a nearby street light, furnished fair illumination.

Doc Savage and his men gazed at the body, astounded by its strange condition.

The four who carried the form in the blanket did not seem very happy about it, either. In fact, they were sweating profusely, and their faces were lead-colored. They looked as if someone had taken the lid off things and let them see the works.

Over by the Phenix Academy buildings, there was another spattering burst of shots, and the searchlight beams waggled around like the antennae of fantastically enlarged insects.

Spad Ames laughed.

"They still think we're on the roof, where we went after we broke out of the room," he said.

"We'd be there, too, if I hadn't found a freight elevator," reminded a man who evidently wanted to call attention to his own merits.

"You're so damn perfect," Spad Ames said unkindly, "you should have found Mark Colorado for us."

At this point, Herman Locatella emitted a horrified squawk. Locatella carried a flashlight, and it had occurred to him to turn the beam on Doc Savage and his men, who were standing with their arms lifted. The others had not recognized Doc Savage, but Locatella knew Doc instantly, and let out the noise, a wordless kind of squawk.

The four sweating pallbearers hanging to the blanket corners, shocked by Locatella's noise, let go the blanket. It dropped. The body it contained hit the sidewalk, making a sound exactly as if a stone statue had been dropped, and one of the doubled-up legs broke of cleanly.

Locatella got words coming.

"This guy you've held up is Doc Savage!" he screeched.

SPAD AMES wheeled, his mouth becoming perfectly round with astonishment. "What—what—"

"Doc Savage!" Locatella jabbed both arms at Doc. "The Man of Bronze—"

Spad understood, and must have remembered some of the things he had heard about Doc Savage. His blackjack was in his coat pocket. He drove a hand for it.

"Watch out there!" Ham yelled. He lunged for Spad Ames, but someone whacked him over the head with a blackjack, and Ham sank and began crawling around foolishly on the ground.

Fortunately, Doc Savage pitched for Spad also. Spad, who was fast on his feet, twisted to get clear. He didn't quite succeed. Doc got hold of his coat, wrenched, and the coat came to pieces. Doc got the part of the coat containing the blackjack.

Monk had been ogling the body in the blanket, and his small eyes had been almost hanging out since he had seen the leg break off when the body was dropped. Monk came out of his trance and plunged into the fight.

Herman Locatella drew a small automatic; he shot Doc Savage six times in the chest and stomach—the bullets seemed to have no effect—before he realized Doc must be wearing some kind of bullet-proof undergarment. His gun—the only gun in the crowd, incidentally—was now empty. Locatella whirled and ran to the car, dived in behind the wheel, and stamped the starter pedal in a frenzy.

Doc Savage, whose movement always had method, worked straight to the bound figure of Ruth Colorado. He scooped up the white-haired girl, carried her into the nearest shrubbery, left her there, and raced back to the fight.

Monk had two men down. He was thumping them and howling. Monk liked his fights noisy.

The mêlée so far had been as confused as the first seconds of a cat-and-dog fight. Now it straightened out.

Locatella got the car engine started. Spad Ames lunged clear of the scrap, and grasping the blanket, he gathered it up, body and all, and jammed it into the car.

While Spad Ames was working with the body, big-fisted Renny had snatched up the part of Spad Ames' coat which had been torn off earlier in the fight. He had felt in the pockets, and found no arrowhead. Renny was very interested in the black arrowhead. Rushing up behind Spad Ames, Renny seized his trousers pockets and tore them bodily out of Spad Ames' pants.

Spad howled and began fighting Renny.

Four of the hired thugs, suddenly deserting the fray, jumped for the car. Two of them struck Renny on the head with sand-filled socks, and Renny folded down. Spad Ames tried to get the arrowhead out of Renny's hand, but the engineer's big fist refused to open.

"Gimme a hand!" Spad rapped, and they heaved the dazed Renny bodily into the car, where two men sat upon him and clubbed him methodically.

Spad Ames grasped the blanket, gathered it up and jammed blanket and body into the car.

The cab rolled.

Monk roared: "They're all getting away!" and raced vainly after the fleeing cab.

But Spad Ames, Locatella, the four hired thugs,

and the fantastically rock-hard body of their companion, all vanished into the fog and darkness with the taxicab. They took Renny with them.

MONK stopped and stamped his feet and shook both fists to express his feelings.

"Just like a rusty ape," Ham said unkindly.

Monk came back, found a flashlight in his clothing, and switched the beam over the surroundings. It was darker, now that the headlights of the taxicab were gone. Monk discovered that two members of the Spad Ames-Locatella gang were spread out, senseless.

"Well, we bagged a couple, anyway," Monk said.

"Whew!" groaned Ham. "Did we get away from them?"

"Yes, we got away—wait a minute!" Monk turned his flashlight on Ham. "Ain't you a little mixed up, shyster? They got away from us."

"Was there a fight?"

"Was there—say, where have you been?"

Ham felt of his head. "Somebody kissed me. I think he used a blackjack."

"They got Renny."

"Great grief!" Ham gasped.

Doc Savage went into the shrubbery, then came out again carrying Ruth Colorado over his shoulder.

There was enough noise in the campus shrubbery to indicate the police were approaching to investigate.

"Here, take the girl," Doc Savage said quickly. "Also pick up the two men on the ground. Get them away from here before the police come."

"I'll carry the girl," Ham said, beating Monk to that job by a small margin.

Monk asked disgustedly: "Where'll we meet you, Doc?"

"At your laboratory," Doc said.

Ham carried the girl. Monk gathered up the two senseless Spad Ames' men easily. They vanished into the night fog.

Within a few moments, several policemen arrived on the spot. They recognized Doc Savage at once, possibly because he happened to hold a high honorary commission in the department; or more probably because he had addressed a mass meeting of police the week before on crime-prevention methods, and his big bronze figure was easily remembered.

"What happened?" an officer asked. "We heard a young riot over this way."

"Some strangers seized the car in which I was riding and also seized Renny Renwick, one of my—ah—associates." He described Spad Ames, Locatella and the others, explained that the car was a cab, gave its license number, and finished, "They had the body of a man with them."

RUTH COLORADO

He started to say that the body of the man seemed to be smoking, and when dropped, had made a sound as if it was rock and one of the limbs had broken off. He changed his mind. They wouldn't believe him.

Not that he would have blamed them for not believing.

"What is going on?" he asked.

"There you've got us," said the policeman. "About half an hour ago, an uproar broke out in the room of a student named Mark Colorado. The night watchman came to investigate, and got slugged on the head for his pains. There was a bunch of men in the room, and they rushed out. The watchman could use his gun, and he drove them onto the roof. The cops were called. We thought the gang was still on the roof. I guess they got off."

"They used a freight elevator," Doc advised, repeating what he had heard one of the raiders say.

The policeman's expression became peculiar. "I don't believe this, but here's what somebody said," he muttered. "They said these guys were carrying a life-sized statue in a blanket, and the statue was giving off smoke. I guess it was only the body they saw."

"Possibly," Doc said.

"What gave them the idea the body was smoking, though?" pondered the officer, puzzled.

Doc asked: "What about Mark Colorado?"

"Someone saw him during the hoopla, but now we can't find him."

"Suppose," Doc suggested, "we take a look at the room where all this started."

Chapter VII
DANGEROUS KNOWLEDGE

ANOTHER of the strange things about the mysterious Colorados was the fact that they had seemed to have plenty of money, and one of the Phenix faculty mentioned this to explain the rather pleasant room which Mark Colorado occupied. Doc Savage said, "Thank you," and looked around.

The radio had been knocked to the floor and stepped on, two chairs were upset and the bedclothing had been scattered, doubtless when Spad Ames seized the blanket in which to carry away his unlucky hired thug. Struggling feet had goosed the rug out of shape.

Doc paused and tested the air noticeably with his nostrils.

"You're right—there was a queer odor in here," a policeman said. "It was stronger, but the window has been open." The officer hesitated. "There was something else, too."

"What?"

"When I first came into the room, the place seemed—er—well, like a tomb. It was chilly in here, it seemed to me. The cold and that odor sort of gave me the creeps. Ah—I hope you don't think I'm being silly. But I distinctly got a creepy feeling."

Doc Savage's flake-gold eyes roved. He had trained his faculties of observation with exercises included in the daily two-hour routine which he took. Having gone over the room, bath and closet, he did something which Spad Ames and Locatella, in their hurried dash into the room, had not thought—he examined the ceiling.

Doc slid the table into the center of the room and climbed upon it. The ceiling, instead of being plastered, was paneled with a sound absorbent material in areas about two feet square. Doc shoved against one of these which was somewhat soiled along one edge—the soiled edge had drawn his attention to the thing.

The panel hinged upward, leaving an opening sufficiently large to permit the passage of a man.

"What is on the floor above?" Doc asked.

"The student labs," a faculty member explained. "Each Phenix student is encouraged to rent and equip a private laboratory if he is sufficiently scientifically inclined. The labs are small rooms on the top floor, and are completely private. We have had instances of students using them to—

ah—distill their own gin. But usually they do worthwhile work."

"Who used this?" he asked.

"Mark Colorado. I remember, now, that he was insistent on having this laboratory."

In one corner of the lab was a pile of excelsior and the remains of a wooden packing case. The case had been sent to Mark Colorado by express. Doc made particular note of where it had come from.

The case had been shipped from Flagstaff, Arizona.

Neither case nor packing gave any indication of what its contents might have been.

Doc Savage completed a thorough investigation of the lab, and another inspection of Mark Colorado's living quarters below, in the course of which he brought out a number of fingerprints, using print powder borrowed from a police identification bureau man who had arrived. He studied the prints closely, fixing their primary type in his mind sufficiently that he could, by calling upon his remarkably developed memory, probably recognize them if he saw them again.

Meantime, no trace had been found of Mark Colorado.

"What do you make of this thing?" a policeman asked.

"It seems rather mysterious so far," Doc Savage admitted, and leaving the college, took a cab to Monk's laboratory. He would have preferred the subway, which was faster, but he was continually being recognized and embarrassed by stares and autograph hunters.

Then, too, he had noticed another cab following him, and he did not want to make the trailing too difficult.

MONK MAYFAIR maintained a penthouse atop one of the giant needle-thin buildings in the Wall Street district, where he had a breathtaking view of the lower city and the harbor. Monk liked to lean on the penthouse balcony railing for hours at a time, and watch the patterns of steamship lights on the harbor water, for Monk, himself as pleasantly homely as a Texas horned toad, was a great admirer of beauty. The type of beauty he admired most was in pretty girls.

In addition to a laboratory which was almost as complete as Doc Savage's amazing establishment at headquarters, Monk maintained rather fantastic modernistic living quarters in this penthouse. One of the features was a suite he had rigged up for his pet pig, an animal he had named Habeas Corpus in order to irritate Ham. There was a mud bath for Habeas' exclusive use, and the mud was special radioactive mud imported from Claremore, Oklahoma, and delicately perfumed.

Doc Savage alighted from his taxicab, and entered the building, then angled over to a corner of the lobby, taking up a position behind a pillar to wait.

Mark Colorado came in almost at once. Doc had not seen him before, but he recognized the young man, although Mark Colorado wore a dark hat yanked down over his white hair. Mark Colorado, then, must have been the occupant of the trailing taxicab.

Mark Colorado was being cautious. He glanced about, then went directly to the elevator, the only one in operation at this time of night, and rang. The elevator arrived.

"This the only elevator running?" he asked.

"Yes."

"Where did you let Doc Savage off?"

"I haven't seen Doc Savage," the operator said.

Mark Colorado did not argue about it. He took the fellow by the throat with his left hand and hit the man's jaw with his right hand, then placed the limp operator in a corner. He closed the door and ran the elevator up himself.

Doc Savage raced to the elevator bank. The remaining cages stood at the lobby level, but the sliding doors were closed. They could be opened by key, and Doc knew where an emergency key was kept hanging on an obscure hook. He got it, piloted a cage upward, and was careful about stepping out into the penthouse vestibule, which was dark, and moving to an open door.

Mark Colorado was flourishing a large hand grenade. He had plucked the key out of this, and was holding the lever down with his thumb.

"You can put your hands up or keep them down," he said. "But if one of you jumps me, I'll let go of this thing."

Monk and Ham gave the grenade wide-eyed looks. If Mark Colorado took his thumb off the firing lever, nothing on earth would prevent that grenade exploding within five seconds or so, and it would probably demolish most of the penthouse, for it was a large grenade.

Ruth Colorado, freed of the cords with which Spad Ames had bound her, was sitting in a chair. There was a radiant pleasure on her face as she looked at her brother, although she was not smiling. She seemed to approve of what he was doing with the grenade.

The two Spad Ames followers who had been unconscious had now revived. They occupied two other chairs, and were tied hand and foot. They ogled the grenade and looked as if they wanted to faint.

The pig, Habeas Corpus, was investigating the ankles of the two prisoners. Habeas had abnormally long legs, a lean body, a long snout built for inquiring into things, and two ears so enormous that they might have been mistaken for misplaced wings.

Chemistry, Ham's pet, sat nearby.

"Where is Doc Savage?" asked Mark Colorado.

Monk frowned. "You had better find out who your friends are around here," the homely chemist advised. "We rescued your sister."

"I watched you do that," Mark Colorado said.

"You—" Monk frowned. "Why didn't you pitch in and help?"

"And let you make me a prisoner, too?"

"Nobody," disclaimed Monk, "is a prisoner around here."

Mark Colorado glanced at his sister and asked: "What about that?"

"They were asking me questions," the girl said. "And they were beginning to talk about using truth serum."

"That," said Mark Colorado grimly, "is what I was afraid of."

MARK COLORADO moved a little and stood under a light, so that Doc Savage, watching from the darkened vestibule, was able to inspect the thing thoroughly enough to be positive that it was genuine.

Both Monk and Ham were perspiring from the strain.

"One of you call Doc Savage in here," ordered Mark Colorado.

"He isn't here," Ham said.

"I know better. I saw you go off and leave him, and I hung around in a cab until he left Phenix Academy. I followed him. While waiting, I asked someone who he was. They told me he was Doc Savage, of whom I have heard and read. It is unfortunate that it had to be Doc Savage."

"Unfortunate?" Ham squinted at him. "What kind of talk is that?"

"You have learned something—"

"Brother, are you mistaken!" Ham interrupted. "We haven't learned anything!"

Mark Colorado said: "You know that Spad Ames is getting a gang together to go back after something he found somewhere in Africa—"

"Africa!" Ham barked. "Who said anything about Africa? It was in the Grand Canyon badlands somewhere."

Mark Colorado showed his teeth grimly. "You see? You do know a great deal."

Monk told Ham disgustedly: "What you better do is shut up before you talk him into letting go of that grenade."

"The fellow is crazy," Ham said. "Anyone who does what he's doing with a grenade is crazy."

"Well, shut up and stop irritating him," Monk yelled, "before he drops that egg!"

Mark Colorado spoke to his sister. He used a dialect which, while not unmusical, was completely unintelligible to Monk and Ham.

Out in the darkened vestibule, perplexed wrinkles appeared on Doc Savage's forehead. The lingo was completely unknown to him, although he could make himself understood in almost any language or dialect, and could speak many of them with native fluency.

Ruth Colorado arose from her chair and picked up the cords with which she had been tied. She went to Monk and Ham in turn and searched them. Then she threw loops over their wrists and began tying them.

"What you think you're doin' with us?" Monk asked uneasily.

"Unfortunately," Mark Colorado said, "you have got to disappear, and not be seen again."

Monk said: "You mean—you're gonna try to kill us?"

"No. You will be taken to the spot which Spad Ames happened to find. You will remain there the rest of your lives."

DOC SAVAGE eased back from the open door, wheeled and entered the section of the penthouse containing Monk's chemical laboratory. Monk and Ham were having their troubles with the Colorados in the residential portion. The laboratory was a series of large rooms done in white, with the apparatus arrayed in spectacular fashion, for while Monk was unquestionably a great industrial chemist, he also loved a show, and one of his proud boasts was that a motion picture producer had recently taken still photographs of the lab to use as a model in constructing a set for some pseudo-scientific picture that was in production.

Chemicals were contained in an array of long metal cabinets in the storeroom. Doc Savage went to the cabinet, and covering his flashlight lens with his palm, except for a small crack of light, he searched. He had worked with Monk here, so he knew the particular container which he wanted.

The bottle which he selected, gallon-sized, held a liquid concoction of chemicals which Doc had recently perfected, but which as yet he had not given a practical test.

Ruth Colorado had finished tying Monk and Ham when Doc returned to the vestibule door with the container of chemical.

Mark Colorado, taking a small pillbox from one of his pockets with his hand which did not hold the grenade, said: "You are going to eat some of these. They are sleeping pills, so don't get worried. Ruth, take the pills and make each one swallow about four."

Doc Savage came into the room then. He uncorked the bottle. He dashed the contents over the back of Mark Colorado's head. When Mark Colorado whirled, Doc sloshed more of the chemical liquid into his face.

Ruth Colorado started to leap forward. Doc

thrust the gallon bottle at her, and the chemical splashed over her face. She gasped loudly, and clamped her hands to her eyes.

Mark Colorado dropped the grenade. The lever clicked, and inside the thing the timing mechanism began to race off the four or five seconds before it would explode. Doc hurled the bottle of chemical against Mark Colorado; the bottle broke and saturated the man.

With a continuation of the hurling gesture, the bronze man lunged forward and down and got the grenade while it was still rolling.

He threw it through the window, hurled it very hard, so that it would continue outward and upward.

His rush had carried him almost to the window, so he went flat on the floor below the sill, where the masonry would furnish a parapet. Monk and Ham, flopping like fish out of water, had already progressed through a door into a darkened room; they continued their flip-flop progress, their idea to get as far away as fast as possible.

There was white flash, crash; the entire window jumped inward over Doc's head. Glass landed on his body, jangled on the floor beside him. Grenade fragments, as dangerous as bullets, chopped at the walls. Habeas Corpus, the pig, and Chemistry, the chimp, dashed for cover.

Mark and Ruth Colorado had raced out into the vestibule, the chemical obviously not having blinded them. Clanging of the elevator door indicated they had entered the lift.

Doc Savage made no effort to stop them.

Chapter VIII
RADIO CLUE

WHEN Monk and Ham were untied, they had trouble making their voices function. "Blast me, I didn't think I could get so scared!" Monk managed finally.

"You red-headed ape," Ham said unkindly, "if you hadn't been busy big-eyeing that girl, Mark Colorado couldn't have walked in on us like he did."

"Well, there's no danger of you having red hair."

"Why not?"

"Nobody ever heard of ivory rusting."

Monk and Ham scowled at each other. After a narrow escape, it seemed that they could quiet their nerves by insulting each other.

When they had gotten rid of some of the scare, Ham said: "Both of those Colorados are nuts, or something. He wasn't fooling with that grenade, and the girl seemed just as calm as he was about it."

"It wasn't quite human, the way they acted," Monk admitted.

"I'll say it wasn't human," Ham agreed. Then Ham realized he was forgetting himself and agreeing with Monk, so he scowled, and snapped, "The girl is all right. She's just got a lot of nerve."

"She had a lot more than nerve," Monk said, and made a shape with his hands. "Boy, what a form!"

"Monk's heart," Ham explained, "sounded like a string of firecrackers."

Monk grinned. "I didn't hear yours making any sound, particularly after her big brother walked in with that iron apple."

Doc Savage had gone outside to the balcony, and by leaning over the cold stone parapet, he could look downward into the lifeless fog that packed the canyon of street that was sixty-odd floors deep. He thought he saw a pale spot that might have been a taxicab headlight move away. He was not sure. The bronze man went back to Monk and Ham.

"Did you learn anything from the girl before her brother arrived?" he asked.

Ham said: "She thanked us for rescuing her. We told her who we were, and she said she was very, very sorry that we had gotten mixed up in this, because it meant that we would have to be taken into the mists."

"Into the mists?" The bronze man's flake-gold eyes seemed to become more animated.

"Into the mists—it sounds silly," Monk interposed. "But that's what she said."

"Was that all?"

"Yes. Of course, we gathered that we were to be taken into the mists, as she put it, because we had found out just a little bit about some tremendous secret. That was the general idea."

"She give information on the black arrowheads?"

"Heck, no! She just told us it was too bad we knew anything at all about black arrowheads."

Monk got up and stamped about the room. "The Colorados got away. Spad Ames got away. So did Locatella. Unless we can get something out of the two prisoners we've got left, we're sunk."

"Which means we may have trouble finding Renny," Ham added.

Doc Savage went into the adjacent room and studied the two hired men of Spad Ames whom they had captured. Some glass had been sprayed over the pair by the grenade explosion outside, and one of them was staring in fascinated horror at a gouge which a grenade fragment had made in the floor near his head.

"Have you any truth serum?" Doc asked.

"Heck, no!" Monk said. "We told the girl we had some, trying to scare her. But we're out of it."

"Long Tom has a new lie detector," Doc said. "Get hold of him."

LONG TOM was Major Thomas J. Roberts, another of Doc Savage's coterie of five associates.

The fifth member, the long-bodied and long-worded William Harper Johnny Littlejohn, was at present in Mongolia following his occupation of archaeology; he was trying to prove or disprove somebody's claim that the human race had first appeared in that part of the world.

In the interval before Long Tom arrived, the police came, but departed when Doc Savage explained that he would rather handle this matter himself, and when Monk promised to pay for all the grenade damage in the vicinity. After the officers left, it occurred to Monk that he had better ascertain just how much damage he had rashly promised to pay for, and he went out to look.

Doc telephoned the central city police station and the headquarters of the state police, but no trace had been found of his taxicab or of Spad Ames and Locatella.

Monk came back in, muttering. "I must be losing my mind, promising to pay for that damage! I'm financially ruined! Ham, you'll have to loan me some dough."

"You broke again?" Ham demanded.

"Listen, when I was a baby they paid a nurse to push me around in a buggy, and I been pushed for money ever since."

Long Tom Roberts walked in. He was a rather wan-looking fellow with the kind of a complexion that made it seem he must have grown up in a mushroom cave. Long Tom's general physical appearance frequently convinced strangers that he had either just left, or was headed for, a hospital bed. As a matter of fact, no one remembered Long Tom ever having been ill, and he frequently whipped much healthier-looking men than himself, two and three at a time.

"I brought it," he announced triumphantly.

He meant his lie detector. Long Tom was the electrical wizard of their group, and his latest brain child was his lie detector, a supersensitive device which measured tiny electrical currents set up in the body as a part of nerve reaction when an individual told a lie. The device was about the size of a portable radio, and somewhat resembled one, except that there was a large dial and a needle, and electrodes which connected to the victim's wrists.

Monk sniffed and said: "Probably that thing won't work."

"You can ride Ham all you want to," Long Tom told him levelly. "But you mess with me and you'll end up like a postage stamp."

"How do you mean—postage stamp?"

"Licked."

Monk fell silent. The truth was that he was afraid of the anemic-looking Long Tom, who occasionally flew off the handle without warning and performed somewhat after the fashion of a wild cat.

They questioned the two prisoners, Doc Savage putting the queries.

"What do you know about the black arrowheads?"

"Nothing," both answered.

"What does the talk about going into the mists, and coming out of the mists, mean?"

"We have no idea."

"Where can we find Spad Ames and Locatella?"

"Don't know."

"To what race of people do the Colorados belong?"

"Can't imagine."

Long Tom's device indicated answers to all four of these questions to be the truth.

"Do you have criminal records?" Doc asked.

"No."

They were both liars there, however, according to the detector.

"We'll take them downstairs," Doc said, "and take a cab to headquarters."

THE trip uptown was uneventful, and so was the ride up in the private elevator to the eighty-sixth floor; but when they approached the door, they saw an envelope that had been stuck to the panel with a bit of chewing gum.

"Now what's this?" Monk grumbled, and opened the envelope. Printed lettering on the one sheet inside said:

HOW DOES THIS STRIKE YOU FOR A TRADE? YOUR FRIEND RENNY IN EXCHANGE FOR MARK AND RUTH COLORADO.

WE TRIED TO BORROW YOUR CAR. REMEMBER?

"Spad Ames wants the two Colorados mighty bad," Monk muttered. "I wonder why?"

No one told him why. Doc Savage went into the laboratory, returned with a hypodermic needle, and used the contents to put both of their captives to sleep.

"Bring them along," the bronze man said.

They used another car from the private garage, this machine a dark sedan that had size, power and the impregnability of a battleship turret without being conspicuous, and drove to a small private hospital on the West Side, where they unloaded the two sleeping prisoners.

The hospital, although no one but the managing director knew the fact, was maintained by Doc Savage as a completely charitable institution for the nearby slum sections. The two captives would be held there until called for.

"These will go to college," Doc told the hospital director, indicating the two senseless ex-members of Spad Ames' gang.

MONK

Monk is the chemist of Doc Savage's little band of fighters. You'd never think he was a scientist—from his appearance. He looks more like the missing link.

Monk is a tough battler, a bruiser who doesn't know when to quit.

He likes the girls, too. In fact, Monk is quite a contradiction all the way through. As witness his almost constant quarreling with Ham, for whom many times he has risked his life.

These cryptic instructions would result in an ambulance calling for the pair before many hours had passed, and taking them to a unique institution for curing criminals which Doc Savage maintained in a remote, mountainous and almost uninhabited section of upstate New York. At this institution, surgeons trained by Doc Savage would perform delicate brain operations which would wipe out all memory of the past. The pair would receive training in some trade, would be taught to hate crime and criminals, after which they would be released to become citizens of some value. No crook—once having matriculated in this unusual "college"— ever returned to crime.

Existence of this "college" was kept from the public for various reasons, one being that the place was a little unorthodox; and this method of curing

criminals, while it was one that Doc felt would eventually be used widely, was somewhat too fantastic for public acceptance.

"Now," Monk said grimly, "if we just had a way of locating Renny."

"We have," Doc said.

"Huh?"

The bronze man switched on the radio which, instead of being located under the dash, was clamped against the car top, just back of the windshield. It was a compact set, both transmitter and receiver, as well as convertible into a direction finder. Doc made the conversion by throwing switches, and stopping the car and fitting a small collapsible loop aërial into the weatherproof socket on top.

Monk suddenly remembered the perfectly obvious fact that all of Doc Savage's private machines were equipped with two-way radio apparatus.

"Doc!" he exploded. "In that taxicab Spad Ames took from us—you didn't leave the radio on by any chance?"

"I left the transmitter switched on," Doc admitted.

Monk emitted a pleased whoop. "Then it's probably still on, because the transmitter don't make any noise, so they wouldn't notice it."

Long Tom said: "Then we can locate the car simply by taking bearings on the transmitter carrier wave with our finder."

Doc nodded; he was busy with the direction-finder.

Chapter IX
TRAILS WEST

BY three o'clock in the morning, the fog had turned to thin rain that poured down in long strings and made sheets on the windshield wherever it was not knocked away by the wipers. The big car ran silently, the tires making, as they threw water, more noise than the engine of the machine.

The road was rough—it was well north of the city—and the car bucked enough to keep them hanging to the support straps. Monk, Ham and Long Tom would have been uneasy had any one of them been driving at such speed, but their confidence in Doc's tooling of the machine was complete, so they were relaxing as much as they could.

"Naturally, they would go north," Ham said grimly. "That way, they would not have to use bridges, ferries or tunnels over the East River or Hudson that are easily watched."

Long Tom emitted a sharp noise.

"Hep!" said Long Tom. "We've passed it up."

He had been manipulating the direction finder steadily; the loop had swung around sharply, following the signal, until it was at right angles to the car.

"We just passed a side road," Ham said.

Doc continued driving. "We will go on a bit, in case they should be watching the road," he explained.

Half a mile beyond, after they had rounded a curve, the bronze man wheeled their machine off the rough blacktop pavement and stopped.

Ham opened the door, grumbled: "Have we got to get out and swim in this?"

"Too bad about them clothes of yours," Monk said.

Doc took the radio along. It could be made portable by loosening thumb screws, an emergency set of batteries being self-contained.

The rain poured down, brush beat their faces and their feet sank in a lot of wet leaves. Trees thickened, and the branches laced a canopy that shut out any light there might have been.

There was a thump, and Monk croaked, "Oof! I mashed my face flat against a tree!"

"Probably improved it," Ham said cheerfully.

Doc Savage suggested: "Use the scanners."

The "scanner" was a device perfected by Doc Savage, and so complicated that only Monk and the missing Renny had any accurate idea of how it functioned. There was a projector that put out "black" light, or light with a wavelength near the infrared spectrum, and which was called "black" because it was invisible to the unaided human eye. The goggles which enabled the wearer to see by "black" light had lenses resembling condensed-milk cans, and functioned through the medium of rotating screens coated with a substance which briefly retained a "picture" formed by the infrared light.

They donned the scanners. Seen through the devices, their surroundings were a vague, unreal panorama of bone-colored objects and intensely black shadows. But it was literally seeing in the dark; no one unequipped with the scanners would realize there was any light at all. Doc Savage had used the devices before; they gave a tremendous advantage in any fight in darkness.

They made good time for twenty minutes through the rain.

"This looks like it," Monk said, and they had been walking in such an unreal world, as seen through the scanner goggles, that his voice caused all the others to jump.

THE cabin was not constructed of genuine logs, but of sawed imitations nailed on over a framework of ordinary lumber, although in spite of that it would be an attractive place seen in better weather. There was a wide porch, and on this stood two men with shotguns.

The taxicab containing the radio they had trailed stood nearby.

"We could walk up," Monk whispered, "and

LONG TOM

"Long Tom"—Thomas J. Roberts—known as the "wizard of the juice"—is the electrical expert of Doc Savage's band of intrepid fighters. Small in stature, his brain holds an enormous amount of learning. It is he who furnishes the electrical equipment and radio devices that have done much to further the success of Doc Savage's triumphs over his enemies—men who wish to further their own ends at the expense and suffering of mankind.

cold-crack them two lookouts as easy as falling off a log."

"Careful does it," Doc warned. "We have had enough fighting and charging around for one night. It is about time we made some progress."

No trace of light whatever came from the cabin itself.

They had been standing there some moments when two automobiles, both sedans, came laboring up in the mud and the rain. The cabin door opened and spilled a great blade of light into the night—it was instantly evident that they had the cabin windows blanketed—and Spad Ames came out.

Locatella alighted from one of the cars.

"Here's the rest of your men, Spad," he called. "Sixteen of them. Sixteen was the best I could do."

Spad Ames swore admiringly. "How you got sixteen together so quick beats me."

"Oh, I have my contacts," Locatella said smugly. "In fact, I keep quite an organization together for little jobs which bob up now and then."

The men dashed into the cabin, and Spad Ames and Locatella switched off the car lights, so that the resulting darkness and the noise of the drizzling rain made it perfectly safe for Doc Savage to approach close enough to overhear.

Spad Ames asked: "What about the machine guns, the bombs and the gas?"

"Already on its way west," Locatella said. "The pilot was willing to take off in this weather, which gives you some idea of the kind of a pilot he is."

"You sent the stuff ahead by plane?" Spad said admiringly.

"Yes."

"And that fellow Renny Renwick? We don't want him dead yet."

"On the plane with our weapons. I figured we should get him out of Doc Savage's reach until we made a trade—or got hold of the Colorados our-selves, after which we can drop him out of a plane or something."

Spad Ames nodded, asked: "What about our-selves? Where do we get planes?"

"We've got them," Locatella said, and laughed. "This cabin is one of my places. It's not held in my name, you understand. It's—well, I've got two or three of them scattered around in case of emergen-cies."

Spad Ames said admiringly: "You don't over-look many bets, do you? But what about planes for ourselves?"

"Come on," Locatella requested.

"Hey, in this rain—"

"It's not far."

Spad Ames and Locatella moved away, entering a narrow path walled thickly with shrubbery and overhung by leafage. They dashed the beams of flashlights ahead of them as they walked, so Doc Savage used care, not only to keep out of range of the lights, but to keep from being silhouetted between the lights and one of the guards on the cabin porch.

Suddenly they came out on the edge of a level meadow across which wind drove the rain in slant-ing, twisting wisps.

The hangar on the meadow edge was large with-out being conspicuous. Locatella worked briefly with a key and the padlock on the hangar door, then rolled the door back.

"Nice, eh?" he asked.

The two lean silver planes inside appeared, at first glance, smaller than they actually were, being streamlined to an extreme degree. They were dual-motored, the engine being the water-cooled type which lends itself to more effective streamlining.

"My personal ships," Locatella explained. "Two honeys—and they ought to be. They cost enough. I've only had them about three months."

"What about machine-gun mounts?"

"Already drilled. All you have to do is clamp the guns in. I have the guns, too, incidentally."

"Then we can take off for the west as soon as we get Mark and Ruth Colorado."

"Nothing to prevent."

Spad Ames rubbed his hands together. "This is swell. Perfect. When I came to the well-dressed Mr. Locatella, I sure didn't make a mistake, did I?"

Locatella gave his companion in crime a big confidential smile. "I'm glad you're satisfied, Spad, old pal." Locatella clapped Spad on the shoulder. "You know by now that you can trust me. So suppose you be a good fellow and tell me what you're after. Yes, indeed, tell me. What about the black arrowheads, and what about this going into the mists? It sounds very interesting."

"The hell with you, my genial friend!" Spad Ames said. "The hell with you!"

AFTER Spad Ames and Locatella—a drought of words had fallen between them—had gone back to the cabin, Doc Savage joined his men, who had been waiting in the brush. Long Tom was holding the two-way car radio in his arms, and Monk was carrying the loop aërial for the device.

"You heard what they said?" Monk asked grim-ly. "Renny isn't here. He's on a plane that they've sent west with a load of weapons."

The homely chemist was gloomy, feeling let down because they had not found Renny, their companion, who was a hostage, at this spot. Ham was unusually quiet, not even trying to think up remarks that would irritate Monk. Long Tom mut-tered: "This is a fine break. I thought we had Renny spotted."

Doc whispered: "There are two ways of helping Renny. One of them is to catch the Colorados before Spad Ames can find them. The second is to trail these fellows to the spot where they meet their arms cargo plane, and affect a direct rescue, if we can."

"Kind of puts us up a tree," Monk muttered. "We ain't got no idea where to find the Colorados. And you don't trail airplanes so easy."

"In this case, we might manage," Doc Savage said slowly.

"You mean—somebody stow away aboard?"

"No." The bronze man indicated the radio. "Use that. It is a transmitter as well as a receiver, and the emergency batteries will operate it steadily for almost forty-eight hours. We can trail that transmit-ter by using another direction-finder."

They concealed the radio far back in the fuselage

of one of the planes. Long Tom, who was thinner than any of the others, crawled into the cramped space and planted the apparatus.

On second thought, Doc Savage concluded to put a radio in each of Locatella's ships, so he went back to the taxicab, and worked with the radio that was in the machine. Transmitter and receiver were separate units, although mounted in the same case. He removed the transmitter unit with its compact assemblage of batteries, and replaced the receiver and the case. It now appeared that the taxi radio had not been tampered with. But Doc carried the transmitter unit back, and they installed it in the other plane.

They put this one inside the right wing. Doc carefully unlaced an inspection port, and placed the set far back where it was not likely to be noticed, then replaced the inspection port cover.

"Now," announced Long Tom, "we're ready for them to take off for the west."

"The trouble is," Monk muttered, "they may stick around here for days, trying to catch the Colorados."

Doc Savage had been considering that angle, and it was one he did not like. He wanted to get Renny out of the hands of the Spad Ames' crew as soon as possible. He much preferred immediate action.

"We will hurry them a little," the bronze man said.

Doc went back to the cabin, placed his men behind trees, gave instructions, then drew a small high-explosive grenade, not much larger than a bantam egg, from a pocket, and hurled it. The earth quaked, the big cabin slid a foot on its foundations, and smashed boards climbed up in the air. A great gobble of echoes came back from surrounding woods and hills.

Doc Savage lifted his voice.

"You're under arrest, all of you!" His words were a great crashing that everyone in the cabin must have heard. "Come out with your hands up!"

He did not expect them to obey, and they didn't. An automatic shotgun ripped out a three-shell burst, and tore bark off the tree behind which Doc Savage had flattened.

The bronze man threw another grenade, a smaller one, tossing it so it would drop on the roof. In the flash, a cloud of swirling shingles was visible.

Men piled out of the cabin. They were armed, mostly with automatic rifles, and they turned loose a deafening roar of fire.

Spad Ames shouted: "Get to the planes, you fools!"

He got his gang organized, and they retreated rapidly through the woods.

Doc, altering his voice until it did not sound like his own, called: "Be careful, men! There are more of them than we thought."

Monk, fooled by the changed voice, growled: "Hey, somebody else is helpin' us!"

"That's Doc, you homely dope!" Ham enlightened him.

The engines of Locatella's big planes began roaring, and both craft shortly moaned up into the black leaking night sky.

"I hope," Monk said cheerfully, "that we scared 'em so bad they'll head straight for the west."

IN addition to the establishment on the eighty-sixth floor of the midtown building, and the basement garage which housed their collection of cars, Doc Savage maintained a hangar and boathouse on the Hudson River waterfront, only a few blocks distant. This structure was ostensibly an ancient warehouse that was not being used; the painted sign across the front had peeled in the weather until its legend, "Hidalgo Trading Company," could hardly be read, and the walls gave little outward sign of being as thick as those of an ancient fortress.

Inside was an assortment of fast planes, a true gyroplane which could arise and descend vertically, and various experimental craft. There was also a small yacht, very fast, a schooner which Doc Savage was storing there for his cousin, pretty Patricia Savage. Pat joined the bronze man sometimes in adventuring, when he did not manage to stop her, for she loved adventure. Other craft included speedboats and a highly advanced experimental submarine which Doc had constructed for subseas exploration and a trip under the polar ice cap.

They selected their fastest plane, a craft that could pound out of its two huge motors more speed than any military pursuit craft, and which was equipped for landing upon earth or water.

Doc had lately installed a large vault which held an assortment of the scientific devices which he used, these being packed in cases ready for quick transportation. The cases were numbered, and Doc, who knew their contents, checked off more than a dozen, which were loaded aboard.

Early daylight was whitening the skull-colored strings of rain as they taxied out on the Hudson. Because visibility was no more than a hundred yards, even with the powerful floods spouting white light, Doc taxied downriver with the wind, then turned the plane—simply cranking up the landing gear converted it into a seaplane—and took the air.

"I'll get on the radio," Long Tom said. He adjusted the dials, worked with the direction finder, then grinned. "They're heading west, all right."

The two pets, Habeas and Chemistry, were aboard; Monk and Ham never left them behind, possibly because, when no other excuse for wrangling could be found, they could squabble over the animals.

Monk said: "How about catching the morning news? I'd like to know who is laying down an ultimatum to whom in Europe this morning."

There was no object in operating the direction finder steadily, so Long Tom tuned in a news broadcast. They learned about the state of affairs in Europe and in China, heard of another politician being kicked out of Kansas City, a murder in Texas, a bank robbery in Florida, after which they got a shock.

"When a man bites a dog, it's news, and when a man steals an airplane, it should be something or other," the radio commentator said. "But in this case, a man and a woman stole the plane. Both of them had snow-white hair, the snowy-white hair being news because the pilot whose airplane was stolen said both thieves could hardly have been more than twenty years old. The plane was stolen in Newark, and the thieves took off in the face of weather conditions that had grounded all regular passenger planes. It is believed they flew west."

The news commentator was followed by an asininely cheerful fellow who wanted all the little early birds to look in the mirror and smile, smile, smile.

"Did you hear that news item?" Monk yelled.

"White-haired girl and boy sound like Ruth and Mark Colorado," Ham said.

"The Colorados seem to be heading west, too," Long Tom suggested.

Chapter X
CAPTURE

THEY flew out of the rain into bright sunlight two hours later. In a place or two over the mountains in Pennsylvania, they saw traces of snow, so it was probably cold outside. The cabin was heated.

Monk dropped into the extra seat in the pilot's compartment. Doc was handling the controls.

"I been trying to figure something, Doc," the homely chemist said. "Back there last night, when you jumped the Colorados in my place you had something in a bottle. You splashed the stuff over them. I thought at first it was acid or gas or something, but it didn't seem to have any effect on them."

"It would not harm them," Doc said.

"What was it?"

"You remember the experiments we were making with a method that banks and armored trucks could use on bandits?"

"Oh!" Monk grinned. "So that's what it was!"

Monk went back into the cabin, and Ham, who was interested in knowing what he had learned, asked: "What was the liquid?"

"It's sure hell, ain't it?" Monk muttered.

"What?"

"The place where the bad people go."

"I hope you don't think that was funny," Ham said sourly, and added several choice opinions of the Mayfair ancestry, including the variety of trees they had probably swung in.

Monk was irritating Ham deliberately, and Ham was entirely willing, so the quarrel lasted across Ohio, Illinois and Missouri.

Over Kansas, Monk ran dry, and sat peering glumly at the vast expanse of flat wheat fields until he was moved to remark: "Brothers, there is sure a lot of land down there."

"And just think," Ham said dryly, "you can only see what is on top."

"I think that was some kind of an insult!" Monk yelled. "Some day, I'm going to—"

Whatever he was going to do to Ham remained untold, because Doc Savage called a sharp summons from the cockpit. The bronze man thought they would be interested in what the radio was saying.

"This is a general message to all planes in the air," Doc said. "A broadcast in cooperation with the police."

"A plane stolen by a young man and a young woman, both of whom had remarkable white hair, has landed on a field at Millard, Missouri," the radio voice said. "The occupants of the plane forced a tank-wagon driver to refuel the craft, then took off again. All pilots are requested to report any trace of the plane, a yellow Airpex monoplane, Department of Commerce Number NC973—645. A yellow Airpex monoplane, number N-as-in-Norma, C-as-in-Charles, nine hundred seventy three thousand, six hundred forty-five."

Long Tom said: "Mark and Ruth Colorado again. They aren't making such good time."

Doc Savage flattened a chart out on the map board, and noted the line which they had flown, trailing the radio transmitters concealed in Spad Ames' two ships. The line was almost straight. He extended it and noted that it passed over a part of the Grand Canyon country that he happened to know was virtually unexplored.

"The Millard, Missouri, airport," Doc Savage said slowly, "is located only a few miles from the Santa Fe Railway. The railway, running in a fairly direct line to California, and passing near the Grand Canyon, is a logical trail for planes to follow."

Doc swung southward fifty miles or so, and landed on a remote piece of prairie near the Santa Fe Railway.

"We can afford to waste an hour or two," the

The youthful white-haired man fired point-blank at the plane!

bronze man said, "on the chance the Colorados will fly overhead."

IT was near noon when Doc Savage, using strong binoculars, discovered a yellow monoplane approaching. Immediately, he boarded his own ship with Monk, Ham and Long Tom, and they climbed up in the sky. They got close enough to the other plane to identify the numbers.

"That's it," Monk said.

Mark Colorado was flying the stolen craft. He banked away, tried flight. But he lacked the speed—his plane was nearly a hundred miles slower—to escape.

Doc flew alongside, gestured orders to land. He was ignored.

Yanking the control wheel, Doc brought his plane up to a point where it flew directly ahead of the Colorado ship, and perhaps two hundred feet distant. He flew in that position, and jerked a lever on the control panel.

The gas which poured out of tanks mounted in the fuselage of Doc's ship was one of the secrets which would probably save America from foreign air raids, if the war need ever arose. It was colorless. It spread quickly. It retained its effectiveness. And when a plane motor sucked the stuff into its carburetor, the gas made fuel vapor noninflammable. The gas would instantly stop any airplane motor of internal combustion type—and no plane today has a motor of any other type.

They saw both Mark and Ruth Colorado start up in alarm as the engine of the plane died.

Mark Colorado managed a safe landing in a wheat field. He climbed out with a rifle; his sister also was armed. They raced to a small ditch nearby.

Doc dived his big ship at them. Rifle slugs smacked against the fuselage, but did not penetrate the double layer of alloy metal skin armor.

"Gas them," Doc directed. "Use anaesthetic."

Monk dropped the anaesthetic gas containers, and these burst around the ditch in which the Colorados crouched. Instantly, both Colorados tried to return to their plane. Mark covered about thirty feet; the girl almost made it.

Doc landed near their unconscious forms.

"Load them aboard," he directed, and climbed into the plane the Colorados had stolen. He did not find any trace of a chart with a destination marked upon it; in fact, there was no chart at all in the craft.

"No wonder they were following the railroad," Monk remarked.

Doc Savage took his own plane off, the slipstream stirring up a cloud of dust that swirled over the yellow craft the Colorados had been flying. Using the radio, he advised the nearest government airways station where the stolen plane could be found.

"Will you take the controls?" Doc requested of Monk, and the homely chemist nodded.

Doc searched the Colorados, Mark in particular. He found a notebook containing notations probably made during lectures at Phenix Academy, a pocket knife, cartridges for the rifle, some silver coins and nearly a thousand dollars in currency.

"With that roll, I would think he'd have hired a plane," Long Tom said, after he had counted the money and whistled.

He removed the thin stainless steel chain from Mark Colorado's neck, and examined the black arrowhead on the end. The arrowhead had not been drilled; it was fastened to the chain by a band which encircled the part that was ordinarily bound to the arrow.

"Is it like the one the girl carried?" Ham inquired.

"Not identical. But apparently made of the same material."

The bronze man stood for some time studying the faces of Mark and Ruth Colorado. Once, he moved Mark Colorado's head in order to get a better view of the man's facial contour.

Ham said: "Their faces look strange, don't they? I can't guess their nationality."

Doc Savage made, very softly so that it was hardly audible within the big silenced plane, a small trilling sound. The note was exotic, as weird as the song of some tropical bird, or the vagaries of a wind in a waste of Arctic ice pinnacles. Most peculiar quality of the trilling was the way it seemed to come from everywhere, rather than from any definite spot in the room; it was distinctly ventriloqual.

The sound was a small unconscious thing which Doc Savage made in moments of mental stress, or when he was comtemplating unusual action, or was very puzzled.

A BIT later, "Locate a wireless station that has a radio compass," Doc Savage suggested to Long Tom. "Preferably one along the Mexican border. We need a cross bearing on the Spad Ames' crowd, which will show us how far ahead they are."

Long Tom worked over the radio controls. What he wanted done was a little complicated when it came to explaining it to distant operators, but finally he had copied compass bearings, and drawn on his own chart the bearing line taken by the distant direction finder—he had located one in El Paso, Texas—so that this line, where it intersected the projected line of their own bearing, gave a fairly accurate guide to the location of Spad Ames' planes.

"About a hundred miles ahead," Long Tom said. "Less than half an hour's flying time."

"We should overhaul them about the time they reach the Grand Canyon country," Doc decided.

Ham lashed the ankles of Mark and Ruth Colorado.

Normal interval of unconsciousness produced by the anaesthetic gas was forty-five minutes. Mark and Ruth Colorado revived somewhat quicker than that. They were very stoical. They merely looked around, then the girl smiled slightly without humor.

"You had plenty of money," Doc said. "Why did you steal a plane instead of hiring one?"

"We wanted Spad Ames to know we were going west," the girl answered immediately. "We did not know where to find him. So we stole the plane to get ourselves in the newspapers."

Doc was impressed again with the strange accent which rather pleasantly fuzzed her words.

"What nationality are you?" he asked.

She only smiled.

Doc said: "By any chance, did you, too, come out of the mists?"

She nodded, but said nothing.

"What does that mean?"

She gave him a rather strange answer.

"A few white men have learned the truth," she said. "But only one has carried his knowledge back to the world—that one being Spad Ames."

Her lips became thin and compressed, and after that she did nothing but watch the two pets, Habeas Corpus and Chemistry.

Monk raised his voice in a yell. He had been peering through binoculars while he flew. Now he lifted his freak voice.

"Three planes dead ahead," he shouted. "Think they're Spad Ames' ships."

"Three?" Doc Savage said sharply.

"Yeah. The third one just flew in from the south. Guess it's the plane carrying Spad Ames' guns and bombs and stuff. Probably they arranged a meeting by radio."

Doc Savage went forward grimly.

"This is what we wanted—to find Renny," he said grimly. "We'll bring those planes down as fast as we can."

Monk glanced downward and shuddered.

"They won't like that very well," he surmised.

IF a great multitude of needles, made of stone and of lengths ranging from five hundred to four or five thousand feet in length, had been placed together in a great bundle with the points uppermost, the result would have been a fair imitation of what was below. Directly ahead, one of the great cracks seemed half filled with fog, which was a little queer. Fog was unusual in this desert.

CHEMISTRY

Ham looked a little queer, and without a word, got a parachute and put it on.

"Good idea," Doc Savage said, and they all strapped 'chute harness to themselves, and upon the two prisoners.

The bronze man took over the controls, pulled the big ship into a climb. The three planes ahead had slowed, for the plane bearing Renny and the weapons was obviously a slow craft.

A few minutes later, the three Spad Ames' planes began circling.

"Looks like they're fixin' to land," Monk said.

Doc nodded. He put his own ship into a long dive, came in a long moaning comet-rush out of the afternoon haze. If there was a landing spot down there below, he intended to disable the other planes with the gas that would stop their motors, and follow down the one which carried Renny.

They saw Doc's ship. He had expected that. He had expected the ships to bank sharply, trying to get into positions for men in the cabins to use machine guns. He kept diving. There was not much chance that they would do damage, for both windows and fuselage of his plane would stop ordinary rifle and machine-gun slugs.

What he had not expected was Ham's sudden howl from back in the plane cabin.

"Ham! Watch out!"

Doc twisted. He was in time to see Mark Colorado heave up, and with his bound feet, kick the dapper Ham head over heels. Monk was already on the floor, where he had been knocked.

It was impossible for Doc to leave the controls.

They were screaming toward the other three planes; there was every chance of collision.

Long Tom was on his knees at the rear, working over the engine-stopping gas containers.

Mark Colorado dived for the plane door. He had freed his hands somehow, but his ankles were still bound. The door, a siding type, could be opened when the craft was in flight. Mark Colorado wrenched it back, fell out.

He was desperate, he had a parachute, and he took a big chance. He managed to fall onto the wing—the door was directly over the wing—so that he hooked his hands over the leading edge.

He clung there until, with his free hand, he worked his parachute loose and hurled it into the propeller. Twisting at terrific speed, the propeller knocked itself into a complex knot.

Mark Colorado lay on the wing. Doc Savage, from the cockpit, could see the man's strangely blue eyes looking at him steadily.

The three Spad Ames' ships were above now. Monk—he had both arms wrapped about his midriff where he had been kicked—staggered to the cockpit.

"Fine stuff!" he gasped. "Those guys can fly rings around us now."

That was true. With only one motor, any one of the three planes above was faster. Men were wrenching the windows open and leaning out, braced against the rip of passing air, holding high-explosive grenades ready for use.

Ruth Colorado came forward, dragging herself by her arms, for her ankles were bound.

"You see that canyon?" She pointed.

"It's narrow," Doc said grimly.

"Very narrow. But you may be able to land in the bottom. It is sand, fairly smooth."

Doc glanced at the great crack in the needled wilderness of stone. He nodded, said: "We will try it."

"That is where Spad Ames crashed when he first came," Ruth Colorado said. "So be careful."

Chapter XI
STRANGE CANYON

THE sand was not level. It was bumpy. The plane made sounds somewhat like a big drum after the wheels touched; then it stopped.

Monk dived through the open door of the ship, landed upon Mark Colorado, and yelled: "I'm gonna turn this guy inside out! Ruin our propeller, will he!"

There was a ripping explosion, a geyser of sand a few yards distant. They were dropping grenades from above. Three more exploded close together on the canyon side, and a shower of rock came jumping down, the larger fragments out-distancing the smaller. Several of them were the size of automobiles.

Monk scooped up Mark Colorado and rushed with him to safety.

"I oughta leave you there for rocks to roll on," Monk declared unreasonably.

Doc Savage shouldered the girl, and ran. Ham and Long Tom tried to get an equipment case out of the plane, looked at the descending landslide of stone, and changed their minds. They raced clear.

The stone struck, knocking the plane about a little, bending it out of shape.

"Blast it!" Monk yelled. "We gotta get our equipment out of that ship!"

Doc Savage stared upward. He thought of the bombs which Spad Ames had told Locatella he would need. They were probably in the munitions ship, which was slanting slowly down toward the canyon.

"Run!" Doc said, and set an example.

The bomb must have been one of the new horrors of military science, a compressed oxygen-demolition bomb. Its concussion knocked them flat. They were deafened for moments, got up with nostrils leaking crimson.

In a hundred places, the blast had loosened the sheer canyon walls. Stone fell, pulling great comet trails of dust after it. Above the ringing in their ears, they could hear the rumbling grind of the slides. Under their feet, sand trembled so violently that dust began to arise from it.

They ran.

Monk, whose short legs handicapped him, began to yelp with each jump. But he did not drop Mark Colorado.

A few big boulders leaped across their path. Smaller fragments showered them. Echoes began coming through the din, sounding like battery after battery of big cannon being fired in succession.

Doc halted, and the others stopped also. Monk ceased yelping.

"You sounded like a coyote after a rabbit," Ham told Monk.

Monk let it pass. He was looking back at the spot where their plane had been standing.

The dust blew away after a while.

"How deep would you say the rock is over our plane?" Long Tom asked dryly.

"Fifty feet," Monk said.

It was a conservative estimate.

MONK opened his mouth, then closed it without saying anything. Their predicament was clear enough without comment. The plane was gone. Spad Ames still prowled around overhead. They could hear his three planes moaning.

"Here's an overhang where they can't see us," Doc said.

They stood in the niche which water had worn in the side of the canyon and waited. One of the planes, flying very carefully, ventured down some distance into the canyon, searching. It climbed out again, apparently satisfied.

Doc Savage looked down at Mark Colorado. The white-haired man's face was placid, and he smiled slightly.

"You seem satisfied," Doc said.

"I am."

"Spad Ames is not your friend."

"Of course not."

"But you helped him by disabling our plane."

Mark Colorado shook his head. "You have the wrong slant on that. I have seen a little of your methods. Enough to know you will be far harder to stop than Spad Ames."

"But why should you try to stop us?"

"You have learned that Spad Ames is after something mysterious," Mark Colorado said slowly. "The mystery has intrigued you. If you had managed to rescue your friend, Renny, up there a few minutes ago, you would not have been satisfied. You would have gone on. You are an adventurer. And because you have an amazing amount of ability, you might have—well, you might have gone through the mists, and learned about the destiny that no man shall know."

Doc Savage deliberately kept his metallic features expressionless. He was very puzzled.

"That sounds like—just words," he said. "Going through the mists. And destiny that no man shall solve the mystery. Words. Just words."

"That is because you do not understand."

Doc Savage glanced upward, listening. "You may be right, at that."

"He may be a little nuts, too," Monk said. "This thing has had a screwy twist from the first."

The planes had not gone away. They were out of sight, but all three motors were droning.

"They seem to be getting ready to land," Doc said.

Mark Colorado nodded. "They will descend farther down this canyon—probably a mile away. There is a spot at that point which is wider."

"You're helping us when you tell that," Doc said. "A few minutes ago, you were fighting us."

"I am not helping you—I am fighting Spad Ames." Mark Colorado smiled again.

Doc turned to Ruth Colorado suddenly. "What do you think about this attitude of your brother's?"

She had evidently been thinking about that, because her answer was prompt.

"The truth about my brother and myself is fantastic," she said. "And it is better for no one to ever know it."

DOC took off his coat, a dark gabardine garment. He ripped it into strips. With the strips, he bound both Colorados.

"Watch them," he said. "Watch them very closely."

"Where you goin'?" Monk called.

"To see about Renny."

High overhead, the eroded pinnacles of stone were tipped with the fire of afternoon sunlight, but here in the depths there was shadow. Not particularly dark shadow, once eyes had become accustomed to it, but murky enough to make the sunlight above seem blinding. Everywhere were the walls of stone, sheer and towering and causing a feeling of breathless awe.

Doc began running. He had been comparatively inactive for hours in the plane, and the exercise was welcome. The air was utterly dry and a little cold.

Noise of running water reached his ears, and soon he saw the stream that caused the sound. A small river, it poured out of the base of the canyon wall with rushing violence and a squirming cloud of spray.

It was on the opposite side of the canyon. He did not cross to investigate.

Judging from the sound, two of the planes appeared to have landed; Doc believed there was only one engine still running, although the multitude of echoes made it hard to be sure. He continued running until the canyon widened abruptly, when he slackened his pace, going very slowly, listening frequently.

Two of the planes had landed. The third was coming in, motor throttled, the pilot banking carefully between the walls of stone. The tricky air currents made balancing difficult. The plane seemed no larger than a house fly buzzing down into a rut that a big truck had made in soft yellow earth.

When the ship was down safely, it taxied over to the other two craft. A camp was apparently going to be set up. A mass of boulders lay on the canyon floor at that point, and the stream was nearby.

Guards scattered quickly, took up positions some distance from the camp, where they could cover the surroundings. They carried automatic rifles.

As soon as he saw Renny being hauled out of the last plane to land, Doc moved. He flattened in a small gully and crawled to the creek. On the way, he gathered rocks until he had his pockets filled.

He had a number of scientific gadgets on his person, devices which were compact, and which he usually carried when fooling around with trouble. He had a gas mask which doubled as a diving "lung." He inserted this between his teeth and applied the clamp to his nostrils.

The creek water was bitterly cold. Rocks in Doc's pocket held him on the bottom. He crawled along. The current, while it did not have the bounding rush of a mountain stream, was fast. Keeping his eyes open, Doc remained in the deepest shadows as much as possible.

The first time he crawled out of the water, he discovered he'd overshot his goal somewhat. Entering the stream again, he crawled back, with extreme difficulty, against the current. Then he lay on the bank, exercising rapidly to get the blue cold stiffness out of his muscles.

Spad Ames was giving loud orders.

"Rig the plane floodlights so they cover the whole floor of the canyon," he ordered. "And step on it. It's gonna be dark before long."

A man said: "Here is that ball of string you wanted."

"After it gets dark," Spad ordered, "stretch that string between you when you stand guard. If anybody should try to crawl past you, there's a good chance of them hitting the string."

"Right."

"Now get that fellow Renny out here."

There was a scuffling sound, and Renny said, "Holy cow!" twice, and a man yelped in agony. Doc took a chance and looked. Renny was tied hand and foot, but it was taking four of them to hold him.

Spad Ames drew a revolver and cocked it.

"I don't know whether Doc Savage is dead or not," he said, "but in any case, I don't think we're going to need you."

DOC SAVAGE lifted up and threw a smoke grenade. Then he threw a gas grenade, another smoke, and kept pitching them. The grenades were waterproof. The gas grenades weren't noisy. The smoke ones were. They sounded louder than shotguns. Violence of their hatching hurled the black smoke yards in every direction. Each resembled, an instant after it exploded, a large black octopus; this soon turned into a cloud.

Doc went into the smoke. A revolver smashed out deafeningly—Spad Ames' gun, probably.

"Renny!" the bronze man called.

Renny answered in Mayan, a language almost unknown to the civilized world, which Doc and his men used when they did not wish to be understood. Renny was safe, lying to the right.

Doc had a pocket knife out when he reached Renny. He slashed ropes, got the big-fisted engineer free. "Can you run?" he asked.

"I hope to tell you!" Renny boomed.

Doc Savage spoke in Mayan. "Go up the canyon. Follow the river. And now—hold your breath! There's gas in this smoke."

Renny went away.

The smoke had spread. Wind would soon sweep it away. Doc tossed more smoke grenades into the wind where the sepia pall would be carried over them.

There was some shooting. Three or four men were coughing. Others cursed. Doc felt about for the planes.

When he found one of the ships, he felt in his pocket and brought out one of the rocks which had a sharp edge. He struck it against the undersurface of one of the wings. Wing skin split. So did the fuel tank. Gasoline flooded down his arm.

There was a small waterproof lighter in one of his pockets, and he got it with the hand which was not gasoline-drenched. The high-test aviation gas caught with a sound that might have been a giant coughing.

Doc had fixed the position of all three planes in his mind. He made for another one. Spad Ames had become silent—gassed, probably. There were plenty of men left for yelling and shooting, however.

Firing the second plane was managed without incident, but when he ignited the third craft, flames seized his arm, made it a bundle of red pain. He ran a few yards, pitched into the sand, and smothered the fire before it did more than scorch his skin.

Suddenly, it was lighter. Wind was sweeping the smoke away. He had no more of the grenades, so there was nothing to do but run for it. He wanted to locate Spad Ames, if possible. He did try, but failed, and had to run for it.

He made the creek safely, and a few minutes later he joined Renny.

Chapter XII
THE KEY

LONG TOM was standing watch, some distance from Monk, Ham and the Colorados. They startled Long Tom, and after he had apparently tried to jump out of the canyon, he grinned at Renny and said: "This was once I never expected to see you again, you big lug."

Renny rubbed his jaw, pondered, then said: "Holy cow!"

That was the extent of their reunion greetings. They moved on toward the spot where Monk and Ham were keeping the Colorados.

Soon they could hear Monk and Ham. The pair were not speaking in loud voices, but they were saying unusually violent things to each other.

"Monk and Ham are swapping animals," Long Tom advised.

"Eh?"

"Ham passed the buck to Monk and it got Monk's goat," Long Tom explained, "It's over who was responsible for Mark Colorado getting loose and ruining the propeller of our plane."

Judging from the text of the conversation, the argument had progressed somewhat from its starting point. Monk was discussing Ham's ancestry, and Ham was protesting.

"Listen, you homely gossoon," Ham advised Monk. "I come from the finest Pilgrim stock."

"You've come a long way, then," Monk said. "What you're trying to tell me is that you're blue-blooded?"

Ham scowled at Monk malevolently. "Exactly."

"You may be so blue-blooded you can give a transfusion to a fountain pen," Monk said. "But what does it prove? To me, you're—*Renny!*" Monk shot to his feet. *"Renny!"*

The meeting, comprising of an exhibition of jumping by Monk, and several "By Joves!" from Ham, was soon over. Habeas Corpus and Chemistry bounced around in glee.

Renny walked over to Ruth and Mark Colorado. It was getting dark fast; even the reflection of the sunlight on the canyon rim was dying. Renny stared at the prisoners.

"Spad Ames and Locatella know you got these two," he said. "Saw them in the plane. They're not happy about it."

"What have you learned about this mystery, Renny?" Monk asked.

"Well, practically nothing. I know why Spad Ames was so anxious to get hold of the Colorados."

"Why?"

"Hostages. He was going to use them as human shields for himself. Mark and Ruth Colorado—and I got the idea that is just a name they took for themselves—seem to be very important personages in this place that we've heard mentioned as behind the mists."

"You don't know what they mean by that silly business—behind the mists?"

"No. Your guess would be as good as mine."

"Spad Ames is plenty anxious to get back into the place."

"Yes. I gather that. It is something pretty tremendous that he is after."

MONK was not too enthusiastic about leaving the watching of pretty Ruth Colorado to the others, but he accompanied Doc, at the bronze man's suggestion.

They went to a point below the source of the river several hundred feet, where the canyon was very narrow.

"Good place to make a stand, if Spad Ames should try to reach us," Monk said.

"They are too heavily armed for us," Doc assured him.

"Then what're we here for?"

He found out. Doc produced a metal tube which was filled with round dark objects which somewhat resembled shotgun shot. He sprinkled these over the sand carefully.

"I get it," Monk said. The stuff was an explosive which was not affected by moisture, and detonated from pressure—an improved variation of the ordinary Fourth of July spit-devil. An intruder could hardly pass this point without stepping on the stuff; immediately there would be a loud, if not very damaging, explosion. Enough noise to give a vociferous alarm.

This, Monk gathered, was to be their precaution for the night. They could get some sleep. Personally, he needed it.

It was dark when they got back. Intensely black. Doc Savage bent over the Colorados, as if testing the ropes that tied them.

He deliberately let his pocket knife drop against Mark Colorado's leg—as though it might have been an accident.

Five minutes later, casually, as if he had just found it out, he said: "My knife seems to be missing."

"You used it to cut my ropes," Renny reminded.

"I might have dropped it there," Doc remarked, as if dismissing the matter.

For the next few minutes, Doc listened carefully. He decided that Mark Colorado had found the knife, was using it to slyly cut himself loose.

"Let's get over here a minute, where the Colorados cannot hear," Doc said, "and discuss the campaign plan."

They assembled fifty yards away, and the bronze man said: "Don't get excited. The Colorados are escaping right now, probably."

"What!" Monk howled, so loud that fifty echoes came back from the surrounding stone pinnacles.

"Sh-h-h, stupid!" Ham admonished.

"Holy cow!" Renny said, trying to whisper. "What's the idea?"

"We will trail the Colorados," Doc explained.

"How?"

"Back in Monk's laboratory in New York, I splashed some chemical over both Mark and Ruth Colorado. At the time, I intended to use the stuff to locate the Colorados in the city, but as it developed, we didn't have a chance to do that. We can use it now."

"What kind of chemical is it?" Renny demanded. "And how—"

"Phosphorescent," Doc told him. "That is, it gives off light, but not visible light. It is infrared phosphorescent."

"Not visible light?"

"Unless you view it through a fluoroscopic eyepiece," Doc elaborated. "You cannot see X-rays ordinarily, you know. But a fluoroscope makes them visible through the fluorescing characteristic of certain materials."

The description was a little too general for Long Tom, who liked his explanations to be specific. "As far back as 1883, a man named Becquerel studied the invisible region of the solar spectrum, with reference to the quenching of phosphorescence by red and infrared light, and he discovered—"

"Kindly spare us, if you don't mind," Renny interrupted. "Right now, I don't feel like hearing a scientific discussion of how and why it works. If it works, swell."

Doc Savage produced a pair of spectacles from a pocket. He broke them at the bridge, kept one lens himself and handed the other to Renny. "Hold that in front of your eyes, and you should be able to distinguish the faces of both Colorados, as a pale spot of light. That is, if they are visible from here."

Renny peered and squinted. "Holy cow!"

"But it has been hours and hours since that chemical was dumped on the Colorados," Ham muttered.

"It does not wash off readily," Doc advised.

Renny took another squint through the small fluoroscopic eyepiece. "If you fellows think the Colorados are escaping," he said, "you're wrong."

They went back. Mark and Ruth Colorado had not moved. Apparently the ropes which held them had not been tampered with.

Doc said nothing. He thumbed on a flashlight, took one of the black arrowheads from a pocket, looked at it thoughtfully, then put it back. He knew both Colorados watched him.

IT was near ten o'clock when Mark Colorado threw the ropes off his wrists and ankles, and approached Doc Savage. The bronze man grew tense, thinking of the knife. The blade was short, but it did not take a long blade to cut a throat. He set himself for defense.

Mark Colorado felt very cautiously, located the pocket in which Doc had put the arrowhead. He took the arrowhead, nothing else.

Both Colorados then crept away in the darkness.

Doc breathed: "You fellows awake?"

They were. "I been layin' here with a rock in each hand," Monk whispered.

"Come on," Doc said.

They trailed Mark and Ruth Colorado. The infrared phosphorescent chemical was so pale that they could hardly distinguish it.

"We're gonna have to improve that stuff," Monk whispered. "How did you figure on using it in New York, Doc?"

"By equipping watchers with fluoroscopic spectacles sensitive to the stuff, and planting them at all train gates, bus stations and airports," Doc explained. "That way, they could spot the Colorados, even if they did dye their hair and alter their clothing."

The Colorados went straight to the spot where the river poured out of the aperture in the base of the cliff.

"Holy cow!" Renny breathed a moment later.

The river had stopped flowing.

Doc Savage went forward suddenly. The others followed. They stood, a moment later, at the mouth of an aperture which was perhaps two and a half feet high and seven or eight feet wide—the hole out of which water had stopped pouring. They learned that much by exploring with their hands.

They listened. Sounds came out of the hole. Noises that would be made by two people climbing.

Monk whispered: "I'm goin' in there! It's a secret entrance, or something!"

With Monk, to get a violent idea was to act upon it. He dropped to all fours and scuttled into the hole. He did not get far.

Came a gurgling roar of water. Also a louder howl from Monk. The river again spouted out of the hole.

Ham unlimbered a flashlight, fanned the beam, then yelled: "There goes Monk!"

The homely chemist was going head over heels. He squawked each time he bounced off a rock, flailed his arms and howled: "Grab me, somebody!" The water had carried him out of the hole with terrific speed; it rushed him fifty yards before he practically bounced out on the bank.

Monk glared at Ham and said: "You laugh, and I'll take that sword cane of yours and ram it down your throat!"

"What happened?" Ham asked innocently.

"You know as well as I do—the water just started coming out of the hole again."

"You see anything?"

"Nothing but dark."

Doc Savage went back to the aperture in the base of the cliff from which the river spouted. He used his flashlight, which was waterproof.

"Holy cow!" Renny ejaculated, and pointed with one of his big fists.

Doc had seen it. An arrowhead, black, more than a foot in length, and inlaid or carved into the face of the cliff.

"That's queer," Monk muttered. "That thing is like the smaller black arrowheads. Why don't we compare 'em?"

Doc Savage still carried the second of the two arrowheads which had been taken from the Colorados. He produced it and held it close to the black arrowhead on the face of the cliff.

A moment later, the river stopped flowing.

DOC SAVAGE'S bronze features remained expressionless in the reflected glow from their flashlights, but the others looked startled.

"That—that arrowhead—stops the water," Long Tom said, putting amazement between his words. "But—but how?"

"Have you a pocket knife?" Doc asked.

"Yes. But what—"

"Hold it against this arrowhead," Doc suggested.

Long Tom stared as the knife blade picked up the arrowhead. "Magnetic!"

"The small arrowhead is made of lodestone, which is naturally magnetic," the bronze man explained quietly. "Behind the large arrowhead on the cliff face is doubtless some kind of a trip which is operated magnetically by the smaller arrowhead, and that in turn shuts off the water by a mechanical arrangement."

"But what—"

The river began flowing again, like a great fire hydrant that had suddenly been turned on.

"Which answers my question," Long Tom said. "The thing shuts off for only so long at a time—just long enough to permit a person to enter or leave."

Monk emitted an angry rumble.

"Shut her off again!" he said. "I'm willing to give that hole another whirl."

They shut off the water, then raced to the hole, sank to all fours, and began climbing.

"Come on, Habeas!" Monk called, and Ham said: "Chemistry, step on it!"

Chapter XIII
THROUGH THE MISTS

THE walls were dark, smooth, and shone with wetness which threw back the white spray of their flashlights in jeweled glitter. The slant was about the same as a stairway, although the steps were higher, about two feet, and of nearly the same depth. The steps and the tunnel wall were not of the same stone as the cliff, but of harder flintlike stone blocks joined together so that the cracks were hardly noticeable. It was perhaps forty feet up to a platform of stone onto which they could climb clear of the water channel.

The platform was wet with spray, slick, and Long Tom fell down. He said several words which the others were not aware he knew.

"Tsk, tsk," Monk said. "Such language!"

Monk then made an involuntary dash for the far side of the platform, for water fell down the shaft with a deafening roar.

There were steps leading upward.

They put their heads together and screamed at each other. "We will go up," Doc Savage said.

The stairway followed above the roaring stream for some distance, then veered sharply to the left,

and they were in a tunnel. The walls were not lined; they were natural stone.

Habeas Corpus, the pig, made tapping sounds as he walked. Chemistry was noiseless, although he chattered fearfully once.

Their flashlights poked out cones that seemed made of thin cotton, an effect due to the presence of something like fog. The vapor puzzled Monk, particularly after they got farther along the passage.

"I thought this stuff was spray from the water," Monk grumbled. "It don't seem to be. I wonder—"

He went silent, for Ruth Colorado was coming toward them. Her form was vague in this mist; she was within three arm lengths before they saw her. It was eerie. She seemed to materialize before them like a supernatural body.

"Go back," she said. "There is a black arrowhead on the wall at the head of the water tunnel, so that you can stop the flow of the water."

She spoke in a low voice. There was tense earnestness in her manner. And when she looked at Doc Savage, there was a warm light in her eyes.

Ham, in the background, kicked Monk on the shin, breathed, "She likes him!" And Monk, because the girl was very pretty and he had been harboring some ideas, turned around and returned the kick to Ham's shin, with interest. Ham's yip of pain echoed faintly.

"Where is your brother?" Doc asked gently.

"He has gone on, and will return with—with the others," the girl said rapidly. "He left me to watch and give an alarm if you followed. I—well—I know you are not our enemy, so here I— Please go. Please!"

Doc Savage was uncomfortable. "As a matter of fact, it had not occurred to us to turn back."

"Why? Surely you came here for no reason except curiosity. It is curiosity, isn't it?"

"Partially—"

"Go away and forget all this—mystery," Ruth Colorado urged. She reached out and gripped both the bronze man's arms. "The price you'll pay for learning the secret is too great. So great that I—I don't want it to happen to you."

There was a pounding earnestness in her voice that caused Long Tom to moisten his lips, and Renny to open and close his big fists nervously.

Doc said: "Curiosity isn't the only reason we are here. We are fighting Spad Ames. We can fight him more effectively if we know what he is after—if we know what is behind all this mystery."

Ruth Colorado searched the bronze man's face, said finally: "I am trying to help you."

"We know that," Doc Savage said gently. "And that is why we are going back."

"Going back!" Renny barked. "But Doc—"

The big-fisted engineer never got his argument

finished. For suddenly, like smoke from a camp-fire, the mists thickened.

And it began to get cold.

Ruth Colorado put back her head and shrieked: "Don't kill us! I am with them!" Then, apparently realizing she had cried out in English, she shifted to the language which Doc had never heard before, and called out shrilly.

It was getting colder with incredible swiftness.

"For the love of Eskimos!" Monk yelled. "What kind of a place is this?"

Doc whirled, rapped: "Back toward the river! We may be able to make—"

"Wait!" The girl was gripping his arm again. "Stay here! They will not—I am with you. You are safe as long—as long as you do not let me go."

Out of the mists came her brother's voice. He spoke English.

"You are a fool, my sister," Mark Colorado said. "You are saving their lives. We will have them on our hands, a perpetual source of trouble."

The girl put her chin up, said nothing.

It stopped getting colder. The fog thinned a little. There was movement in the mists, beyond range of their flashlights.

"Do not resist them," the girl said.

Monk took two large rocks out of his pockets, said: "This won't be resistance. It'll be a massacre!"

It wasn't exactly a massacre, but it was brisk while it lasted. The mists suddenly thickened, and forms came flying out of them, long and grotesque forms that hardly seemed human in the strange vapor. Monk whooped, dived to meet the first one. He drove a fist. The attacker dodged expertly, took Monk around the waist, slammed him to the tunnel floor.

Two figures charged upon Doc Savage. The bronze man side-stepped. He made no effort to strike out, being interested in hearing what kind of weapons they had, and in what the assailants looked like.

The attackers were naked, except for short trousers that fitted as snugly as tights. All had remarkably white hair. And their bodies, lithe and corded with rippling strength, were greased.

Doc laid hold of one of them. The fellow was as slick as a catfish. Doc grabbed again, this time for the white-haired assailant's hand. He got it. The hand was covered with sand, so that it would hold a grip. Clutching the fellow by the hand, Doc swung him, knocked another down.

Monk had gotten up, was chasing a man, grab-bing him again and again, only to have the greased body slide out of his angry fingers.

Ham was probably being most sensible of all. He danced back, managed to unlimber his sword cane, and began pricking each attacker to rush him.

He made no effort to cut off heads or arms or run victims through—he merely broke skin with the tip of the blade, which was coated with a chemical that would cause quick unconsciousness.

Mark Colorado called out loudly, speaking the strange dialect. He must have called for help, because there was an overwhelming rush of semi-naked, white-haired men.

As Monk explained it later, he got along all right until he was fighting at least thirty men at once, and he might have been all right then, except that he kicked a greasy foe, got grease on his foot, then slipped and fell when he tried to stand on the foot.

This was probably a slight exaggeration. They were only fighting about forty opponents, all told, when they were overcome.

Chapter XIV
MIST MEN

AFTER he had opened his eyes, Doc Savage lay for some time without moving, although all his sensations were of motion—turning over and over and around and around with slow dizzy speed, and in space—while actually he was lying still. The dizziness went partly away. He moved, first his arms and then his legs, and learned he was not tied. After that, he was quiet again, shifting his eyes and listening.

He got the impression he was in a very small place.

It was dark. The darkness had a blue-black qual-ity. Once, the bronze man thought there were small lights swimming overhead, but he touched his eyes with his fingers and discovered it was only the result of being struck on the head—the same visual phenomena occurring when a fingertip is pressed to the side of the eyeball. He did not know exactly what he had been struck with. Seven or eight semi-naked assailants had been holding him at the time. A rock, probably.

There was breathing near him; then someone cleared a throat. Unconscious people do not clear throats; they only cough.

"Monk," Doc said.

"How long you been conscious?" Monk asked.

"A few moments. And you?"

"Longer. I think they beat on your head a while after they got you down. I seem to remember that."

"Any idea where we are?"

"Some place I'll bet we'll wish we weren't," Monk said. "No. Last I remember, we are going around and around with those guys in the tunnel."

Monk thought of something, called, "Habeas! Habeas Corpus!"

Somewhere near, but not in their tiny enclosure, the pig began squealing. Chemistry, the chimp,

**Grotesque forms suddenly appeared out of
the strange vapor and charged Doc and his men!**

emitted some forceful opinions in his own language.

Doc Savage lifted up. His head bumped the top. He explored with his hands, found stout wooden poles. He also located Ham, Long Tom and Renny.

"They hurt?" Monk asked.

"Not bad, apparently. They haven't revived yet."

The pig and the chimp continued to make a noise, and this drew attention. Footsteps approached, and there were low, guttural voices. Yellow light suddenly flooded Doc and the others.

They were in a cage made of tough wooden bars—the bars were ocotillo, the desert cactus shrub also called coach whip and devil's walking stick—that were almost as tough as iron. A curtain covered the thing, and this had been lifted.

The men outside were seminaked, white-haired; and they carried a few torches which gave off gory red light and strings of smoke which mixed with the darkness and the smoky-looking air.

Mark Colorado had removed his civilized clothing. He wore, like the others, nothing except an article that resembled bathing trunks.

Mark Colorado leaned against the bars, holding a rock so its red light flickered over them.

"I am really sorry about this," he said. "I wish you had taken my warning—and not attempted to find the answer to this mystery."

Monk grabbed the bars and shook them. He yelled: "Somebody is gonna be a danged sight sorrier before we're through!" and continued to shake the bars until someone gave his knuckles a whack with one of the lighted torches, after which the homely chemist bounced around among the sparks and yelled so loud that the surroundings gobbled with echoes. "What's the idea of puttin' us in cages?" he squawled. "We're not apes!"

"There might be a difference of opinion on that point," Ham suggested.

Monk, too angry to think of a response, sank back and snarled: "I wonder what they done with our clothes?"

It was a little embarrassing, too, because all of them were as naked as the day they were born.

THE cages had wheels. But the region over which they were to travel, they discovered, had no roads. Strange white-haired men got behind and pushed until they came to the top of a steep hill, after which they gave the cage a shove. The careening ride down the hill was something to remember. The cage jumped, bounced, did everything but swap ends. At one point, it must have been coasting fifty miles an hour; it seemed like five hundred.

The captors galloped after them, and after the cage stopped rolling, surrounded them and scowled malevolently.

"They don't seem to like us," Long Tom decided.

"The sentiments are mutual," Long Tom announced.

One of the white-haired men put his hands to his mouth and emitted a low, weird caterwauling cry. A summons of some kind, evidently, because a crowd suddenly surrounded the cage.

The newcomers were attired in long capes of something that resembled suede leather. They wore tall conical headgear of the same material. Both capes and headgear were deep crimson in color; hence the effect was somewhat astounding.

Monk yelled: "How about giving us some clothes, you guys!"

They made no answer, but gathered around the cage to stare. There was, it became increasingly evident, nothing friendly in their manner. One made an expressive gesture, drawing a finger across his throat. Two others spat.

Mark Colorado stepped close to the cage and spoke in a whisper.

"Do not do anything to anger them," he warned.

"If I get out of here," Renny promised, "I'll do more than anger them."

"You idiot!" Mark Colorado yelled. "I'm trying to save your lives."

"Oh, sure," Renny said skeptically.

"Don't worry. If it wasn't that I promised my sister, I would wash my hands of you. I didn't ask you to follow us here."

The remark, being true, was something to think about.

Laying hold of the cage, the crowd shoved it along. A score of torches shed crimson light that enhanced the bright scarlet of the robes. And abruptly a cobbled pavement was underfoot; then buildings shoved up around them in the mist.

Every building, every part about each building, was square or rectangular. They were like boxes piled one atop the other, large boxes on the bottom, smaller ones on top. The colors were brilliant and varied; greens and yellows and blues were plentiful, but nowhere was there a red structure.

Not all of the people here were garbed in red. Twenty of them, at a rough estimate, wore scarlet, Doc Savage decided.

"The guys in red seem to be the big shots," Monk remarked. He raised his voice: "Hey, you funny-looking clowns! How about some clothes? I'm getting cold."

Someone hurled a torch at the cage, and hot sparks showered them plentifully.

The crowd seemed to approve; it howled in glee.

"Say, maybe the guy was right about behaving ourselves," Monk muttered.

They came abruptly to a red building, larger than the others, a great perfectly square box of a structure.

"The jail house, I guess," Renny hazarded.

He was not exactly correct. There was a pit in front of the red building. Ropes were attached to their cage, and it was rolled over the pit rim, with no regard whatever for their comfort. The cage bottom was evidently hinged so it could be yanked open with a rope, for they suddenly tumbled out on hard stone, and the cage was yanked upward again.

It was incredibly dark in the pit.

Something thudded near them. Doc investigated. "Seems to be a bundle of skins," he reported. "Probably what we are supposed to wear."

THERE were five of the skins, each barely large enough for a man to wrap around his waist. Having donned these makeshifts, they looked up, and decided that the pit was circular, since the thing was edged by burning torches. The mists seemed to be thinner here, although the air still had a befogged appearance.

"Holy cow!" Renny rumbled, peering up at the torches. "What kind of a place have we gotten into, anyway?"

"Kind of a lost valley, or something," Long Tom hazarded.

"Sure, sure, but what are these people? They look a little like Indians, only their skins are too light. And who ever heard of Indians having white hair?"

An interruption arrived in the form of a hurled torch. The missile apparently had been pitched at the sound of their voices. It came close enough that the splash of the sparks showed their figures. Instantly, a dozen torches were hurled.

They scattered hurriedly.

Monk growled: "I'm gonna play their game with 'em."

The homely chemist seized one of the torches, wound up like a baseball pitcher, and knocked a tall red cone of a hat off of a tormentor's head.

An entirely new voice addressed them.

"Hey, pards," the voice said. "You're just stirrin' up a mess. If they can devil you, they'll stay there and throw things all night."

"Who the blazes are you?" Monk exploded. He tried to fan a torch into flames for light, but only succeeded in making himself a target which drew a shower of sticks and small stones. He threw the torch away.

"You hombres kinda mosey over this way," the strange voice suggested, "and maybe we'll get us some peace around here after a while."

They felt their way toward the voice, until they encountered the stone pit wall, along the base of which was a stone shelf slightly under a yard in width.

"You rannies might as well make yourselves at home," the voice advised. "This here bench is gonna be your bed, table and home for a while."

The voice was that of a robust old man.

"Prospector?" Doc asked.

"Yep. Easy for you to guess, wasn't it? Reckon I should've knowed this was a heck of a country to hunt gold in, before I started in. What're you fellers? Surveyin' crew, maybe?"

"We were just curious, you might say," Doc explained.

"Curiosity kills cats, don't it? It's gonna get you gents a long and peaceful life. 'Tain't bad here, though. Kinda monotonous, at times."

"They keep you in this pit all the time?"

"Nope. Unless you do somethin' you ain't supposed. I tried to climb out of the valley. Near as I can figure, that was about a month ago. Blast the luck!"

"They caught you, eh?"

"Wouldn't've, only I used some bad judgment. Took me a partner, see. Should've knowed better. We made us a rope, and lassoed a pinnacle. My partner climbed up first. Then he untied the rope, and let me fall back."

Doc said: "The partner was not Spad Ames, by any chance?"

"Why, heck! How'd you know?"

THEY were startled enough to remain silent for some moments. The old prospector must have done some thinking in the interval, because he made a disgusted noise.

"That durn coyote! I was years figgerin' out the path to escape, and I only took this Spad Ames because I'm gettin' old and about as active as a terrapin."

Doc suggested: "What about this Spad Ames?"

"Hain't much to tell about that jasper. Him an' another scallawag like 'im fell near here in their airplane. Partner was named Waldo Berlitz if I remember right. He found one of these hermit Indians, an' up an' killed him. So the Indian's friends turned Waldo Berlitz into a stone man—"

"Into a stone man!" Monk ejaculated.

"Yep," said the old-timer matter-of-factly. "Then they ketched Spad Ames an' brought 'im here. Spad Ames was a slick one. He learned a lot by playin' up to 'em. I think he was goin' to come back, if he ever got away. Won't—if he knows what's good for 'im."

Doc asked: "How long have you been here?"

"Since fall of 1916."

"Holy cow!" Renny exploded.

"Yep. Voted for Woodrow Wilson for second term as president, then headed into the badlands. Woodrow said he'd keep us out of war. Heard afterward they had the War anyway."

"Wait a minute!" Monk exploded. "We're getting sidetracked. What about that stone-man business?"

"Nothin' about it. They just made him into a stone man."

"You don't really mean stone?"

"Drop 'em and they break. I calls 'em stone. Use your own judgment."

Monk scratched his head and scowled up at the pit rim. They were still flourishing lighted torches up there, but could distinguish no targets at which to hurl them. Monk snorted.

"Now look, old-timer—just two things can explain what you're telling us."

"Eh?"

"You're kiddin' us—"

"I ain't kiddin'—"

"Or you're nuts."

"Figure I'm locoed, eh?" The old-timer sighed without concern. "That's what they always figure when they first land here. Later, they found out they're wrong. You'll find it out too, my squeak-voiced friend."

Doc asked: "How do they manage this—ah—turning a man to stone?"

"Wouldn't know. Ain't ever seen 'em do the job."

The bronze man abandoned that line of inquiry for another, asking: "You say there are others here?"

"Half a dozen. Two of 'em are Hopi Indians who strayed too far from their home-huntin' ground. There's another prospector, two Mormons who were runnin' away from their wives, an' one old geezer who was an arky—arky—whatcha call it?"

"Archaeologist?"

"That sounds like what he call hisself."

"Where are they?"

"Oh, they got houses to themselves. Do a little more work than the regular inhabitants. Ain't an uncomfortable way to live, though. My mistake was in tryin' to escape. What I shoulda done is married an' settled down. Only I ain't never trusted women."

"Married? You mean that they let their captives intermarry?"

"Sure. The prospector an' the arky—arky—what you call him—is married. So are the two Mormons, with one wife apiece, an' always arguin' they're entitled to more'n that."

Monk snorted again.

"This place may not be so bad at that," he said thoughtfully.

"Don't forget Spad Ames," Ham reminded him.

Chapter XV
THE HERMIT INDIANS

THE old prospector, possibly irritated by the aspersion Monk had cast on his sanity, suddenly refused to talk further until they had given him the latest news from the outside world. He sat there and listened to the troubles in Europe, the latest crooked politicians to go to jail, the difficulties in China and the baseball situation.

Suddenly, he demanded what they meant by the reference to Spad Ames.

Doc told him.

"That's bad," the old-timer muttered. "That Spad Ames was a rattlesnake in rabbit fur. He was a new kind of ranny for these hermit Indians. That's how come he learned so much, then got away."

"What is Spad Ames after?" Doc asked.

"You mean—why did he come back?"

"Yes."

"You got me, partner. The south end of this valley, I never been in. They don't let us mosey around there none. They got somethin' down there that's kinda mysterious. I know that's where they turn a man into stone, though. But that's 'bout all."

"And you have no idea how that stone-man business is managed?"

"Nary a idea."

The old-timer was cantankerous. He decided he needed some sleep, and sleep he did, curling up on the hard stone; and before long he was emitting snores that had the resonant volume, if not the musical quality, of a saxophone.

Doc Savage said: "We might as well get some sleep ourselves."

So they stretched out on the stone shelf, and were wide awake until dawn. The circumstances in which they were involved were such that sleep seemed unimportant.

As Long Tom muttered once: "When a man's got something as startling as this to think about, he'd be a sucker to sleep."

It was all unreal, as if they had stepped in a theater and were seeing a thundering musical comedy, full of strange happenings. There was no feeling that anything was natural, or as it should be. Everything was fantastic, difficult to accept.

The would-be tormentors with the torches loitered around the pit rim for an hour or two, then grew disgusted and wandered away.

Dawn came, and they got a closer look at their pit. The sides were sheer, as smooth as glass, and about twenty feet in height. The pit was, roughly, sixty feet in diameter.

They got nothing to eat that morning.

The absence of food piqued the old-timer.

"Why, dag nab it!" he complained. "You hombres is fetchin' me bad luck. First mornin' in my life they never fed me vittles."

"You mean," Doc said, "that we are getting worse treatment than their prisoners usually get?"

"You sure as heck be."

"That's queer," Ham said thoughtfully. "Why should they have it in for us in particular?"

SUNLIGHT eventually came down into the valley, turning the mists to cream; then everything lightened and took on a glowing that was reminiscent of a blue neon light. The mists did not seem quite as thick by day. They had thought it would be impossible to see through them a distance of more than fifty feet, whereas vision could actually penetrate twice that distance.

There was a breeze, and the mists swept along overhead, blowing like fog, long streamers squirming over the pit edge. The stuff was partially fog, but it had a vague and not unpleasant odor.

The faint scent of the mists was one which Doc had caught before—in Mark Colorado's room at Phenix Academy, that first time Spad Ames had attempted to seize him.

"Where does this fog come from?" Doc asked.

"Tain't fog. Leastways, not entirely," the old-timer advised. "Fog goes away. This don't, never."

"Where does it come from?"

"South end of the valley. Part I was tellin' you about—where I never been."

"Same part of the valley where they turn men to stone, as you put it?"

"Yes."

Monk put in: "You know, if some of this ain't explained to me before long, I'm gonna get a headache. There in New York, Mark Colorado apparently turned one of Spad Ames' men to stone. If I hadn't seen the fellow with my own eyes, I would think this stone-man talk was crazy."

The day dragged on, and from time to time, white-haired people appeared at the pit rim and stood staring. Now and then, someone flung a rock.

The white-haired girls, as Monk particularly noted, were not at all hard on the eyes.

"I wonder what gives them their white hair?" the homely chemist pondered.

"Take a look at me," the old-timer suggested.

The prospector was as ancient as they had expected, with a face as wrinkled as a discouraged prune and a rather gnarled body. His hair was snow-white.

"You ain't no collar ad," Monk said. "Whatcha mean—take a look at you?"

"My hair."

"It's white. But white hair on an old goat your age ain't so unusual."

"I ain't so danged old!" yelled the prospector indignantly. "And my hair was as black as a pole kitty when I come here. Three months after I got here, it turned white!"

Doc said: "You mean that the mists turn the hair white?"

"Yep. Figure so."

"Probably some chemical in this mist," Monk hazarded, "that whitens the hair. Might be the chemical that gives the odor to the vapor."

Long Tom, who liked his food, had been brooding about the lack of a breakfast. "How do they eat around here?" he wanted to know.

"They farm. They make me and the other prisoners work in the fields, durn 'em. Course, they work themselves."

"This country is as dry as the Sahara," Long Tom reminded. "They must irrigate."

"Plenty of rain."

"What?"

"They have a shower nearly every day," the old-timer explained. "Long in the afternoon, usually."

"Holy cow!" Renny interjected incredulously. "But it hardly ever rains in the surrounding desert!"

"I ain't lyin' to you jaspers," the prospector insisted. "It rains. And it's right cool in the valley in the summertime, when it's hotter'n the hinges of Hades outside."

"That doesn't sound reasonable," said the big-fisted engineer.

"I ain't explainin' it. I'm just tellin' you."

It was past midafternoon when they heard shooting in the distance.

IT was a machine gun. The weapon gobbled like a ten-ton turkey, short bursts frequently repeated. There were shorter, more vicious smacks of high-powered rifles.

The explosions came then. Four of them; they were great, deep-throated roars that trembled the ground.

"Spad Ames," Doc said in a low voice.

Height of the surrounding canyon walls made darkness approach slowly. And soon after shadows came creeping, a grim cluster of the white-haired Indians gathered around the pit rim.

They did not throw things this time. Their manner was more grim than that. They shouted a few words.

The old-timer made a silent whistling mouth.

"Bad," he said. "They're talkin' about killin' you fellers."

"Why?" Doc asked.

"You're from the outside. They've never liked outsiders. And now this Spad Ames is attacking the valley, and they're workin' up a big hate for all outsiders. That includes you fellers."

An uncomfortable silence fell. They set on the stone shelf, and watched the faces on the pit rim until increasing darkness blanketed the place.

"Their language," Doc Savage said thoughtfully, "must be an extremely ancient dialect."

"Yep," the old-timer agreed. "I talk some Injun

RENNY

myself, but I never heard this lingo until I got here. You know what I think?"

"What?"

"You've seen them cliff dwellin's scattered around over this part of the country, ain't you?"

"Yes."

"Well, think these people are descendants of them cliff dwellers. Ain't sure, of course. But they've been in this valley for hundreds of years. They've got everything in here they need, and the place is easy to defend. Only that one entrance, closed by the river when they want it to be."

"They're not ignorant people," Doc said.

"Course not. They send a young brave and a squaw out now and then to be educated. Them two you call Mark and Ruth Colorado were the last pair—they're son and daughter of the chief."

"If Mark and Ruth Colorado have the chief for a father," Monk put in hopefully, "they might be able to help us."

"I gather they're all that's keepin' you alive." The old-timer jerked a thumb up at the rim of the pit. "I've learned their language, you know. They ain't talkin' so favorable about you fellers."

When it was very dark, Doc said: "Let's make a pyramid, fellows. It's time we were looking over this place."

Monk grunted, got close to the wall, doubled over and braced his hands against his knees. Renny climbed atop his shoulders. Using great care, Ham topped them.

There was a clattering sound, and something fell into the pit. They hastily unmade their pyramid, lest they be discovered. Monk felt around in the darkness to ascertain what had fallen into the pit.

"Blazes!" the homely chemist said. "Is somebody up there a mind reader?"

He had found a rope ladder which someone had dropped so that it dangled into the pit.

Ruth Colorado's voice addressed them from above.

"You can climb out," she said. "We have a proposition for you."

Chapter XVI
THE POOR PROPOSITION

CRIMSON seemed to be the regal color in the valley. The room had walls and ceiling and floors of exactly the same shade of crimson. It was a large room, forty feet or so in each dimension, except the ceiling, which was about fifteen feet.

In addition to Mark and Ruth Colorado, there were fourteen others present. Doc counted them while he listened to the chief talk.

The chief, a tall, lean fellow, healthy and active, bore considerable resemblance to the Colorados. Obviously he had been educated outside the valley, because he spoke fairly understandable English.

He had made a long talk without saying much. Evidently they had plenty of time in the valley for long-winded conversation. At the end, he got down to the point.

"The council voted to end your lives," he said, "but my son and daughter have persuaded them to reconsider. We will make a deal. If you will capture this Spad Ames and Locatella and all their men, you will be permitted to live as prisoners here the rest of your lives."

When the proposal soaked into big-fisted Renny, he emitted a disgusted rumble.

"Generous, ain't you?" he boomed.

Doc Savage asked: "Just what was the idea of voting to kill us in the first place?"

"We do not wish any more outsiders here," the chief said grimly. "We get along very well by ourselves, and have for a long time."

"Killing us will hardly prevent others coming, will it?"

"If we had killed Spad Ames, we would have avoided a good deal of trouble," the chief pointed out logically.

"But we are your friends, whether you think so or not,"

"That is what Spad Ames said. We believed him."

"We're wastin' our breath arguin' with these geezers," Monk muttered.

Doc said: "What you hope we will do is get rid of all your enemies, then meekly be prisoners the rest of our lives!"

"What is wrong with that?" countered the chief. "It seems very generous to me."

"Not to us," Doc said. "However, we might make counter proposals and reach a more fair—"

The old chief shoved up his chin arrogantly.

"We are not interested in bargaining," he said. "You will do as we say."

The bronze man's flake-gold eyes got small fires in them, but his voice remained steady enough. "Do you know just what you are going up against in this Spad Ames?"

"We do not fear him."

"Being brave and using good sense are two different things. Spad Ames has plenty of men with him, and he is armed with modern bombs and probably poison gas."

"You mean that you cannot overcome him?"

"I did not say that. We can try. Have you got the clothing you took from us, and the stuff that was in the pockets?"

"Of course."

"On the weapons that we had with us will depend our chances of overcoming Spad Ames."

The chief said something in the dialect. Two of the red-garbed men went away, came back bearing a basket containing the clothes of Doc and his men.

Slyly, the chief sorted through the stuff and removed machine pistols which Monk, Ham and Long Tom had been carrying. He kept these.

"We're not taking chances with you fellows," he remarked.

Doc Savage decided none of the stuff was missing. He went through it, poking with one finger, noting high-explosive grenades, various chemical and small devices. He touched a number of the things, but always with a fingertip.

"All right," he said.

A man picked up the basket and started away. He covered four or five yards, made a mumbling noise, and put the basket down. Then he fell loosely beside it.

The men jumped up excitedly. They were very animated for a few moments, then they began collapsing two and three and four at a time.

DOC had been holding his breath; his men were doing likewise. They had seen one of the objects he had touched—a small cylindrical bomb of anaesthetic gas which had a timing mechanism which caused it to open several moments after the lever was flicked.

Monk upended the basket, began sorting their clothing. They donned some, discarded other of the garments as unnecessary.

"This is a fine mess," Renny grumbled. "We've got to fight all these guys, beside Spad Ames and his crew. Either outfit would be a handful."

"What next?" Long Tom wanted to know.

"Holy cow," rumbled Renny. "I'm interested in this south end of the valley."

"We'll go there," Doc said. "But first, we'll go back to the pit."

"The pit—why there?"

"The old-timer," the bronze man explained. "We need a guide."

There were none of the white-haired Indians around the pit rim. Doc found the rope ladder, coiled on the rim, and dropped it down.

The old-timer was not glad to see them.

"You hombres is a tarnation source of trouble," he complained. "I didn't wish you no bad luck, but I wasn't hankerin' to see you again."

"Want to guide us around this place?" Doc asked.

The old-timer chuckled. "Sure. Might as well."

They set off through the darkness, the old-timer leading and making fast time. Evidently he had exaggerated somewhat about being no more active than a terrapin.

When they reached the steep hill down which the cage had rolled with such jouncing violence the night before, their guide stopped.

"I ain't useful from here on," he said.

His voice did not hold a great deal of enthusiasm about venturing farther toward the south end of the valley.

"Would you help us by waiting here, and giving an alarm in case we're followed?" Doc asked.

"Sure as tootin'."

They left him there. The hill was smooth, slippery and difficult climbing. "Wonder we didn't get killed in that cage," Ham said grimly.

Doc said: "That shooting and bombing this afternoon was down in this end of the valley. Evidently Spad Ames was trying to force an entrance."

The bronze man made the remark because of dull thumping sounds which he could hear occasionally. The noises were irregularly spaced. He went toward them, moving ahead of the others, using extreme caution.

The thumping noises became audible to the less intensively trained hearing of the others.

"Sounds like shooting," Monk muttered.

"Wait here," Doc said in a low voice.

He found the mouth of the tunnel five minutes after he had left the others. The thumping noises guided him. As nearly as he could ascertain with his hands, it was a great gaping aperture. Extremely cold air blew out of the opening.

Doc went back to the others.

"You wait outside," he directed. "No need of all of us getting trapped in there." Then he added sharply: "Wait! There are torches coming!"

ABOUT a dozen natives came from the direction of the village of box-shaped stone houses. There were three torch bearers in the group. They were hardly excited enough to be pursuers.

They strode into the tunnel, and Doc followed.

The bronze man kept close enough on their heels to get some benefit of the torchlight. That was probably fortunate, because there were points where the passage worked along the edge of great pits. This was a natural cave for the most part, eroded by underground water in the course of innumerable centuries.

The sounds he had been hearing were shooting.

Suddenly, there were many men ahead. They were gathered about a steeply sloping tunnel, behind a barricade of huge boulders. There were other boulders behind the barricade—ammunition, it appeared; for at intervals, men would seize one of the stones and pitch it over the barricade, where it went thumping down the steep shaft beyond. Sometimes one of the missiles caused pained howls; more often, there were answering shots.

The Spad Ames gang must have blasted open the secret entrance closed by the river flowing out of the cliff. They had penetrated this far, and were being stood off by the primitive device of rolled boulders.

None of the white-haired Indians carried weapons. For that matter, the old-timer had explained that for generations there had been no need of weapons in the valley.

The ineffectiveness of gas—Spad Ames undoubtedly had gas—puzzled Doc Savage for a moment. Then he noticed the strong current of chill air, concluded this wind was blowing the poisonous fumes out as fast as they were released.

Suddenly, Doc whipped back and sought cover.

A file of white-haired men was approaching. They had clambered down out of a shaft which led upward. Each carried a burden. As they passed, Doc paid particular attention to the peculiar substance which they were carrying.

The stuff had a greenish-yellow hue, resembling sulphur somewhat. It was in sizable blocks, as if the lumps had been mined from a great mass.

Each of the carriers was very careful to keep his hands wrapped in many folds of coarse cloth.

As they approached, Doc hurriedly delved into his clothing for an article he always carried—a long, stout silk cord, to one end of which a collapsible grapple was fixed. Ordinarily he used the device for surmounting walls.

He flipped the silk line out from the niche in which he had hidden himself, made it fall in a loop on the cavern floor. Waiting, he held the two ends.

He began to think that none of the burden bearers were going to step in the loop he had made. But finally one put his foot down in the proper spot. Doc jerked. The bearer upset. Doc hurriedly hauled in the silk line, got it out of sight before they discovered it.

The man who had fallen said a great many words in his native language, all of it forceful. Then he got up and scowled at his lump of greenish-yellow material, which he had dropped. It lay in two large pieces, and some smaller ones.

He gathered the two lumps together, left the smaller ones, and went on with the others.

Doc glided out of the niche, used his flashlight—it had been recovered along with his clothing and gadgets—and made the beam very small, dashed it only momentarily.

Spreading his handkerchief, the bronze man raked some of the greenish-yellow substance onto the fabric, not using a finger for the raking, but the flashlight.

He returned to his men.

"WE were beginning not to like waiting," Long Tom informed him.

There was more shooting back in the cavern, continuous but irregular, as if a child might be playing aimlessly with a drum in the depths.

"Sounds like a nice little war going on in there," Monk suggested. Wars always interested Monk.

Doc Savage spread his handkerchief on the ground and put a flashlight beam on the yellow-green particles.

"About the same color as sulphur," Ham suggested.

"Or the color your face is gonna be after I choke you one of these days, providin' you keep messin' with me," Monk told him.

Doc scrutinized the material intently. He had no pocket magnifier, something he would have liked to use. He smelled the stuff.

It had an odor, but not particularly strong.

Very carefully, he rolled a small particle of the stuff onto the palm of his hand—and suddenly dropped it.

With furious haste, and some slight trace of pain on his metallic face, the bronze man scrubbed his hand in the sand. He rubbed it against his trousers leg, scrubbed it again.

"Holy cow! The stuff bite you?" Renny peered with great interest.

Doc Savage snapped the fingers of the hand several times, then put a light on the palm so the others could see.

An unpleasantly large blister was already rising.

"Should have known better," he said thoughtfully. "Already had a pretty good idea of what the stuff was."

"You had—Wait a minute!" Monk forgot to whisper, and gave a squawk of excitement. "You know what it is?"

"Not the exact chemical composition," Doc said. "A chemical analysis will show that."

"But I don't get it!"

Instead of explaining, Doc said: "Listen!"

They held their breaths, instinctively extinguishing their flashlights in alarm, and it was very still; except for two deep thumping noises from inside the cave, and also very dark, although they could hear the night breeze moving through nearby crags, and the odor of the mists was a faintly pleasant redolence.

"I don't hear nothin'," Monk said.

Doc, who had trained his hearing with years of scientific exercise, caught a faintly cautious voice some distance away calling: "Doc Savage! Hey, where the heck are you?"

"Old-timer!" Doc called.

The old prospector scrambled up to them. "They found out you got away," he said. "And they've got a war party on your trail."

"Fat chance they've got of findin' us," Monk said.

"That's where you're wrong, good-lookin' feller," the old-timer told homely Monk. "They've got bloodhounds."

"Bloodhounds?"

"Well, these dogs ain't the long-eared kind of pot licker, but they can trail a man. Listen."

The night stillness was broken abruptly by the long kiyoodling howl of a dog taking up a trail.

"They can't trail so good in the mists, and they had lost the trail," the old-timer explained. "They've got it again now. We better be doing something."

Doc wheeled toward the tunnel mouth, and the others followed him, for greater convenience each man holding to the belt of the man ahead of him. They entered the tunnel.

"Dag nab it!" the old-timer exclaimed delightedly. "Did you find a way out of the valley?"

"With the best of luck," Doc said, "it may be sort of an indirect route."

Chapter XVII
THE STRANGE CAVERN

DOC did not go directly to the barricade where the natives were holding Spad Ames' men back. Instead, he turned off into the shaft down which he had seen the file of men come bearing the strange greenish-yellow chemical.

The shaft was narrow, crooked, the work of some prehistoric trickle of water. Once, when Monk happened to splash his flashlight beam upward, he stopped and pointed.

"Look up in there, Doc," he suggested.

High in a cranny overhead was a small vein of the greenish-yellow chemical.

Doc said: "There were probably veins of the stuff all through this peak to begin with, and water washed it away, leaving this cavern. That underground river which comes out at the base of the cliff—you remember how cold the water was?"

"What has cold water got to do with it?"

"Come on. I may be able to show you."

The vague odor grew more noticeable as they progressed, and it dawned on the others why Doc Savage had come in this direction.

"That smell is getting strong enough that the dogs won't be able to trail us," big-fisted Renny rumbled cheerfully.

They came to a larger chamber, a place so vast that its length dimension was lost in the mists, although its width appeared to be at least two hundred feet, Doc found upon scouting.

The left wall of the chamber was composed for the most part of the greenish-yellow chemical.

Several of the white-haired Indians were working with long sticks, digging holes, then prying loose lumps of the chemical. Their torches threw pale-red light.

"Come on," Doc whispered.

They moved very cautiously and, not using their flashlights, passed the workers. The floor of the chamber slanted upward shortly, and they began to hear sounds of running water. Then they were climbing stones laid in masonry.

The dam reached nearly to the ceiling—there was, in fact, only a narrow aperture at the top, and that could be closed by a great pivoted stone slab of a door.

A small underground river was rushing down, beating against the dam, and glancing off into another channel.

"This must be the stream they used to close the secret entrance," Monk decided.

Doc voiced his own opinion. "At one time, the stream flowed into the cavern through which we just passed. The natives managed to dam it and divert it into another arm of the network of caves, and made their secret entrance."

The bronze man was thoughtful a moment.

"That gave them access to the chemical deposit," he added. "And lately, they must have considered making arrangements with the outside world to market the chemical commercially."

Renny said: "Holy cow! What is the stuff, Doc?"

INSTEAD of explaining directly, the bronze man cleared up details that had been puzzling the others.

"Mark Colorado had some of the chemical at the Phenix Academy," the bronze man said. "There was a packing case in his room, so probably the stuff was shipped to him in that. He evidently planned to market it, as I said. It was an excellent idea, because no natural deposit of the stuff has been found anywhere else. A commercial mixture probably somewhat similar has recently been marketed, however."

"Wait a minute!" Renny exploded. "You say something similar to this stuff is on the market?"

Doc Savage nodded. The others were staring at his bronze features, limned in flashlight glow.

"It has long been the dream of chemists to discover a refrigerant which could be safely handled," Doc said. "You are all familiar with dry ice, or solidified carbon dioxide, which has a temperature of one hundred and nine degrees below zero."

"What has dry ice got to do—" Renny paused, swallowed, said: "I begin to get this."

"The recently marketed material," Doc continued, "is a combination of bicarbonate of soda and other substances, which the formula owner is keeping secret, which forms a powder. When water is added to this powder, it becomes violently cold. One pound of it is claimed to have the cooling power of at least fifty pounds of ice."

They thought this over. A great deal was becoming clear.

"This greenish-yellow stuff," Monk said, "becomes cold when you add water to it."

"Very cold," Doc agreed. "As cold, apparently, as liquid air, the temperature of which is extremely low. As you know, a piece of beefsteak, for instance, when dipped in liquid air, instantly becomes so cold that it is as hard as stone and may be broken like glass."

Monk gave a bark of astonishment. "That explains the so-called stone men! They were simply frozen with this stuff!"

"Exactly," Doc agreed grimly. "Water was added to the greenish-yellow chemical to put it in operation, then the stuff was poured over the men. As soon as it exhausts itself, the stuff doubtless evaporates, just as do liquid air and dry ice. Dry ice doesn't melt, as you know; it evaporates."

"That smoking effect around the bodies that everybody thought had been turned to stone," Monk suggested, "was simply the intensely cold chemical still evaporating from the body and clothing. Right?"

Doc nodded.

Then the bronze man gave his idea of the explanation for the unusual climate of the valley.

"The deposit of this chemical must be enormous," he said. "Water seepage reaches it continually, and the intense cold escapes through cracks in the stone, in the form of the mists which we noticed."

"And the rain the old-timer, here, said they had so often—"

"Is simply due to the cold valley air condensing what moisture there is in the atmosphere. The normal process by which rain is formed, accelerated somewhat by the cold seepage from this deposit."

They heard shouting, then, and screaming. The cries, garbled by the fantastic acoustics of the cavern, were as weird as the howling of a coyote pack on a moonlight night. There were explosions. Shots. More cries.

"Sounds as if Spad Ames had broken through," Doc said.

With the others, he raced back toward the tunnel intersection. As they passed through the great chamber where the natives had been mining the cold chemical, they saw that the miners had deserted their tasks and raced away.

Doc knew, of course, that they had been planning to use the chemical to freeze Spad Ames and his men, if they tried to rush the barricade.

Apparently they had not been very successful.

THE fighting was furious in the main tunnel leading to the barricade. And the natives were retreating.

"Back!" Doc warned.

The bronze man had a few high-explosive grenades left. He ran down the subterranean passage a short distance—not toward the fighting, but in the direction of the valley. He covered fifty yards, selected his spot, put one of the grenades in a crack in the wall, then whirled and ran back.

"Get down!" he rapped at the others.

The explosion ripped out, followed by a sound as if broken glass was being ground together, and the roof came down at that point. Rock dust boiled in the glare of their flashlights, mixing darkly with the lighter foglike vapor that came from the cold chemical.

Monk didn't approve. "Blazes!" he howled. "Now we're blocked off from the valley!"

"So is Spad Ames," Doc said grimly.

The first cluster of retreating white-haired Indians raced past. Doc and the others, extinguishing their flashlights and flattening against the side wall, escaped notice. The fleeing group reached the point where the roof had collapsed, instantly set up a terrified bedlam of howling.

"They seem a little disturbed," Monk said.

"Sh-h-h, you homely missing link!" Ham warned. "They find us, and we'll be disturbed, too!"

The fugitives came racing back, dived into the tunnel which led to the huge chamber and the chemical deposit. Other natives in flight appeared, and followed them. The word had evidently gone down the line, in the strange gobbling language, that the other tunnel was blocked.

Doc watched them flee past. Except for running sounds the defenders made, comparative silence had fallen.

The last man in flight, it developed, was Mark Colorado. He must have recovered from the anaesthetic, followed the dogs as they trailed Doc and the others to the subterranean passages, and joined the defenders.

Doc stepped out, grasped Mark Colorado's arm. The bronze man put a flash on his own face so the other would recognize him.

"Oh—we knew you must be in here somewhere!" Mark Colorado gasped. "We—you've got to help us!"

"What happened?"

"They had poison gas. We were holding them back at a long shaft by rolling stones, until we could get ready to use the freezing stone upon them. The shaft was crooked, and they could not shoot the grenades to the top. But they caught a badger."

"Badger?"

"Yes. Tied a poison gas bomb to the badger, then turned the animal loose, and the scared creature climbed up the shaft. It was among us before we knew it. Half—half of our men are dead."

Doc said: "Come on. We can't hold them off here."

They followed the natives who had fled toward the great chamber, one side of which was composed of the vast deposit of cold chemical.

"We can get out into the valley by this route?" Doc asked.

"How—how did you know that?"

"The breeze. There is a strong draft through here. There has to be an opening somewhere beyond."

"Yes," Mark Colorado explained. "There is a dam across the river, and we can follow the river for a short distance, then there is another opening which leads into the valley."

They could hear the Spad Ames crowd behind them.

WHEN they were half across the great room, they were shot at. One of Spad Ames' men did the firing, using an automatic rifle. The bullets shrieked very close, and clamor of the weapon in the cavern was ear-splitting. They extinguished their lights, scattered.

"Get to the dam as quick as you can!" Doc shouted.

They raced forward. Renny became confused in the intense darkness, and ran against the chemical deposit with one hand, and there was enough perspiration on his skin to cause the stuff to induce terrific cold that felt as if a white-hot iron had touched his fingers. He howled in pain.

Doc showed a light briefly. Renny joined them. They scrambled up the steep stone backslope of the dam, found the narrow opening, and crowded through.

There was a native with a torch and a club on the other side. He snarled, lifted the club. Mark Colorado knocked him down, then barked at the man in their lingo.

"I told him," Mark Colorado explained, "to get the others out of here. Or do you want them to stay and help fight?"

"Tell them to get out," Doc directed. "You can stay and act as guide, if you don't mind."

Mark Colorado shouted directions, and the native retreated, joining the others. The sounds they made grew fainter.

There were other noises, however, on the other side of the dam.

"Spad Ames and Locatella are coming!" Monk barked.

"Get back," Doc directed. "Get off this dam."

Then the bronze man sent a loud shout back into the great cavern.

"Ames!" he shouted. "Spad Ames!"

Spad Ames answered profanely, said: "Damn us! We've been wonderin' what happened to you!"

Doc yelled: "Get back! Don't try to rush us! We'll give you that one chance."

Spad Ames swore. Then he laughed. And he drove the beam of a powerful searchlight against the dam. He made a mistake about the nature of the dam proving that he had apparently never been in this part of the underground labyrinth before.

"They got a barricade!" he yelled. "Blow it down, guys!"

Doc moved. He moved at least as fast as ever before in his life, and retreated from the dam. He splashed into the river, crossed it, joined the others, shouted: "Run! They're going to blast the dam!"

The others were already running.

Spad Ames' bomb, evidently a big grenade thrown by hand, let loose a ripping crash. They had pitched it through the aperture in what they thought was a barricade, not a dam, and the thing had landed in the water. Spray flew over Doc and the others. The dam came apart.

For a few minutes, there was only rushing water.

Then the shrieks began coming. And the vapor. The cold. The incredibly agonizing cold. The yells grew more horrible.

The bitter cold kept increasing.

"Run!" Doc warned. "There is a tremendous deposit of that chemical. We might be frozen if we stay here."

They raced, falling frequently, through the cavern passage.

After a while there were no more shrieks behind them.

And later they came out into the misty pleasant darkness of the valley.

Chapter XVIII
TO HERMIT OR NOT TO HERMIT

THREE days later, the last searching party of white-haired people came in from the desert, climbing the long ropes which had been lowered over the cliff. They were not particularly cheerful.

Three of Spad Ames' men, fellows left behind as lookouts, had escaped through the desert, it seemed. These three were all that survived. Spad Ames, Locatella, the others, had died of cold in the great cavern, or in the passages beyond.

Doc Savage listened to a translation of the report. He had picked up a few words of the language, but not enough to more than catch the gist of what was said.

Mark Colorado did not seem disappointed. "That should remove the last objection to your leaving here," he said. "The older men seemed to think we should go on trying to keep the existence of this valley a secret."

Pretty Ruth Colorado was not so enthusiastic. She nipped her lips, said finally: "We will hate very much to see you go."

Ham nudged Monk, whispered: "What she means is that she hates to see Doc go."

If the bronze man was aware of any particular feeling on the young woman's part, or if he had any thoughts of his own in that direction, he carefully refrained from showing them. His life work was dangerous; it allowed no feminine entanglements, for enemies would strike at him through anyone who became close to him. He stuck always to his determination: no women. It was not always easy, and not always was he entirely successful. The remarkable training which he had received from childhood at the hands of scientists had gone a long way toward making him a superb physical machine, but it had not succeeded in relieving him of human emotions.

Renny had a report: "We can rebuild that dam, by going in with electrically heated suits that will protect us against the cold. Or we can wait for a very dry season, when the river stops flowing, and build the dam again. That was the way it was constructed in the first place."

Doc had consulted at some length with the chief of the valley Indians. As he had suspected, they had planned to market the chemical commercially—that was the real reason for the presence of Mark and Ruth Colorado in Phenix Academy. It had been hoped the Colorados could develop suitable containers for the stuff, using Phenix laboratory facilities, and later arrange marketing facilities.

After some argument, Doc's proposition was accepted. The chemical product would be marketed through an organization which the bronze man could arrange. If possible, no outsiders would be allowed to enter the valley, as long as the inhabitants so wished.

Part of the preparations which Doc and his aides made before leaving consisted of another argument—this one about whether the prisoners in the valley should be permitted to leave.

Doc finally won out.

Then they learned that the prisoners did not care about leaving.

The old-timer expressed it the most coherently.

"I don't see where I'd be any better off outside," he said. "Dag nab it, they got right tolerable-lookin' squaws here, you gotta admit. And I got me one picked out."

"You want to stay?" Monk asked.

"Thanks, gents, but figger I will."

Monk had been looking over the native feminin-ity rather intensively, and he understood how the old-timer felt.

"You know," Monk said, "I think you got some-thin' there."

THE END

Coming in DOC SAVAGE Volume #11:

The Man of Bronze battles a faceless fiend whose sinister pronouncements threaten destruction through the eerie COLD DEATH

Then, Doc Savage embarks on a desperate race to Antarctica to block THE SOUTH POLE TERROR

Don't miss these two pulse-pounding thrillers in *DOC SAVAGE* #11!